New York Times and *USA Today* bestselling author

Laura Griffin

"DELIVERS THE GOODS." —*Publishers Weekly*

Praise for *AT CLOSE RANGE*

"An emotional, exciting page-turner. Griffin deftly balances the mystery and the love story."

—*The Washington Post*

"A compelling mystery that will grip the reader from the start with her crisp storytelling, natural dialogue, and high-stakes tension . . . fiercely electric."

—*RT Book Reviews*

"Explosive, seductive, and totally empowering . . . *At Close Range* has it all."

—*Romance Junkies*

Praise for *DEEP DARK*

"It is the perfect blend of mystery, suspense, and romance. . . . It is fast paced, with great writing and crime scenes that will make you want to keep your light on when you go to bed."

—*Cocktails and Books*

"*Deep Dark* is a book to be devoured and savored with each new development. It is the perfect combination of mystery, terrifying suspense, and hotter-than-hot romance."

—*Fresh Fiction*

"I encourage you to check out [*Deep Dark*], which combines sizzling attraction with terrifying suspense."

—*The Amazon Book Review*

Praise for *SHADOW FALL*

"An expert at creating mystery and suspense that hooks readers from the first page, Griffin's detailed description, well-crafted, intriguing plot, and clear-cut characters are the highlights of her latest."

—*RT Book Reviews*

"Great lead characters and a spooky atmosphere make this a spine-tingling, stand-out novel of romantic suspense."

—*BookPage*

Praise for *BEYOND LIMITS*

"A page-turning, nail-biting thriller from the very first scene to the very last page."

—*Fresh Fiction*

"*Beyond Limits* has daring escapades, honest emotions, and heart-stopping danger."

—*Single Titles*

Praise for *FAR GONE*

"Perfectly gritty. . . . Griffin sprinkles on just enough jargon to give the reader the feel of being in the middle of an investigation, easily merging high-stakes action and spicy romance with rhythmic pacing and smartly economic prose."

—*Publishers Weekly* (starred review)

"Crisp storytelling, multifaceted characters, and excellent pacing. . . . A highly entertaining read."

—*RT Book Reviews* (4 stars)

"Be prepared for heart palpitations and a racing pulse as you read this fantastic novel. Fans of Lisa Gardner, Lisa Jackson, Nelson DeMille, and Michael Connelly will love [Griffin's] work."

—*The Reading Frenzy*

"A tense, exciting romantic thriller that's not to be missed."

—Karen Robards, *New York Times* bestselling author

"Griffin has cooked up a delicious read that will thrill her devoted fans and earn her legions more."

— Lisa Unger, *New York Times* bestselling author

Praise for the Tracers Series

EXPOSED

"Laura Griffin at her finest! If you are not a Tracer-a-holic yet . . . you will be after this."

—*A Tasty Read*

"Explodes with action. . . . Laura Griffin escalates the tension with each page, each scene, and intersperses the action with spine-tingling romance in a perfect blend."

—*The Romance Reviews*

SCORCHED

"Has it all: dynamite characters, a taut plot, and plenty of sizzle to balance the suspense without overwhelming it."

—*RT Book Reviews* (4½ stars)

"Starts with a bang and never loses its momentum . . . intense and mesmerizing."

—*Night Owl Reviews* (Top Pick)

TWISTED

"The pace is wickedly fast and the story is tight and compelling."

—*Publishers Weekly*

"With a taut story line, believable characters, and a strong grasp of current forensic practice, Griffin sucks readers into this drama and doesn't let go."

—*RT Book Reviews* (Top Pick)

UNFORGIVABLE

"The perfect mix of suspense and romance."

—*Booklist*

"The science is fascinating, the sex is sizzling, and the story is top-notch, making this clever, breakneck tale hard to put down."

—*Publishers Weekly*

UNSPEAKABLE

"Laura Griffin is a master at keeping the reader in complete suspense."

—*Single Titles*

UNTRACEABLE

"Taut drama and constant action. . . . Griffin keeps the suspense high and the pace quick."

—*Publishers Weekly* (starred review)

BOOKS BY LAURA GRIFFIN

The Alpha Crew Series

*Cover of Night**

*Alpha Crew: The Mission Begins**

The Tracers Series

At Close Range

Deep Dark

Shadow Fall

Beyond Limits

Exposed

Scorched

Twisted

Snapped

Unforgivable

Unspeakable

Untraceable

Also by Laura Griffin

Far Gone

*Unstoppable** (first appeared in *Deadly Promises* anthology)

Whisper of Warning

Thread of Fear

One Wrong Step

One Last Breath

*ebook only

TOUCH OF RED

Laura Griffin

Pocket Books
New York London Toronto Sydney New Delhi

Pocket Books
An Imprint of Simon & Schuster, Inc.
1230 Avenue of the Americas
New York, NY 10020

This book is a work of fiction. Any references to historical events, real people, or real places are used fictitiously. Other names, characters, places, and events are products of the author's imagination, and any resemblance to actual events or places or persons, living or dead, is entirely coincidental.

First Pocket Books paperback edition November 2017

POCKET and colophon are registered trademarks of Simon & Schuster, Inc.

For information about special discounts for bulk purchases, please contact Simon & Schuster Special Sales at 1-866-506-1949 or business@simonandschuster.com.

The Simon & Schuster Speakers Bureau can bring authors to your live event. For more information or to book an event, contact the Simon & Schuster Speakers Bureau at 1-866-248-3049 or visit our website at www.simonspeakers.com.

Manufactured in the United States of America

10 9 8 7 6 5 4 3 2 1

ISBN 978-1-5011-6237-4
ISBN 978-1-5011-6238-1 (ebook)

For Abby

TOUCH OF RED

CHAPTER 1

It was like any other Wednesday night. Until it wasn't.

Samantha Bonner had just finished sweeping up. She'd emptied the dustpan and sanitized the sink and wiped down the pastry case. The burned smell of coffee beans hung thick in the air, overpowering the vinegar solution she'd run through the machines. But it was quiet. She stood for a moment and let the silence surround her, glad to be free of the acoustic-guitar music that had been looping through her head all day.

Sam grabbed her purse and locked up. Crossing the rain-slicked parking lot to her car, she darted a look into all the dark corners. It was a safe neighborhood, but you never knew.

She pulled out of the lot, relieved to be on her way home after pulling a double shift. Raindrops pitter-pattered on her windshield as she made her way through downtown. She switched the wipers to low, and her phone lit up with an incoming call. Amy.

Sam stared down at the phone a moment. Then she put the call on speaker.

"Sam? Can you talk?" Amy sounded undone. More than usual.

"What's up?"

"It's Jared. He wants to move back in."

"He called you?"

"He came by to drop off Aiden. I didn't let him in or anything."

Sam didn't respond as she pulled up to a stoplight. In most areas, Amy wasn't a pushover. But her two-year-old boy missed his daddy, and his daddy knew it. He used the kid as leverage.

"I know what you're thinking," Amy said now. "And I just want to talk through it, figure out what I'm going to tell him. Can you come over for a bit? I can make us some coffee."

The mere thought of coffee made Sam want to retch. "Sure," she said anyway. Amy was sniffling now, and Sam didn't have the heart to say no.

"Or we could talk on the phone," Amy said. "You're probably busy. Tonight's your night off, isn't it?"

"No, I closed up."

Sam slowed for a bend in the road. Stately oak trees and manicured lawns soon gave way to weeds and chain-link fences. Then came the railroad tracks. White-collar to blue in less than a mile. The people in Sam's neighborhood commuted to work at all hours and didn't stop for lattes on the way.

"I'll be over in a little." Sam turned onto her street. "Give me twenty minutes."

"Are you sure?" Another sniffle.

"I'm sure." Sam pulled into her driveway and rolled to a stop in the glow of her back-porch light.

"Thanks, Sam. I mean it. I just need to hash this out. I mean, what if he's legit this time? I owe it to Aiden to at least think about it."

Sam kept her skepticism to herself. For now. She slid from her car and noticed the white bike propped against her back deck as she walked up the driveway.

"Sam? You there?"

"I'm here."

She mounted the steps and spotted a blur of movement. Pain exploded at the base of her skull.

Sam dropped to her knees and pitched forward. A big arm wrapped around her neck, hauling her back. The smell of tobacco registered in her brain, filling her with bone-deep fear as the arm clamped around her windpipe.

"Sam?" Amy's voice was far away.

Pain roared through Sam's skull. She struggled to move, to breathe. A glove-covered hand tipped her head back, exposing her neck.

No.

Sam clawed at the arm, trying desperately to buck, to kick, to scream for help. *No, no, no!* From the corner of her eye, she spied her phone on the ground. She tried to call out but the cries died in her throat.

"Sam, are you there?"

Fear became panic as she saw the glint of a blade.

"Samantha?"

• • •

Brooke Porter beat the detectives, which surprised her. But then again, she'd made good time. When the message had come in coded 911, she'd dropped what she was doing and rushed straight over.

She parked beside a police unit and grabbed her evidence kit from the trunk as she surveyed the location. It was a small bungalow, like every other house on the block. In contrast to its neighbors, this home had a fresh coat of paint and looked to be in decent repair. Potted chrysanthemums lined the front stoop, where a uniformed officer stood taking shelter from the cold drizzle.

Brooke darted up the sidewalk and ducked under the overhang. The officer was big. Huge. Brooke had met him before, but for the life of her, she couldn't remember his name.

"Jasper Miller," he provided, handing her a clipboard. "Your photographer just got here."

So, he knew she was with the Delphi Center. The San Marcos Police Department typically called Brooke's lab in to help with their big cases.

Brooke scribbled her name into the scene log. "You the first responder?"

"Yes, ma'am." He nodded at the driveway. "Victim's around back. Looks like she was coming home from someplace, and he surprised her at the door."

Brooke eyed the little white Kia parked in the driveway. She wanted to see things for herself and draw her own conclusions.

"Medical examiner's people got here about five minutes ago," Jasper added.

"And the detectives?"

"On their way."

She handed back the clipboard. "Thanks."

Brooke picked her way across the stepping-stones in the grass, trying not to mar anything useful—although the rain had already done a pretty good job of that. At the top of the driveway several uniforms stood under a blue Delphi Center tent that had been erected beside the back porch.

Brooke's stomach tightened with nerves as she lifted the crime-scene tape and walked up the drive. She noted the chain-link fence, the thick shrubbery, the trash cans tucked against the one-car garage. Plenty of places for someone to hide.

A camera flashed as she reached the tent. The Delphi Center photographer had already set up lights and started documenting the scene. Brooke unloaded some supplies from her kit. She zipped into coveralls and pulled booties over her shoes, then tugged on thick purple gloves as the uniforms looked on silently.

Beat cops thought she was an oddity. She showed up at death scenes with her tweezers and her flashlights and her big orange goggles. She plucked bits of evidence from obscure places and then scuttled back to the lab to do her thing . . . whatever that was.

The detectives got her. Well, maybe not totally. But they'd at least learned to appreciate what she could do for them. Which ones had been assigned to this case? And where the hell were they?

Brooke pulled her long dark hair into a ponytail. She picked up her evidence kit and sucked in a deep breath to brace herself before ducking under the tent to take her first look.

Blood was everywhere.

"Holy God," she murmured.

A woman lay crumpled at the back door, her neck slashed open to the bone. Her hair, her clothes, even the wooden decking beneath her, were saturated. Dark rivulets had dripped down the stairs and were now coagulating in little pools on the lower slats.

"Watch your step." She glanced up at the ME's assistant crouched beside the body. He was reading a thermometer and making notes on a pad. "It's slippery."

Brooked walked up the stairs and eased around him, taking care not to step in any puddles. Maddie Callahan stood beside the door, photographing a scarlet arc against the white siding.

Arterial spray.

She lowered her camera and glanced at Brooke. "The detectives here?"

"Not yet."

The breeze shifted, and Brooke got a whiff of blood, strong and metallic. She glanced again at the gaping wound and stepped back to grab the wooden railing.

Maddie looked at her. "You okay?"

"Yeah."

Brooke should be immune to this stuff by now. But that *neck*.

She steadied herself and looked around. A set of blood-spattered car keys lay near the victim's hand. Brooke glanced at the woman's face, partially visible beneath blood-matted blond hair. Brooke didn't see a weapon near the body. Any trail the killer might have left as he'd fled the scene had likely been obscured by rain. The back door stood ajar. Had he fled through the house?

She turned to the ME's assistant. "Was this door open like this when you arrived?"

He glanced up, looking annoyed. "Yes. We haven't been inside."

Brooke turned to the victim again. Her head lolled weirdly to the side, and flies were already hovering despite the cool temperature. Brooke stepped past the ME's assistant and slipped into the house.

She found herself in a dark utility room that smelled of fabric softener. The room was small but clean, without so much as a scrap of laundry on the floor. She switched on her flashlight and swept it around. No footprints.

She stepped into the kitchen, maneuvering around an open pantry door.

"Was this open, too?" she asked Maddie.

"That's right. And I haven't shot the kitchen yet, so don't move anything."

Brooke stood still, giving herself a few moments to absorb the scene. She always tried to put herself in the perpetrator's shoes. Had he been in here? If so, what had he touched?

The kitchen was dim except for a light above the sink. Using the end of her flashlight, Brooke flipped a switch beside the door, and an overhead fixture came on.

No dirty dishes on the counter or food sitting out. Eighties-era appliances. A drying rack beside the sink contained a glass, a plate, and a fork. On the counter beside a microwave was a loose key and a stack of mail. She stepped over to read the name on the top envelope. Samantha Bonner.

Brooke zeroed in on the key. It was bronze. Shiny. Unremarkable, except that it was sitting there all by itself.

In the breakfast nook, a small wooden table was pushed up against a window. A brown bottle of root beer sat on the table unopened. Just below room temperature, judging from the condensation.

Brooke returned her attention to the pantry. Soup, soup, and more soup, all Campbell's brand. It was like looking at an Andy Warhol painting. Chicken. Tomato. Cream of mushroom. The shelf above the soup was stocked with paper goods. The bottom shelf was filled with healthy cereals and gluten-free crackers and a package of those pink and white animal cookies with the colored sprinkles.

"Brooke?"

"Yeah?" She leaned her head out to look at Maddie.

"Just finished shooting the back door if you want it."

"I definitely want it." Brooke returned to the utility room. She put on her orange goggles and switched her flashlight to ultraviolet, searching the floor for any fluids that might not be visible to the naked eye.

Nothing.

She examined the knob a moment, then selected a powder from her kit. On the porch outside, the ME's assistant was busy covering the victim's hands with paper bags for transport back to the morgue.

Brooke glanced back at the kitchen, her attention drawn to the key again. It looked like a house key, and she wanted to know if it fit this door. But she couldn't touch it until Maddie finished her photos.

Brooke opened the jar of powder and tapped some into a plastic tray. Using her softest brush, she loaded the bristles and then gently dusted the knob. She worked slowly, methodically. When she finished dusting, she cast her light over the fluorescent powder and was pleased to see a pristine thumbprint on the side of the knob.

"Maddie, can you get this for me?"

"Sure."

Maddie stepped over and photographed the knob from several angles. When she finished, she moved into the kitchen with her camera.

Brooked took out a strip of clear polyethylene tape and carefully lifted the thumbprint off the curved surface, taking care not to smudge it. She picked out a black card for contrast and gently placed the tape against the card.

One lift done, probably a hundred to go. She closed her eyes a moment and inhaled deeply. When she got laser focused, she sometimes forgot to breathe.

Brooke heard the detectives before she saw them—

two low male voices at the front of the house exchanging clipped police jargon.

Sean Byrne and Ric Santos. She'd know them anywhere.

Brooke labeled the card and tucked it into her evidence kit. So, Sean and Ric on this one. They were experienced and observant. Sean noticed everything she did, even when he seemed to be interviewing witnesses or talking to other cops. He observed where she spent her time and how, and if she lingered in a particular spot, he always asked about it later.

Brooke noticed him, too. With his athletic build and sly smile, it was hard not to. But mostly she noticed his attitude. He had an easygoing confidence she found attractive. Nothing ever seemed to rattle him.

Of course, being a cop, he also had an ego.

The voices grew louder as the detectives neared the kitchen. Brooke didn't look up, but she felt a jolt of awareness as Sean stepped into the room. His conversation stalled, and she could practically feel his gaze on her.

• • •

Sean watched Brooke for a moment, then turned to Jasper.

"You say the neighbor found her?"

"That's right. Lady let her dog out, and he started barking like crazy, so she went outside to see what was going on and spotted the victim in a pool of blood there on the porch. Name's Samantha Bonner. She works at a coffee shop."

Sean raked his hand through his damp hair, scattering water on the floor. "Married? Kids?"

Jasper shook his head. "Neighbor says she lives alone."

Sean unzipped his SMPD Windbreaker and glanced at Brooke again. She was on her knees by the back door, lifting fingerprints. Just beyond her was the victim, and the ME's people were already unzipping the body bag.

Damn.

Sean was accustomed to seeing Brooke surrounded by blood and gore, but this was bad. He studied the victim, noting the position of the body, the clothing.

Brooke closed her evidence kit and got to her feet as Sean approached.

"Hey."

"Hi." She looked him up and down. "Where were you guys?"

"Got stuck behind an accident near the bridge. Tow truck's blocking the road, so we had to hoof it." Sean ran his hand through his hair again.

"Don't drip water all over my crime scene."

He smiled. "Yours?"

"That's right."

For a moment they just looked at each other, and Sean tried to read her expression.

"Detective? Can we bag her?"

Brooke shot a blistering look at the ME's assistant, clearly not liking his glib tone.

Sean stepped into the utility room to take a look at the back porch. The whole area was a bloodbath.

"Jesus," Ric said, coming up beside him. "You get all this, Maddie?"

"Yes, I'm finished with the porch," the photographer called from the kitchen.

The ME's guy looked at Sean again. "Detective?"

"Yeah, go ahead."

Sean turned around. Brooke was watching him now,

her evidence kit clutched at her side. He motioned for her to follow him into the living room.

Brooke was short and slender, with pale skin and a plump pink mouth he'd always wondered about. As she looked up at him, he noticed the worry line between her brows.

"What's wrong?"

Her eyebrows shot up. "You mean besides the fact that this woman was practically decapitated on her doorstep?"

"Yes."

She took a deep breath and glanced around. "This crime scene bugs me."

"Why?"

"Look at it. See for yourself."

Without another word, she stepped around him and went back into the kitchen to crouch beside the pantry door.

Sean pulled some latex gloves from his pocket and tugged them on as he surveyed the kitchen. It was clean and uncluttered, except for a stack of mail on the counter beside a key. He studied the key for a moment, but resisted the urge to pick it up.

He opened the fridge. Yogurt, salad kit, pomegranate juice. On the lower shelf was a six-pack of root beer with a bottle missing from the carton. That was the bottle Maddie was snapping a picture of now as it sat on the breakfast table.

Sean glanced through the open back door as the ME's people started loading the body bag onto a gurney. The victim's clothes had been intact, and she'd shown no obvious sign of sexual assault. At first glance, it looked like the killer had grabbed her from behind and slit her throat. Given the lack of blood inside the house, Sean figured the attacker had fled down the driveway to the street or maybe hopped the back fence.

Ric stepped into the kitchen again. "Her purse is on the back porch. Wallet's inside, but no cell phone."

"You check the car?" Sean asked.

"Not yet. Let's walk through the house first."

"Don't move anything," Maddie said. "I haven't been back there yet."

After another look at Brooke, Sean led the way back. The simple layout had rooms off a central hallway. Sean flipped on a light in the first room. It had a wooden desk and a metal folding chair. On the desk was a notebook computer, closed and powered off. On the far side of the room stood a shelving unit crammed with books.

"Looks like a home office," Sean said, moving on to the bathroom. He paid close attention to the floor as he went, but saw no blood or footprints or even dust bunnies.

The bathroom smelled like ammonia. Sean switched on the light.

"House is squeaky-clean," Ric observed.

"Yep."

The pedestal sink gleamed. Sean opened the medicine cabinet. Toothpaste, cough drops, tampons. Ric eased back the shower curtain to reveal a shiny tub with several bottles of hair products lined up on the side.

They moved on to the bedroom, where they found a neatly made queen bed with a light blue comforter and two pillows in standard pink pillowcases that matched the sheets.

"Not a lot of pillows," Sean said.

"What's that?"

"Pillows. Most women put a lot on the bed, don't they?"

"I don't know. My wife does."

Sean studied the room. It smelled like vanilla. On the dresser were several plastic trays of makeup and one of those bottles of liquid air freshener with the sticks poking up. Sean spied a sticky note attached to the mirror and leaned closer to read the feminine handwriting: *One day, one breath.*

Was it a poem? A song lyric? Maybe Samantha's own words?

The closet door was ajar, and Sean nudged it open. Six pairs of jeans, all on hangers. A couple dozen T-shirts, also hanging.

Ric whistled. "Damn. You know anyone who arranges their T-shirts by color?"

"Nope." Sean looked around the bedroom again. "Pretty basic. Not a lot here."

He walked back through the house, noting a conspicuous absence of anything that would indicate a male presence. No razors on the sink or man-size shoes kicking around. No beer in the fridge. The living room was simply furnished with a sofa, a coffee table, and a smallish TV.

"Looks to me like she lives alone." Ric turned to Jasper. "You say she works at a restaurant?"

"Coffee shop, according to the neighbor lady." Jasper took out a spiral pad and consulted his notes. "Java House over on Elm Street."

"I've never been in there." Ric looked at Sean. "You?"

"Nope."

Sean glanced around the living room, which was devoid of clutter. Maybe the victim didn't have a lot of money for extras, but even so, most women tended to decorate their homes more than this. Sean hadn't spotted a single framed photograph in the entire place.

The strobe of a camera flash drew his attention to the kitchen again. Brooke was right. This scene seemed odd. Sean had worked a lot of homicides over the years, and most boiled down to money, drugs, or sex.

Sean had seen no sign of sexual assault. No drugs or drug paraphernalia or even alcohol. No hint of illegal activity. No evidence of a boyfriend.

A remote control sat on the coffee table. Sean had watched Brooke in action enough to know it would be one of the first items she collected to dust for prints.

"I don't see any blood trails or signs of struggle inside," Ric said. "Doesn't feel like the assailant was in the house."

"I'm not getting a read on motive."

"I know." Ric shook his head. "Doesn't look like a rape or a robbery. No cash or drugs around."

"We need her phone. I want to search her car and the surrounding area."

"I'll go check the car," Ric said.

He exited the front, and Sean returned to the kitchen. Brooke wasn't there. Maddie knelt in the pantry with her camera, and Sean noticed the pantry door was missing.

"What happened to the door?"

She glanced at him. "Brooke took it."

"Took it where?"

"Back to the lab."

Sean stared at her. "You mean she's gone?"

"She needed to test something. She said it was urgent."

"Yo, Sean, come here," Ric called from outside.

Sean walked out the front, glancing at his watch.

Why had she left already? This scene would take hours to process and they were just getting started.

Ric was in the driveway near the Kia. Another Delphi CSI in gray coveralls crouched beside the car.

Ric glanced up at Sean. "Jackpot."

CHAPTER 2

Brooke stepped through her front door and peeled off her jacket, scattering rain all over her wood floor. She tossed the jacket on a chair and made a beeline for the sink to wash her hands for the umpteenth time tonight. Fingerprint powder was everywhere—on her clothes, her skin, under her nails. She'd find it in her bra, too, when she undressed later. The superfine particles permeated everything, readily adhering to almost any surface.

Brooke shut off the water and stared for a moment at her reflection in the window above the sink. She looked drained. Exhausted. She *was* exhausted, and she should have been hungry, too, but right now the thought of food sent a shudder through her.

A soft scratching at the back door made her turn around. Midnight was hungry, even if Brooke wasn't. She grabbed a scoop of cat food and crossed her darkened living room to open the slider, first pulling out the metal rod she kept there to deter burglars.

Midnight wasn't even her cat, really. He belonged to her neighbor on the other side of the duplex. Leila had adopted him last Halloween after he'd shown up with singed fur and a broken tail. She kept him outside because their landlord didn't allow pets, and she'd asked

Brooke to feed him for a few days while she was out of town.

Midnight was wet and pitiful looking. Brooke crouched down to stroke his ears, but he ignored her attention as he went after his chow.

A sharp knock on the front door made Brooke jump. Who would show up this late? The most obvious answer put a knot in her stomach as she crossed the house.

It wasn't her ex on the doorstep, but Sean, she saw through the peephole. She felt a wave of relief, quickly followed by nerves. What was he doing here so late? His hair was damp and the shoulders of his leather jacket were dark with rain.

She opened the door. "You're done already?"

He smiled. "Already? It's nearly one."

She stared up at him, trying to think of what to say.

"I got your text," he said. "You just get off work?"

"Yeah. You?"

"Yeah."

She watched him a moment, debating with herself before pulling the door back. "Come in."

He stepped inside. She suddenly realized she had a sexy, rain-drenched man standing in her living room, and she didn't have a clue what to do with him. Sean had been by here once before to pick up a report, but he'd never come inside. Now that he was here, he seemed to fill up the space with his strong presence.

Brooke glanced around. As opposed to her office, which was immaculate, her house was a mess. Shoes littered the floor. Soda cans perched on the tables. A basket of laundry sat in the hallway, where she'd parked it to remind herself that she was almost out of underwear.

"You lit out of there quick."

She looked up at him. "I had to get back to the lab to run something."

"And?"

"And what?"

"And what was so urgent? Your text was vague."

"I don't know yet. I'll tell you when I do."

His eyebrows arched. "Seriously? You can't give me a hint?"

"Sorry."

He gazed down at her, and she felt a warm flutter. His eyes got to her. They were hazel, and he had the kind of thick dark lashes that were wasted on a man.

She thought he'd twist her arm about the lab work, but instead he looked away.

"So. You eaten yet?" he asked.

"Um, no."

"Want to get something?" He was inviting her out to dinner. At nearly one in the morning. "IHOP's open."

It was, but she was still processing the fact that he was asking her out.

Brooke was taking a break from men. And from badge-wearing alpha men in particular. But she didn't want to tell him that because he'd probably take it as a challenge.

He smiled. "Whoa, why'd you get all tense? It's just pancakes."

"Thanks. But I should get to bed. And anyway, I'm not too hungry after everything tonight."

His expression turned somber. "Yeah, I know what you mean."

Sean ran his hand through his hair and sighed. He looked tired. His eyes were bloodshot and his jaw was covered in stubble. He'd had a long day, as she had, and she felt tempted to invite him to hang out for a while and have a beer. But she didn't know him well enough to predict how he'd interpret that. Probably like most guys would, like she was offering him sex.

Another moment ticked by, and he reached for the door. "I'll let you get to bed." A cold gust of air whipped through her T-shirt as he stepped outside. "I'm sure you've got an early start tomorrow."

"I do."

"By the way, we found drugs in her vehicle."

She blinked up at him. "You did?"

"About two grams of coke."

"That's strange."

"Why?"

She rubbed her arms to ward off the chill. "I don't know, it seemed like she was in recovery."

"What makes you say that?"

She shrugged. "No alcohol in the kitchen. And the Serenity Prayer needlepoint. They say it at AA meetings."

"Where was that?"

"On the wall near the breakfast table."

"Huh. I didn't see the prayer, but I definitely noticed the lack of substances. It's unusual."

She scoffed. "Definitely an unusual case."

His gaze narrowed. He eased closer, and Brooke's pulse picked up. She could feel his body heat and smell the rain on him.

"You know something, don't you?"

"Maybe. I'll call you if I get it nailed down."

He watched her for a long moment. Then he reached over and touched her chin, and she felt a rush of warmth. "You've got something here."

"Swedish black."

His eyebrows tipped up.

"Fingerprint powder." She cleared her throat. "It gets everywhere."

He smiled and stepped back. "Go to bed, Brooke. I'll catch you tomorrow."

• • •

Sean strode through the door of the station house and checked his phone.

"Any word yet?"

He looked at Ric as they walked down the corridor of offices. "No," Sean said.

He'd expected to hear from Brooke before the autopsy wrapped up, but he'd had nothing from her and it was almost noon. He was going to have to track her down.

"Hey, you okay?" Ric asked.

"Yeah. Why?"

"You look stressed. How's the leg?"

"Fine," Sean said, even though it wasn't. It felt like someone had jammed an ice pick into his knee, which was more or less true.

Sean had been shot during a takedown four months ago. He'd broken his leg in the same incident when his truck skidded off the road. The leg turned out to be a bigger deal than the bullet wound, and he'd had to have a pin inserted in the bone and go through weeks of rehab. Although he'd passed his physical and been cleared for work, he still wasn't 100 percent. He wasn't about to tell anyone, but Ric had figured it out.

Sean checked his phone again as they entered the bull pen. He wanted to hear from Brooke. She was good at her job. Freakishly good. She saw things most other people missed, and Sean wanted to know what had snagged her attention last night and sent her racing back to the crime lab.

"Conference room in five," Ric said.

"I need to grab some coffee first."

Sean headed for the break room and stopped cold at the sight of Brooke. She was with Jasper, who looked like a giant standing next to her, and she was laughing at something he'd said. Damn, was he seriously flirting with her right there in the bull pen?

Sean walked over. "Hey, what's up?"

Brooke looked relieved to see him. "Oh, good, you're back. They said you were in Austin."

Sean shot Jasper a look. "We're meeting in the conference room." The rookie took the hint and excused himself, and Sean turned to Brooke. "The autopsy wrapped about an hour ago."

"Was it bad?"

"Long. I could use some coffee. Here, come on." He ushered her into the break room, where the pot was almost empty, of course. "You want some?"

"No."

He grabbed a styrofoam cup and poured the last dregs. It looked like sludge, but he didn't care—he just wanted a few moments alone with her. She was the first good thing to happen to him all morning. And not just because she looked good and smelled good, which she definitely did. She was in jeans and a thin black sweater, along with some black lace-up boots that were totally hot. She was standing close enough for him to get some of that scent she wore, something soft and feminine that always drove him crazy.

But the really, *truly* good thing about seeing her was that she was a busy woman. Much too busy to waste her time coming to the station unless she had something important to share.

"I got those results back."

He noticed the spark in her eyes. It was something important. "And?"

"I'd like to go over my findings, if you have a minute."

He sipped his coffee, watching her, and something told him her findings weren't simple. He eyed the file folder sticking up from her oversize purse.

"Come on back." He pitched his cup into the trash. "You can sit in on our meeting, tell all of us."

Sean led her into the conference room, where the rest of the case team was already assembled around a table. In addition to Sean and Ric, they had a third detective assigned to the case, Callie McLean, plus Jasper to help with the legwork. Lieutenant Reynolds sat at the head of the table. Sean doubted he was there to work—probably just wanted an update. The chief of police hated press conferences and probably planned to have Reynolds take the podium for the briefing later.

"You guys know Brooke Porter with Delphi," Sean said as she took a seat. "She's got some updates on the lab work for us."

Everyone knew Brooke, at least by name. His teammates nodded greetings as Sean grabbed the seat beside her.

"Let's start with the autopsy first." Reynolds looked at Ric. "You were there?"

"Sean and I drove up at six," Ric said.

Travis County Medical Examiner's Office in Austin handled most of the autopsies in their county, which created logistical headaches, especially since the pathologist liked to start cutting people open at the crack of dawn.

"The formal report should be ready tomorrow," Ric said, "but we have the basics. First off, he confirmed her identity. Samantha Bonner, twenty-three."

Reynolds jotted some notes on a legal pad. "And what do we know about her?"

"She's single, no kids. Works as a shift manager at a coffee shop here in town," Ric said. "And we stopped over there on our way back in. Her boss tells us she was also taking classes at the university."

Reynolds shook his head. "Just what we need. A dead college student. The media's going to be all over this."

Sean felt Brooke tense beside him.

"As for cause of death," Ric continued, flipping open his notebook, "sharp-force injury to the neck. Specifically, transection of the left and right carotid arteries, and incision of the left and right jugular veins."

"So, he slit her throat," Reynolds said.

Ric nodded, although that description seemed mild to Sean. Brooke's was closer to the truth. He'd damn near cut her head off.

"From the angle of the wound," Sean said, "the ME thinks he grabbed her from behind and tipped her head back."

Brooke shuddered.

"Murder weapon is a large knife with a serrated blade," Ric added. "Probably a hunting knife."

Across the table, Callie grimaced. She'd been on the scene last night, but the body had already been removed, so she hadn't seen the full extent of the carnage. You could tell a lot from the amount of blood everywhere, though.

Reynolds looked around the table. "What else? We have the murder weapon?"

"No," Sean said.

"We canvassed the area," Jasper put in. "We didn't find it, so it looks like he took it with him, although we didn't find any blood trails leading away from the body. But that may be because of the rain."

Ric flipped another page in his notebook. "No defensive wounds on her hands or arms. No sexual assault."

"The pathologist thinks the whole attack lasted a few seconds," Sean said. "He thinks it was an ambush."

Reynolds blew out a breath. "What about witnesses?"

"We interviewed the neighbors," Callie said. "Nobody saw anything until the woman next door let her dog out and spotted the body there on the back porch. There's a chain-link fence between the two houses."

"Well, shit." Reynolds looked around the table. "You're basically saying that this girl was murdered on her doorstep and nobody saw a damn thing. What about the lab work?" His gaze homed in on Brooke.

She folded her hands on top of her file, and Sean admired her calm in the face of the lieutenant's bluster. "The ME sent us her fingerprint card this morning. We lifted prints from the doorknobs, both interior and exterior, and all those come back to the victim. Also, we found no blood trails or bloody shoe prints inside that would indicate the perpetrator entered the house after the attack."

"Why would he?" Reynolds looked at Sean. "You said it was an ambush."

Sean cleared his throat. "Well, the back door was open, so it looked like someone might have been inside."

"Open as in unlocked, or *open* open?"

"Standing open," Sean told the lieutenant. "Right, Brooke? You made the scene before I did."

She nodded. "The crime-scene photos confirm that. The door was open with the victim's body a few inches away. Our CSIs collected other fingerprints, too. On her car door, for instance. Those belonged to her, as well."

"What about the baggie from the car?" Ric asked.

"I haven't seen the results of the drug test, but I printed the plastic bag this morning. I got one good print and it belongs to the victim."

The lieutenant's bushy eyebrows popped up. "Wait, drugs?"

"A little over two grams of cocaine," Ric said. "It was in the glove box."

"So, what's your case theory, then?" Reynolds looked around the table. "Are you thinking it's a drug thing?"

"We don't have a case theory yet," Sean said. "And I don't think it's a drug thing."

"Why not?"

Sean hesitated a beat. "That's not the impression I get based on the evidence so far."

Reynolds blew out a sigh. "So, we've got *no* murder weapon. No witnesses. No blood trails, no bloody shoe prints, no fingerprints except the victim's. We've got no case theory, except maybe drugs, but you're not convinced." Reynolds tossed down his pencil and crossed his arms. "Sounds to me like we got a whole lot of nothing."

"Actually, that's not accurate."

Everyone turned to Brooke.

"I think you have a witness."

CHAPTER 3

Five pairs of eyes bored into her.

"I believe the witness is a child."

"A *child*?" The lieutenant turned to Ric. "You said she lived alone."

"No husband, no kids," Ric said.

Brooke looked at Sean, whose attention was fixed on her. She could tell he understood the gravity of what she was saying. "Why do you think it's a child?" he asked.

She glanced around the room at all the gazes. Interested, definitely. But skeptical, too. Cops were skeptical by nature. Brooke didn't mind, but it meant she had to make a strong case.

"When I first entered the home, I noticed a key on the counter."

"You guys collected it for evidence before we could test it out," Sean said.

"I tested it," Brooke told him. "It fits the back door. When I entered the house, I also noticed the pantry door was open and there were some crumbs on the floor."

"Wait," Sean said. "You're saying—"

"I think the child was standing in the pantry, hiding there behind the door while the murder took place a few feet away."

Silence fell over the room.

"Why do you think it's a kid?" Ric asked. "If someone *was* there, it could have been an adult."

"It wasn't."

More skeptical looks.

"The prints on the pantry door were low, about twenty-eight inches off the ground. So, that's either a child or a short adult. As I was dusting the door, I noticed cookie crumbs on the floor—frosted animal cookies—and I immediately thought about a kid standing there. So on a hunch I took the door, the cookie package, and the spare key back to the lab and confirmed it: nine good prints, all belonging to a child. Two on both the key and the cookie package and five prints on the door."

"Wait a minute." The lieutenant held up his hand. "Even *if* you've got some kid's prints in the kitchen, what makes you assume the kid's a witness?"

"I don't assume. I know."

"How can you be sure this child was there last night?" Ric asked. "Maybe it's the victim's niece or nephew, or some kid she babysits, and the prints were left a week ago."

"They weren't," Brooke said firmly.

Sean darted a look at Ric, and Brooke felt a surge of frustration.

"Just . . . listen." She scooted forward in her chair. "Do you all understand how fingerprints work?" She glanced around the table, but no one would admit to not knowing. Of course not. "Fingerprints are basically ridges on the skin. Latent prints, the ones invisible to the naked eye, are made up of oil and sweat and other substances that we deposit on a surface when we touch something. *Children's* prints—like the ones at that murder scene—are different from adults' prints. The fatty acids are more volatile and break down faster. So kids' prints are much more fragile than adults' are, which is why in kidnapping cases you can fingerprint a suspect's vehicle days or even hours after a child was in it and not get anything. It depends on time elapsed, heat, humidity—a lot of things—but the prints can just vanish."

Brooke paused to let all that sink in.

"That explains the rush."

She turned to Sean. "What?"

"You left the crime scene before everyone else."

She nodded. "I had to get back to the lab quickly to run everything using a different method. We're talking about very delicate evidence. Powders and brushes can be destructive. So I used a technique called infrared microspectroscopy. You visualize the print by using beams of infrared light to detect substances, such as salts, fatty acids, and proteins." She pulled a photograph from her file. The bright-colored image was of a thumbprint from the pantry door. "See the ridge detail? The red and orange indicate oil from the skin."

She slid the photo to the lieutenant, who passed it to Ric.

"My tests confirmed that we are, in fact, dealing with the prints of a prepubescent child. I performed the procedure again this morning, and the red and orange have already faded significantly as the biological material breaks down, making the minutiae of the print much harder to discern." She passed them another photo. "See? If those fingerprints had been left weeks or even days ago, they'd be long gone."

Sean watched her, but his expression was guarded.

"Walk me through it," Callie said. "Let's say it's a boy. You think he let himself in with a spare key and then . . . what?"

"The spare key would be my guess, yes. He lets himself in the back door, which has a glass window. Then let's say he goes to the fridge and grabs a root beer. And then he goes to the pantry and reaches for some cookies. He's in there munching on one when Samantha Bonner pulls into the driveway. Moments later, she's attacked on her doorstep, and the kid is cowering behind the pantry door, watching or at least hearing the whole thing. After the killer flees, the kid steps outside—explaining the open back door—and finds Samantha dead."

No one said anything. Brooke wondered if they were thinking about what had had her tossing and turning most of the night. The child would have been utterly terrified.

"A potential eyewitness is big," Ric said. "We need to interview the victim's friends and family and find out what kid could have been at her house last night. And maybe the kid was there with a parent."

"It would have to be a parent there on foot," Callie said. "I mean, if the killer sees some car parked in front of her house, he's not going to carry out the attack, right?"

Brooke let out a breath. Buy-in. Finally. They were at least pretending to accept her findings.

She glanced at her watch and pushed her chair back.

Sean gave her a sharp look. "Where are you going?"

"I need to get back to the lab."

"You mind if we hang on to these pictures?" Ric asked.

"Sure, I've got them on my computer. Those are for

you." Brooke looked around the room. "Good luck with the investigation. And locating this witness."

She slipped out and felt an immediate wave of relief not to be holed up in the little conference room. Talking to a table full of detectives was nerve-racking.

"Brooke, wait."

She turned around, and Sean caught up to her near the break room. He rested his hands on his hips and stared down at her.

"That was a bombshell." There was something in his voice. Was it respect? Or doubt? "Why didn't you tell me last night?"

"It wasn't confirmed last night. Now it is."

He gazed down at her as the office buzzed around them. His silence stretched out, and her stomach started to flutter.

"I should go. I have a meeting at one."

He nodded. "Thanks. You've been a big help." He held out his hand.

She smiled, amused by his formality. Then they shook hands, and her amusement was replaced by a warm tingle. His hand enveloped hers, and she felt a rush of sexual awareness.

"Sure." She stepped back. "Anytime."

• • •

Sean watched her cross the bull pen. She didn't look back as she pushed through the door.

An eyewitness.

A *child* eyewitness.

If she was right, then her findings were certainly useful. But then Sean had a problem. A potentially explosive one.

"Detective?"

He turned to see the receptionist hurrying toward him. "Hi, Marjorie. What's up?" It wasn't good, whatever it was, he could tell by the look on her face.

"There's a woman out front. She wants to talk to a detective on the Samantha Bonner case."

"Who is she?"

"She wouldn't say." Marjorie looked annoyed as she adjusted her glasses. She wore them on a chain around her neck, which always reminded Sean of his grandmother. "But she's very distraught."

Sean started toward the lobby. "Did she say why?"

"She seems to think she was on the phone with the victim at the time she was murdered."

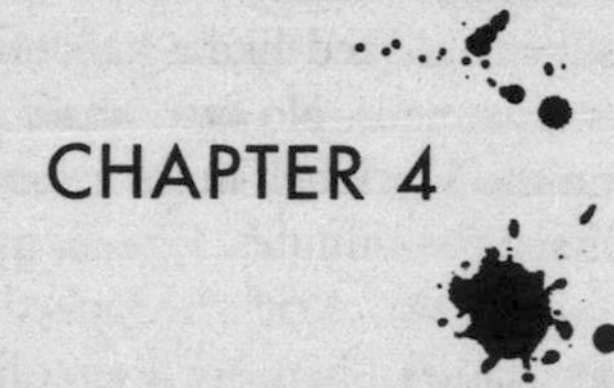

CHAPTER 4

Distraught was right. And she looked overwhelmed, too.

The woman was young, maybe midtwenties, with brown hair pulled back in a messy ponytail. She was juggling a kid on her hip, a diaper bag over her shoulder, and a handful of wadded tissues that she was using to mop up the tears on her cheeks. She sniffled and nodded her way through the introductions.

Sean led her into an interview room.

"Is it true? They didn't give a name on the news, but it's Sam, isn't it?"

Sean looked at the kid. Aiden, she'd said. Sean was no expert on kids, but this one had droopy eyes and a runny nose. "Is Aiden okay?" He pulled a chair out for the mother.

"He's got an ear infection. We were just at the clinic, and he's all out of sorts."

"Go home, Mommy. I wanna watch *PAW Patrol*."

Sean stuck his head out the door. The only people not on the phone were Jasper and Callie. So . . . six-foot-three uniform or petite, plainclothes detective?

"Callie." Sean motioned her over. She had a wary look on her face as she neared the door.

"I've got to interview a witness," he said in a low

voice. "Can you entertain her kid for a couple minutes?"

"Do I look like a nanny?"

In truth, she looked like a powder puff. Five-two, blond hair, blue eyes. No one would guess she was a ballbuster and a black belt in tae kwon do.

"I just need ten minutes. Fifteen, max. It's the Bonner case."

"Is this *the* kid?"

"Nah, too young."

She peered around Sean into the interview room. "Aw . . ." She made a little clucking noise. "He's just a toddler."

She glanced at Sean, and he knew he had her. It was the tongue cluck. But all maternal softness disappeared as she pointed a finger at his chest. "You owe me, Byrne. Big-time."

"Whatever you want. His name's Aiden, by the way."

Sean opened the door wider, and Callie walked over to the boy, who was running a red race car along the table.

"Hi, Aiden. I'm Miss Callie." She looked at the mom. "Think he'd like to see our kitchen? We've got some apple juice."

Amy whispered something to her son. After a moment of hesitation, he took Callie's hand and let her lead him from the room.

As soon as the door whisked shut, the tears started flowing again. Amy's brown eyes were puffy and bloodshot.

Sean took the chair across from her. He hated this part of his job, hated the look people always gave him when they wanted him to tell them they were wrong about something they already knew.

"The victim has been identified as Samantha Bonner."

She squeezed her eyes shut and nodded. She was silent for a few seconds and then blew her nose. "God, this can't be happening. It can't. I just talked to her last *night*."

"When?"

"About eight forty-five." She shook her head. "She was supposed to come over."

"I need you to check the time on that."

She dragged the diaper bag into her lap and pulled out a black cell phone. "Eight forty-two. The call was four minutes."

Sean opened his notebook and jotted down the time. They hadn't recovered Samantha's phone, which made Sean wonder if the killer had been in communication with her and stolen the phone to cover his tracks.

"Take me through that conversation. Did she call *you*?"

Amy took a deep breath. She flipped her phone over and seemed to collect herself as she clutched the tissue that was already disintegrating.

"I called Sam. She was on her way home from work. I asked her to come over for coffee." Amy closed her eyes again. "I needed to talk to her."

"And where was she when you called?"

"In her car. She told me she'd just closed up. The place she works, it closes at eight, but she has to clean everything, refill the condiments and napkin dispensers, all that side work. It takes about forty minutes."

"And did she say she would come over or . . . ?"

"Yes. I mean, that was the impression I got. I don't remember exactly, but the call got cut off and she never came."

"Cut off?"

"It dropped. At least, that's what I thought." A pained look came over Amy's face. "You think maybe . . . someone *else* hung up on me?"

"I don't know." Sean watched her eyes. "What do you think?"

"I . . . I'm not sure. Sam has a cheap phone. It's always cutting out and dropping calls." Amy shook her head. "I texted her after, and that's when Aiden started crying—he woke up with another earache, and I got sidetracked. He gets them all the time. The doctor said he should have tubes put in, but we haven't done that."

"Could you write down that phone number for me?"

"Sam's number?"

"Yes, ma'am."

Sean slid his pad across the table and she scribbled down a number.

"And how long have you known Sam?"

"Only a year. But we talk almost every day. Sometimes twice. She's my sponsor. You know, AA."

So, Brooke was right. "And how was she doing with the program?"

Amy snorted. "Better than me."

"Do you know if she had any problems besides alcohol? Any drugs?"

She shook her head. "Not Sam."

"You sure?"

"Absolutely."

Sean didn't know how she could be so certain, but he wanted to move on, so he flipped to a clean page in his book. "Do you know if Sam has any family living in town?" They'd had trouble locating her next of kin.

"I don't know. If she did, she never said anything, and I think she would have."

"And did she have any children?"

"No." Amy dabbed her nose with the tissue. "She's never been married."

That wasn't what he'd asked, but he let it go. "Are there kids she liked to spend time with?"

"Well, she spends time with Aiden."

He nodded. "Any others? Maybe kids of neighbors or friends from AA? Anyone she babysat?"

Amy shook her head, looking confused now. "Why?"

"We're trying to get a picture."

"Sam loves kids. She's great with them. *Was.*" Amy closed her eyes. "She went trick-or-treating with us this year."

Sean waited, watching her. He'd become an expert at reading people, and this woman looked genuinely shocked by everything. And she hadn't been evasive with his questions.

"Was Sam having trouble with anyone that you know about?"

Amy shook her head.

"Was she dating anyone?"

"No."

"Seeing anyone casually?"

The door opened and Callie poked her head in. "Sorry to interrupt, Detective." She gave him a too-sweet smile and then looked at Amy. "Someone brought in doughnuts this morning. Is it all right if Aiden has one?"

"Sure. Thank you."

Callie disappeared, and Amy looked at him. "Sam didn't have a boyfriend. Not since I've known her. Guys were always hitting on her, but she wasn't into it."

"Why not?"

"I don't know."

"You think she had a problem with someone in her past?"

"I don't know. Maybe." Amy tipped her head to the side. "I always thought she had some skeletons in the closet, but doesn't everyone?"

Sean didn't answer that.

"Come to an AA meeting, if you don't believe me." Amy shook her head, and he got a glimpse of some resilience underneath all the tears.

"What about family connections?"

"I think she mentioned her mom once, but it wasn't like they were close."

Amy flipped her phone over and looked at the time. "I'm sorry. I'm supposed to work soon." She rubbed her forehead. "God, I really need to go to a meeting."

"Where do you work?"

"The Cotton Gin. My shift starts at two." She stood up, and Sean stood, too. "Can we finish this later if you have more questions?"

"That's fine." He was sure he'd have more questions, but it would be good to let her mull things over. "If you think of anything else that would help, call us." He handed her a business card.

She looked at the card and bit her lip. "One more thing. The news said . . . they said she was stabbed?" Amy gave him a pleading look.

Sean nodded, and her face crumpled.

"Oh, that's horrible. *Horrible*. Sam doesn't deserve this. Nobody deserves this."

The door opened, and it was Aiden and Callie. The boy had a gold police-badge sticker on his T-shirt and icing on his chin.

"Aiden tells me his ear hurts," Callie said.

"Come here, sweet pea." Amy scooped him up and shifted him onto her hip. "We'll get you your drops, okay?" Then she looked at Sean. "I hope you find the person who did this. I hope you find him and nail him to the wall."

• • •

Brooke swept her UV light over the seat for the third time, and for the third time she found nothing. She crouched beside the car and examined the floor-boards.

"Any chance we can get some lights on in the next hour?" Roland Delgado asked.

Brooke glanced across the lab at him. He was seated at his computer in the corner. His spiky dark hair looked jet-black, and the screen cast his face in a blu-ish hue. Up to now he'd been patient with the on-again, off-again lighting in the lab as Brooke examined Sa-mantha Bonner's car.

Brooke shoved up her goggles and flipped on the light switch, illuminating the cavernous room. "This doesn't make sense. This doesn't feel like a drug addict's car to me."

"Oh, yeah?" Roland didn't take his eyes off his screen. "What does a drug addict's car feel like?"

"You know. Messy. Disorganized. Crap everywhere."

"Not everyone's a slob."

"Okay, but two grams of coke in the glove box, and nothing anywhere else? I'd expect to find a trace of something. I mean, what do addicts do when they go make a buy? They pull over and get a fix, right? Or they race home to do it. Are we supposed to believe this woman went out and bought more than a hundred dollars' worth of coke and then left it in her car overnight? Who does that?"

"I dunno."

"Plus, she makes twelve bucks an hour. So why's she buying cocaine in the first place and not something cheaper? The whole thing doesn't add up."

Brooke crossed the lab to the fume hood and took another look at the plastic baggie inside the rectangular glass chamber. She'd fumed it again using cyanoacrylate, but hadn't developed any additional fingerprints besides the one distinct thumbprint at the top of the bag.

"And look at this baggie. One thumbprint, and it belongs to the victim."

"So?"

"So, it doesn't make sense."

"Evidence doesn't lie, Brookie."

"What about prints of whoever she bought it from?"

"Maybe he wore gloves."

"Yeah, I'm sure."

"Hey, it can happen." Roland still hadn't looked up from his screen. "He could be one of those rare drug dealers who hasn't fried half his brain cells."

"Okay, but *one* thumbprint and it conveniently belongs to the victim? I mean, how do you even hold a bag that way?"

Roland swiveled around in his chair. "Are you saying it's a plant?"

"I don't know."

"Why would someone plant coke in her car?"

"I don't know. To throw off investigators, maybe? To confuse them about motive?"

Roland leaned back in his seat and laced his hands behind his head. "You're the one who's confused, Brooke. It's the detectives' job to figure out motive. You're a trace-evidence examiner. You should worry about examining *trace evidence*. Full stop."

Brooke rolled her eyes. They'd had this argument before. But Brooke couldn't work a case—or couldn't do her *best* work—unless she thought about the big picture. She discovered a lot more clues that way.

Roland grinned at her. "You're trying to throw the whole case into a tailspin, aren't you?"

"I'm not trying to throw anything into a tailspin. I'm trying to make sense of it. Her house is just as weird. No drugs there, either."

"Maybe she only recently had a relapse."

"We vacuumed the sofa, the chairs, the rug. We tape-lifted the tabletops. We swabbed the sinks. Nothing. All we found were some coffee grounds and a few dog hairs on the couch."

"So, she wins the Good Housekeeping Award. So what?"

"No drugs in her purse. Not so much as an aspirin. But she *did* have three one-year sobriety chips from Alcoholics Anonymous."

Roland shook his head. "You're determined to make life complicated. Why do I bother?"

"Don't you want to help solve the case?"

"Yes. By analyzing trace evidence. That's my job. Let the detectives do theirs."

Brooke sighed. "How's that footwear impression coming?"

"I submitted it. Still waiting to hear back. It's only a partial, so it takes longer."

Maddie walked into the room. "Hey, I thought you guys would be gone by now."

"Gone where?" Roland asked.

"Over to Schmitt's. Didn't you get the email? It's Kelsey's birthday. A bunch of us are meeting there."

"Kelsey's birthday, huh?" Roland checked his watch. "Who all's going?"

"Gee, let's see." Maddie gave him a teasing smile. "*Kelsey* is going. And Ben. Oh, and I think that new woman in the forensic anthro lab? The young blond one? What's her name?"

"Sara Lockhart," Brooke said. Roland had been ogling her for weeks and clearly saw his chance. He was already shutting down his computer as Maddie waved and ducked out.

"You coming?" he asked Brooke.

"I don't know." She didn't feel like sitting at a beer garden tonight.

"Oh, come on. One beer."

"I'll probably stay here a while."

"Come on, Brooke. What time did you get here today? Seven?"

"Six."

"Jesus, you trying to make us all look bad? Pack it in. Go home already. Or better yet, come have a brew with your friends."

"I should get home."

"Your loss." He clamped a hand on her shoulder and gave her a serious look. "But know this, Brookie-Brooke. You used to be fun."

He walked out, leaving her alone in the huge room. She looked at her worktable, blanketed in case files.

Four open cases right now, including the still-fresh homicide that had consumed her since last night when she'd first gotten the call.

Brooke looked around the lab. It was still and quiet, and the smell of cyanoacrylate hung in the air. Usually, she liked working at night because she could concentrate better.

But a break sounded tempting. So did spending time with her friends. Problem was, Schmitt's was a cop hangout, and she could easily imagine bumping into someone she *didn't* want to see.

You used to be fun.

"Screw it," she muttered, pulling off her goggles and tossing them on the table. Roland was right.

• • •

Within five minutes of arriving at Schmitt's, Brooke saw that Roland had no interest in Kelsey's birthday and every interest in hitting on Kelsey's new lab assistant. Sara Lockhart had pretty green eyes and a friendly smile. Brooke liked that Sara had no trouble holding her own when Roland tried to talk her into a game of pool.

"Not now, thanks," she said, and then jumped back into the conversation at the far end of the table. Despite the chilly weather, Kelsey had chosen to sit outside at a picnic table under the oak tree wrapped in twinkle lights. Most of the guys from work were inside playing pool, which left Maddie, Sara, and Brooke with the birthday girl.

A waiter delivered Brooke's beer and walked off.

Maddie lifted her eyebrow. "He's cute." She gave Brooke a hopeful look.

"Yep. Too bad he's not on the meal plan."

"Meal plan?" Sara asked.

"Brooke's on a man diet," Kelsey explained.

"It's more of a fast." Brooke slurped the foam off her Guinness. "I just got out of a bad relationship. Two, actually. I seem to have a talent."

Sara nodded. "I see. Bad as in . . . commitment-phobe? Cheater? Man-child? Just reciting what jumps to mind based on personal experience."

"Hmm . . . The most recent one, I'd say, is in the man-child category. The one before that . . . probably commitment-phobe. But it wasn't just me. He was afraid of commitment in all its forms. Jobs, bills, personal hygiene."

Sara made a face.

"He was an unemployed drummer," Brooke said.

"I think that's redundant." Maddie looked at Sara. "My first boyfriend was a drummer, so I can relate. Sort of. Actually, I traded him in for a doctor, who turned out to be even more of a toad, so I probably shouldn't be chiming in."

"But she's now happily married to a very hot FBI agent, so it all worked out," Kelsey said.

Maddie smiled. "Yes, it did."

Sara turned to Brooke. "So, what happened with the drummer?"

"Joshua. Basically, I woke up one morning and realized I'd been paying his bills for a year while he smoked pot on my couch. So I broke up with him. And I decided I was done with guys that had no motivation. Then I went to the other guardrail. Matt."

"This is the recent guy?"

Brooke nodded. She felt a knot in her stomach, which shouldn't still be happening. It had been four months. "He had a job and everything. Actually, two.

He's a cop and a volunteer firefighter. But he was a little intense."

"Controlling," Kelsey said.

"Intensely controlling." Brooke sipped her beer. "So, what about you?"

Sara smiled. "I'm very single. And very happy that way." She clinked Brooke's glass. "No offense to all the newlyweds. There seem to be a lot at Delphi. There must be something in the water."

Brooke looked around the table at her friends. Sara had only just met everyone, and she'd already noticed that their friendship group at Delphi was mostly newlyweds. Slowly but surely, everyone was meeting their soul mate and pairing off. Brooke was happy for them. Truly. Every one of her friends had been through some sort of relationship trial by fire to get to their current state. Brooke didn't see those same things in her future, though. She didn't know if she ever wanted to be married, and she was sick of thinking about it, sick of dealing with relationships at all. Hence, the man diet.

A few minutes later Roland reappeared, and Brooke could tell he'd won by the deflated expression on Ben's face.

"Okay, who's next?" Roland asked. "Brooke, how about you and Ben versus me and Sara?"

Ben slid onto the bench beside Brooke. "I'm out."

"Same." Brooke lifted her beer. "I'm still working on this."

"Come on. Really?"

"Really."

"I'm out, too," Sara said. "I'm having too much fun talking."

Roland took the spot across from Sara and signaled a server.

"Whoa." Maddie put her hand over Brooke's. "Speak of the devil," she whispered.

Brooke followed her gaze to the bar.

Where Matt was pulling up a stool.

Brooke's stomach clenched. "Unbelievable."

"You think he saw your car?"

"Ha. Yes, in a manner of speaking."

Matt ordered a drink and pretended not to see Brooke as he chatted up a pair of women beside him. He was in his typical off duty attire of jeans and cowboy boots. Brooke turned away and sipped her beer.

No doubt he'd noticed every person she was with, including Roland. He'd never liked that she and Roland worked together. Matt had a jealous streak and had frequently accused her of having a secret thing with Roland, even though Brooke had never cheated on anyone, ever.

Maddie leaned closer. "Has he been following you?"

"No."

Maddie lifted her eyebrows.

"He hasn't. He just keeps . . . showing up places. The grocery store. My gym. *Our* gym, I should say. Maybe it's a coincidence."

"Or maybe he's following you."

"No, sometimes he's there before I am. Small town, right? I should get used to it." Brooke pulled a twenty from her purse. "Listen, I need to head out. Throw my money into the pot, will you?"

Brooke slid from the picnic table and said a quick good-bye to Kelsey, trying not to put a damper on the birthday festivities.

When Brooke started to leave, Maddie was at her side. "I'll walk you out."

"I'm fine. I'm parked in the front row."

"Really, I insist."

When they were on the sidewalk, Brooke spotted her little Prius. Matt's oversize pickup was parked right beside her car, making it look like a toy.

"Subtle, isn't he?"

Maddie gave her a worried look. "Are you sure everything's okay with him?"

"Actually, no." Brooke glanced back at the door. "I thought maybe he installed a Snitch on my car or something. I took it to the shop, but they didn't find anything."

"Oh, my God, Brooke. That's insane. Let me talk to Brian."

"No. The last thing I need is an FBI agent confronting him."

"But if he's harassing you . . ."

"I'm being paranoid."

"Maybe you're not. Maybe he's tracking you some other way. Like your phone."

Brooke's stomach sank. She hadn't thought of that. "I'm so fucking done with this." Gritting her teeth, she popped her locks and managed to get the door open just enough to squeeze through.

"You should have Alex take a look at your phone. If there's anything on there, you can bet she'll find it." Alex Lovell worked in Delphi's cybercrimes unit and had plenty of tricks up her sleeve.

"I'll get her to take a look."

Brooke slid behind the wheel, and Maddie watched her leave. As Brooke pulled out of the parking lot, she let out a sigh of relief. No unwelcome taillights in her rearview mirror. And she was headed home.

She felt tapped. She glanced at the clock and was surprised to see it was only 8:35. Almost exactly twenty-four hours since Samantha Bonner had been ambushed on her back porch.

Brooke rolled to a stop at an intersection, vividly remembering the blood-soaked crime scene. That poor woman. Brooke wondered if she'd had enough time to realize what was happening to her.

When the light turned green, Brooke pulled a U-turn. She wasn't ready for home yet.

CHAPTER 5

Sean curved around the bend and dipped down over the low-water bridge, passing the spot where some guy had smashed his car into a tree last night. Sean turned onto Cypress Hollow and spotted Brooke's white Prius in the glow of a streetlight near the victim's house. He pulled over and parked as Brooke got out of her car.

She glanced up and down the block as she approached him. She had on the same clothes as earlier—including the sexy black boots—and her hair was back in the ponytail she always wore for work. Looked like she hadn't been home yet, either.

She stopped and gazed up at him. Her eyes were a mesmerizing blue-green color that seemed to change with her surroundings. Right now they were deep blue.

"Hi." She seemed . . . anxious. Maybe because only a few hours ago a woman had been slaughtered just footsteps away from here.

"Hi."

"Did you find the child?" she asked, studying his face.

"No."

She looked away. The child witness was not a hypothetical. Not to Brooke. It was a living, breathing person. A very vulnerable one.

"We were here all afternoon," Sean said, pulling her gaze back to him. "We talked to the neighbors. There are some children around, but none that fit."

"How old?"

He nodded across the street. "People over there have a baby and a three-year-old."

"Too young."

"And a block over there are some teenagers ranging in age from sixteen to nineteen."

Brooke stared down the street and sighed. She started toward the house, and Sean fell into step with her.

"Thanks for meeting me," she said.

"I was on my way here anyway. It's been twenty-four hours."

Sean liked to see a crime scene in close to the same conditions as when the crime occurred. There was no rain tonight, but the lighting would be similar, and probably some of the same people and cars would be coming and going as residents went about their evening routines.

Sean let Brooke go up the front steps ahead of him. He took out his pocketknife to slice through the police seal over the door, then used the key the landlord had given him.

Brooke stepped inside first. Someone had left a box of gloves on the floor near the door, along with the crime-scene log. Sean signed in and passed the log to Brooke before pulling on some gloves.

He stood for a moment and looked around. The house was cold. Still.

"There's something off about this." Brooke turned to look at him.

"I was thinking the same thing."

Sean caught a faint trace of vanilla, but none of the superglue smell that usually lingered at Brooke's crime scenes. She'd taken the evidence back to the lab for fuming this time.

"When will the scene be released?" she asked.

"Few days. Maybe tomorrow. Depends when the DA can get out here."

The case was grabbing headlines already, and the county prosecutor was eager to get a piece of it. She'd want to see the scene for herself, along with her staffers.

Brooke walked down the hallway toward the bedrooms, and Sean crossed the living room to check out the television. The remote had been collected for fingerprinting, so Sean used the button on the set to power it on. *The Simpsons* was beginning.

Brooke walked over and stared at the TV, and Sean took a moment to study her profile. Her neck looked way too distracting with her hair pulled up that way. Even more distracting was the thin black sweater that clung to her breasts. He shouldn't be having these thoughts about her at a death scene where the blood was barely dry. But he couldn't help it. Most times he got to see her they were in the aftermath of some kind of violence.

Brooke stepped into the kitchen and went straight for the freezer. She examined the ice trays and poked through the bags of frozen vegetables. The freezer was a common place to hide drugs or money, but investigators hadn't found anything.

"We did all that," he said. "Same for the air vents, the toilet tank, and the crawl space."

She glanced at him over her shoulder.

"I had our drug dog out here, too. He didn't alert on anything."

She walked past Sean to stand in front of the open pantry, where she combed through the soup cans.

"What are you thinking?" She looked at him.

"Same thing you are. I'm not buying the drug connection."

He filled her in on the interview with Sam's friend from AA, and Brooke's mouth dropped open. "You're *kidding* me."

"No."

"You think she was *on* the phone with Samantha when the murder happened?"

"Could be. It's hard to pin down the timing that precisely, but it's possible. Anyway, you were right about the AA thing. And this friend doesn't think Samantha was into drugs at all."

"So, what then? You think the evidence was planted?"

He scoffed. "Not by us."

"The killer?"

Sean didn't say anything. He tucked his hands in his pockets and watched her work through it.

"I see evidence she was a recovering alcoholic and a healthy eater and a neat freak, maybe even OCD," Brooke said. "But not that she was a drug addict."

"People fall off the wagon."

She shot him a look. "You sound like Roland."

She walked through the utility room and unlocked the back door, then stepped out onto the porch. The brown-black stain covered the area near the door. The landlord, who had talked to Ric that afternoon, was in a hurry to get the place cleaned up and vacated so he could get a new tenant in. Business as usual.

Brooke stared down at the blood, and Sean felt a

pang of uneasiness. He didn't like seeing her standing there.

"Very emotional." She knelt down and looked at the wood, where the stain went deep into the grain.

Sean crouched beside her. "You mean because of all the blood?"

"The violence of what he did to her," Brooke said quietly. "So much rage."

Sean knew what she meant, and he'd seen that kind of emotion before. "Makes me think of a jealous ex. Some guys are allergic to rejection."

She glanced up at him. Then she looked out at the driveway. "Are you familiar with Locard's principle?"

"Every contact leaves a trace."

"Exactly." She stood up, and Sean did, too. "A perp leaves behind evidence. But the reverse is also true. We haven't found much of him. The attack happened fast, no sexual assault, he didn't go inside." Brooke's gaze locked on Sean's. "But if you get a suspect, if you get me his clothes or his shoes or his car, I *will* find a trace of her on him."

Her voice vibrated with determination, and Sean had no doubt she'd do it. Brooke was smart and tough and good at her job.

Underneath her toughness, he detected some skittishness, though. He didn't know what it was about, but he was determined to get past it. He wanted to get to know her better.

She turned and picked her way down the creaky wooden steps.

"Speaking of dogs," she said, "we found dog hair on one of the sofa cushions."

"She didn't have a dog."

"Maybe she had a visitor who does. Maybe an

ex-boyfriend, or her friend Amy, or possibly the child we're looking for."

"You sure it's a dog and not a cat?" he asked. "I noticed a striped tabby hanging around here."

"Animal hair varies by species. Microscopic examination reveals different scale patterns on the hair cuticle. It's definitely a dog."

Sean wasn't going to argue. He knew jack shit about scale patterns on hair cuticle. But it seemed odd for the victim to have dog hair on her couch when she didn't have a dog. "You know what kind of dog?"

"Long, light hair. Possibly a Labrador mix."

Sean filed it away as she went to stand in the spot where Samantha's car had been parked. The Kia was now at the Delphi Center garage.

"You guys start on the car yet?"

She nodded. "We didn't get much. It's clean and well maintained. Recently had an oil change. Again, not the usual MO for a drug addict. There's something else we're working on, though."

Sean perked up. She had that tone she always got when she was onto something, but didn't want to get his hopes up. "What is it?"

"Let me show you."

She led him to the trash cans at the side of the one-car garage. Last night Sean had checked out the dilapidated structure, which was used as a storage shed for torn screens and old paint cans.

"We believe the victim was ambushed," Brooke said. "So the killer had to have been hiding somewhere nearby, then approached her from behind for the attack. I think he was crouched here behind the trash cans. Roland found a footwear impression that corroborates that theory."

"I thought we didn't have any footprints because of the rain?"

"This wasn't in the dirt. Roland recovered a small styrofoam box, like you get for fast food, flattened right here beside the trash can. You'll see it if you go through all the crime-scene photos. Looks like someone stepped on the box while he was crouched here. It's only a partial impression, but the herringbone tread pattern looks consistent with a small portion of a footprint made in blood on the bottom step of the deck. So, we're thinking it's the killer."

"Any idea the shoe size?"

"No, and we're not optimistic on that because it isn't a full print. But we're running the tread pattern through the database to see if we can get the type of shoe. We're lucky with the styrofoam—it's pretty impervious to the elements."

"I'll take any luck we can get, at this point."

A woman at the end of the driveway caught Sean's attention. She was pretending to walk her dog as she watched what they were doing. The woman was short and heavyset, and she had a yappy terrier on the end of the leash.

Sean strolled over to her. "Evening, ma'am."

She nodded warily.

"Detective Sean Byrne." He gave her a smile. "Do you live on this street?"

"On the end there. Right before the hollow."

So, this would be Mrs. Morton, the widow who lived alone. Sean had read Jasper's interview notes.

"Have they caught him yet?" She squinted at the house.

"We're working on it. Ma'am, have you seen any suspicious people or vehicles around here lately? Maybe even today?"

She shook her head. "Except for the news van. They were here this morning, but they haven't been back since."

"And were you home last night?"

"I was at church. Wednesday potluck. Then I stopped by the store. I came home about nine and unloaded a few groceries."

Sean nodded. "Do you remember any cars you might have passed?"

"The officer yesterday asked that. I don't remember any."

"Hear any noises or commotion?"

"Well, it was raining. Not a lot, but enough to keep people indoors instead of walking their dogs and whatnot." She tipped her head to the side. "When I was unloading the groceries, I heard a screech of brakes down by the bridge. People are always taking that turn too fast and running off the road there. Someone did it last night, too."

Sean's pulse picked up. "What time was this noise?"

"Like I said, about nine. Maybe a little before."

The first responder had arrived at nine fifteen. The wreck that held up Sean and Ric had happened even later than that.

Sean took out a business card. "Thanks for your help tonight. If you think of anything else—"

"I'll be sure to call." She took the card.

Brooke joined Sean at the end of the driveway as Mrs. Morton and her terrier walked off. "What was that about?"

"Come on."

Sean headed down the street toward the hollow. They passed the widow's house, and then the fenced yards gave way to overgrown bushes. The air smelled like wet leaves, and a thick layer of kudzu covered everything except the road and the guardrail.

Sean approached the tree where the guy had crashed his car last night. The front of the black sedan had been crumpled like an accordion. Up ahead, Sean could make out the fresh yellow wound in the tree trunk.

"What time did you get to the scene last night?" He looked at Brooke.

"Around nine forty. Why?"

"Ric and I reached the neighborhood just before ten and got stuck behind a wreck."

"Yeah, you said."

"That witness heard brakes down here around nine."

They stopped beside the guardrail that was bent and twisted. Black skid marks led directly to the tree.

"There's a second set of skids here," Brooke said.

Sean turned around. She was standing on the opposite side of the road about ten yards back.

Sean crossed the street, pulling out his flashlight. He swept the beam over the guardrail. The railing was bent in one place, but the damage looked old.

"Doesn't look like the car left the roadway," she said. "But it clearly swerved and braked."

Sean glanced around. No streetlights here, only the reflectors along the curved metal barrier that had been smashed into time and time again. He walked all the way to the end of the guardrail, moving his light over the vegetation. Some of the weeds were bent and broken.

Sean waded into the brush, his stomach growing heavier with every step.

"Where are you going?"

He didn't answer as he pushed aside some branches and crouched down to look at a blue baseball cap with a Red Sox logo on it. Behind him, Brooke gasped.

The land dropped off sharply. Sean picked his way down, shining his light around. The beam landed on something white. Sean held his breath as he peeled away the branches.

"Sean?" Her voice was small and fearful.

He stared down at the mangled metal, then turned to look at her. She was a dark silhouette at the top of the ridge.

"Sean, what is it?"

"A kid's bike."

CHAPTER 6

Roland walked in and plunked a Slurpee on her work-table. "Wild cherry."

Brooke didn't look up. The print she was attempting to lift required her undivided attention. "Thanks. Next one's on me."

"Forget it. You've got visitors, by the way."

She glanced up. "Who?"

"Two detectives, a man and a woman."

She narrowed her gaze at him. Why didn't he just say who they were?

Roland smiled, and she knew he was needling her. Maybe he'd picked up on the weird tension between her and Sean.

As if on cue, Sean stepped into the laboratory, followed by Callie McLean. Both wore visitor's badges.

Brooke put down her fingerprint powder. "Hi." She didn't bother to hide her surprise.

"We decided to stop by."

She glanced at Callie, who was looking around the lab curiously. To Brooke's knowledge, she'd never before been down here.

Sean stepped closer, his attention drawn to the red brick on Brooke's worktable. "What's that?"

"A murder weapon."

"Don't tell me you're trying to get a print off that thing?" Sean said.

"You sound like a very annoying sheriff's deputy who told me not to bother."

"Never tell Brooke she *can't* do something," Roland said from across the room. "Only pisses her off."

Callie stepped over to take a look. The brick had dried blood on it because it had been used to bludgeon a man to death. Brooke had already used an alternative light source to locate a trio of prints on the side of the weapon. The challenge was lifting the prints from such a textured surface. She had dusted the area with black magnetic powder and photographed it, and now came the hard part.

"You guys mind waiting a sec? I have to finish this before my casting material dries."

"Not at all." Sean smiled as he stood back to watch.

Brooke wasn't used to having an audience, but she tried to stay focused as she dipped a plastic spatula into a small bowl of liquid silicone. "Right now it's the consistency of toothpaste." She carefully coated the area. "When it dries, I'll be able to lift the prints. They'll show up black against the white putty. I'll then reverse the images using digital photography and run the prints through the database."

"Impressive," Sean said.

"Hopefully. We'll know in a few minutes." She finished applying the material and turned to look at her audience. "So. What can I do for you, Detectives?"

"We're checking in on our evidence," Sean said. "You managed to get to it yet?"

"First thing this morning." Brooke stepped over to the maimed bicycle in the vehicle bay beside Samantha Bonner's Kia. Even the kickstand was bent.

Callie circled the bike. "Wow. This thing is trashed."

"We got transfer paint off the frame. The paint is dark red, but you knew that already. We're waiting on a make and model of the vehicle."

Callie glanced at Brooke. "You can get make and model just from the paint?"

"Oftentimes, yes. The sample is analyzed not just by pigment, but also the layering involved—the undercoat, topcoat, clear coat—to narrow down the particular type of vehicle."

"What about his fingerprints?" Sean asked.

Callie looked at him. "*His*?"

"It's a boy's bike, so we're going with that assumption." Brooke looked at Sean, who was watching her steadily with those hazel eyes.

"No prints. It's the same problem we had at the crime scene. Very fragile evidence, and the rain doesn't help us." Brooke turned to Callie. "Based on the size of the bike and the lack of fingerprints, it's probable it belongs to a boy between eight and ten."

"Maybe our mystery witness?" Callie asked hopefully.

"It's possible. The timing works. A neighbor heard a screech of brakes about nine p.m. We saw skid marks leading to the area where the bike was recovered. *And* a close examination of some of the crime-scene photos shows a tire mark on the driveway."

"I've got them here," Roland said from his computer.

Everyone gathered around his chair as he scrolled through a seemingly endless series of photographs. The shots started at the base of the driveway, capturing the car and the house, and then nearing the back door where the body was found.

"That's a lot of photos," Callie said.

"Shoot your way in, shoot your way out," Brooke said. "That's Maddie's motto."

"Here." Roland stopped on a close-up shot of the driveway near the deck. A thin brown line on the asphalt appeared to be a muddy tire track.

"Zoom in on that," Sean said.

Roland enlarged the image. It definitely looked like a mark made by a bike tire.

"The rain washed it away before anyone got a good look at it, but at least we have it on film," Roland said.

"Does this mark match the bike?" Callie asked.

"Hard to say 'match' when all we've got to go on is a photograph," Brooke told her. "But I would say it's consistent with the bike we found in the hollow, which suggests the rider of the bike was at the crime scene."

Callie tipped her head to the side. "So, the scenario is that this kid sees something terrifying, leaves the scene in a hurry and isn't paying attention, and gets hit by a car as he races away?" She looked at Sean for confirmation.

"You're assuming it's an accident," Sean said.

"You're not?"

"Maybe the car belongs to the killer."

Brooke shuddered. The possibility had kept her up all night. Had Samantha's killer *seen* the child witness fleeing the house and tried to chase him down? If so, had the child escaped or not? A whole team of officers had combed the area last night, but they'd recovered no further clues beyond the crumpled bicycle and the youth-size Red Sox cap that Sean had found in the hollow.

"I hope you're wrong about this," Callie said. "But no matter what, we need to find this kid."

"We're also working on a shoe impression we recovered near the trash cans," Roland said. "The feds maintain a database, and I submitted what we have. Haven't heard back yet, but I can tell you it's a herringbone tread pattern."

"We'll be able to get a brand for you," Brooke said. "I can send you a picture, too, when it comes in."

The lab phone rang, and Roland reached for it. "Trace evidence." He listened for a few moments and looked at Brooke. "Sure, I'll tell her." He hung up. "That was Dave upstairs. He finished with the paint sample. Comes back to a Ford pickup or SUV, dark red."

"Damn," Callie said. "There have to be a lot of those in town. And statewide? We're talking about thousands."

"Date range '96 to '05," Roland added. "That should help narrow it down."

Alex Lovell stepped into the lab and looked surprised to see so many people. Her gaze settled on Brooke. "I got those results back."

Brooked nodded.

"Whenever you get a minute." Alex gave her a meaningful look and slipped out.

What had Alex found? Whatever it was, Brooke couldn't think about it right now.

She turned to Sean. "One last thing—and it may or may not help you. The bicycle is a boy's Mongoose mountain bike, around ten years old. Given that we think the boy riding it is around that age, it's safe to say the bike's a hand-me-down or possibly purchased at a resale shop. I know it's a long shot, but—"

"We'll check into it," Sean said.

"We need to move on this vehicle lead." Callie's

phone chimed, and she pulled it from the pocket of her blazer. "Sorry, I have to take this. Thanks for the fast turnaround, you guys."

Callie stepped out, leaving Sean behind with Brooke and Roland.

"Walk me out?" Sean nodded at the door.

Brooke followed him into the dim hallway. The trace-evidence lab occupied a remote part of the Delphi Center, and she wasn't used to so many visitors coming and going.

Sean propped his shoulder against the cinder-block wall and gazed down at her. "What's wrong?"

"What do you mean?"

"You're tense."

"I'm worried." About the child, she meant, but she didn't have to say that. Sean knew.

His gaze was steady, and she looked up into those sharp eyes that missed nothing. Was he this perceptive with everyone, or just her?

He reached over and tucked a lock of hair behind her ear. "We'll find him, Brooke." He rested his hand on her shoulder.

"I know you will."

• • •

Brooke went directly to the cybercrimes unit on the Delphi Center's top floor. The lab seemed strangely deserted for a Friday morning.

"Where is everyone?" Brooke asked as she approached Alex's cubicle. A row of vintage *Star Wars* figures lined the wall she shared with the neighboring cube.

"We pulled an all-nighter. Child-porn ring out of Dallas."

"God. I don't know how you do that."

"Same way you do." Alex pushed over a chair for Brooke to sit in. The slender brunette had a low-key way about her that always put Brooke at ease. "I hear you caught the Samantha Bonner homicide. Sean and Ric are on it?"

"They've got a whole team."

"Are we running all the evidence? I haven't seen a computer or a cell phone, but if they send something over, I can bump it to the front of my line."

"Thanks. I'll tell Sean."

"Here." Alex nodded at the phone on her desk. "Have a look at what I found."

Brooke eyed her phone with apprehension. It sat atop the mouse pad, and Brooke's glittery-white phone case was off to the side. "Did you have to take it apart?"

"Actually, no. Turns out your culprit is a stealth app."

"Stealth?"

"It's not visible. Unless you installed it, you wouldn't even know it was there."

"*You* did."

"I know what to look for. Thwarting electronic surveillance is my specialty."

"Electronic surveillance." A bitter lump rose in Brooke's throat.

"That's right."

Before joining the Delphi Center, Alex had run a PI firm that specialized in helping women in trouble disappear. Many of her clients were in abusive relationships and needed to drop off the radar.

Brooke had never imagined herself in that category. She wasn't. Not really.

"Brooke?"

"Sorry, what?"

"I said, have you heard of Tagger?"

"No."

"It's a spying app."

Damn him.

Damn him, damn him, damn him.

He'd gotten hold of her phone. When had he done it? And how had he known her password?

"Can you prove who put this app on there?" she asked Alex.

"That's what sucks. We can't. It's completely traceless until someone comes up with a program to crack it, which hasn't happened yet. Believe me, I've looked around."

"When did he do this?"

"I can't tell. But it could have been done remotely, so the possibilities are pretty wide-open. You think it's your ex?"

"Who else would it be?"

Alex stared at her.

"What?"

"You've told me he's controlling, but . . ."

"But what?"

"Is there anything else?" Alex asked. "Anything physical? You could press charges."

"No."

"You could. Trust me. I'm married to a cop, and he could help you."

"Thanks, but it wasn't like that. It never got to that point." Not really. "I saw where it was heading and I got out. At least, I thought I did."

Alex nodded. "Good for you."

Right. Good for her.

Brooke wished she could feel good about it, but instead she felt angry. And embarrassed. Yeah, she'd gotten out, but not before he'd maneuvered himself into a position to control her life from the inside out. And he was still doing it.

Tears of frustration burned her eyes as she stared at her phone. "So . . . what does this app do, exactly? He's able to see where I am? Listen in on my calls? What?"

"He knows your location anytime your phone is with you."

Brooke's chest clenched. "Son of a *bitch*. I hate him."

He'd been tracking her movements when she went out with friends, or to the gym, or on a solitary run to clear her head. God forbid she ever went on a date again.

No wonder he'd been showing up all the time.

"The good news is, this app's GPS only. He hasn't hijacked your camera or anything."

Her heart skittered. "That's really possible?"

"Unfortunately, yes."

"Guess I'm lucky, then, huh? And, hey, what would it matter anyway, since he's seen everything already?"

"It's your privacy, Brooke. It matters."

She looked away. "Sorry. I'm just . . . pissed." She wiped her cheeks, embarrassed now all over again for crying in front of Alex.

This was not her. None of it. Brooke didn't cry over guys.

She didn't let guys control her or jerk her around. Or tell her what to wear or how to cut her hair or what to eat, for Christ's sake. Except that she *had*, and now everything had gotten so out of hand.

The crazy thing was, she'd actually thought she loved him at one point. How had she been such a terrible judge of character?

Alex focused on the phone, swiping at the screen

while Brooke got her emotions under control. She'd thought she'd put all this behind her, and now it was back again.

"You've got two options," Alex said matter-of-factly, as though Brooke weren't sitting there weeping. "Option one, remove the app."

"Sounds like a no-brainer."

"The problem with that option is that he'll know that *you* know he put it there, which could prompt communication." Alex paused. "When it comes to cases like this, where the guy is controlling and obsessive, where there's any sort of stalking behavior, communication is what you want to avoid. It only feeds his delusion that you're in a relationship together. He's trying to get a reaction out of you, and you don't want to give him one. You're better off ignoring him."

Brooke's chest burned. "So, I'm just supposed to let him spy on me indefinitely?"

"I'm not saying that. Another option is to accidentally 'lose' your phone. Go paddleboarding and drop it in the lake or something."

Brooke squeezed the bridge of her nose. "Damn it, I don't have time for this! I'm working a homicide case."

"If he thinks it was lost or stolen, then he won't suspect you've figured him out when you switch to a new device."

"I can't afford a new device. Anyway, I like this one. I bought this phone less than a year ago, and I paid good money."

Alex nodded. "Okay. I hear you. But I've seen this before. You're essentially calling him out on what he did, and that might spark a confrontation. Are you willing to risk that?"

Brooke wrestled with the question. What was wrong

with her? She used to be so decisive. He'd undermined her faith in her own decision making.

"It's your call, Brooke. Whatever you want me to do, I'll do." Alex gave her a calm, reassuring look, and Brooke had never been so grateful to have her for a friend.

Brooke stared down at the phone—*her* phone—and she felt a surge of fury.

"Remove it. I don't care what he thinks. He can go screw himself."

CHAPTER 7

"This could be a waste of time, you know."

Sean glanced at Callie as she maneuvered the unmarked police unit through afternoon traffic.

"If she's wrong about the kid witness," Callie elaborated.

"*She* meaning Brooke."

"That's right. Or even if she's right about the kid witness, but wrong about him being on that bike, then we've wasted most of the day."

It was a fair point. They'd spent the better part of the day systematically working the list of locally registered vehicles that fit Brooke's description. They were on number thirty-two of more than one hundred. In a homicide investigation, early days were critical, and Sean hoped to hell they hadn't wasted one.

"It's a solid theory," he said. "Outside the box, but solid."

"Solid but not provable. That's my point."

He looked at her. "Not provable *yet*. If it pans out, we might have ourselves an eyewitness."

Callie stopped at a red light, and Sean checked out the gas station on the corner. No people with dark red pickups or SUVs gassing up or buying snacks.

"So, you have a thing for her?"

He looked at Callie.

"Don't act like you don't know what I'm talking about." Callie smiled. "I've worked with you for a year now."

"And?"

"And I'm a detective. I detect things. Such as vibes between people."

The light changed, and Sean looked out the window. *Between* people. So, Callie didn't detect that this thing—whatever it was—was only one-sided. Sometimes Sean wondered. Brooke seemed guarded around him, immune to his efforts to get her to loosen up. It wasn't a problem he usually had.

A lot of women had a thing for men in law enforcement, but not Brooke. She'd never seemed particularly impressed by Sean's job, which made him all the more determined to impress her in other ways. Sean wanted to get to know her. He wanted to get past the cool and aloof attitude she showed the world.

"You take the Fifth, huh?" Callie turned onto a street. "Why am I not surprised."

Sean gave her what he hoped was a neutral look and then read off the street number. "Should be up here on the left."

Callie neared the house, and low and behold, a dark red F-150 was parked right in front. No need to sneak up the driveway and set off a bunch of dogs.

Callie rolled to a stop and Sean hopped out. He circled the vehicle, a late-nineties pickup with an extended cab. He noted a scratch in the paint where someone had keyed the driver's-side door, but no dents. And no paint transfer, white or otherwise.

He returned to the car, frustrated. This process was tedious. They'd called every body shop in town this morning searching for the hit-and-run vehicle, but no one had seen it. That would have been too easy.

His phone buzzed as he slid back into the Taurus. "Byrne."

"I've got something for you."

Brooke's voice dissolved his tension. He liked the sound of it. And he liked that she knew she didn't need to identify herself.

"Lay it on me, and I hope it's good."

"I can narrow the list for you. Factoring in the wheelbase, we believe you're looking for a pickup truck, not an SUV."

Sean paused. "You went back and measured those tread marks. Why didn't I think of that?"

"Because you didn't spend your first year as a CSI investigating motor-vehicle accidents for the sheriff's office. I haven't always had this cushy gig at Delphi."

Cushy. Right. Sean knew what kind of hours she worked. With the exception of Wednesday night, Brooke was always one of the last to leave a crime scene. And she often went back for a second pass if the evidence she'd collected the first time didn't yield any leads. Brooke was fiercely dedicated to her work, and Sean admired her for it.

And, yes, Callie was right. He had a thing for her.

"Thanks for the tip." He wanted to ask Brooke what she was doing later, but he'd wait until he was alone.

"No problem. Call me if anything breaks, okay?"

"Same for you." He ended the call and looked at Callie. "Pickup trucks only, not SUVs."

"Go, Brooke. What's that do to our workload?"

Sean scanned the list. "Cuts it in half."

• • •

Brooke surveyed the storefronts. A dry cleaner, a nail salon, a doughnut shop. She had already tried the Dairy Queen on the corner and the convenience store across the street, but those had been dead ends. Her best bet was Sunrise Donuts.

Brooke had left work early to canvass Samantha Bonner's neighborhood. Roland would lecture her if he knew what she was up to. This wasn't her job. But Sean's team was overwhelmed, and Brooke couldn't let perfectly good leads go unpursued—not when a child's safety was at risk.

She entered the shop and was immediately hit by the scent of fried sugar. She didn't even like doughnuts, but her stomach growled in response.

A pimply-faced teen in a yellow apron stood behind the cash register. Beside him was a portly man who looked remarkably like the guy from the old Dunkin' Donuts commercials. *Time to make the doughnuts.* He was loading a sheet of fresh, perfectly glazed pastries into the case.

"Are you the manager?" Brooke asked cheerfully.

"Yes."

She flashed her official-looking Delphi Center ID badge. He glanced down, but didn't study it closely.

"I'm looking for a neighborhood boy who may have been in here recently. Around ten years old? He rides a white bike and wears a blue Boston Red Sox cap."

The manager fisted his hand on his hip. "What's this about?"

She smiled. "I'm afraid I'm not at liberty to say."

"We get a lot of kids in here. Especially after school." He glanced at the window, and Brooke followed his gaze. He did, indeed, have a number of young customers clustered around the metal picnic tables outside.

They looked too old, though. One girl held a pink leash with a sleeping beagle on the end of it.

"It's possible this boy might have had a dog with him?" Brooke looked at the manager.

"Sorry. Don't know him." He finished arranging pastries and looked at her. "You want to order something?"

"Uh . . . yes. A chocolate glazed. With sprinkles."

He nodded at the kid behind the register and then shuffled into the back room.

"Anything else?" the teen asked.

"And a bottle of water, please."

She glanced back at the outdoor tables. Not a single one of the customers there looked to be younger than fourteen.

"I know that kid you're talking about."

She turned around. "You do?"

"He comes in about once a week. Gets a dozen doughnut holes and always pays with quarters."

She glanced at his name tag. *Evan.* "And do you know his name?"

"Nope."

"Does he come in with a parent? Or maybe a sibling?"

"Nope."

"Does he hang out with anyone else here?"

"No. Just shells out his quarters and takes off."

Brooke's heart was racing now. She couldn't believe this. And she wanted to call Sean, but instead she calmly pulled out a ten and paid for her food.

"What's he look like?"

The teen rubbed his chin. "Skinny little guy. Red hair. Freckles. And the white bike, like you said. When he's on foot, sometimes he brings a little white dog with him."

Her pulse jumped. "What kind of dog?"

"I don't know. Think it's a mutt."

He handed back her change, and she dropped it into the tip jar.

"Want me to call you if I see him again?"

"Thank you, Evan." Brooke took out her business card. "You read my mind."

• • •

Sean was pulling out of the parking lot when he got a call from Ric.

"Get anything?" Sean asked.

"Nothing. What about you guys?"

"Struck out. Callie's going to do some drive-bys tonight, a few houses where the vehicles weren't there on our first pass."

"We had a lot of those," Ric said. "Okay, let's circle back in the morning. And I just got word from the ME's office. The official autopsy report is done. He emailed it over."

"Anything new?"

"I haven't read it yet. He sent some stuff over to Delphi, though. The bloody clothing, the nail clippings. If she'd had time to put up a fight, I might be hopeful for DNA."

"What about the tox screen?"

"I asked. Said it should be a few weeks."

Sean wanted it sooner. Reynolds was still pushing the drug angle, probably hoping the public would think the killing was gang related. Sean needed anything he could get—such as a tox-screen negative for drugs and alcohol—to bolster his case that the drugs were a plant.

"Maybe we can get a rush on it," Ric said, following the same train of thought as Sean.

"I'll contact the lab tomorrow. One of their techs owes me a favor."

"Good. You on call tonight?"

"Yeah. You?"

"I'm off. See you in the morning."

Sean hung up and wended his way home. He needed to hit the weights tonight and work on his leg, but what he really wanted to do was go to Brooke's.

He thought about how she'd looked last night at the crime scene. The case was weighing on her. He could tell. He'd learned to read the signs.

Sean wasn't sure when he'd become so tuned in to her. Sometime before the shooting that nearly ended his life.

Brooke had been the first person to visit him in the hospital. He'd been doped up on pain meds, in and out of consciousness after one of his surgeries. She'd been in his room, sitting silently in a chair while a TV droned in the background. He'd drifted out and the next time he'd come to, she was gone.

She'd never mentioned it. She probably didn't think he'd been aware of her, but he definitely had. Sean had sensed her there before he even opened his eyes. It was one of the strangest moments of his life, and all these months later he still couldn't get it out of his head.

He picked up his phone and called her.

"Hey, I was about to call you," she said. "I found something. At least, I think I did."

"What is it?"

"Our witness. The child. He's a regular at Sunrise Donuts. You know the place over on Sycamore right by Dairy Queen? I talked to the kid who works there—"

"Wait, hold up. You interviewed people?"

She paused. "Yeah. So what?"

"So, you're not a detective. You can't go around interviewing witnesses." She was doing his job for him. Worse, she was putting herself in a position to potentially cross paths with a murderer.

"Do you want this lead or not?"

"Damn it, Brooke."

"Fine, I'll give it to Callie."

"I want it. Do you have a name?"

"No, but I have a description."

Even a mere description was the best lead they'd had all day.

Information was only as good as the source, though. Sean had become an expert at reading people and sorting through their lies and evasions. Yet another reason it bothered him that Brooke had gone out and interviewed someone who should have been talked to by a trained detective.

"How reliable is the source? Scale of one to ten?"

"I'd say he's, I don't know, maybe an eight?"

"How'd you get him to talk to you? Tell me you didn't pretend to be a cop."

"I was just friendly. I chatted him up. Why are you pissed off?"

"I'm not."

"Yes, you are."

Sean tried to tamp down his reaction. He wanted her involved, but in the laboratory, not out pounding the pavement.

"Have you had dinner?"

The question seemed to throw her, and she didn't answer right away. "I ate something earlier."

"Let's meet for a drink, then. How about Schmitt's?"

Silence.

Sean looked down at his phone. "Brooke?"

"Yes?"

She was on her guard again, and he didn't know why. Damn it, one of these days he was going to convince her to have an actual meal with him. "It's just a beer. You can catch me up on this lead you developed by impersonating a detective."

"I told you, I did *not*—"

"Relax, I'm kidding. Will you please meet me at Schmitt's?"

He waited. And waited. As the silence stretched out, he tried to figure out when, exactly, she'd gotten him so worked up he was holding his breath over whether she'd agree to have a beer with him.

"You know Flannigan's?" she asked.

"The pub over on Oak Street."

"I'll meet you there in twenty minutes."

• • •

Brooke didn't have time to go home and change out of her yoga clothes, and part of her was relieved, because going home would give her the chance to bail out. She was taking a break from dating. But this wasn't a date, it was only a drink.

So why was she parked in the Flannigan's lot, rummaging through her gym bag, desperate for something to wear?

She eyed the door of the bar. Then she glanced around the parking lot before stripping down to her sports bra and pulling on a clean T-shirt. She tucked some loose strands of hair into her ponytail and checked the mirror.

Not great, but passable. Sean would be in his work clothes most likely—a button-down shirt, with his sleeves rolled up because it was the end of the day. Or maybe he'd be wearing that black leather jacket he'd worn to her house the other night.

Who cared what he was wearing? This was beer with a friend. Same as last night, except it was Sean instead of her coworkers.

Brooke spotted him as she stepped through the door. He turned around on his stool the moment she walked in. Maybe it was that weird connection they had going.

Or maybe he'd simply seen her in the mirror behind the bar.

His gaze locked on her as she crossed the bar. Sure enough, he'd worn the leather jacket, and she felt a twinge of excitement as the sexiest man in the room zeroed in on her.

"Saved you a seat."

She took the empty stool. "It's crowded."

"It's Friday. Considered by many to be the start of the weekend." He looked her over. "You changed."

"I had a yoga class."

Sean flagged the bartender, and she sauntered over with a flirty smile on her face. "Get y'all something?"

Sean nodded at Brooke.

"I'll have a Guinness, please."

"Make it two."

The bartender left, and Brooke turned to Sean.

"Yoga and Guinness." He smiled. "I like that."

"Gotta feed your soul."

"So"—his smile faded—"you want to tell me how this went down?"

"How what went down?"

"You finding our mystery witness."

"I haven't found him yet."

"It's only a matter of time now that we know where

to look. What'd you do, canvass the neighborhood?"

"Not really." Brooke shifted her gaze to the large Irish flag on the wall. Beneath it, in a row of cozy booths, couples were enjoying their drinks, and she felt a tug of envy.

She glanced back at Sean and shrugged. "Basically, I just did some poking around."

Two beers appeared in front of them, cold dark brews with frothy heads. The bartender smiled. "Anything else, Blue?"

"We're good, thanks."

She winked and walked off.

"Blue?"

"She knows I'm a cop."

Brooke managed not to roll her eyes.

Sean lifted his beer and clinked the glass against hers. "Here's to you."

"Why?"

"That was some decent work you did today."

"Gee, thanks, Blue."

"I'm serious. You took what sounded like a far-fetched theory and turned it into a real lead." He leaned closer. "But next time, stick with the physical evidence. Leave the interviews to the detectives."

The beer was cold and bitter and soothed the tension lingering in her chest. "You're very territorial about this."

"Not territorial. Protective."

"Of the case?"

"Of you." His bluntness startled her. "You shouldn't be mixing with potential suspects. It isn't protocol and it definitely isn't safe."

"I hardly think this kid is your suspect."

"Yeah, but you don't know how he fits in. Could be

it's his dad or his uncle or his older brother. We don't know how all the players tie together. If this kid was in her house—"

"He was."

"How do you know that?" His words had an edge now. "For all we know, this kid with the baseball cap got knocked off his bike the night of the murder, but has nothing to do with Samantha Bonner."

"Do you really believe that?"

"I don't believe anything yet. I'm still building a case theory."

She looked at him for a long time, considering it.

The bar was loud and getting louder. It wasn't the normal place to discuss a homicide investigation, or anything else of a macabre nature. But here they were.

He sipped his beer, watching her. "So, fill me in. What's this description you got?"

She gave him a rundown of her conversation with the teen at the doughnut shop.

"You notice any cameras?"

"What, like security cams?"

He nodded.

"No. But I doubt there would be any. It's a doughnut place, not a liquor store."

"I'll check."

"Why?"

"Maybe they have this kid on tape."

"If they do, you wouldn't actually release that, would you?"

"Depends. Video footage can be one of the fastest ways to ID someone."

"*No* video." She put her hand over his. "Promise me, Sean."

"I doubt we'd go that route, given the circumstances. We don't want to put a target on his back."

Brooke's stomach knotted. "There might be a target there already if the killer knows there was a witness. And if that witness happens to be the same kid who was bumped off his bike—"

"A lot of ifs."

Brooke couldn't disagree. Yet she couldn't shake the certainty that they were onto something. The fingerprints, the tire mark, the trashed bicycle. It all added up to a dangerous situation for this child, whoever he was.

"We'll find him," Sean said, reading Brooke's mind. How did he always seem to do that? She looked into his eyes and felt that warm pull.

Sean leaned close to her. "Can I ask you something personal?"

"Maybe."

"Are you always like this?"

"How do you mean?"

"So involved in your cases. Revisiting the crime scene, combing the neighborhood for witnesses. You're going way above and beyond here."

"Do you ever go above and beyond?"

"Yeah, and sometimes it lands me in trouble."

"Well, you get it, then. It's not all lab work. A lot of what I do happens outside the laboratory. Thoroughly exploring the crime scene is critical to the job because evidence is transitory. It can disappear before you even know it's there."

"This can't be your only case, though. I'm guessing you have a few other open files?"

"More than a few. We're always backlogged."

He watched her expectantly as he sipped his beer.

She looked away, skimming her gaze over the people around her. A lot of them were her age or younger, out living it up on a Friday night. Brooke couldn't remember the last time she'd gone anywhere with a man for the express purpose of having fun.

Two years with Matt had changed her. She was wary now, skeptical of people's motives. And worse, reluctant to trust her instincts when it came to men.

That pissed her off because she'd had so much confidence before. She'd felt so in charge of her life.

Sean was watching her steadily. Those eyes of his seemed to look straight into her soul.

"It's the kid thing," she said, getting back to the matter at hand. "I hate when children get caught up in the twisted stuff adults do to each other."

"You really believe he's involved."

"Yes, I really do."

"Another round?"

The bartender was back, and Brooke was surprised to see they'd drained their beers. And also surprised that her hand was still resting on top of Sean's.

Brooke reached for her purse. "I should get home."

"This is on me."

Sean took out his wallet, but she ignored him and left money on the bar to cover her drink and the tip. She didn't want him to think this was a date.

The place was filling up, and they had to squeeze their way through the crowd to get to the door. When they were out in the cold, damp air, Brooke took a deep breath. What little relaxation she'd achieved at her yoga class was long gone.

Without a word, Sean started walking her toward her Prius. No oversize black pickup pinning her in tonight, thank God. She cast a look around the parking lot.

"What kind of yoga do you do?"

She glanced at him. "Bikram."

He winced. "Too hot."

"You've tried it?"

"Running's much better for working up a sweat. Yoga's good for stress, though." He glanced at her. "Like you said, gotta feed your soul."

She would never have guessed he practiced yoga. It didn't fit her image of a tough-guy cop. Given his build, she'd always pictured him pumping iron in a gym.

"So, tomorrow's Saturday. Prime time for doughnuts," she said as they reached her car.

"We'll have someone check out the shop. Maybe he'll show."

"I can try to swing by there, too. Before I head to the lab."

"Brooke."

"What?"

He cupped her face in his hand and kissed her.

For an instant, pure shock. Then she registered the warmth of his fingers against her cheek, the press of his lips. His mouth moved against hers, and she opened for him—just like that, no hesitation. The most natural thing ever.

The touch of his tongue sent a surge of heat through her. Sean was kissing her. And all she could think was how right it felt, how *perfect*, and she let herself sink into him.

She liked the way he kissed her, liked the feel of his hand against her face as he tilted her head for a better angle. It went on and on until she was clinging to him, gripping his shirt in her fingers.

He eased back, and she blinked up at him, dazed.

"Wow," he said in a husky voice.

"Wow."

He rested his forehead against hers. "I've been wanting to do that for weeks."

She leaned back. "You have not."

"Okay, months."

She stared up at him. The corner of his mouth curved in that sly smile, and she reached up and pulled his head down for another kiss.

He kissed her back, and the sweep of his tongue brought another rush of heat. He glided his hands down to cup her hips and eased her back against the car, lining their bodies up, and she burrowed her hands inside the warmth of his jacket. He felt so good, everything about him. He was strong and solid and warm. She slid her hands around his waist and up his back to pull him even closer, and she was pressed between the cold hardness of her car and the hot hardness of Sean's body.

"Brooke."

She kissed him, desperate *not* to talk right now. She only wanted to keep the kiss going. She wanted to keep tasting him and feeling the rasp of his stubble against her skin. She pressed her breasts into him, craving his heat, wanting more of him as her entire body started to throb. When she rocked her hips against him, he made a low groan deep in his chest.

His hand slid up to her breast, and the brush of his thumb over her nipple made her squirm closer.

"Come home with me."

She didn't answer, and he kissed her again. She melted into him. But then he pulled away, and she saw the intensity in his eyes.

"Brooke, come home with me."

She jerked back, snapping out of the trance. "I'm sorry. I can't do this."

He watched her, searching her face.

"I'm taking a break from men."

Confusion came into his eyes. "Why?"

"It's complicated." She glanced around. God, what was she doing? One drink, and here she was throwing herself at him in the middle of the parking lot.

He stepped back, giving her space. She opened the car door and scooted around it, putting it between them so she wouldn't lose her resolve and kiss him again.

His phone buzzed, but he ignored it. He watched her with a look of concern as she slid behind the wheel. "Are you all right?"

"Fine." She forced a smile. "I'll call you tomorrow about the case."

• • •

Sean watched her pull out of the lot, cursing himself. He shouldn't have rushed her. He should have taken it one small step at a time, like he'd planned.

But one taste of her and his plan had gone up in flames. She was so hot, everything about her, and he couldn't resist touching her. He always knew they'd have chemistry, but he'd never expected *that*. He hoped to hell he hadn't screwed it up.

His phone buzzed again and he pulled it out. Callie. "What?"

"Hey, hey. What's your problem?"

"Nothing." He took a deep breath. "Everything okay there?"

"Better than okay. I got a lead from Samantha Bonner's phone dump."

"Let's hear it."

"I went back three months. She has a half dozen

calls from her boss, and a bunch more from one of her coworkers at the coffee shop, Kaitlyn Spence. Then she's got almost daily calls from Amy Doppler, her AA friend. But listen to this."

"I'm listening."

"She's also got calls from a *Jared* Doppler. Three late-night calls on Monday of last week. And Jared, my friend, has a rap sheet. Five years ago he did six months in lockup."

Sean's pulse quickened. "For what?"

"Aggravated assault. You'll never guess his weapon of choice."

"A knife."

CHAPTER 8

At noon the next day Sean pulled his pickup into a parking space beside Callie's SUV. She got out and jumped into his passenger seat.

She looked him over. "You're dressed up." He was in the dark suit he always wore in court. "How was Samantha's funeral?"

"Depressing." Sean hated funerals, but sometimes they came with the job.

Callie handed over a file folder, and Sean opened it in his lap as he loosened his tie. The plan was to go over some background info before they approached the target at his workplace.

Sean skimmed the phone records, focusing on the three highlighted calls from Jared Doppler. "Interesting timing."

"I thought so, too. Late enough to be a booty call." Sean glanced up, and Callie's expression turned slightly defensive. "Why else would he call her at one in the morning?"

"Drug buy?"

"Okay, good point." Her cheeks flushed. "I didn't think of that."

Sean smiled and tucked his tie into his pocket.

"Why was the funeral depressing? Besides the obvious."

"It was small. Who's this number here?"

"The registrar's office at her university. Mind if I have some coffee?"

"Sure." Sean finished with the phone records and then flipped through to Jared's rap sheet.

"Eww! It's stone cold."

He glanced up. "What'd you expect? I bought it at seven this morning."

Sean had spent an hour at the doughnut shop, but no sign of the kid. Or Brooke. He'd been on the lookout for both of them, but had completely struck out.

Callie put the coffee back in the cup holder. "How small is 'small'?"

"Eight people, including the priest."

"Yikes."

"Couple people from her job and an AA friend who sat with Amy. Plus her foster mom and a social worker."

"Any suspects?"

"With the exception of her boss and the priest, it was all women."

"What's the story with the foster mom and the social worker?"

"I don't know yet. After we finish here, I plan to find out." Sean handed back the paperwork. "Okay, I'm good. You ready?"

"Let's do it."

They got out of the truck and approached the hardware store, which was part of a local chain. Not as big as Home Depot, but sizable enough to attract a decent crowd on a Saturday afternoon.

Sean looked at Callie, who was in her typical detective outfit—black slacks, plus a blazer to conceal her firearm. Her shiny gold detective's shield was clipped at her hip.

"You take the lead," Sean said. "If my instincts are right about this guy, you're going to get under his skin."

She shot him a look as he held open the door.

The store smelled like fresh paint. They started at the customer-service counter, where they asked for Jared Doppler. He appeared a few minutes later with a scowl on his face, and Callie held up her police ID. After some tense words with a manager, Doppler led Callie and Sean outside. He went around the corner of the building and turned to face them, crossing his arms over his chest.

"You trying to get me shit-canned?"

Callie shook her head. "Not at all, Jared. We just have a few questions for you. If you don't want to talk here, we can always do it at the station."

Doppler dug a pack of smokes from his shirt pocket. "What questions?"

"How do you know Samantha Bonner?" Callie asked.

"I don't." He lit a cigarette and blew out a stream of smoke.

Sean flipped open his notebook. "Never met her?"

"Nope."

He jotted that down as Doppler eyed him with suspicion.

"Never talked to her?"

"Sure, I talked to her once or twice." He gave a shrug. "But I don't *know* her or anything. She was friends with my wife, not me."

"Don't you mean *ex*-wife?"

Doppler looked at Callie.

"We have that you two divorced—what was it, Detective Byrne? Five months ago?"

"Six."

Doppler sucked in a drag and squinted. "Whatever." He blew out the smoke. "She was Amy's friend."

"And you never actually met her face-to-face," Callie stated.

"That's right."

"Okay, what do you know *about* her?"

"She was an alcoholic, same as Amy. She filled Amy's head with a bunch of mumbo jumbo about getting in touch with her higher power, or some such shit."

Callie glanced at Sean, then back to Doppler. "According to Samantha's phone records, Jared, you called her three separate times just ten days before she died."

He sucked in a drag, but didn't respond.

"All on the night of November fifth." Callie glanced at the notebook. "You called at one sixteen, one eighteen, and one twenty-two in the morning. The last call lasted twelve minutes."

"So?"

"So, you want to tell us what you talked about?"

He stared at Callie for a moment. Then he looked at Sean. "I told her to butt out. To stop calling my wife and mind her own business."

"Ex-wife."

Jared glared at Callie.

"It didn't take twelve minutes to tell her that," Sean said. "What else did you talk about?"

"Nothing. I just told her to butt out of our business."

Callie lifted an eyebrow. "And if she didn't? What'd you plan to do then?"

"What the hell is this? Did Amy say I *threatened* that bitch?" Doppler pointed his cigarette at Callie. "Because I didn't."

Sean was starting to get pissed off, but Callie smiled calmly.

"I guess we'll never know, will we, Jared? Because 'that bitch' is dead."

"Where were you at eight forty-five Wednesday night?" Sean asked.

Doppler didn't look surprised by the question. "I was with someone."

"Really? Who?" The note of disbelief in Callie's voice made Sean smile.

"Her name's Jenny Landry." Doppler tossed his cigarette butt to the ground and pulled out his cell phone. "I texted her at eight forty. I've got it right here." He showed his phone to Sean. "I headed over to her place at eight forty-five."

"We need her address," Sean said.

"Hyde Creek Apartments. She's in unit twelve."

"And when did you leave there?"

"Nine thirty."

Callie whistled. "You're fast."

"Back to the phone calls with Samantha," Sean said. "Had you been drinking when you talked to her?"

Of all the questions, this one seemed to make Doppler the most defensive. "I don't know. Why?"

"Just wondering."

"I'd maybe had a few beers."

"Two? Three? Six?"

"I don't know. A few."

"Any chance you have a drinking problem?" Sean asked.

"Did Amy tell you that?"

"Your rap sheet told us," Callie said. "You've got a pair of DWIs."

"I don't have a drinking problem. Or any other kind

of problem unless I get fired from my job." He glared at Sean. "Are we done here?"

"I don't know. Detective McLean, are we done?" Sean looked at Callie.

"We're done for now, but we'll be checking your alibi, Jared."

"Have at it."

"And I'm going to need you to stay available."

• • •

Sean and Callie stared after him as he stormed off.

"Can't imagine why he's divorced," Callie said.

They started across the parking lot to their cars.

"What'd you think of his alibi?" Sean asked.

"Lines up perfectly."

"Yeah, I noticed."

"We'll see if his girlfriend can back it up."

"He wouldn't have given us her name otherwise."

Callie glanced at Sean. "You're saying he knew we were coming?"

"Probably. Guy's an ex-con and he recently communicated with a murder victim."

"I'll talk to this girlfriend of his, see if she'll corroborate his timeline," Callie said. "Unless you want to do it?"

"She's all yours."

"Speaking of girlfriends, how's it going with Brooke?"

"It's not."

"Why not? Did you ask her out yet?"

"She says she's taking a break from men." Sean popped the locks on his truck. The sooner he ended this conversation, the better.

"And?"

"And what?"

Callie laughed. "And don't you want to know why?"

"Hell yeah. I'm working on it."

"Ask her out again. See if she'll open up to you. Maybe she's on the rebound and you can be her shoulder to cry on."

Something told him Brooke didn't want a shoulder. Something also told him that the hard-sell approach wasn't going to work with her. He had to be subtle. And patient.

The opposite of how he'd been last night when he'd practically begged her to come home with him.

A text landed on Sean's phone as he slid into his truck. "Hey, here's something from Jasper." He read the message. "Someone found a knife near Samantha Bonner's house."

"Are you serious? What kind?"

"He doesn't say. There's no blood on it, though."

"Who found it?"

"Mrs. Morton's dog came across it when they were walking near the train tracks."

Callie looked at Sean. "You think it's the murder weapon?"

"Might be."

"That would be *huge*."

"Yep."

"Why aren't you excited?"

"I don't get excited this early. It could be a steak knife, for all we know. We need to get it to Delphi for testing." He checked the time. "Damn it. I can't go right now. I've got an interview in ten minutes."

"I can run it over there."

"You mind?"

"Not at all. What else do I have to do this afternoon? It's not like I've got some hot date to get ready for."

"I can do it after my interview."

"No, let me. You've got enough on your plate. I can take the lead on this one."

Sean started up his truck. "Thanks. Let me know what you hear."

"I will. And good luck."

"With what?"

She rolled her eyes. "With Brooke. It's only Saturday. The weekend is young."

• • •

Farrah Saunders had changed out of her funeral clothes, and Sean almost didn't recognize the social worker when she walked into Java House. She wore a camo-print jacket with jeans, and her curly blond hair was pulled back in a loose bun.

Sean stood up as she took a chair at the little table. "Coffee?"

"No, thank you." She checked her watch. "I have to be on a fishing boat in an hour, so I need to make this quick."

"That case, thanks for making the time, Ms. Saunders."

Her expression told him she caught the sarcasm. "Call me Farrah. And it's no problem."

Sean watched her body language as she glanced around the coffee shop.

"Did you know Sam worked here?" he asked.

"She mentioned it once. She was a barista?"

"She'd been promoted to shift manager."

Sean had picked this location as a sort of test. He wanted to get a read on how much this woman knew about Sam's current life.

"I saw you at the funeral talking to Sam's foster

mom." Sean flipped open his notebook. "Diane Jacobs. So, Sam went by the name of her birth mother, I'm guessing?"

"That's right."

"Were her birth parents married?"

Farrah watched him warily, but didn't respond.

"This is public record. I can find all this out, but it would be a lot faster if you told me."

Farrah started to respond, but the scream of a coffee grinder cut her off. She waited until the noise stopped. "Her birth mother was single. She never married."

"Any other kids?"

"No. At least not that I'm aware of."

"And when did Sam move in with the Jacobs family?"

"When she was fourteen."

"Before that, did she always live with her birth mom?"

"No."

"So . . . she lived with a relative? Another foster family?"

"She lived with her aunt for several years, but it didn't work out."

"Why not?"

Farrah watched him for a long moment. Then she leaned forward. "Look, Detective. An important part of my job is protecting my clients' privacy."

"I understand. But your client is dead now, and it's *my* job to figure out who killed her."

Farrah shook her head. "Sam's records are confidential. If you need to see them, you can file a request—"

"That could take ten business days to process, I know." He looked at her. "This is a murder case, Farrah. That means we're on a ticking clock here. Every day that goes by without a suspect makes it more and more likely that whoever killed Sam will get away with it. And that means an extremely violent person is out there roaming the streets." He paused to let that sink in. "This isn't just about Samantha Bonner. I have a duty to this community. So do you."

She folded her arms over her chest. "You're good at this. A little thick on the guilt, but it's effective."

He held her gaze but didn't say anything.

"Fine." She huffed out a breath. "I can give you some basics. But if you want detailed specifics, you're going to need to file that request."

"Okay, then." Sean wrapped his hand around his coffee cup. "Tell me the basics."

"How about you tell *me* what you're looking for? It might be quicker for everybody."

"I'm sure you saw some of the details of Sam's murder on the news."

"Yes."

"Then you know it was brutal. We think the killer knew Sam personally. The thing is, none of the friends or coworkers we've interviewed have been able to tell us about a boyfriend or any men in her life."

"I don't know about all that." Farrah shook her head. "It's not like we were friends, really."

"You were one of eight people at her funeral."

She unfolded her arms and rested her hands on the table. "Sam was special. She'd managed to beat the odds. Or at least, I thought she had. She dropped me notes from time to time to let me know how she was doing."

"And how was she doing?"

"Very well." Farrah glanced down. "I *thought* so, at least. She was holding down a job. She'd started college part-time. Did you know she was studying social work?"

"I heard that." He watched her, trying to read her expression. "What was Sam's life like growing up?"

Farrah looked uneasy. "Hard. I can't get into specifics . . . but I can tell you many of my cases are children who have to be removed from their homes because of drug or alcohol addiction. They go into the foster system, which—as we all know—is far from perfect. Despite our best efforts, sometimes the kids end up in homes where they're even more at risk than in their original setting."

"'At risk,' as in sexual abuse?"

"Yes."

Sean watched Farrah's eyes, trying to pick up every little clue. "This was when Sam lived with her aunt and . . . I'm guessing her uncle?"

Farrah nodded. "I can tell you want a name, but it won't help. Her uncle's been dead for years. Since shortly after Sam moved out of his home, actually."

So much for a viable lead. But at least Sean had got Samantha's caseworker talking. "What about the next home? The Jacobs place?"

Farrah's face brightened. "Sam thrived there. She really did. That's why she stayed in touch with her foster mom, I think."

"Did they have other kids?"

"It was just Diane, and, yes, she had several other foster kids. All girls. Sam seemed to do well there. She started making good grades. She joined the choir. She graduated high school with honors over in Burr County."

"And then?"

"And then what?"

"And then sometime after graduating with honors she ended up in a twelve-step program. Sounds like she had some setbacks."

Farrah tilted her head to the side. "Do you know how many of my kids end up with drug and alcohol problems in adulthood? It's amazingly common. The unusual thing about Sam was that she caught it early and decided to get help. I don't see that as a setback."

Sean sighed. Between the incomplete answers and the generalizations, they were talking in circles. Farrah glanced at her watch, and Sean felt a surge of impatience.

"Let me be straight with you, Farrah. I need names."

"And as I told you—"

"Off the record. I'm not asking you to testify in court here. I'm asking for a lead. Can you think of anyone in Sam's life—past or present—who might have been a problem for her?"

Farrah looked blank.

"Or not a problem. Maybe just a man in her life who was in the background?"

Sean was grasping at straws now. But much of Samantha Bonner's life was a mystery to him, and her caseworker was one of the few people who had any real information.

"There's no one I can think of offhand. I could look back through her case file. But like I alluded to before, the person who abused her as a child is dead now."

"What about recently? Was she having trouble with a boss or a boyfriend?"

"I don't know about that. We really just exchanged notes from time to time." Farrah looked at her watch again. "Listen, I'm sorry, Detective, but I have to go."

"Do me a favor and check that file for me." Sean took out a business card. "If you find anything—"

"I'll let you know."

• • •

Brooke left the lab feeling drained. And totally uninspired by the mountain of laundry she had waiting for her. She'd meant to tackle it that afternoon, but between the doughnut shop and the Delphi Center, she'd barely been home.

She eyed the clock. Seven thirty already. She hadn't heard from Sean all day. She decided to check in, and he answered on the first ring.

"I wanted to see if you went by the doughnut place today," she said.

"I was there this morning. No sign of him. You?"

"I went by twice this morning and once this afternoon. No one fit the description." She paused, suddenly feeling awkward about calling. The last time she'd seen him, he'd kissed her breathless. "So . . . I'm on my way home. Anything new with the case?"

"A lot. We got our first suspect."

"Really?"

"It's not panning out, though. His girlfriend came in for an interview, and his alibi holds."

"Damn."

"I know."

"I take it you're at work, then?" she asked.

"Nah, I'm headed to Gino's to get a pizza. Want to join me?"

"Oh. I don't know."

"Well, are you hungry?"

"Yeah, actually."

"You could meet me there. Or I could pick you up."

She didn't say anything, and the quiet stretched out.

"It's just pizza, Brooke."

He sounded amused by her reluctance. And he was so laid-back about it, why was she hesitating? She'd called *him*. It wasn't like he was pressuring her.

"You don't mind driving?" she asked.

"No problem. I'll be by in a few."

By the time Brooke pulled onto her street, she was having second thoughts.

She shouldn't get into something with him. She needed a break from relationships and sex and all the twisty dynamics that went along with everything. She needed to stand on her own. She'd made a promise to herself when she broke up with Matt that she'd take some time to get her footing back. So what the hell was she doing with Sean?

Just pizza. Last night had been *just beer*, and look where that had gotten her. All day she'd been thinking about kissing him. She was thinking about it now, too, as she swung into her driveway and spotted his headlights turning onto her street. So much for dashing inside to change clothes or do her hair or maybe put on some makeup—which was for the better.

Sean glided to a stop in front of her house, and she went around to the passenger side and climbed in.

"Whoa." She looked him over. "What's with the suit?"

"Funeral." He pulled away from the curb.

"Already? That seems fast."

"It was. Think they were trying to dodge the media."

Brooke glanced around. She'd never been in Sean's truck before. It was toasty warm and filled with guy clutter. She noticed the muddy work boots in back, the gym bag, the skateboard.

"It's my nephew's," he said, noticing her noticing. "Although I *do* know how to skate, in case you were wondering."

"I wasn't." She smiled at him, all *GQ*-looking in his dark suit, and she couldn't picture him on a skateboard.

He glanced at her. "You're one of those girls, huh? I bet you stayed away from skaters. We were the troublemakers."

"I think it's more accurate to say skaters stayed away from me. I was a science geek."

"Yeah, I bet you were." He smiled. "In a good way."

"Hmm . . . I don't know if it was 'good' for my social life. I didn't go to a single dance in high school."

"You're kidding."

"No."

Why had she just told him that? She wished she'd kept her mouth shut. She glanced over, and he was grinning.

"Those guys must be kicking themselves now."

"Yes, I'm sure not a day goes by."

"Seriously, look at you. You're beautiful and successful. You've got a cool job at a world-famous crime lab."

She darted a glance at him.

"What?"

"You're so full of it."

"I'm just stating the obvious."

She shook her head and looked away as he pulled into Gino's parking lot. They got out, and Sean took a moment to shrug out of his suit jacket and stash it in the back of the cab. Meanwhile, Brooke skimmed the parking lot for Matt's oversize pickup.

When she glanced back at Sean, he was watching her. He stepped closer, looking concerned. "What's wrong?"

"Nothing."

They walked to the restaurant in silence, and Sean held the door for a family going in ahead of them. It was a little thing, but she definitely noticed. So many guys didn't bother with manners.

Gino's smelled like roasted garlic, and Brooke's mouth started to water as she read the menu board posted above the counter.

"I'm thinking we need a large," Sean said. "What kind do you want?"

She almost told him to choose what he wanted, but caught herself. "Mushroom and extra pepperoni. Thick crust."

Sean placed the order and took a plastic number, and Brooke didn't fight him when he got out his wallet. She insisted on paying for their beers, though.

Several cozy booths were available, but Brooke led him to a tall table in a lively corner of the restaurant beside a pair of dartboards.

"You play?" Sean set down their bottles.

"Yes, but I'd hate to embarrass you."

He lifted an eyebrow. "Trash talk, huh? I'll be right back."

She watched him as he walked over to the bar. Being near him again brought their kiss back in vivid detail. The way his mouth had fit over hers, his taste, the snug press of his body . . . Every cell inside her had been screaming, *This. Finally.* It had felt so completely right, like every kiss before it had been a weak imitation of what a kiss should be.

Brooke sipped her beer as Sean returned to the table with a handful of darts.

"You want to play a game or just throw until the food comes?" he asked.

"How about first to one hundred?"

He leaned his elbow on the table and watched her, and she tried not to get distracted by how good he looked with his sleeves rolled up and a day's worth of stubble darkening his jaw. Other women were noticing him, but his gaze stayed fixed on her—so firmly she felt butterflies in her stomach as she tried to concentrate on the dartboard.

She hit an eighteen.

"Not bad."

She shot him a look. Her next throw hit a twenty. The third dart bounced, so she stopped for a beer break.

"So, how many nephews do you have?" she asked.

"Eight."

"Get out. *Eight* nephews?"

"And three nieces." The pride in his voice told her he was totally serious.

"How many siblings are in your family?" She plucked her darts from the board and handed them over.

"Four sisters and a brother. I'm the youngest of six."

"Aha. No wonder you're a charmer. I bet you got away with all kinds of stuff growing up."

"Guilty."

Brooke tried to imagine being in a family that large. She couldn't picture it. "What do they all do?"

He narrowed his gaze for a moment, focusing on the board. He hit a fifteen and turned to look at her. "Let's see, we've got a nurse, a cop, two teachers, and a firefighter." He swigged his beer.

"Jeez. You sound like a Richard Scarry book. Your sister's a cop, too?"

"That's my brother. My sister's the firefighter."

"Really? That's so cool."

"You'd like her. She's an ass-kicker like you."

"Right."

"You don't think you're an ass-kicker?"

"Um, no."

"I've seen you at crime scenes bossing around cops twice your size. You scare the hell out of people."

"No, I don't."

"You do. Everyone's terrified to touch anything."

"They should be. We can't have people tromping around destroying evidence."

He smiled, and she felt a warm pull. The attraction was right there, simmering between them every time she got near him. It wasn't just his looks. As good as he looked, that was only a small part of it. It was the way he moved, the way he talked, and—most important—the way he looked at her. He seemed interested, maybe even intrigued, as though he wanted to hear what she had to say.

He was looking at her that way now, so of course her mind went blank.

Brooke wrapped her hand around the cold beer bottle. "So. How'd your sister decide to become a firefighter?"

"I don't know." Sean threw a nineteen. "She's always kind of marched to her own drum."

"Good for her."

He threw a bull's-eye as if it were no big deal and jotted their scores on the nearby chalkboard.

"What about your family?" He handed over the darts.

"We're pretty small. Just my mom, my dad, and my brother. He's six years older, so we weren't exactly close growing up."

"And now?"

"Not really. I mean, they are, I guess. Everyone's a doctor but me."

"The medical kind?"

"PhDs. Chemistry, physics, and electrical engineering."

"Wow." Sean folded his arms over his chest and somehow managed to look even sexier. "You're all scientists."

"I'm not like them, though. I'm not in academia."

"Yeah, well, I've seen your business card. You've got some pretty impressive letters after your name."

She hadn't realized he knew about her master's in forensic science. But she should have known. He paid attention to details. Including details about her, apparently.

She turned her attention to the board and threw a ten, which didn't count.

"What's wrong with not being in academia?"

"Nothing, really. But I don't discuss my work with my family."

"How come?"

"I deal with rape kits and shell casings and blood spatter all day. It's too . . . I don't know . . . *raw*, I guess you'd say."

He watched her over his beer as he took a sip.

How had they gotten on this topic? Siblings and parents and family dynamics? She hadn't intended to venture into personal territory tonight. She was trying to keep this friendly, not flirty, but his comments weren't helping. *You're beautiful.* It was such a line, but still it put a sweet tingle in the pit of her stomach.

"Speaking of work," she said, "you said a lot happened with the case today."

He nodded. "I told you about our maybe suspect, although I'm skeptical. We also found a potential murder weapon."

"The knife? Where was it?"

"I don't know if it's *the* knife. Callie took it to Delphi for testing. We'll see what we get."

"We have it already? I didn't see it come in."

"I think it's in the DNA lab right now."

"I'll check in with them tomorrow."

He glanced at her, and she realized she'd revealed that she planned to spend her Sunday at work.

Sean didn't comment, maybe because he was as bad as she was.

Brooke shifted her attention to the board. She finished her turn with no points to show.

Sean retrieved the darts and lined up his next shot. "So, I have a question for you."

The warm tone of his voice made Brooke's nerves flutter.

"About this break you're taking from men." He looked at her.

"What about it?"

He threw a dart.

"Bull's-eye for the win," she said. "I must be getting rusty."

He plucked the dart from the board and returned to the table.

"I'm wondering, is it like a brief hiatus? Or more of a long-term ban?"

"I don't know. It's as long as I need."

He held her gaze, and she felt her heart thudding. His look was so intent, as though he had a lot riding on her answer.

"Sounds like there's a story there. You want to talk about it?"

"Not really."

He nodded. "Your call."

Your call. Two words Matt never said to her.

Sean gazed down at her, and the warm pull was back. He hadn't touched her at all tonight. Not once, only with his eyes. But something about them was magnetic, and she couldn't look away.

A server appeared with a giant pizza, and Brooke jumped on the distraction.

"Mushroom double pepperoni?"

"That's us."

CHAPTER 9

Sean drove through town, happy to have Brooke riding in the seat beside him, but not at all happy that he was about to drop her off.

"Thanks for not pressing the issue."

He glanced at her. "Sure."

"Honestly, I'm just sick of talking about it lately. Rehashing it with my friends. Maybe another time."

"I'm a patient man."

She laughed. "No, you're not."

"I am."

She turned in her seat to face him. "The day I met you, you demanded I put a rush on your evidence for you. Less than twenty-four hours later, you were back with more evidence, and you needed it ASAP. Then you proceeded to pester me for daily updates."

"Okay, but that was a double homicide. It was an unusual case. Anyway, I was talking about my personal life."

"So, you're a bulldog at work, but in your personal life, you're totally chill?"

"Exactly."

He glanced at her, and he could see she didn't believe him. But it was true. Months of rehab had forced him to dig deep within himself for things he didn't know he had. Patience. The ability to withstand pain. Gratitude.

Gratitude was a big one. He hadn't realized how much he took people for granted in his life until they showed up to help him without even being asked. It was humbling as hell.

The experience of nearly getting killed and having to work to get his life back had changed him. He was more analytical now and took a longer view. He appreciated people and experiences more.

This thing with Brooke was a perfect example. The chemistry they had together—it wasn't every day you felt something like that. In his thirty-three years, he'd never before felt it. It was rare, and he was clued in enough now to realize it.

Not that he planned to tell her. If he did, she'd probably run for the hills. There would be no more pizza or dart games or beers after work. She'd made it clear she needed some space, and Sean was determined to give it to her, even if it hurt—literally *ached*—to be around her and not touch her. He could make himself wait.

Sean pulled up in front of her house and parked.

"Thank you for the pizza," she said. "And the darts. And the ride."

"Anytime. Thanks for the beer."

She opened the door, and he resisted the urge to do the same. He really, really wanted to walk her to her door.

"Good night, Sean."

"Night."

He watched her go up the sidewalk.

Regret pummeled him. He should have kissed her. He should have done it now, tonight, when last night's kiss was still fresh in her mind. But she was on her porch now, rummaging for her keys, about to go inside alone, and who the hell knew when she'd agree to have dinner with him again?

The pizza.

Sean grabbed the box from the back and shoved open his door.

"Wait." He jogged up the sidewalk with the box in hand. "Your leftovers."

"Oh. Thanks, I forgot."

She looked up at him, and he had his second chance. He gazed down at those mesmerizing eyes of hers.

She yelped and jumped back.

Sean glanced down to see a mangy black cat glaring up at him.

"Oh, my God, you *scared* me!"

"Who's this?"

"This is Midnight." She turned and unlocked the door, and the cat darted inside. "He's not even my cat."

"Better tell him that."

"Midnight, come here."

She stepped inside.

Sean followed. "Want me to put this in the kitchen?"

"Sure, that's—" She gasped and halted.

Sean bumped into her and caught her elbow. "What's wrong?"

She didn't answer. She stood motionless, staring at her living room. It looked the same as last time he'd been in here—a tight space furnished with a sofa, an armchair, and a coffee table. In the center of the table was a beer bottle.

"Brooke, what is it?"

Without a word, she strode across the room and snatched up the bottle.

Sean closed the front door and followed her into

the kitchen, where she stood at the sink pouring the beer down the drain. She opened a lower cabinet and dropped the bottle into the trash.

Sean set down the pizza box. He leaned back against the counter and watched her. She had her back to him. Tension radiated from her body, flowing directly to his.

"*Brooke*?" He couldn't keep the edge out of his voice.

She turned around. "My ex was here. That was his calling card."

"He was here while you were gone? Without your permission?"

"Apparently." She looked at Sean and sighed. "Just . . . drop it, okay?"

"Are you fucking serious? That's breaking and entering."

"Not if he used a key."

She crossed the kitchen and went through the utility room to the back door. Sean followed her, watching as she stepped outside and crouched down to run her hand over the metal downspout near the steps.

"What are you doing?"

"I keep a hide-a-key back here." She stood up with a small plastic box that had a magnet attached. She slid it open.

Empty.

Brooke muttered a curse. Then she strode back into the kitchen. Sean locked the door—for all the good it did—and joined her by the sink.

"Brooke—"

"*Don't* say it. Obviously, I need to get my locks changed."

Sean leaned against the counter, struggling to get a grip on his temper.

"I didn't realize he knew about my key."

Sean stared at her. He hated the apologetic look in her eyes. "Who is this guy?"

She shook her head.

"You should slap a restraining order on him."

She snorted. "No."

"I can help you get it done."

"Forget it."

"Like hell I'm gonna forget it. He's fucking threatening you in your own home."

She closed her eyes. Her chest rose and fell as she took a deep breath.

Yoga breathing.

Like that was going to help her deal with this asshole. Sean clenched his teeth, trying to rein in his temper.

"I don't want to get into this right now," she said calmly.

"Looks to me like you don't have a choice."

Sean wanted her to talk to him. He wanted to help, but he didn't have any information. "Who is he, Brooke?"

"You don't know him."

"Does he have a criminal record?"

"No."

"Is he violent?"

"No."

It was only a nanosecond of hesitation, but Sean caught it. *God damn it.* Fury swelled in his chest.

He stepped closer, but she ducked around him. "I could use a drink. Would you like a glass of wine?" She selected a bottle of red from a rack on the counter and then took out a corkscrew. Sean wanted to do it for her, but she seemed to need something to do with her hands, so he stood back and watched as she uncorked the bottle.

He opened a few cabinets and found some glasses. "When did you break up?"

She took a deep breath and poured the wine. "Four months ago."

Four months.

About the time he'd started hanging out with her. She'd seemed guarded when they'd first met.

She still seemed guarded.

She handed Sean a glass, then leaned back against the counter and looked at him.

"I can help you file a report."

"There's nothing to report."

"Brooke, come on."

"He didn't break in here. And he's not violent, he's just . . . controlling. And he's having a hard time letting go."

"You need to slap an RO on him."

"Oh, yeah? Because those work so well all the time?"

She was right. They didn't always work. In fact, Sean had handled more than one murder-suicide case where a freshly issued restraining order was found *at* the crime scene. Brooke had probably seen the same.

"Don't look at me that way," she said.

"What way?"

"It's not like you're thinking. He never hit me or anything. If he had, I would have done something about it." She took a deep breath and looked away. "I'll call a locksmith tomorrow."

"That's good." Sean set his wine aside and stepped close to her. "I don't want you here alone tonight. And now I know what *you're* thinking, but that's not a line."

She looked up at him.

"Will you stay with me tonight?" He held up his hands. "I'll take the couch. I swear."

She looked conflicted.

"Or you can have the couch. I'm offering friend to friend here. If Ric needed a place to crash, say if Mia threw him out—"

"Like that would ever happen."

"If it did, I'd give him my sofa. That's all I'm offering."

"Thanks, but . . . it's probably easier if I crash at my brother's."

"Where's he live? I'll take you."

"Then I won't have my car."

"Fine, I'll follow you."

"Thanks, but that's completely unnecessary."

"I'm not actually asking here, Brooke. Wherever you go tonight, I'm going to make sure you get there safely, so there's no point in arguing about it."

"Fine. Thank you." She set down her wine. "Let me pack a bag."

• • •

Brooke pulled into her brother's driveway and parked behind his Prius. It was like hers, but black—a detail that probably wasn't lost on Sean, who noticed everything.

He pulled up to the curb and got out, surveying the condominium complex. The brand-new construction was meant to look old, and every redbrick unit had a black gas lamp out front.

"Who's the yellow Mini?" Sean asked, eyeing the car at the top of the driveway.

"Owen's girlfriend."

Brooke glanced up and down the street, but didn't see a single black pickup, oversize or even regular-size.

Sean followed her up the cobblestone path and opened the wrought-iron gate into the courtyard.

"Does your brother own a firearm?"

She glanced over her shoulder. "He's a chemistry professor."

"So, that's a no?"

"That's a no."

"Alarm system?"

"No."

Brooke pressed the bell, and chimes sounded behind the heavy black door. A faint yapping noise ensued, and Lin pulled open the door. With heels and hair mousse, she was five feet tall. At the moment, she wore pink pajamas—no shoes—and held a white Chihuahua in her arms.

"Brooke. Hi." She adjusted her horned-rimmed glasses.

"Sorry to barge in."

"No problem." The dog yapped and squirmed. "Owen didn't mention you were coming over."

"Hey, Lin, Brooke's coming over," Owen called. He appeared in the doorway, grinning. "Sorry, I got sidetracked." His grin faded when he saw Sean. "Owen Porter." He reached around Lin and offered a handshake.

"Sean Byrne."

Owen looked at Brooke expectantly. "So . . . you said something about a break-in?"

"Nothing stolen. Think we scared him off." Brooke smiled. "I need to get a locksmith out tomorrow."

Brooke could feel the tension coming from Sean as Owen ushered them into the foyer. The house smelled like popcorn, and Brooke remembered the two liked to watch movies on Saturdays in their media room.

"I don't want to interrupt you guys or anything," Brooke said. "I know where everything is, so . . ."

"Stay as long as you want," Owen said to Sean. "We'll be upstairs finishing our movie."

Owen and Lin headed up the stairs with the Chihuahua trotting behind.

"You didn't tell him?"

Brooke turned to look at Sean. "I didn't want to get into it in a text message."

Sean shook his head and turned to examine the door. The hardware was shiny and new. "Decent locks." He walked across the foyer and examined the keypad. "They have an alarm system here."

"Yeah, I don't think it's activated."

His jaw tightened as he glanced around the house. It was expensive and spacious. More than enough room for two professionals and a miniature dog. Also, it was a safe neighborhood.

Brooke set her duffel down beside the stairs.

Sean surprised her by taking her hand and leading her into the darkened living room.

"Does your family know you've been having trouble with your ex?"

She sighed. "No."

"Will you tell your brother, please?"

"Yes."

He gazed down at her, and the moment stretched out. His eyes looked so serious, and she wished she knew what he was thinking.

"I'm sorry dinner turned into . . . all this other stuff."

"Brooke." He sounded exasperated.

And he was still holding her hand. His fingers were warm and strong, and she liked the feel of them folded around hers.

She tugged her hand loose, and he pretended not to notice.

"Will you be okay here?"

"Fine. They have a really comfortable sectional." She nodded at it, and when she glanced up at Sean again, he was looking at her like he had the other night before he'd kissed her.

She had things to say to him, but when she tried to form a sentence, her throat tightened. "Thanks for following me over."

"You're welcome." He reached over and tucked a lock of hair behind her ear. "So, you're working tomorrow?"

"I've got to catch up on some things at the lab."

"I'll call you in the morning. Talk to your brother."

"I will." It wasn't fair to stay here without filling him in on what was going on, even though she dreaded the conversation. He'd never liked Matt to begin with.

Sean eased closer, and Brooke's heart gave a kick as he leaned down and kissed her. It was a brief brush of his lips, but then she slid her hands around his waist and pulled him close, and everything heated. She pressed against him, and he deepened the kiss. She loved the way he tasted, the way he held her. She loved the way his tongue moved against hers, the way his fingers combed into her hair.

She didn't know why she was doing this. She definitely needed to stop, but she couldn't bring herself to pull away from him.

It ended way too soon, and he eased back, watching her closely. "You can change your mind. My offer still stands."

She stepped away, letting her hands drop. "I'm fine here."

He looked at her for another moment, then turned to leave.

"Sean."

"Yeah?"

"The thing is, my life's kind of a mess right now. I'm not looking to get involved with anyone."

"That's okay."

"How is that okay? Why do you want to spend time on something that's not going anywhere?"

"Maybe I like where it's going."

"Why? I told you I don't want to start anything new. And I'll save you the suspense—I'm not good at casual relationships, so sex is not happening."

"So noted."

She stared up at him, and he didn't even blink.

"Lock up behind me." He gave her a long look and pulled open the door. "Good night."

CHAPTER 10

The sectional wasn't as comfortable as Brooke remembered, and she flailed around most of the night. Just before dawn, she gave up and shuffled into the kitchen, where she poked through some cabinets until she found a mug and the pods for the fancy coffeemaker.

After a brief conversation with Owen last night about her unwanted intruder, Brooke had tried to wind down with some channel surfing. But nothing could calm her nerves, especially when her brother's words kept playing through her head:

I always knew I didn't like that guy.

Evidently, Owen's dislike had intensified last Thanksgiving when Brooke had skipped out on dinner with her family because Matt didn't want to deal with "the whole Thanksgiving scene." Brooke had acquiesced. It was the first of many occasions when Matt had pressured her to spend time with him alone instead of with her family or friends.

Why had it taken her so long to see those incidents for what they were? He'd been trying to isolate her from people who cared about her, and she'd allowed it to happen. The whole thing made her feel guilt toward her family and also disgust with herself.

"Hey there."

She jumped and turned around.

Lin smiled at her. "Sorry to scare you."

"I didn't hear you come down. Did I wake you?"

"No, I'm an early riser." Lin took a stool at the granite island. "Unlike Owen and Chico, who can stay sacked out till noon."

"You want some coffee?"

"Not yet, thanks."

Brooke dropped a pod into the coffeemaker and fetched some cream from the mammoth refrigerator. She liked to tease Owen about his kitchen, which was outfitted with top-of-the-line appliances even though he barely knew how to make a sandwich.

"So, give me the gossip. What's up with you and the cop?"

Brooke glanced at Lin. "How'd you know he's a cop?"

"I knew it!"

Brooke tried to pin down what Sean might have said or done last night to give himself away. He hadn't been wearing a badge. He'd been armed, as always, but she doubted Lin had had a chance to notice the bulge under his jacket during their brief meeting in the dim foyer.

"It was the eyes."

The coffee finished brewing and Brooke collected it from the machine. She took a stool beside Lin's. "The eyes?"

"Uh-huh. I dated a cop before I met Owen. They're a hyperobservant bunch."

Hyperobservant. Sean definitely fit that description.

"He noticed everything," Lin said. "It used to drive me crazy."

Brooke sipped her coffee and watched the woman she hoped would one day become her sister-in-law.

She couldn't picture Lin with someone in law enforcement. "What happened with him?"

"It was fun. Brief, though." Lin shrugged. "We were never a fit, really. And then I met Owen and—" She gave a wistful sigh. "The first time he talked to me it was just . . . magic."

Wow, *magic*? Owen?

Lin laughed. "You should see the look on your face. You didn't know your brother was a girl magnet?"

"I'll have to take your word for it."

"So, back to the cop. Are you two serious?"

"*No.*"

Lin pulled back. "Alrighty then."

"We're not dating. Last night was random. We're really just friends."

"Hmm."

"What?"

Lin shrugged. "That's not the impression I got."

Brooke watched her as she took a sip. Lin was a clinical psychologist—potentially another PhD in the family—and Brooke was curious to get her take on things. But she had to be careful because anything she revealed could ultimately get back to Owen.

"The thing is, Matt and I just broke up, so the timing's all wrong."

"That was, what? Three months ago?"

"Four, actually. But that relationship started right after things ended with me and someone else, and that was part of the problem, I think. I rushed into something new when I should have given myself some time."

"So, now you want some breathing room."

"Exactly," Brooke said. "I don't want to do that all over again. I don't want to repeat the whole cycle."

"What cycle?"

"My cycle. The thing I keep doing. Everything starts out great, and then I wake up one day about a year in, and everything's all a mess, and I wonder, 'How the hell did I end up with this guy who's all wrong for me?' "

Lin watched Brooke carefully, probably analyzing every word and no doubt diagnosing something dysfunctional about Brooke's MO with men.

Lin tipped her head to the side. "So, do you believe Sean's all wrong for you?"

The question surprised Brooke. "No. I mean . . . I don't know, really. He's just . . ."

Sean was different. He was strong without being overbearing. And he respected her space. But he also seemed determined to wait her out, even though she'd told him this thing between them wasn't going anywhere.

Maybe I like where it's going.

Brooke didn't know if she believed that, not when he got that hungry look in his eyes, that look that made her insides all warm and fluttery.

He seemed resolved to wait, as though he knew that she'd ultimately change her mind. She should be annoyed, but instead she felt anxious.

What if he was right? What if he hung around long enough and she caved in to this burning attraction between them?

Then, once again, she would have taken no time to stand on her own before plunging into something new. She didn't want to do that this time. She wanted to prove to herself that she didn't require a man in her life. She didn't need rings and picket fences and all that other stuff her friends had. She was fine on her own.

"Well?" Lin prompted. "He's just . . . ?"

"He's different. At least, I think he is. We don't know each other all that well."

"He wants to change that, I'm guessing."

"The thing is, the timing's not right." And that was putting it mildly. Up until recently she'd thought Matt might finally be moving on, but now she knew he wasn't. She thought of the beer bottle and had to stifle a shudder. That was so his style, sneaking into her house just to prove he could rattle her. The whole thing was a power trip.

She didn't want to think what he'd do if he thought she had a new boyfriend. That would make a bad situation worse.

Brooke shook her head. "I don't really want to get into anything right now. It would be a big mess."

"What's a big mess?"

They turned around to see Owen standing in the doorway looking groggy and disheveled.

"My love life," Brooke said.

Her brother winced. "Do I need to hear this?"

"No."

"At least tell me it doesn't involve Matt."

"It doesn't. I told you, we're over."

He shuffled to the fridge and grabbed a jug of orange juice. "Does it involve Sean from last night?"

"*No.* It doesn't involve anyone. I'm officially single. In fact, I'm thinking about joining a convent."

"Good. Music to my ears."

• • •

Sean figured he'd be the only detective working Sunday morning, but Callie's personal vehicle was in the lot behind the station house. He parked beside it and found her at her desk in the bull pen, staring at her computer.

"What brings you in on a Sunday?" Sean asked.

She leaned back in her chair. "Same as you. This case is a bitch. I hardly slept last night."

Sean had had the same problem, but his lack of sleep had more to do with Brooke. "I went by the doughnut place."

"Yeah, me too. No sign of the redheaded kid." She sighed. "I'm beginning to wonder if this mystery witness really exists."

"You better hope he exists. He's our only lead. Jared Doppler's girlfriend was in for an interview yesterday, and she backs his alibi."

"Yeah, and how firm is she?"

"I'd say firm."

"Damn. I really wanted to nail that guy."

Sean sat on the edge of her desk and folded his arms over his chest. "So, Callie. You know some of Brooke's friends at the Delphi Center, don't you?"

Callie looked instantly suspicious. "I know Alex and Maddie. Why?"

"Brooke's ex-boyfriend is hassling her, and I need to get the dope on him."

Callie frowned. "Hassling her how?"

"He was in her house last night while she was gone. It freaked her out a little."

"That would freak me out more than a little. Who the hell is he?"

"That's what I don't know. She won't talk about him with me."

"She probably figures you'll break out your badge and go bust the guy's chops."

"Hey. Would I do that?"

"Absolutely. Why don't you admit you have it bad for this girl?"

"Fine, whatever. Will you get me a name?"

"What, you mean hit up some women I barely know for gossip about another woman I barely know? Because, you know, being female and all, I'm into that?"

Sean just looked at her.

"Why don't you get Ric to help you? His wife works at Delphi. She might know Brooke."

"I'm planning to ask him, too, but I want to see what you can find out."

Callie rolled her eyes. "Fine, I'll do it. But you owe me, Byrne. Again. You're racking up a lot of debt."

"I know." He paused. "In the meantime, what's new with the case? You hear anything on the knife?"

"Not yet." She checked her phone. "Their knife expert is supposed to call me once he's had a chance to look at it. You know Travis Cullen?"

"No."

"He's probably off this weekend, like most normal people, so I'm not expecting to hear anything until tomorrow at the earliest."

Sean's phone buzzed, and he pulled it from his pocket. "Ric," he told Callie as he answered the call. "Hey, what's up?"

"Can you meet me at the station house? It's important."

"I'm here now. Why?"

"We need a team meeting. Mia just called me from the lab."

Sean's pulse kicked up. "What is it?"

"She finished running those DNA tests from Samantha Bonner. We have a hit."

• • •

Callie watched as Ric's wife blew into the conference room.

"Sorry, I'm late." Mia dropped a computer bag on the table. Her cheeks were flushed and her strawberry blond hair looked windblown. She pulled off an oversize barn jacket and draped it over a chair as she glanced around.

"Everyone's here but Lieutenant Reynolds," Ric said, claiming the seat beside her.

"You guys can brief him." Mia checked her watch. "I have to pick up the baby from my sister's in an hour."

Callie watched as Mia set up her computer, impressed by the woman and also envious. Mia somehow managed to juggle the top job at the Delphi Center's DNA lab, marriage to one of the best men Callie knew, and now motherhood. And she didn't even look tired.

Well, maybe a little tired. She took a gulp from a Venti-size coffee before settling in for her presentation.

"All of you probably know that the pathologist sent over some items from the autopsy. The victim's bloody clothing, and also the rape kit, which included nail clippings." Mia looked around the room. "The rape kit was negative for semen. And we swabbed all the clothing, but didn't come up with any blood that wasn't the victim's. The nail clippings, however, yielded a lead." She took a deep breath. "We recovered biological material *not* belonging to Samantha Bonner."

"She clawed him," Sean said.

"That's what it looks like."

Mia tapped some keys on her computer, and the black and white bands of a DNA profile appeared on the screen behind her.

"I thought the ME said there were no defensive injuries," Callie said. "That she didn't have time to fight back."

"She didn't sustain defensive injuries, such as scratches or parry wounds, but that's not to say she didn't *cause* any injuries. Based on what we found, I'd say she managed to get a few good swipes in."

"So you found blood under her nails?" Sean asked.

"And skin cells, yes. We ran the sample through the database and came up with a partial hit."

Callie leaned forward. "Partial?"

"That's right. Have you heard of familial DNA? There have been several high-profile cases. The Grim Sleeper case in LA, for example."

"How exactly does it work?" Callie asked.

"I should probably start by clarifying a few things about how we run DNA. Basically, when we analyze genetic material, we can't look at the entire chromosome. That would take too much time. Instead, we look at certain genetic markers where people's DNA is highly variable. You follow?" Mia glanced around the table. Then she turned to face the image on the screen. "The DNA from under Samantha Bonner's fingernails shares eight of thirteen key markers with a DNA profile that is already in the database. In other words, it's a partial match."

"So, it's not the killer," Sean said, "but someone related to him."

"Most likely, yes. Based on the level of similarity between these two profiles, I believe you're looking for a close relative. A son, an uncle. Possibly a cousin."

Sean whistled. "Damn, that's a good lead."

"I contacted the submitting agency on this," Ric said.

"Who is it?" Callie asked.

"Austin PD. The profile in the database belongs to a James Ryan Mahoney, age twenty-seven." Ric slid a piece of paper across the table to her. "He was convicted of aggravated assault up in Austin three years ago."

Beside her, Jasper opened up his laptop computer and started typing.

"He serve time?" Sean asked.

"Two years," Ric said.

"According to this, he now lives in Kyle, Texas, right north of here," Jasper chimed in, reading from his computer screen.

"Interesting coincidence," Sean said. "Are you sure he's not our guy?"

"Absolutely." Mia gave a firm nod. "And it's not necessarily a coincidence if you consider that James Mahoney might be from around here, so some of his family members probably live locally."

"And do we know for sure that this DNA profile belongs to a *male* relative of the guy who's in the system?" Callie asked.

"That's right. This profile includes a Y chromosome."

"According to DPS records, we've got . . . damn, nineteen Mahoneys in this county alone." Jasper glanced up.

"Narrow it to males," Callie said.

Jasper refined the search as Callie looked on. "Okay, ten males. And that's just registered drivers in this county. What if we expand it to neighboring counties?"

"And what if his name isn't Mahoney?" Callie looked at Mia. "You said it could be a cousin, right? So if bloodline runs through the mother, then the perp may have a different last name."

"That's entirely possible."

"Hey, check this out. One of these Mahoneys used

to share an address with James Ryan Mahoney. I bet they're brothers."

Sean sat forward. "What's his name?"

"Bradley John Mahoney. Age twenty-nine."

"Any criminal record on him?"

Jasper pecked around for a few moments. "Looks like . . . nothing."

"Nothing at all?" Sean asked.

"Not even a traffic ticket."

"Damn."

Callie sat back in her chair, both discouraged and intrigued. If this Bradley Mahoney was their guy, she would have expected a criminal record. Most people didn't go from being law-abiding citizens to committing murder. But at least they had a suspect now. And possibly additional suspects, if they could trace more of the ex-con's male relatives.

"This is a great lead, Mia," Sean said.

"Yeah, and we appreciate you working this on a Sunday," Callie added.

"No problem." Mia checked her watch. "One other thing before I go. Familial DNA is a gray area from a legal perspective. A lot of courts aren't allowing it in. So, you need to watch your step in terms of how you use this."

"How do you mean?" Jasper asked.

"I mean, I can tell you with confidence that you have a partial match here. I corroborated my findings with a colleague. But I'm also obligated to tell you that you should run this by the prosecutor before you move forward."

"Why?" Sean asked.

"This area of the law is controversial. A lot of civil-liberties people and privacy advocates aren't happy about how this technology is being used by police, and they're making noise about it. Fourth Amendment issues, unreasonable search and seizure, that sort of thing."

"The DNA profiles are in the database for a reason," Sean countered. "These are people who have been arrested or convicted of a crime."

"Yes, but using those profiles to shine a spotlight on relatives who may or may not have done anything criminal . . . that's a whole other matter. It's dicey, and I'm sure the DA is going to have some opinions on how to proceed." Mia checked her watch and closed her computer. "I'm sorry, but I have to take off. If you guys have any more questions . . ." She looked at Ric.

"We know where to find you."

• • •

Sean watched Mia leave. Then he turned to Ric. "We need eyes on this guy ASAP."

Ric nodded. "He may not be the killer, though."

"If he isn't, he's related."

"Wait, hold on." Callie leaned forward. "Did you hear what Mia said? We have to contact the prosecutor. If we play this thing wrong, we could botch up the case."

"*That* was your takeaway?" Sean shook his head in frustration. "Mia just handed us the best lead we've had so far. This isn't some phantom witness or a vanishing fingerprint. We're talking about *actual* DNA found *under* the victim's fingernails from when she tried to fight off her killer. Far as physical evidence goes, it's a slam dunk."

"Maybe so, but using it to target a suspect isn't a slam dunk." Callie looked from Sean to Ric. "You want to screw up a court case? We can't just rush out and start arresting people named Mahoney. I mean, what if we're wrong? At the very least, we get ourselves in a bunch of legal trouble. And we could end up tipping off the real perpetrator that we're onto him."

"I'm not about to start arresting people." Sean pushed his chair back. "But I'm also not going to sit around waiting for some lawyer to give me permission to do my job."

CHAPTER 11

"Where are you?"

Sean put his phone on speaker and dropped it into the cup holder. "I'm parked outside his gym," he told Callie.

"And where is that?"

"Fifth and West."

"Don't go anywhere."

Sean stared through the windshield at the gym's entrance, then shifted his gaze to the silver BMW parked at the front of the lot. Bradley Mahoney had driven over here an hour ago even though the gym was only six blocks from his condo. Guess he didn't want to exert himself on the way to his workout.

The Riverbend condominium complex was a gated community on the south end of the riverfront district, an area known for restaurants, bars, and trendy coffee shops—including Java House, which was three short blocks from Mahoney's home.

Coincidence? Sean planned to find out.

While he'd been stuck in the parking lot observing the neighborhood, Sean had come up with multiple scenarios in which Samantha Bonner might have crossed paths with her killer, such as serving up his coffee every morning. Mahoney might have noticed the pretty barista and asked her out. Or maybe they frequented the same dry cleaner's. Or sandwich shop. They could have come into contact anywhere in the neighborhood where he lived and she worked. If there was an intersection point between them, Sean would find it.

The passenger-side door opened, and Callie slid into the truck.

"Damn, it's cold in here. Why isn't your heater on?"

"I've been here an hour. What have you got?"

"A lot." She handed over a stapled stack of papers. "Bradley J. Mahoney, attorney-at-law."

"Shit, you're kidding."

"No."

Lawyers were connected, especially in a town this size. Sean hoped they weren't going to have to deal with Mahoney's hearing through the grapevine that he was a person of interest in a homicide investigation.

"Turns out he *did* have a traffic ticket," Callie said. "Two, actually, both for speeding. And he got both dismissed. My guess is he's got a contact at the courthouse who made these go away."

Sean flipped through the papers, thinking about what else Mahoney could have made go away. As a general rule, Sean hated lawyers, even the ones on his side. They worried more about probable cause and admissibility than keeping dangerous people off the streets.

"What kind of law does he practice?" Sean asked, thumbing through the paperwork, which included an article in the state bar magazine: "Five Tips for Winning Your Case before Trial." Bradley J. Mahoney was listed as a coauthor.

"From what I can tell? Mostly personal injury and workers' comp."

"Married?"

"No. And no kids, that I could find."

Sean skimmed the printout of Mahoney's driver's record. Sean had already pulled it electronically while he'd been waiting outside the gym. He studied the driver's license photo, looking for something menacing in the man's eyes. But he just looked like some bored businessman who'd wasted his morning waiting in line at the DMV.

"I like his age," he told Callie. "Twenty-nine."

"Yeah, and you notice his size? Six-two, one-eighty."

"Plenty big enough to ambush Samantha Bonner with a hunting knife."

"That's right. And I'm sure you noticed his address. Those Riverbend condos are what, three blocks from Java House?"

"That's right." Sean glanced at the gym, but still no sign of their suspect. "I want a credit-card dump. Maybe he's been in there before."

"You won't get it without a warrant."

"I know."

"And you won't get a warrant without Rachel's help. Ric talked to her, and she's not big on this familial-DNA thing. She told him it's a can of worms."

Ric had already called Sean and relayed the DA's concerns, once again reinforcing all the reasons Sean hated lawyers. Rachel did everything by the book, which sucked from a detective's perspective.

But Sean had to admit that her obsession with rules helped bolster her impressive conviction rate, which Sean *did* appreciate because it meant that many of his collars served time. As lawyers went, Rachel wasn't all bad.

"The DA doesn't like big suspect pools," Sean told

Callie. "Right now we're at ten people, and that's only in this county."

"So, what are we going to do?"

"Narrow it down for her."

"And how do you propose we do that?" Callie gestured toward the gym. "The two of us have wasted three solid hours already on *one* guy. We don't have the time or the manpower to stake out every Mahoney on the list."

Sean looked at her. "You ever heard of surreptitious evidence collection?"

Her gaze narrowed. "Yeah."

"I talked to the building management over at Riverbend. Trash day is Monday."

"That's all you, Byrne. Don't think for a minute I'm going Dumpster diving. You already owe me favors. And speaking of favors, I got a name for you, and you're not going to like it."

Sean tensed.

"Matt Jorgensen."

Sean watched her, letting the words sink in. "I've heard that name before. He have a sheet?"

"No. He's a deputy sheriff over in Burr County."

Sean's gut clenched. "Where'd you get this?"

"Maddie. Apparently, she's met him and she's not a fan."

"She said that?"

"I think her exact words were 'Thank God they broke up. The guy's a prick.'"

"Fuck," Sean said, combing his hand through his hair.

"That was pretty much my reaction."

Sean gritted his teeth. Why hadn't Brooke told him? He glanced out the window and shook his head. A goddamn sheriff's deputy. No wonder she'd balked at the idea of getting an RO. Maybe she figured she'd be better off ignoring him or handling the situation alone.

Well, she wasn't alone now. She was getting Sean's help with this guy whether she wanted it or not. The trick would be finding a way to help her that didn't piss her off. It would be much easier if he could convince her to let him.

Sean glanced at his phone. He wanted to call her right this minute and see if she'd gotten those locks changed.

"Hey, Callie, thanks so much for spending part of your Sunday doing me a favor," she quipped.

Sean glanced at her. "Thanks."

"You're welcome. And for the record, I'd be happy to help you follow up on this, whatever you plan to do. I like Brooke and I hope she shakes loose of this guy."

Sean looked at his phone again. Then he glanced at the gym as the door opened and Bradley Mahoney stepped out.

"Heads up," Sean said.

Mahoney wore black workout clothes, and sunlight gleamed off his shaved head. He had his phone pressed to his ear and a water bottle in his hand.

"Dang, look at the size of him," Callie murmured. "No way he's one-eighty."

"I'd put him at two hundred, easy."

Sean watched as Mahoney finished his call, then guzzled water. He tossed the bottle in a nearby can and started across the parking lot to his car.

"Where are you parked?" Sean asked.

"One row back."

Sean turned around and spotted her SUV. "Wait until he leaves. Then tail him. I'm guessing he's going home after this, but you never know. Maybe he has a girlfriend or something, which would be a lead."

Callie put her hand on the door handle and waited. Mahoney got into his car and backed out of the space. He exited the lot, turning left on Fifth.

"Okay, now."

She turned to look at him. "What about you?"

"I'm going after that water bottle."

• • •

Brooke left Sunrise Donuts hungry and discouraged. She'd stopped by half a dozen times this weekend and failed to spot anyone even remotely resembling their redheaded mystery witness. Her new pal, Evan, was off today, too, so she'd had to talk to the manager, who was getting annoyed with her frequent visits. And Brooke was getting annoyed with buying doughnuts she didn't want.

She slid into her car and tossed a water bottle on the floorboard, adding to the collection there. She'd felt compelled to at least purchase a beverage every time she went in.

Her phone chimed, and she checked the number. Sean. She tried to tell herself the warm zip of excitement was because she hadn't talked to him all day and she needed an update on the case. It had nothing to do with her recent discovery that he was an amazing kisser.

"Hi," she said.

"Hey there." Just the sound of his voice made her skin flush. How did he do that with only two words?

"So, how's your day going?" Brooke drove across the street and pulled into Dairy Queen.

"Fine. What are you doing?"

"About to get a bite of lunch. Why?"

"A little late for that, isn't it?"

"Not really." She got out of her car and scanned the kids clustered at picnic tables near the doors.

"How'd it go with the locksmith?"

"It didn't."

"What happened?"

"He moved the appointment. Now he's meeting me over there at five."

"Who are you using?"

"Turn Key. They had good reviews."

"If he doesn't show, I have a friend I can call."

The smell of french fries made Brooke's stomach grumble as she stepped into the restaurant. "Thanks, but I've got it covered. What's up with the case today?"

"We've had some developments. I'll fill you in later. Listen, I have to go. I just wanted to check on that locksmith. Let me know if you need me to contact my friend."

"I'm sure that won't be necessary."

"If it is—"

"Then I'll let you know."

He went quiet.

"Thanks for the offer," she added.

"Sure. I'll call you later, okay?"

They hung up, and Brooke stood for a moment, staring at the menu board. She wasn't thinking about what she wanted, she was thinking about the worry in Sean's tone.

He knew.

It probably hadn't taken much for him to find out who her ex was. It wasn't like it was a secret or anything—she'd just never mentioned his name in front of Sean.

Oh, well. She'd known Sean would find out sooner or later. The man was a detective. There was probably very little she could hide from him if he was determined to look. And he'd definitely seemed determined lately. About a lot of things.

"Ma'am?"

"Sorry." She stepped up to the register. "Um . . . I'll have a chicken-strip basket with onion rings."

I'll call you later. Did that mean tonight? Would he ask her out again? Or maybe he'd show up on her doorstep with that sexy smile and invite her out for "just beers" again?

"Wait. Change that. Make it fries instead of onion rings."

Just in case.

The woman rang her up, and Brooke glanced to her side, where a young boy stood at the neighboring register. The sight of his rust-colored hair made Brooke's pulse skip. It skipped again as he dumped a pile of coins on the counter and slid them, one by one, toward the cashier.

"You're fifty-nine cents short," the cashier told him.

The kid dug into his pocket and came up with another quarter, which earned him an eye roll.

"Thirty-four cents short."

Brooke stepped over with a twenty-dollar bill. "Here, let me."

CHAPTER 12

The boy had a buzz cut and freckles, and Brooke estimated his age at ten, maximum, because of his small stature. Despite his youthful appearance, he had a streetwise way about him as he glanced at Brooke and exited the restaurant. He stopped at a picnic table, where a little white dog waited, tail thumping, at the end of a leash.

Brooke paused beside the table.

"Thanks for the money." He darted a suspicious look at her as he sat down and unpacked his food.

"No problem." She glanced around. "They're pretty crowded. Mind if I share your table?"

He gave a shrug and unwrapped his burger. He'd ordered two plain cheeseburgers. The first one went beneath the table, where the little dog quickly devoured it.

Brooke sat on the bench across from them.

"Cute pup. What's his name?"

"Fenway."

She smiled. "Like the park."

He nodded and slurped his soft drink, watching her.

"I'm Brooke."

"I'm Cameron."

"Nice to meet you, Cameron. Where'd you get all the quarters?"

"Around." He popped a fry into his mouth, then leaned down and gave one to Fenway.

Brooke opened up her food, although she felt too wired to eat. Her heart was racing as she sat across the table from this kid who had been a faceless figment of her imagination up to now.

"It's not really that hard." He popped another fry into his mouth. "I mean, you have to know where to look, but I do, so . . ."

She sipped her drink and watched him. "So . . . it's like a hobby? Hunting for loose change?"

He nodded.

"Sounds lucrative."

"Vending machines. That's where you go. There's a lot around town. You ever been to Wash-o-rama?"

"Over on Main Street?"

"Yeah."

"Can't say that I have."

"That's the best place. It's my first stop. Then the car-wash place, the library, then Holiday House. Then the arcade at the truck stop, but only if I have time. Sometimes it's a waste. I think someone who works there checks the machines."

"Wow, that's a lot of stops."

He shrugged. "Not really. I mean, not if it's a weekend."

"The motel is on the interstate. Your parents let you go all the way over there by yourself?"

"It's just my mom. And she doesn't care. As long as I stay out of trouble while she's gone."

Brooke picked at her chicken. "Gone, like at work?"

"Yeah." He dipped a fry in ketchup and handed it down to Fenway.

"Where does she work?"

His gaze narrowed. “Why?”

“Just curious.”

“This coffee place. Not Starbucks or anything, but it’s pretty good. It’s over on Elm Street.”

“Java House?”

“You know it?”

“Yeah.” She watched him and forced herself to nibble a french fry. “So . . . you drink coffee?”

“No, but if I go there after school, they always give me free hot chocolate.”

Brooke wished she could think of what to say to this kid. She wanted to know his full name and his address. And she wanted to talk to his mother immediately and tell her that her son was mixed up in something dangerous. But she couldn’t just sit here and interrogate a minor without a parent present. Plus, if her hunch was right, he’d get spooked in no time and she might never see him again.

She searched his face and his hands, looking for any hint that he’d been injured recently in a bike crash. His gaze stayed on her as he chomped his burger.

“Does Fenway like chicken?”

“He likes anything.”

Brooke tore off a bite and leaned down to offer it. The dog hurried over and licked it off her hand, and Brooke took a moment to stroke his ears.

“What breed is he?”

“He’s not, he’s a rescue. Mom says he’s got some of everything. You have a dog?”

“Just a cat. He’s a rescue, too.”

The boy scarfed the rest of his food, and Brooke could tell she’d made him uncomfortable with all her questions. His mom had probably taught him about stranger danger.

He stood and crumpled his food wrapper. "Well, we should probably get going."

She forced a smile. "More vending machines to check?"

"Yeah. If I see you again, I'll pay you back."

"Don't worry about it. It was nice meeting you, Cameron. Thanks for sharing your table."

"Sure, no problem."

• • •

Sean was relieved not to see Brooke's car when he pulled into the Delphi Center. Hopefully, she was home right now meeting her locksmith. He suspected she wouldn't hesitate to blow off the appointment if she got sidetracked at work.

Sean grabbed the paper evidence bag off his front seat. It contained a sixteen-ounce water bottle—luckily the only one he'd found perched at the top of the garbage bin. Because Mahoney had tossed it in a public place, he had no reasonable expectation of privacy, so Sean didn't need a warrant for anything found on it—such as the DNA that would either implicate the man in a homicide or rule him out.

Sean's phone buzzed with a call from Brooke.

"Hey. You get your locks done?"

"Not yet. Something's come up."

Sean stopped short. "What's wrong?"

"I identified our witness. His name's Cameron, and he lives at 267 Cherrywood Road. And get this. His mother works at Java House."

"You *interviewed* him?"

"No."

"How do you know all this?"

"I spotted him at Dairy Queen. He has red hair and

freckles and a little white dog, Sean. He fits the description to a T!"

Delphi's weekend security guard pushed open the door and held it, and Sean gave him a nod as he stepped into the lobby.

"There have to be a lot of redhead kids around town, and some of them probably have dogs, too. How can you be sure it's our kid?"

"I snagged his food wrapper and ran it back to the lab earlier this afternoon. The prints match."

"Jesus, Brooke. I can't believe you did that."

"I'm a CSI. That's what I *do*."

"Yeah, but you're not a cop. And I already told you about interviewing witnesses—"

"It wasn't an interview. It was a casual conversation."

He could tell he'd put her on the defensive, and he didn't give a damn. He needed to get through to her. She was putting herself in danger, not to mention jeopardizing the case.

"Sean, you have to get over here. Or send Ric over. Someone needs to talk to this kid's mother."

"Don't tell me you're at his house."

"Why not?"

"How the hell did you get his address if you didn't interview him?"

"It was on his dog's collar. When we were talking—"

"Brooke. Listen to me. You shouldn't be talking to potential witnesses or staking out houses. I don't want you involved in this."

"Too late. I am involved. And I found your witness for you, so you need to come see him. His mother has to be oblivious to all this. Why else would she let him roam around in public all day when someone just tried to run him down on his bike?"

"We don't know that for sure."

"I sure as hell do. Now, could you please send someone over here?"

Sean gritted his teeth and looked at his watch. "I'm tied up with something right now."

Silence.

"It's important," he added.

"What's more important than this eyewitness?"

"We've got a new suspect, and I think I can prove his involvement." Or disprove it. "I'll call Ric. Maybe he can get by there and talk the mom into bringing the boy in for an interview. With any luck, she'll agree to let a forensic artist sit down with him, and maybe we'll get a suspect sketch."

"I don't want him interviewed, I want him protected! Someone tried to kill him the other night, and he needs to be in some kind of protective custody or something."

"We don't have the resources for that, Brooke. As much as I wish we did. We're spread paper-thin already trying to keep an eye on a whole list of suspects while we pin down their involvement."

She went quiet. Sean glanced up and noticed the guard was watching him, blatantly eavesdropping. Sean stepped over to the reception counter and signed in. The sooner he got this evidence dropped off, the sooner he could deal with Brooke, who was obviously dead set on making his evening as complicated as possible. Why couldn't she have called him with this lead instead of going over there? Now she was committed. He could hear it in her voice.

The silence continued, and he figured she was seriously ticked off by his less-than-thrilled reaction to her discovery.

"So this Cameron kid, did you get a last name?"

"No."

"Do you know his mother's name?"

"No."

"Well, how old is he?"

"I'm not sure. Ten, I'm guessing."

The guard handed Sean a visitor's badge, and he clipped it to his jacket as he headed down the hall to the evidence room to check in his package. He'd ask Mia to bump it to the top of her list in the morning.

"Kaitlyn Spence," Sean said. "I'd bet money on it."

"Who's that?"

"One of the two Java House baristas who went to Samantha's funeral. The other one is only eighteen, so she couldn't have a kid the age you're describing. I'm betting Kaitlyn's his mother."

"Okay, but why was Cameron at Samantha's house that night if the coffee shop was closed? His mother would have been home, right?"

"Hell if I know. We need to interview these people, like I said. Is she there now?"

"I don't know. I don't think she is. It's a little house with a carport, but I don't see any cars."

"Is the kid there?"

"I think so. His dog was in the backyard, and I can see a TV on in the living room."

"And you're sure it's him?"

"*Yes*, Sean. I matched the prints."

"I'll call Ric. Meantime—"

"Don't tell me to go home. I'm not going anywhere until someone with a badge gets here. Wait, hang on."

"What is it?"

"There's a car pulling into the driveway. Just a sec."

Sean gripped the phone. He hated her in the middle of this. "Brooke?"

"It's his mom, I think. Tall and thin. Auburn hair. She's wearing a brown apron, like she just got off work."

"That's Kaitlyn Spence. Let me get Ric over there to talk to her."

"Someone needs to tell her what's going on with her son."

"We'll take it from here. You stay out of it."

She didn't say anything.

"Brooke? *We* will handle it."

"Fine, then hurry up and handle it."

• • •

Kaitlyn Spence walked across the weedy lawn and up the steps to her door. The woman looked tired. Just like her house. Just like her car, which had dings on the side and was missing the back bumper. She let herself in without a key, and Brooke cringed as she realized Cameron had been sitting inside an unlocked house.

Brooke's phone chirped as a text landed from Sean.

Ric on his way. Can u send the plate?

Brooke looked at the Hyundai. Then she got out and glanced around, hoping she didn't draw attention as she took a leisurely stroll past the driveway. She snapped a quick photo of the license plate with her phone and also committed it to memory in case the picture turned out fuzzy. After about half a block, she turned around and walked casually back to her car. Once inside, she checked the photo and texted it to Sean. He probably wanted to run a criminal background check on Cameron's mother. The thought wouldn't have occurred to Brooke, but Sean was much more suspicious of people than she was.

The front door opened, and Kaitlyn emerged looking completely different. Her long auburn hair was piled in a knot on top of her head now. She wore a black shirt, a black miniskirt, and tall black boots, along with a different apron—also black.

She had *two* jobs? Clearly, she was going out for the evening, and it looked like she was dressed to wait tables. Brooke checked her watch and cursed. She looked up and down the street, but no sign of Ric.

Damn it. How long would she be gone? And had she bothered locking the door? And what would Cameron do on his own all night? Maybe he'd get bored and go roaming around town hunting for loose change.

Kaitlyn opened her car door, and Brooke jumped out.

"Ms. Spence?"

She turned around. Her look was curious but not unfriendly, and Brooke fixed a smile on her face as she approached her.

"Hi. You don't know me but . . . I need to talk to you about your son."

Her brow furrowed. "What about him?"

The front door opened, and Fenway shot outside. Cameron stepped out behind him and stood at the top of the porch steps, looking at Brooke as Fenway jumped in hysterical circles at her feet, probably hoping for another chicken nugget.

"Fenway, *no*." Kaitlyn walked over and tried to grab the dog's collar as she glanced up at Brooke. "Who did you say you are?"

"My name is Brooke Porter. And I work with . . . some people who need to talk to you about something."

"Fenway, *here*!" Cameron shouted, coming down the steps. But the dog was too busy barking to obey.

Kaitlyn gave Fenway's collar a sharp tug as she looked up at Brooke. "I'm sorry, you're . . . who? And how do you know my son?"

From the corner of her eye, Brooke spotted a dark shape moving down the street. And then everything happened in slow motion.

Cameron reached for the dog's collar.

Kaitlyn stood and looked at Brooke with confusion.

The black pickup moved closer, and Brooke's stomach plummeted as she spied the long black gun barrel poking from the window.

CHAPTER 13

A gunshot rang out.

"Get *down*!" Brooke screamed.

She took a running leap at Cameron and they crashed to the ground in a heap. The air flew from Brooke's lungs, and Fenway was on her instantly, barking and nipping with his sharp teeth.

Brooke flattened herself over Cameron as he yelped and kicked. Kaitlyn's shrieks surrounded them.

"Stay down!" Brooke yelled.

More barks. A squeal of brakes. Teeth clamped around Brooke's elbow, and she tried to shake off the dog.

"Cameron! *Cameron!*"

His mother's voice was shrill with panic as she grabbed Brooke's arm and pulled her off her son. Brooke cast a frantic glance at the street, but the pickup was long gone.

"*Cameron!*"

Brooke turned to the boy. Blood trickled from the side of his mouth and he looked dazed.

Kaitlyn crouched beside him, yelling and crying and running her hands over his head. Blood streamed down Kaitlyn's arm, and Brooke couldn't see where it was coming from.

"Oh, my God! Are you okay? Are you hurt?" Kaitlyn touched her hands to her son's face, smearing his cheeks with red.

"What was that? Mom, what happened?" He grabbed Fenway and pulled him against his chest.

Brooke pushed to her feet, but her knees buckled and she sank to the ground. Her heart pounded as she fumbled to pull her phone from her pocket.

"Call 911!" Kaitlyn shouted. "Cameron, answer me, baby! *Are you hurt?*"

"I'm okay." He blinked up at her. "But . . . Mom, you're bleeding."

• • •

Brooke cast an anxious glance around as she leaned against her car.

"Could you describe the vehicle, ma'am?"

She looked up at Jasper. "A black pickup truck," she said for the umpteenth time. "It was old. I didn't get the make or the model."

"When you say 'old'—"

"Nineties or earlier. I don't know, really. I only saw it for a second."

Jasper jotted something in his notepad.

Brooke looked around impatiently. She'd been through this already with the responding officer. She shifted her gaze to the middle of the street where that officer was now using a police department camera to snap a picture of the skid marks at the end of the block. Brooke had already taken the same shots with her cell phone so she could trace the tire marks without having to wait for the police to get around to it.

"Ma'am?"

She sighed. "Would you stop with that, please?"

"Sorry. Brooke." Jasper shifted on his feet. "Do you remember the window color? Was it tinted? Clear?"

"The window was rolled down. I don't remember."

"Did you get a look when it sped away, maybe?"

"No. I didn't see him leave. I just heard him. I was on the ground with Cameron."

Brooke looked at the house now. Even from the street she could hear Cameron's little dog inside barking up a frenzy as police swarmed the property. Both ends of the street had been barricaded, and uniforms were combing the asphalt for shell casings.

"Brooke?"

"Sorry. What?" She snapped out of her daze and looked at Jasper. He was being incredibly patient with her as her attention hopped around like a rabbit on speed.

"I said, don't you want to get that checked out?" He nodded at her arm. Brooke had wrapped it in a T-shirt from her car.

"I'm good."

He gave her a disapproving look as he flipped shut his notepad. "Suit yourself. If you *do* go to the hospital, maybe swing by the station house after. You could look at our vehicle photos and something might jump out."

A gray pickup halted beside the barricade. Brooke's heart skittered as Sean got out and homed in on her instantly. His look of relief turned to determination as he strode over.

"Why aren't you at the hospital?" He looked her up and down. She'd mentioned the dog bite when she talked to him on the phone earlier.

"Because I'm fine." Especially now that Sean was here. Even with all the police milling around, she felt better with him near her.

He took her good arm and shifted her behind the door of her car, as though to shield her from stray bullets. "That dog could have rabies, Brooke."

"He doesn't. Cameron's mom said he's had all his shots."

Sean didn't look placated.

"How are they?" Brooke asked.

"Ric's with them. Kaitlyn is getting stitches where the bullet grazed her. She's lucky she wasn't killed." Sean's eyes held Brooke's, and she knew what he was thinking.

Brooke was lucky, too. And Cameron. Just thinking how close they'd all come to something catastrophic made Brooke break out in a cold sweat. She looked away, hoping Sean wouldn't pick up on her distress. It had been almost an hour, and her pulse was still pounding as though she'd just run a sprint.

"Hey." He took her hand. "Look at me."

She did. His hand felt warm and infinitely reassuring, and she couldn't bring herself to tug hers away this time. It was all she could do not to wrap her arms around him and bury her face against his chest.

"Let me get you out of here," he said in a low voice. "I'll take you to get your arm treated and then have an officer take you home."

She wanted him to take her home. But of course he couldn't do that because he had way too much going on now. This was his case. She got it. But that didn't make the reality any easier to swallow. It was going to be a long, anxious, *solitary* night.

Brooke pulled her hand from his.

"I don't need to get it treated. It's a scratch, I told you."

"Mind if I look?"

She shrugged. He carefully lifted her arm and unwrapped the T-shirt. The pink fabric was dark with blood where he peeled it away from the wound.

He gave her a grim look.

"It's no big deal. I cleaned it up inside the house. I'll put some ointment on it when I get home." She replaced the makeshift bandage. "Tell me more about Kaitlyn. Has Ric interviewed her?"

Sean watched her a moment. "Yes."

"And Cameron?"

"Callie talked to Cameron. She's good with kids."

"And?"

"And Cameron says he went by Samantha's house that night. He said he rang the doorbell, but she wasn't there. Then he headed home and crashed his bike on the way."

Brooke's heart sank. "He really said that?"

"Yes."

"He's lying."

"He's terrified. We need to get a child psychologist in to talk to him, see if we can get the real story out of him."

"Well, what was he doing there?"

"His mother said he goes to Samantha's house sometimes to hang out while she's at work, sort of an informal thing. Samantha gave him a key, which makes me doubt his whole story that he rang the doorbell that night."

Brooke shook her head, frustrated. "What about protection for them?"

"I'm working on it."

"What does that *mean*?"

"It means I'm working on it."

Brooke looked at the weedy lawn that was now a

crime scene. The sight of the bloodstained grass made her stomach tighten. "Sean . . . I feel like I led him here."

"Who?"

"Whoever it is that's after Cameron."

"You didn't."

She searched Sean's face, looking for clues that he believed that. "How do you know?"

"Because you didn't. We're not even sure this drive-by is related to Samantha's murder."

"But . . . why not? What else would it be related to? The killer had to have seen him flee the scene. He *knows* he has a witness, and he's coming after him."

"Take a step back, Brooke. It's a drive-by shooting. Maybe there's a drug connection here. Or some kind of gang violence. We have to look at everything, and right now we don't know nearly enough about Samantha Bonner or Kaitlyn Spence, or who would have wanted to target either of them."

"What about Cameron? *He's* the target here. He's an eyewitness, and someone's trying to silence him."

"Maybe. We have to look at all possibilities." Sean paused. "Which is why I need to ask you something you're not going to like."

She drew back. "What?"

"Any chance you might have been the target?"

Brooke went cold.

"You told police the vehicle was a black pickup. Matt Jorgensen drives a black pickup."

Her mouth dropped open.

"You ex could be involved here. You have to at least consider the possibility."

"No. Never in a million years."

Sean stared at her, his face unreadable.

"It isn't possible."

"Anything's possible."

Brooke shook her head, frustrated beyond words. She slid behind the wheel of her car.

"Where are you going?"

"To the police station. To comb through vehicle photos. To identify the truck from this shooting so that we can develop *real* leads and stop wasting time on wild theories."

"I can take you," Sean said. "It's on my way to the hospital."

"I'm fine."

"Brooke—"

"Stop worrying about me!" She started up her car. "The person you should be worried about is Cameron Spence!"

CHAPTER 14

When Brooke finally made it home, she was bleary-eyed from looking at endless photos on a computer screen. She parked in her driveway and jogged through the drizzle to her neighbor's door on the other side of the duplex. Their landlord had agreed to meet the locksmith for Brooke and leave the new key with Leila, but he was adding the charges to next month's rent.

Leila answered the door with a smile on her face and a glass of wine in her hand. Her smile dropped as she took in Brooke's bedraggled appearance.

"What happened to you?"

"Long day."

"Well, I just opened a bottle of Chianti if you want to come in."

"Thanks, but what I really need is a hot shower."

"Okay, one sec. Your key's in the kitchen."

Brooke waited, shivering, on the porch, and Leila returned with a shiny set of keys.

"Here you go."

"Thanks. And thanks for dealing with Kopcek. How was he?"

Leila rolled her eyes. "An ass pain, as usual. He noticed the cat food on my porch and pitched a fit."

"Damn. Sorry to call him over here."

"No biggie. That locksmith guy was hot, so I didn't mind." Leila winked. "I might have to lock myself out of my car next week."

"Sounds fun."

"If you change your mind about the wine, you know where to find me."

"Thanks."

Brooke let herself in using her new key. She closed the door and locked it behind her with a smooth snick. Then she looked around, noticing bits of sawdust on the floor. She glanced at the coffee table. No beer bottle this time.

Brooke pulled off her damp sweater, stripping down to a black tank top. She tossed the sweater on top of an overflowing laundry basket. She didn't have the energy to think about chores tonight. Tugging her ponytail loose, she headed through the kitchen and into the utility room. She tested the new key and peered through the window, surveying the shadowy yard for a moment before closing the blinds.

Standing in the cool darkness, Brooke was reminded of the crime scene from a few days ago. Five days. So much had happened since then. It seemed like ages since she'd been on her knees in that utility room, surrounded by the stench of blood and fighting off nausea as she fingerprinted the doorknob only inches away from a woman's butchered body.

Some guys are allergic to rejection.

A chill went through her as she remembered Sean's words.

Over the years Brooke had worked hundreds of crime scenes. Some mundane. Some gut-wrenching. Samantha's stood out because of the sheer emotion Brooke had felt just being there. Even on her second visit twenty-four hours later, she'd felt it. That crime was about rage, pure and simple. The motive might still be fuzzy, but the emotion behind it was crystal clear, at least to Brooke.

She stepped to the sink to wash her hands and glimpsed her reflection in the kitchen window. She looked shell-shocked, which shouldn't have surprised her because she'd been shot at tonight.

Shot at.

Recounting the details to the first responder and then to Jasper, Brooke had felt detached, as though she were reporting something that happened to someone else. But now that she was in her own home, surrounded by familiar sights and smells, she didn't feel detached at all. She felt an overwhelming sadness for her family over what had almost happened. Brooke knew better than most how guns could rip apart lives in only an instant. She'd seen the gurneys and heard the wailing mothers, and she was acutely aware of the stark finality of death.

Don't go there. It didn't happen.

Brooke grabbed a dish towel to dry her face and saw that her hands still had a tremor.

The doorbell chimed, and she turned around. She hesitated a moment, then crossed the house to check the peephole. Relief flooded her at the sight of Sean's broad-shouldered silhouette on her porch. She flipped on the outdoor light and opened the door.

"Hi." His gaze went to her bandaged elbow. "Can I come in?"

She stepped back to let him inside. His hair and his jacket were wet with rain, and he dripped water on her floor, just as he had the other night.

He closed the door behind him and gave her a long

look before taking her hand and lifting it to brush a kiss over her knuckles. The unexpected gesture sparked a firestorm of nerves inside her.

"Come here." He pulled her against his chest and wrapped his arms around her. His leather jacket felt damp and cold, and she rested her cheek against the warm flannel of his shirt.

He kissed the top of her head.

"What's this for?" Her voice was muffled, but she couldn't bring herself to pull away from him. He smelled way too good.

"This is what I should have done earlier instead of standing there arguing with you."

She took a deep breath, absorbing his scent, his strength. She loved the way his arms felt around her.

"Tell me the truth. Are you all right?"

"Better." She didn't say *fine* this time because that would have been a lie. That shooting had shaken her to the core.

She pulled back and looked up at him. "How are you?"

"Tired. How's the dog bite?"

"All bandaged and disinfected. It's no big deal."

Sean didn't look as if he believed her.

"Where are Cameron and his mom?"

"Somewhere safe."

" 'Somewhere'?"

He looked at her for a moment before answering. "My sister's an ER nurse in Austin. She helped me get them settled at a shelter up there. They'll be fine for a night or two until we sort this out."

Brooke felt relieved, but not completely. Who knew how long it might take to "sort this out," as he put it? They couldn't stay at a shelter forever.

"We need to talk, Brooke."

She tensed. "About what?"

"Matt Jorgensen."

She sighed and looked away. "I don't want to talk about him tonight."

"This can't wait."

"What happened to Sean Byrne, King of Patience?"

He rested his hand on her shoulder. "As the guy who wants to date you? I can give you all the time you want. As the cop investigating a shooting in which you could have been killed—"

"I *wasn't* the target."

"We don't know that. And until we do, I need every scrap of relevant info. So, I'm sorry, time's up. We're going to talk about this."

His voice was all-business, and she knew it would be pointless to argue.

She pulled back from him. "Fine."

"Fine." He gazed down at her. "You eaten yet?"

"No."

"Me neither."

After a halfhearted debate, they decided on a diner near the university. The ride there was silent and strained, and Brooke spent most of it staring out the window of Sean's truck at the rain-soaked streets. When they arrived, he asked for a corner booth where they'd be able to talk with some measure of privacy.

Brooke scooted in first, and Sean slid around until he was right beside her. Before she'd left the house, she'd pulled a thick sweatshirt over her tank top, both to ward off the chill and to keep Sean from staring at her bandaged elbow.

A young waitress stopped by and asked for their order.

"I'll have a milk shake," Brooke said. "Double chocolate."

Sean looked at her, then glanced at the server. "Make it two."

When the waitress disappeared, Sean leaned back and rested his arm on the back of the booth. "Ice cream for dinner?"

She shrugged. "Comfort food. It's been a crap day."

His brow furrowed, and she wished she hadn't reminded him. He looked all serious now, and she glanced away, bracing herself for an interrogation. Nothing about this felt like a conversation between friends, and it wasn't.

As the guy who wants to date you . . .

Was that truly what he wanted? She'd known he wanted something from her, but she'd thought it had more to do with sex. Was that a line, or was he sincere? Maybe she was being overly skeptical, but that was how she was now—always second-guessing her instincts and questioning her judgment when it came to men.

Sean was watching her closely, and she resisted the urge to squirm in her seat.

"So, what did you want to ask me?"

"Let's start with the vehicle. At the station you identified the truck as a '95 Chevy Silverado, all-black."

"That's right."

"Are you sure about the age on that?"

"It's an estimate. Give or take a few years."

"Only a few?"

She huffed out a breath. "What are you getting at?"

"Jorgensen drives a black pickup."

"I know what his truck looks like. He drives an F-250. That's *not* the truck I saw today."

Sean just looked at her.

"I told you, it wasn't Matt. He'd never do something like this."

"How do you know?"

"Because I *know*, all right?" Her chest tightened. "I was with him for two years. We didn't exactly break up on good terms, but he wouldn't try to *gun me down* in the street, for God's sake. He's not capable of that."

"What's he capable of?"

Sean watched her, his expression unreadable. This was his cop face, and again she felt like she was in an interrogation. She looked away from him. A tear leaked out, and she brushed it away.

"I'm sorry we have to talk about this," he said quietly.

"It's fine. Let's just get it over with. What do you want to know?"

"Why did you guys break up?"

She took a deep breath. "I didn't like our pattern."

"So, you're the one who ended it?"

"Yes."

"Were you living together?"

"No, thank God. That would have been harder." She sighed. "He wanted me to move in with him, but I never felt good about it. I don't know. I'd lived with someone once before, and it didn't work out, and I didn't want to go through all that again."

"You said you didn't like your pattern."

Sean watched her, waiting for her to elaborate. He was looking so closely, picking up every nuance of her body language. He was good at reading people, and he'd know if she tried to sugarcoat anything, so she might as well tell him the truth.

"He had a temper." She cleared her throat. "He would yell. Throw things. Get up in my face. He wasn't like that at first. I don't know what happened, really, but it changed."

She looked at her hands and tried to collect her thoughts as all the old feelings came back. "Stuff would escalate, and my reaction only made things worse."

"What was your reaction?"

She paused to try to describe the utter calm that would settle over her. "It wasn't a conscious thing, really. It was just what I did. He would get louder and more pissed off and all red in the face, and I would go completely calm. I wouldn't say a word or react or anything. It used to drive him crazy."

"You were in control and he wasn't."

"I don't know. Probably." She glanced up at Sean, then looked down at her hands. "There was this one time, we were at the yogurt shop down the street from my house. We got in an argument over something stupid and he was being unreasonable. So I rolled my eyes and walked away from him. That set him off. He followed me down the sidewalk and started shoving me from behind, saying he wasn't done talking to me. He kept shoving me and shoving me, and I kept walking faster and faster so I wouldn't trip. And every jab was like a shock because I couldn't believe he was making this scene in public."

She glanced up, Sean's face was tight.

"We got to my house, and I told him to go home and cool off. I told him if he ever touched me like that again, our relationship was over."

"Did he leave?"

"He got in his truck and peeled off. And that was it. The next day he came over and acted like everything was fine. And it was for a while."

The waitress appeared with two tall shakes topped with whipped cream. Brooke stirred hers with the straw and took a sip to cool her throat.

"Then a few months later it started up again. He'd been working all these weekends. Midnight callouts. He was under a lot of stress at work."

"That's no excuse."

"I know." She glanced at Sean. "Finally, one Saturday we both had the afternoon off, so we went to the river where some of his friends were hanging out at the sand volleyball court. You know the one by the campground?"

Sean nodded.

"So, we were standing beside the court, and it was the same old same old. We got in a disagreement about something minor. I told him he was wrong, and he picked up this big bottle of water and poured it over my head." She remembered the icy liquid trickling down her neck and her back. She remembered her face heating. She'd been so stunned, and she'd wanted to disappear. "I mean, it was *water*. The most harmless thing in the world."

Sean was looking at her now, his gaze intent.

"I was so shocked I just stood there. And I realized this was it. This was the end. He wanted to humiliate me in public and he did."

"What did you do?"

"Nothing. I laughed it off. I acted like it was a joke. But inside I knew that was it for me. It was only going to get worse."

She took a sip of her shake, letting the cold soothe her nerves. Sean still hadn't touched his.

"We finished the afternoon with everyone. Went home. I told him I was tired, so he could just drop me off. I think he knew something was up, but he went along with it. The next day I called him and told him I wanted a break. I didn't have the guts to tell him in person. I wasn't sure how he'd react."

"What did he do?"

"We talked in circles for a while. He told me I was being unreasonable. Overreacting. He told me I didn't understand the stress he was under at work. Whatever. I've got work stress, too. And I deal with cops all the time, so I *know* what the job's like. Yeah, it's stressful, but that doesn't give you a pass to treat people like shit."

She took a deep breath. "So, that's it. The whole crappy story. Aren't you glad you asked?" Another tear leaked out and she swiped it away. "I don't know why I'm like this. I'm not sorry it's over or anything. My instincts told me it was going to get worse, not better, so I know I did the right thing, even though it's been bumpy."

"Define 'bumpy.'" She didn't miss the edge in his voice.

"Everything you'd expect. He came over drunk a few times. I pretended I wasn't home. We've had some heated phone calls. He followed me around some."

Sean's gaze narrowed. "He followed you?"

"He's not doing it anymore. I haven't had a conversation with him in two months."

Sean was watching her closely, but she couldn't tell what was going on in his mind. She decided to omit the part about the spying app on her phone. Alex had removed it, and Brooke didn't want Sean to know she'd been gullible enough to miss something like that. She'd agreed to talk, but that didn't mean she had to share every unflattering detail.

"What are you thinking?" she asked.

"I'm glad you told me."

"That's not all you're thinking. What else?"

He put his hand over hers, and the warmth of it made her feel a pang of yearning.

She pulled her hand away and rested it in her lap. "Matt has plenty of flaws. I'll be the first to tell you that. But you should trust me when I say he's not capable of that shooting today."

"You'd be surprised what people are capable of."

"He's been in law enforcement six years, Sean. He does good things, and he's a volunteer firefighter. He's got third-degree burns on his arms from rescuing a little girl from a house fire. I'm not defending everything about him, but that shooting? You're wasting your time looking at him for that. That's linked to Samantha Bonner's murder somehow. I know it is. That's the avenue you should be pursuing."

"We are." Sean pulled his shake toward him and finally took a sip, downing a third of it in one gulp.

"And?"

"And, as much as I hate to admit it, the drive-by reinforces my lieutenant's theory that this whole thing is drug related."

"What about the theory that someone's gunning down an eyewitness to a murder?"

"If the target was Cameron? Yes, that makes sense. If the target was Kaitlyn, maybe not."

"It was Cameron."

The waitress was back with the check. Sean grabbed

it. Brooke tried to leave money, but he waved her off. "No way. This was my idea."

They left the diner in silence, but it was a different kind of silence from before. Brooke felt relieved. Lighter. Like two heavy sandbags had been lifted off her shoulders.

Sean opened the passenger door for her, and she slid into the truck. He stood beside her for a moment.

"What?" she asked. "What's that look?"

He leaned in and kissed her. It was soft and sweet, and completely opposite of their other kisses, where she'd felt like he wanted to eat her alive.

He leaned his forehead against hers. "You amaze me."

"Why?"

"Everything."

"Right."

He pulled back and shook his head, as if he didn't want to bother arguing. He eased her door shut and then went around to his side and slid behind the wheel. She watched him as he fired up the truck and smoothly backed out of the space.

He was so strong, so confident all the time. She felt strong, too, whenever she was around him. Right now, for instance. At this moment she felt full and energized—as though sharing her experience with him had taken some of its power away.

It started to rain again as they exited the parking lot, and Sean switched on the wipers.

"So, where to?" He glanced at her. "You want to go home yet?"

"That depends." She looked at him.

"On?"

Her stomach did a nervous dance, but she ignored it. "Does your offer still stand?"

He stared straight ahead as they neared a stoplight. The truck was quiet—just the *swoosh-swoosh* of the wiper blades as they rolled to a halt.

He looked at her. "My offer?"

"I'd like to go to your place."

CHAPTER 15

Saying she wanted to go home with him and actually doing it were two different things, Brooke discovered as they drove through town in silence.

He'd answered her request with a brisk nod, but now she felt unsure. All her bold, fizzy confidence seemed to have evaporated. What if she was being too pushy? Maybe he didn't want this tonight.

She darted a glance at him, but his face was a stony mask as he navigated the late-night traffic. A muscle twitched at the side of his jaw, and she looked away as the doubts closed in on her.

He slowed and turned onto a tree-lined street. Along one side were one-story houses, fairly new construction. The other side was condominiums. Sean swung into one of the condo driveways, and Brooke glanced around at the narrow brick units that backed up to acres of woods.

"You live on the greenbelt?"

"Yep."

He cut the engine and looked at her. She couldn't read his expression in the dimness, and her doubts bubbled up again.

"What's wrong?" he asked gruffly.

"I feel like I invited myself over."

"No. *I* invited you."

He unclipped his seat belt and reached for her, pulling her into a kiss, and the warm press of his mouth gave her the reassurance she wanted. She eased into him, loving his kisses, which had somehow become so addictive in only a few days. Running her fingers through his hair, she pulled him as close as they could get with the console between them. He cupped her head in his hands and changed the angle of the kiss. His mouth was hot and avid against hers, and he tasted of chocolate.

"Mmm. You taste good," she whispered, pulling him even closer.

"Hold that thought."

He released her and slid out of the truck, going around the front to her side as she watched him through the rain-slicked windows. He opened her door and tugged her out as she grabbed her purse.

"Watch your step." He shut the door behind her and pulled her along the wet brick path to a front courtyard. She stood beside him, shivering in the rain as he unlocked the door. A bright floodlight lit the courtyard, but the house was dark inside as they stepped over the threshold. A beeping alarm greeted them, and he crossed the foyer to tap a code into a keypad.

Brooke glanced around as her eyes adjusted to the dimness. A Saltillo-tile foyer led into a spacious living room dominated by a big black sofa and a stone fireplace with a TV mounted above it. Floor-to-ceiling windows lined the back wall, and through them she could see a lit balcony overlooking the woods. It was a real place, a grown-up place, and she felt oddly surprised by it.

"This is nice."

"Thanks."

"I like—"

He silenced her with a kiss. It was hungry and insistent. His strong arms came around her, and she felt herself being guided back and eased against the hard wooden door. Excitement surged through her as he kissed her and gripped her hips, pinning her body against the wood.

He pulled back a fraction. "I wanted you here last night. You have no idea how bad I wanted that."

"Why?" she asked in a breathy voice.

"I wanted to prove that I could keep my hands off you. You said I was impatient, and I wanted to show you I could wait."

She rolled her hips against him. "What do you want now?"

He kissed her, hard, and his hand slid under her sweatshirt. "Now"—his fingers glided over her breast, stroking her nipple through the thin tank top—"all bets are off." His voice was rough and desperate.

She dropped her purse to the floor and pulled him in for another kiss, thrilled that he sounded so needy for her. She loved everything he was doing—the fierceness of his kiss, the warmth of his hands, both of them now, sliding under her sweatshirt. The expert stroke of his thumbs made her knees weak, and she twined her arms around his neck to keep from slipping to the floor.

"You smell so good all the time," he murmured against her neck.

She kissed him again, glowing with the compliment as his hands slid down to cup her butt.

"Hold on." He scooped her up and made her gasp with surprise.

She wrapped her legs around him as he walked her into the living room, where he lowered her onto the sofa and eased down on top of her. His body was solid and heavy, and despite all the layers, she could feel the hard press of his erection between her legs.

"Sean."

"Yeah?"

"Too many clothes."

He muttered something against her neck and went to work wrestling her sweatshirt over her head and flinging it away. He settled back on top of her, sliding his hand under the thin fabric of her top. She loved his mouth and his hands and the masculine hardness of his body. Everything he did made her want to be closer to him, as close as she could possibly get, without a single layer between them. She wanted to feel the heat of his skin under her fingertips. She worked his flannel shirt from his jeans and slid her hand under to be rewarded with the hard texture of his muscular abs.

His fingers found her nipple again, and she pressed against him with a whimper. Her breasts weren't big, but they were sensitive, and she wanted his mouth on them, but she didn't want to ask. Instead she pushed him away so she could pull off her tank top, revealing a sheer pink bra that left little to the imagination. Thanks to her laundry situation, she was down to her fancy underwear.

His eyes went dark and he kissed her, cupping her breast in his hand as she felt the hot pull of his mouth. She arched against him and combed her fingers into his hair as he made her entire body start to pulse with need. He found the clasp at her back, and even the whisper-thin fabric disappeared.

"Me too," she said, sitting up to undo the buttons of

his flannel shirt. Before she could finish, he pulled it over his head and tossed it to the floor, and her throat went dry as she saw his torso for the first time. She traced a finger over his sculpted pecs, but he seemed too distracted to notice as he settled over her again and dipped his head down to kiss her.

"I love your breasts."

"*Mine?*"

He looked up at her from between them, that sexy half smile on his face. "You see any others here?"

"They're small."

"They're fucking perfect." He closed his mouth over her nipple, sending a jolt of lust through her that had her squirming and panting and pulling him by his hair. He knew she liked what he was doing, and he seemed to enjoy teasing her, alternating his attention from one side to the other, all the while pressing against the throbbing juncture between her legs. The combination was making her dizzy. She closed her eyes and let herself enjoy it as she ran her fingers over his shoulders and savored the feel of his weight on her. His hand glided down to her waist and she felt him unbuttoning her jeans.

"Is this okay?" His gaze was dark and serious, and the tone of his voice touched her.

She nodded.

She kept her eyes locked on his and heard the rasp of her zipper. Then he moved down the sofa on his knees, unzipping her boots, one by one, and removing them from her feet, followed by her socks. Then his hands were back at her hips again and he slowly slid the jeans down her body, and that's when the tremors started.

She couldn't stop them—they were an involuntary

response to the cool air against her skin, and the heat of his gaze, and the electrical charge between them as the moment unfolded. He stretched out beside her, tracing his finger from her lips to her sternum and down over her belly button to the last remaining scrap of fabric she wore.

She feathered her fingers through his hair, watching his eyes move over her along with his hand. His touch sent warm shivers through her, and mixed with the nerves, it was like he'd flipped a switch inside her and made her whole body start to vibrate. She wanted to tell him, but she didn't know how to describe the feeling. Anyway, he could probably see the effect he was having on her because he was right there beside her with his thigh pressed against hers.

She looked up into his eyes and smiled.

He kissed her. It was soft at first, but then he eased onto her, and everything intensified. She stroked her hands over his back and felt his muscles ripple under her touch. She loved his body. His mouth. She loved the weight of him pressing her into the cushions and the scent of his hot skin. She hooked her leg around him, pulling him against her until it hurt. She slid her hand between them and ran her fingers over his zipper, and he pushed himself against her hand.

"Sean?" She unsnapped his jeans and dipped her fingers inside to stroke his hard length. He moaned against her neck, and she pulled her hand away. "Sean, I don't have anything."

He pulled back, looking dazed, and then his eyes locked on hers. "Be right back." He kissed her and quickly got to his feet. She watched as he disappeared down the hallway, leaving her alone.

Reality swept over her. She glanced around the dim

room. She was in Sean's house. On his sofa and almost naked. She heard the faint sound of a drawer opening and closing as she waited for him, barely able to breathe. Her heart was racing out of control, and her limbs were trembling, even her hands. Was she having a panic attack? Was that even possible right now, when she was so turned on? Maybe her body was trying to tell her she was making a mistake.

Anxiety washed over her. She didn't have to go through with this. It was late in the game to change her mind, but she knew he'd respect what she wanted.

Him. That's what she wanted. She felt nervous and excited and even a bit terrified of what this might do to their relationship, but she wanted *him*. And when his dark silhouette appeared in the hallway, all the anxiety faded in comparison to how much she wanted him.

He'd gotten rid of his clothes except for black boxer briefs, and she admired his body again as he dropped a strip of condoms on the table and lowered himself over her.

He kissed her, brushing her hair away from her face. "You all right?"

"Yeah."

He looked her in the eye. "You sure?"

"Yes. Find what you needed?"

"Oh, yeah."

She kissed him to prove she was fine, and they picked up right where they'd left off before her flurry of doubts. She stroked her hands over his hard muscles, down the indention of his spine, over his hips. She dipped her fingers into the back of his waistband and pulled him close.

He rolled onto his side and slid his hand down her

body and between her legs, and she felt a hot rush of desire. When he cupped his hand over her, she nearly shot off the couch.

"Sean—"

He kissed her, pressing against her as she squirmed and moaned. Then he shifted to sit up. With one smooth motion, he lifted her onto his lap and helped her straddle him, then started kissing her neck and her breasts.

His hands glided up her back as he held her close, and she tipped her head back as he kissed her and lavished more attention on her breasts than she'd ever thought possible. His fingers slid down between her legs, and she rolled her hips against him.

"Take these off." She pushed at his shorts.

He did as she asked, and she wrapped her arms around him as she heard the tear of the condom wrapper. Then she lifted her hips. He reached between her legs to move the silk aside and guided her onto him, entering her body with a deep thrust that left her breathless.

"You okay?"

She moved her legs, trying to get comfortable.

"Brooke?" His voice was strained as she shifted her weight.

"Yes. Like that."

He clasped her hips and moved her against him as he kissed her mouth. She arched into him, loving the friction where their bodies were joined. He pulled her even closer, and the rasp of his chest against her breasts nearly sent her over the edge.

"Sean." She surged against him again and again, and the sensation of him filling her was so impossibly good that she felt her control slipping. "*Sean.*"

She clutched her arms around him as everything shattered. He held her through the aftershocks, then she slumped against his shoulder.

He brushed her hair back from her face and looked at her, smiling.

"Sorry. Couldn't wait."

"Good." He kissed her. Then he lifted her off his lap, lowered her back onto the cushions, and finally pulled the last scrap of silk off her body before settling between her legs. She draped her arms over his shoulders and closed her eyes as she braced herself for the next part, and he pushed into her with one hard stroke.

Brooke wrapped her legs around him, and they moved together, finding a rhythm again. She'd thought she was done, but when she opened her eyes to look up at him, the raw male desire she saw in his face made her hot all over again, and a whole new tension started to burn and build inside her.

She closed her eyes and tipped her head back.

"Brooke, look at me."

She did.

He took her hands and stretched them over her head and held her gaze as he drove into her over and over, until she thought she'd scream. Then she did scream, and he came into her with a powerful thrust and collapsed against her.

Silent seconds ticked by as she lay dizzy. He was heavy and crushing her, and she didn't care at all as she traced her hands over his strong back. In all her life, she'd never felt like this. Ever. She couldn't form a thought. Or utter a word.

Her mind was blown.

• • •

Callie ended her week the same way she'd started it. Working.

She jammed a stack of paperwork into her bag and headed out of the bull pen, giving a wave to the officer manning the phones tonight. He'd been leaving the station to go home when she'd arrived this morning.

Pathetic.

Callie trekked through the drizzle to her Jeep, pondering when, exactly, her life had gotten so out of whack. Not so long ago she'd had interests outside of work. Hobbies. A social life. But all of those things had more or less disappeared in the year since she'd earned her detective's shield. Not that she wasn't glad for the promotion—she'd busted her ass for it, and she loved her job. But sometimes she wished she had something in her life besides work. Such as a hot guy to keep her company on a cold and rainy night.

Ah, pipe dreams. She needed to focus on reality—such as what she planned to eat tonight, because she was going home with a growling stomach to an empty fridge. Delivery or carryout? She checked her watch. Delivery was her only option unless she wanted to swing by the grocery store.

What the hell. Nothing like a late-night trip through the produce section to lift her mood.

Callie got into her Jeep and tossed her stuff onto the passenger seat. She started up the engine as a faint chirp sounded from the depths of her bag. She dug out her phone and spotted Gabe's number. Her nerves skittered.

Be careful what you wish for, she told herself as she swiped her thumb over the screen to read his text.

Wazzup girl?

She hadn't heard from him in months, but she knew

exactly what he wanted, and a teeny, tiny part of her wanted it, too.

Working, she replied.

When do u get off?

Her body tingled at the words. Gabe wasn't exactly subtle, so she was probably imagining the innuendo, but still.

Later, she typed, lying right through her fingertips.

Can i c u?

Callie muttered a curse. What should she tell him? He was persistent, and with good reason. She'd caved in to him before.

Gabe was a personal trainer and he was beyond gorgeous. Not the brightest bulb on the Christmas tree, as her grandfather would say. But in the looks department? Wow. Not to mention he was very skilled in certain areas.

But, Callie had decided to move on. She'd decided she was tired of shallow and short-term.

???

Not 2nite.

Ur killing me.

"Crap." She should call him and get it over with, or he'd be pinging her all night.

He answered on the first ring. "Heeeey, Callie girl."

"Hey."

"I was just thinking about you."

"Listen, I'm working tonight."

"When do you get done?"

"Late."

"Late's good."

"Tonight's not, though."

"For real?"

"I've been working all weekend and I'm whipped."

He made a low groan, and she ignored it.

"I'm really tired, you know? My job's been crazy lately."

"Yeah, okay. Whatever. Call me if you change your mind."

He hung up, and she stared down at the phone, wondering if she'd made a mistake. She hadn't. This was good. This was mature. What she had with Gabe definitely qualified as shallow, and she needed to move on.

She shoved her Jeep in gear, more depressed than ever about the prospect of going home to an empty house and a stack of paperwork. When her cell chimed, she snatched it up.

"Gabe, seriously, come on."

Silence. She glanced down at the phone, and her stomach lurched.

"Detective McLean?"

The voice was low and masculine, but it definitely wasn't Gabe's.

"This is her. *She*." She cleared her throat. "I'm Detective McLean."

"This is Travis Cullen at the Delphi Center crime lab. I'm calling to notify you that we've completed our work and your evidence is ready for pickup."

"Um . . . okay. You know it's eleven o'clock, right?"

"I was told this was urgent. Someone in your department put a rush on it?"

"That would be me."

"Well, I rushed it." He sounded annoyed with her.

She felt a twinge of guilt that he'd clearly spent his Sunday working. But, hey, she'd been working, too, so what did she have to feel guilty about?

"I need to go over my findings. I can meet you here at the lab tomorrow at 0800."

"Sounds fine."

"See you then." He clicked off.

Callie stared down at the phone, replaying the conversation and the deep, authoritative tone of his voice.

Tomorrow at 0800.

Something told her she shouldn't be late.

• • •

Brooke lay on her side with Sean's arm draped over her waist. The living room was drafty, but his body was keeping her warm.

She looked at him over her shoulder. His eyes were closed, but she knew he wasn't asleep.

"Sean?"

"Hmm."

"Do you think they're safe?" She didn't have to explain whom she meant.

"Yes." He opened his eyes. "Why?"

She turned away and stared into the dimness of his living room. "I still feel like it's my fault that whoever it was found them there."

His arm tightened around her. "Don't." He heaved a sigh. "You're not responsible for all the shit people do. That's on them."

He wasn't only talking about the shooting today. Something in his tone told her he meant Matt, too. She couldn't believe she'd told Sean everything, even the things she'd never told her girlfriends. Why had she done it? She'd always wanted Sean's respect, but now he knew that she'd allowed her long-term boyfriend to walk all over her.

She closed her eyes. They were so different, Sean and Matt. How had she ever lumped them together merely because they shared the same profession? Matt was rigid and controlling and had to be right all the time. At the heart of it, that was what most of their fights had been about—his being too insecure to admit when he was wrong, even when he made a simple mistake. Everything was always Brooke's fault.

She felt a wave of guilt. Here she was cuddled up naked with Sean, and she was thinking about Matt. It wasn't right, and the fact that her brain was jumbled with all these thoughts reinforced what she'd known all along, which was that it was too soon for her to get involved with someone new. Her life was spinning. Everything felt out of control, and she *hated* feeling that way. Tears burned her eyes and she squeezed them shut.

Sean kissed her shoulder. "What's wrong? You got all tense."

"Nothing."

He went still. "Are you crying?"

She didn't answer. He rolled onto his back and pulled her against him.

"Sorry." She sniffled, furious with herself for doing this right now.

"It's no big deal." He shifted so her head was cradled on his biceps. "I've got four sisters. Tears do not scare me."

She wiped them off her cheeks before they could leak onto him. "I'm not usually like this. I don't know what's wrong with me tonight."

"Well, let's see . . . you're stressed at work. Someone almost killed you today. I dragged you out with me and made you dredge up a bunch of bad stuff from a relationship you're still grieving over—"

"I'm not sorry it's over."

"Yeah, but it lasted two years, right? That has to hurt."

She nestled her head against his chest, liking the

deep sound of his voice against her ear. "Have you ever been in a relationship that long?"

"No, I'm just guessing." His hand rested on her abdomen, sending a warm shiver through her. "And then there's this thing happening right now. Pretty intense, huh?"

"Yes."

"So, your whole day has been emotional overload. It would shake up anyone."

She sighed. "How can you be so understanding?"

"I told you. Sisters. They were a pain in the ass growing up, but I guess something useful rubbed off on me."

"You're a good listener."

"Thank you."

Brooke discovered she felt better. Again.

He kept his hand on her stomach, and she closed her eyes, listening to the steady thrum of his heart. It felt so good to be held like this at the end of a terrible day. Or—she imagined—at the end of any day. She felt a pang of longing that was becoming familiar. She wished her life weren't such a mess right now.

"It's late," she said quietly. "I should go."

"Stay awhile."

She bit her lip. "That's probably not a good idea."

"I think it's a great idea. Does my opinion count for anything?" His tone was light, which came as a relief. The last thing she wanted to do right now was hurt his feelings.

"If I stay we'll fall asleep. I'll end up spending the night, and that'll just . . ."

He shifted to sit up on his elbow. "What?"

"Confuse things." She studied his face in the dimness, hoping her words wouldn't upset him. But he didn't look upset, he looked perfectly calm. "Today was crazy. Everything. But fundamentally, nothing is different. I still don't want to get tangled up in anything."

He stroked his hand down to her hip, making her breasts tighten. "Can I ask you something?"

She nodded.

"Do you feel good right now, after what we just did?"

"Yes."

"Did you have fun?"

"*Yes*. Obviously."

He smiled. "Then what's confusing? We're two people who happen to like each other and we're having some fun together."

"Oh, yeah?" She tried to match his lighthearted tone. "What makes you so sure I like you?"

"I don't know. Maybe the way you were screaming my name a minute ago?"

Her cheeks flushed at the reminder. "I'm serious. I'm really worried about this, and you act like it's so simple."

"It is simple. We can keep things casual. No pressure."

"Yeah, right."

"You don't believe me?"

"I don't believe *me*. I've never been good at casual. I tend to analyze things and fixate on potential problems."

"Well, don't."

"I can't help it. That's why I'm good at my job. I analyze everything to death and I stress out all the time."

His hand slid from her hip up to her ribs, trailing fire along the way. "You know, I've got something for that." He kissed her mouth. Then her neck. Then her collarbone.

"What?"

He cupped her breast in his hand and toyed with it,

knowing full well how sensitive she was. "The perfect stress relief." His gaze held hers as he moved down her body. "Better than hot yoga."

"That's big talk."

"It's true."

Apprehension swept through her because she knew exactly where he was going with this, and she wasn't comfortable. He kissed her sternum, then hovered over her navel. He traced his tongue over it and she tried to clamp her thighs together, but he held her still.

"Relax."

"Sean—"

"Please?"

She leaned her head back and did just what he asked, giving herself over to the heat of his mouth and the exploration of his hands, even though it wasn't relaxing at all—it was maddening. Every stroke of his tongue and his fingers made her more and more desperate for something just out of reach.

How had he done it so soon? How had he zeroed in on her exact pleasure points when everything was new between them? He'd somehow become an expert at how to kiss her and touch her and coax her into sharing every part of herself. She couldn't think about how he'd done it because she was quickly losing the ability to think at all, and the pressure built and built until she couldn't stand it and she needed him with her.

"Sean." She scraped her fingers through his hair. "Sean, please. I need you up here."

He moved up her body and lowered himself onto her, and she gasped at the hard pressure.

"Wait." He grabbed a condom from the table and quickly pulled it on, then he was inside her again, moving against her, and everything felt so full and perfect she couldn't stand it even a minute more.

She clutched him against her, sinking her teeth into his shoulder to keep from screaming this time, and he reared back and came into her with a fierce push that sent them both into oblivion at the same moment. Then once again she was shaking beneath him as she clung to his shoulders and gasped for air.

When she could breathe, she let her eyes drift open, and he was propped on his elbows, gazing down at her. She let her arms fall limply at her sides.

"Mmm . . . namaste."

He kissed her. "Better than yoga?"

"Hmm. Much better. I'm so relaxed I don't think I can move."

"In that case, it's probably easier if you stay tonight."

She sighed. "You're probably right."

CHAPTER 16

Brooke awoke to an annoying buzz.

Sean's phone.

The bed shifted as he got up, and she turned her face into the pillow, shutting out reality for just a few more minutes of sleep. . . .

"Brooke."

The mattress sank, and she opened her eyes. She was in Sean's bedroom, surrounded by deliciously cool sheets that smelled like him.

"Brooke, honey, wake up."

She lifted her head. He was sitting on the edge of the bed in jeans. No shirt. Yellow light spilled in from the bathroom.

"What is it?" She sat up and pulled the sheet with her.

"I've got a callout. I need to run you home."

She processed the words as she glanced around the room. Where the hell were her clothes?

He stood, fastening his jeans. Then he reached for a shirt draped over a chair in the corner.

She spied a pile of her clothes on the end of the bed. He must have brought them in here while she was dozing. She grabbed her sweatshirt and dragged it on. "What time is it?"

"Six fifteen. Can you be ready in five minutes? We have to hit it."

"Yeah." She stood up and winced.

"You okay?"

"Yeah."

It was like a hangover, but different. She felt stiff and groggy, as though she'd slept for days, but it had only been a few hours. Her knees were bruised from tackling Cameron Spence to the ground, and the cut on her elbow burned.

She spent several minutes in the bathroom, trying unsuccessfully to avoid the mirror. She looked horrid, and she wished she had a ponytail holder to do something with her hair. She twisted it into a knot and returned to the bedroom to look for her boots. She found them in the living room, along with her socks.

Brooke sank onto the sofa to put them on as Sean stood by the fireplace, talking on his phone and watching her.

He ended the call as she stood and grabbed her purse. "Ready."

Sean led her out to the driveway. The air was cool and damp, but the rain had stopped and the sky was beginning to lighten.

They rode in silence as Brooke's brain clicked into gear. From Sean's end of the conversation, it sounded like a homicide. Something near the lake. Brooke checked her phone. She hadn't received anything yet, but the detectives often got the call first. Anyway, it might not involve the Delphi Center.

She stared out the window at the slick pavement that shimmered purple and pink as the sky brightened.

"Sorry to wake you."

"No problem."

She glanced at him. He looked remarkably alert for having been asleep ten minutes ago. Brooke had developed the same skill over the years, but this morning she felt off.

He turned onto her street, and her stomach twisted. Casual. No pressure. But what did that mean in the light of day? She'd spent the night naked in his arms, and she felt a wave of panic as she remembered everything they'd done together.

He swung into her driveway, and she had the door open before he came to a halt.

"Hang on."

"You don't need to—"

But he was out and coming around to her side before she could finish the sentence.

"Sean, I'm fine. Don't make yourself late."

He ignored her and walked her to the door. She saw his gaze skimming over her hedges, her windows, her porch. She unlocked the door and turned to face him.

He glanced over her shoulder into the house. "Everything look okay here?"

"Everything's fine. Go."

He kissed her forehead. "I'm going to be tied up today."

"Me too."

"I'll see you when I see you."

• • •

Sean drove across the dam and hooked a right onto Ridge View. Two point three miles, according to Ric's directions. Sean skimmed his gaze over the roadside, looking for anything unusual leading up to the crime scene. He didn't see anything, but the shadows this time of morning played tricks.

Would Brooke and her crew show up here? Sean didn't know. With it being a homicide, there was a fair chance Delphi would ultimately get involved.

He thought about the way she'd looked standing on her porch a few minutes ago. Last night had been a breakthrough. And not just the sex, all of it. He pictured her on his sofa in the dimness. He'd done everything he knew to get her to relax with him and let her guard down, and it had worked. Mostly.

Convincing her to spend the night—without her realizing how desperately he wanted her to—had been a challenge. And he had more challenges ahead of him, if this morning's drop-off was any indication.

When Sean rolled out of bed, everything had been fine. He'd taken Ric's call, no problem. Then he'd stepped back into his room, and the sight of Brooke asleep on his pillow had hit him right in the solar plexus. But no sooner had he registered the punch of emotion than everything changed. Within seconds of her waking up and realizing where she was, Sean had seen the walls start to go up again. It had gotten worse on the ride home, until she'd actually *flinched* when he kissed her good-bye.

That brief moment had sucked, big-time, especially after she'd been so into him last night.

So something had changed, but Sean didn't know what. The sex had been hot—*that* he knew for sure—but now she had regrets. Sean didn't know what was wrong, but he guessed it had to do with everything she'd told him back at the diner.

Sean clenched his teeth. Matt Jorgensen. The first thing he'd done after learning the guy's name was check out his record. He was twenty-eight, the same age as Brooke. He'd been with the sheriff's department six years and spent four as a volunteer firefighter. He had a clean record—on the surface, at least—and had built a solid career.

The man himself was solid, too. According to his DPS record, Jorgensen was six-three, 230 pounds.

He was a head taller than Brooke, and the thought of him yelling and getting in her face made Sean livid. The thought of him laying a hand on her made Sean want to rip the guy's head off.

Sean rounded a bend and spotted a police cruiser parked on the shoulder. He shoved his thoughts aside for later as he passed the cruiser and pulled over on the opposite side of the road by Ric's truck. No sign of the ME yet.

Sean got out and grabbed an SMPD Windbreaker from the back of the cab. Zipping into it, he stuffed a pair of latex gloves in his pocket and crossed the road, following the distant squelch of police radios. The terrain was steep and muddy, and Sean used branches to brace himself as he picked his way down to the river's edge where Ric was standing beside a uniformed officer.

Ric saw him and tromped over.

"What do we have?"

"Caucasian female. A utility worker spotted the body from the dam." Ric turned and nodded at the brown river churning behind him. The water level was up from all the rain they'd been having. "She's tangled in the tree over there."

"Age?"

"Hard to say. She's in bad shape."

Sean muttered a curse. Anyone who'd spent any time in the water was liable to be unrecognizable, which made it tougher to get a positive ID.

"By the clothing and jewelry, I'd guess maybe twenties," Ric added.

Ric led him through the tangle of mesquite and sagebrush along the shoreline. Sean glanced up at the dam, where a cluster of people in hard hats had stopped their work to watch the action.

Another uniformed officer stood beside a clump of trees where someone had strung up yellow crime-scene tape.

"We're going to need some divers to cut her loose," Ric said. "And probably a forensic anthropologist to make an ID."

Sean picked his way around a cypress tree and stopped. The body was trapped between two tree trunks. A black jacket seemed to have gotten hung up on one of the branches. Ric followed right behind as Sean trekked closer and caught a glimpse of blond hair tangled with leaves and twigs. Dread filled Sean's stomach as he pushed aside some bushes to get a better look at the jacket, the lifeless arm, the pale hand.

The rings.

Sean's breath whooshed out. "Holy hell."

"What is it?"

"I know her."

• • •

Callie nursed her coffee as she stared through the tall windows of the Delphi Center lobby. The rain had cleared overnight, and the rolling hills basked in the rosy light of morning. It was a nice place to work. Beautiful, even, if you could forget that the building sat in the middle of a body farm. Callie watched as a vulture swooped down over a clump of trees, probably checking out one of the anthro department's research projects.

Decomposing remains. Ick. Working here was definitely not for the faint of heart.

"Calista McLean?"

She whirled around, and her pulse jumped at the sight of the impossibly attractive man standing there. How had she not heard him approach?

"Hi." The word came out as a squeak. She thrust her hand out to offer him a handshake, but ended up offering him her coffee cup.

He gave her a puzzled look, but didn't move to touch her. "I'm Travis Cullen."

He was tall and broad-shouldered, with short dark hair that hinted at a military background. He wore a black golf shirt with the Delphi Center logo on the pocket, tan tactical pants, and tan A.T.A.C. boots—which probably explained his stealth approach.

"Good to meet you. Everyone calls me Callie."

He nodded. "Follow me."

The command sent a warm ripple through her, and she followed him to a bank of elevators. He stepped on and jabbed a button. Callie's stomach dropped as they whisked down a few levels. The doors slid open and she stepped off first so she could walk beside him, not behind.

"So. You're the knife guy."

He cast her a sideways look as they walked down a corridor with cinder-block walls. "Who told you that?"

"The evidence clerk who checked in my package the other day. Why? You're not a knife expert?"

"Technically, I'm a tool-marks expert. Knives, hammers, bolt cutters, axes. Anything that leaves a mark."

She stifled a shudder.

He glanced at her, apparently reading her mind. "Not all of my cases are homicides."

"That's . . . comforting to know, I guess."

He opened a door and ushered her into a room with a worktable in the center. Atop it sat a crowbar and a piece of white wood, about two feet long.

She halted beside the table.

"That came in this morning. The detective wants to know whether that tool they recovered from a suspect's car is responsible for the gouges on the windowsill."

"So . . . a burglary?"

"Home invasion and sexual assault. That's why it jumped to the front of my line."

"It's not ours, is it?"

"The case is out of Williamson County. Here, come on back."

She followed him through the room and into a smaller one, this one lined with floor-to-ceiling shelves.

Callie stopped short. "Whoa."

Every shelf was filled with all the tools he'd mentioned before—and then some. Her gaze settled on the nearest section, which held a vast array of saws.

"This is our collection."

"*Collection*? Seriously?"

He nodded.

"That sounds extremely creepy."

She walked up to a small table with a spotlight shining down on it. On a clean sheet of butcher paper was a knife with a long silver blade and a black handle. Callie stared down at it, at a loss for words. She glanced up to find him watching her. "This is it?"

He stepped up beside her. "You hadn't seen it before?"

"One of our officers collected it. I was just the one who brought it in."

"This isn't actually *your* knife. It's a sample. I wanted you to see it intact before I show you what I did."

She looked at him expectantly.

"What you're looking at here is a fixed-blade hunting knife, full tang. It has a four-inch serrated stainless-steel blade and a polymer handle."

"And this is like the one I brought in?"

He nodded. "Except this one's straight from the factory, never been used. It's part of our reference collection."

Collection. There was that word again, and it gave her the willies.

She glanced around at all the various knives and axes and other lethal weapons. Travis Cullen towered over her, and she knew he, too, was a lethal weapon—she could tell simply from the way he moved.

"You okay?"

She glanced at him. "Yeah. You were saying? About the knife? Any chance it's unique?"

"No. Fact, far as hunting goes, it's one of the most common knives out there. Sells for between forty-nine and fifty-nine dollars at sporting-goods stores across the country. Comes with a black plastic sheath."

"Damn. At least tell me you found some prints or some blood or something to help us out."

"No prints. That was the first thing we checked. Looks like it was wiped down."

"Perfect. No fingerprints and the blade was clean."

"I didn't say 'clean.' Under the scope, you can see tiny white fibers from the material used to wipe it—most likely, a cotton T-shirt. You can also see faint traces of blood along the edge."

Callie's pulse picked up.

"We swabbed that, sent it up to our DNA lab."

"To Mia?"

"What's that?"

"In the DNA lab," Callie said. "She's married to Ric Santos, one of our detectives on this thing."

"That explains the quick turnaround. I don't know who ran the tests, but whoever it was found human and animal blood."

"Human?"

"Yes, and it's the victim's. They confirmed it upstairs."

"You're telling me we have our murder weapon. I want to see it. Is it upstairs?"

"Nope, right here. Come have a look."

He led her across the room to another table. This one was the same height, but the black slate tabletop sat beneath a Plexiglas shield, like at a salad bar. Travis switched on a light, illuminating another sheet of butcher paper, this one with knife parts scattered across it.

He pulled on a latex glove. "I disassembled the knife to examine the components."

Until this moment, Callie hadn't thought of a knife as having components. "You just . . . unscrewed the handle?"

"These are rivets." He picked one up. "The black pieces are the handle slabs. Then you have the blade, the tang."

"Tang?"

"The steel piece goes all the way to the butt of the knife, so it's called a full tang. Makes it more durable. And the tang"—he pointed to it—"that's where we found a second DNA profile, blood that had seeped through the crevices. Our lab tells me *that* profile matches the one found under the victim's fingernails."

"No way."

He looked at her. "Way."

"So . . . you think he maybe nicked himself when he attacked her or—"

"This blood was old and pretty degraded, from what I understand. So more likely, he nicked himself some other time when he was using the knife. Could have been cutting a rope or dressing a deer. This knife's got some wear and tear on it, so it's probably been used for at least a few years."

"But they were able to get a profile?"

"It's all in the report. They ran a bunch of tests, and the results check out."

"Wow." Callie had been hopeful, but hadn't dared to hope for anything this good. "This is big. Really big. I see now why you called me at midnight."

He leaned back against the counter and folded his arms over his big chest as he looked her over. "It was more like eleven."

"Whatever. I'm glad you did. My team is going to freak!"

His mouth curved up in a barely there smile.

"What? You're laughing at me." She pulled out her phone. "I'm excited, okay? We have our murder weapon. You totally made my day."

"I'm not laughing at all," he said, although he was definitely smiling at her now. "Just glad I could help."

CHAPTER 17

Sean pulled into the Delphi Center parking lot and scanned the cars. No sign of Brooke's white Prius. He wondered what she was doing today and whether he'd get a chance to see her. Given the morning he'd had, he figured his odds weren't good.

Callie swung into the lot and slid into an empty space beside him.

"Thanks for meeting me," he said as she got out.

"No problem. I was just out here a few hours ago. The guy manning the gate is getting sick of seeing me."

Sean looked at her as they trudged up the steps to the main entrance. "So, that mean you heard back about that knife?"

"Jeez, Sean."

"What?"

"Don't you listen to your voice mail? Yes, I heard back about the knife. I left you a message."

Sean opened the door for her. "Sorry. Been preoccupied. So, is it our murder weapon?"

"It is."

He approached the reception desk and showed his ID. "We're here to see Kelsey Quinn."

The receptionist smiled. "I'm afraid Dr. Quinn is out this afternoon."

"All afternoon?"

"That's correct. She's at a training seminar."

This wasn't good news. Sean knew Kelsey, and he'd been counting on that connection to help speed things along. "Who's handling Kelsey's autopsies?"

"That would be her new assistant, Sara Lockhart."

"I'd like to see her, then."

"And do you have an appointment?"

Sean just looked at the receptionist.

"Sorry." She blushed. "Let me make a call and see . . ."

As she jumped on the phone, Sean turned to talk to Callie, who was grinning at him.

"What?"

"You flustered her," she whispered.

Sean sighed. "So, you were saying? About the murder weapon?"

"They lifted traces of the victim's blood and another profile, presumably the killer."

"How can we know that?"

"Because—get this—the second DNA profile on that knife matches the DNA found under the victim's fingernails."

"Really?"

"Really." Callie beamed at him.

"Damn, that's big."

"I know."

"Now we need to match that profile with a suspect."

"Easier said than done. Did you talk to Ric?"

Sean frowned. "No. What?"

"He just called me. The water bottle we submitted isn't a match with the DNA from the victim's nail clippings."

"Shit."

"I know. So, we can cross off Bradley Mahoney, which means we have to go hit our list again. And we aren't even sure which of these guys are actually blood relatives, and which of them just share a name. We've got some legwork to do."

"Jasper's working on it."

"Excuse me, Detective?" He turned around, and the receptionist was gazing up at him. "Dr. Lockhart is booked solid this afternoon. Would you like to leave a message for her?"

"No. I need to see her."

"But—"

"Tell her I only need ten minutes."

The receptionist bit her lip and picked up the phone.

Sean turned around, and Callie was grinning again. "Pushy, pushy."

"I don't have time to wait around all week for a bunch of official reports. We need this now."

"Yeah, but you're going to piss off Kelsey's new assistant. Not good strategy. You're going to be working with her."

"I'll take my chances."

"Excuse me, Detective? Dr. Lockhart will see you now." The receptionist smiled and placed a pair of visitor's badges on the counter. "You can go on back."

"Thank you."

They clipped on the badges and headed down a long sloping hallway. He opened the door to the forensic anthropology wing and was hit by a blast of cold air.

"You seem edgy today."

He looked at Callie, but didn't answer. Not that it was a question, really.

"Something up with Brooke?"

He glared at her.

"I'll take that as a yes."

They turned the corner and spotted a woman in a white lab coat striding down the hallway.

"You must be the detectives." She stopped in front of them and folded her arms over her chest. As opposed to Kelsey, who was a tall redhead, this woman was short and blond. She was no less intimidating, though, as she looked him over.

"Sean Byrne." He extended a hand, but she ignored it. "And this is Detective Callie McLean."

"Delighted to meet you," Dr. Lockhart said, clearly not delighted at all.

She opened the door to her right and led them into Kelsey's office. At least, Sean had always thought of it as Kelsey's. Several desks shared the space, and Dr. Lockhart sank into a chair behind the nearest one, which was blanketed in paperwork.

"Have a seat," she ordered.

They did, and Callie shot Sean a look of annoyance. She'd been right, and now both of them had gotten off on the wrong foot with this contact.

"Sorry for the interruption. I'll try to make this quick." He smiled, but the doctor looked unmoved. "We're here about the autopsy from Lake Wiley."

"The one I completed five minutes ago. I haven't finished my report yet."

"I understand. We just need your preliminary findings."

"I haven't finished my *preliminary* report yet. I was literally washing my hands when you showed up here without an appointment."

Sean gave her what he hoped was a charming smile. "Yeah, we don't usually do that. We've got a situation today."

She lifted an eyebrow.

"We've got two death investigations going right now, and I believe they're connected."

"How can you possibly know that? This victim hasn't even been ID'd yet."

"Victim?" Callie leaned closer. "So, it's definitely a homicide?"

"Yes, as a matter of fact, it is."

"What about cause of death?" Sean asked. "I saw her at the scene, but it was hard to tell what happened. The body was in rough shape."

"As are most of our cases. Forensic anthropologists don't typically get involved unless the remains are in poor condition. Which leads me to the question—again—how can you know who she is when we don't have a formal ID yet?"

"Jasmine Jones."

Callie glanced at Sean. Even she looked surprised that he'd tossed out a name.

"I saw her Saturday morning at the other victim's funeral."

"How do you know it was her? This woman was badly beaten and she'd spent at least a day underwater."

"Her Jewelry. She had silver rings on both hands. Lots of them. They were distinctive."

"Listen, Detective—"

"It's Sean."

"Sean." Dr. Lockhart leaned her elbows on the desk. "Jewelry can hardly be considered conclusive for identification purposes. We have to run her fingerprints. We submitted them, but they may not even be in the system."

"They are. Jasmine Jones has been arrested on possession charges, as well as prostitution. I *know* who she is. Now, could you please tell me what happened to her?"

Sean waited, watching her, but Dr. Lockhart still didn't seem inclined to open up. This was his pet peeve about scientists. They had to be 100 percent proof-positive certain before they'd go ahead with anything.

Except for Brooke. She went with her gut, same as Sean did—one of the many reasons he'd always liked working with her.

"So. Cause of death," he said, trying to dig up some patience. "Was she drowned? Strangled? Stabbed?"

"Manual strangulation."

Sean sat back in his chair, relieved to have an answer at least.

"There's evidence of bruising in the tissue around her neck, and she was not breathing when she went into that water." The doctor looked at Callie, then back to Sean again. "There's also evidence she struggled with her attacker. Hence, the facial injuries. She had multiple contusions, and her right zygomatic bone was fractured."

"Her cheekbone?" Sean asked.

"That's correct."

"Time of death?"

"Hard to say. At least twenty-four hours in the water. I'd say the death occurred shortly beforehand, within an hour."

"Any evidence of a fall?"

She paused. "Why do you ask?"

"The dam."

Callie looked at him. "You're thinking he strangled her and dumped her off the dam?"

"That's the only upstream bridge. It's about fifty feet high, so it seems like the body would show signs of impact."

"It would," the doctor said. "And I can tell you she also suffered several cracked ribs that would be consistent with a drop like that, particularly if the drop occurred postmortem."

Sean looked at Callie. "I hate being right about this shit."

The doctor gave him a disapproving look as she pulled a phone from the pocket of her lab coat. "The prints are in." She read a message. "Jasmine Michelle Jones, twenty-two, of San Marcos." She glanced up. "Right again, Detective."

• • •

Their next stop was the Burr County Administrative Center, which housed an array of offices, including Child Protective Services. Once again, Callie pulled her car into a space beside Sean's truck, and they trudged across the parking lot together.

She cast a sideways glance at him. His eyes were bloodshot, he needed a shave, and his shoulders looked tense under his black leather jacket.

"So, this thing with Brooke," she said, earning another glare. "I'm guessing it didn't go well?"

"No comment."

"Well, can *I* make a comment?"

"What happens if I say no?"

She pursed her lips, trying to think of a response that would get her what she wanted, which was information.

"What the hell, make your comment."

"She's probably gun-shy."

He just looked at her.

"I mean, isn't she getting out of a long-term thing? And it didn't end well, obviously, so can you blame her for not wanting to dive right into something new? It probably has nothing to do with you."

He made a grunting noise.

"That's it? Your response is a grunt?"

He sent her a cranky look. "My *response* is that this is an interesting insight coming from you. What happened to 'ask her out' and 'the weekend is young'?"

"Well, did you?"

"Yes."

"And did it go okay?"

"She's dodging me."

What did that mean, exactly? Men were so hard to read. Was she dodging his calls? His visits? Or was it more of a conversational dodge, like she didn't want to define the relationship? Callie wasn't usually this meddlesome, but she liked Sean and she wanted to help him with his love life, because he was so obviously botching it up.

"So, what's your plan now?" she asked as they reached the building.

"To keep trying."

The determination in his voice made her smile. "You really like her, don't you?"

He pulled open the door and held it for some people exiting, ignoring Callie's question and essentially ending the conversation.

They stepped into the lobby. The place was dated and dingy and smelled like industrial cleaner. Callie looked around for a directory.

"There she is." Sean strode ahead. "Farrah," he called.

The woman turned around. She was tall and rail thin, with curly blond hair that she wore loose around her shoulders. She looked surprised to see Sean. Then the surprise gave way to impatience as she glanced at her watch.

"This is Detective Callie McLean," Sean said to her. "Callie, this is Farrah Saunders."

The woman gave Callie a wary look before turning her attention back to Sean. "I've been in court all morning. I haven't had time to go through that file yet."

"We're here about Jasmine Jones," Sean said.

"Jasmine Jones."

"That's right. I saw you talking to her at Samantha Bonner's funeral. You know her?"

"Yes. Why?"

"In what capacity?"

Farrah's brow furrowed with confusion. "I thought you were here about Sam?"

"And Jasmine," Sean said. "She was found dead this morning."

Farrah blanched. "You mean—"

"She was murdered. We believe her death might be related to Samantha Bonner's."

The woman's jaw dropped and for a moment she simply stood there. Then she seemed to get her bearings. She glanced around the lobby. "Come back to my office."

Farrah led them through a glass door and then through a corridor lined with gray cubicles. It was midafternoon, and most people were at their desks, either tapping on keyboards or talking on the phone. She stopped at a door and ushered them into a small private office.

The two guest chairs were stacked with binders and files, but Farrah seemed oblivious as she walked behind her desk and sank into a chair.

"I don't know what . . ." She looked at Sean. "Are you sure it's Jasmine? I just saw her on Saturday."

Sean and Callie moved the binders and files to the floor and took seats.

"I'm sure," Sean said. "They made a positive ID with fingerprints at autopsy."

Farrah blanched again at the word *autopsy*.

Callie watched her, picking up everything she could about the reaction. Somehow Farrah Saunders was a link between two young women who had been murdered over the last five days. They weren't sure what the link was, but Sean intended to lead the questioning, while Callie was here to observe and form impressions.

First impression? This woman was shocked by the news. Callie had interviewed plenty of witnesses, and Farrah's reaction seemed genuine.

"Was Jasmine one of your cases?" Sean asked the social worker.

She shook her head distractedly. "Clients, not cases. And, yes, she was."

"When?"

"When she was a minor." Farrah stared off into space. "That would have been . . . three years now?"

"She was twenty-two."

"Four years ago, then." Tears filled Farrah's eyes and she looked down at her desk. "Excuse me, I'm just . . ."

"It's okay." Callie gave her a sympathetic look. "Take your time."

Farrah plucked a tissue from the box on the file cabinet behind her. She dabbed her eyes and took a deep breath. "Sorry. Go ahead."

"When was the last time you saw Jasmine before Samantha's funeral?" Sean asked.

"It's been years. Four, I guess. Around when she turned eighteen."

Callie took out a notepad and jotted that down so Sean could focus on the questions.

"And how did she know Amy Doppler?" he asked.

"Who?"

"Amy Doppler. The woman she was sitting next to at the funeral."

"I have no idea. I don't know Amy."

"She's one of Samantha's AA friends."

"Oh. Well, that could explain it. Jasmine had a serious drinking problem."

"At seventeen?" Callie asked.

"At fourteen. It got worse over the years." Farrah sighed. "That was one reason she bounced around between foster families. She had a lot of issues, and no one could seem to handle her."

Callie tried to imagine a fourteen-year-old with a serious drinking problem. She couldn't. When she'd been fourteen, she'd been an honor student and a starter on the volleyball team.

"So, did Samantha know Jasmine through AA, too? Or foster care?"

"I don't know."

Sean paused, and Callie knew he was struggling for patience.

"Could you think back to her case? Were they ever placed in the same foster home at the same time?"

"I'd have to check."

"Please do that. And the drinking problem she had, what was that a reaction to? Had she been abused, molested, anything like that?"

Farrah darted a look at Callie's notepad. "Jasmine suffered sexual abuse when she lived with her biological mom. I suspect there was probably more abuse along the way, although I don't remember anything documented."

"I need a list of those families," Sean said. "I need everyone in those households, and same for Samantha."

Farrah nodded.

"What other kind of problems did she have? Drugs? School?"

"Well, she was in juvenile detention at least once. I remember that. She assaulted a teacher, and he pressed charges."

"He?" Callie looked up from her notepad.

"A coach, I believe. She broke his nose with a lacrosse stick."

"I want his name," Sean said. "What was the deal with that? Why'd she assault him?"

"Supposedly, the assault was unprovoked, although I'm not sure I believe that. I always thought maybe he tried something with her, but that's not what she reported. Anyway, she spent about six months in JD. I'd have to look at her file to be sure. And that was just the start of it. She had other incidents throughout high school."

"Such as?"

Farrah sighed. "Booze in her locker. Vandalism. Shoplifting. I'd have to look up the rest of it, but she was constantly in trouble. Really, it's a wonder she graduated. She would have spent all four years in juvenile detention, but Judge Mahoney kept giving her second chances."

Callie's gaze jerked up.

"*Who*?" Sean asked.

"Eric Mahoney. The juvenile-court judge. He's a bleeding heart for troubled kids."

Sean stood up.

"What's wrong?" Farrah looked startled.

"We have to get back." He looked at Callie. "Detective McLean and I have a staff meeting." He turned to the social worker again. "I'm going to need the names of those foster families, as well as that coach. Can you email that over as soon as possible?"

"Sure." Farrah looked flustered. "Whatever I can do."

• • •

The tension was palpable as Brooke stepped into the conference room. She took an empty seat next to Jasper and glanced around the table. She'd expected to see Sean at this meeting, and she told herself she was relieved, not disappointed, that he wasn't here.

"That's not my point," Ric was saying.

"I know it's not," the district attorney shot back. Rachel was smart and opinionated and a formidable opponent in the courtroom. She'd put Brooke on the witness stand on numerous occasions. "But it's *exactly* the point a defense attorney is going to make at trial. I guarantee it."

"She's right," Lieutenant Reynolds said from his end of the table. "It'll get tossed."

Rachel turned her attention to Brooke. "Thanks for joining us. I've got some questions for you about the forensic evidence in the Samantha Bonner case. I understand you processed the prints?"

"That's correct." Brooke looked at Ric, hoping he'd told the prosecutor about all the latest developments.

"The DNA lead from the victim's fingernails didn't pan out," Ric said. By the edge in his voice, Brooke guessed that had been the subject of the argument she'd just interrupted. "Now we're looking for something else we can use to focus in on a suspect."

"Those child fingerprints," Rachel said. "Will they hold up in court? I'm not familiar with the technology."

"IR microspectroscopy," Brooke said. "Basically, you use infrared light to visualize the print. The technology is fine. That's not the problem."

The prosecutor leaned back. "What *is* the problem?"

"Well . . . everything." Brooke looked at Ric, hoping for support. His expression was unreadable, so she turned back to Rachel. "Based on the location of the prints, and the time frame they were left there, it's probable the child was at the crime scene at the time of the murder. He's potentially an eyewitness, and as such, he's in grave danger." She looked at Ric. "Did you tell her about the shooting last night?"

"*Attempted* shooting," the lieutenant said. "The boy wasn't hurt, and we haven't established who the target was."

"But—"

"The fingerprints," Rachel said, cutting Brooke off. "Are they solid enough for court? I understand these prints don't exist anymore, so I need to make sure our documentation is impeccable if we intend to use them."

"Everything's solid. I've got plenty of photographs and they're all time-stamped. But, again, that isn't the issue here. Cameron Spence is eleven years old. This whole ordeal has been traumatic for him, and we're not even certain he knows anything—"

"He knows plenty." Rachel looked at Reynolds. "Isn't that what the child psychologist said? The boy seems scared, but underneath all that, he's hiding something?"

"That's a *theory*," Brooke said. "It's not an established fact. Maybe he didn't see anything, but regardless, a close friend of his family is dead, and this child is going through a trauma right now, and the last thing he needs is to get pulled into this case."

"I understand your concern," Rachel said, "but I at least want to talk to him. We need to base this investigation on *usable* evidence, which means something that isn't going to get tossed out by a judge. We need to sit him down with a sketch artist and see what he's got."

Brooke's chest tightened. "I don't recommend that at all."

The prosecutor quirked an eyebrow. "Is that right?"

"That's right."

Rachel smiled. "Well, we appreciate your input on the forensic evidence." In other words, she didn't give a shit what Brooke thought about the rest of it. "Thank you for taking the time to come by," she added pointedly.

Seething with frustration, Brooke stood up. She shot a look at Ric before exiting the conference room and pulling the door shut behind her.

The bull pen was bright and crowded, and Brooke stood still for a moment to compose herself. She thought of Cameron being hauled in here for an interview and felt sick to her stomach.

Callie strode into the bull pen, followed closely by Sean. Brooke's heart did a flip-flop in her chest as his gaze homed in on her. He crossed the sea of cubicles, and the intense look in his eyes told her something big had happened.

"What are you doing here?"

"I . . ." She cleared her throat. "Rachel asked me to come in and go over the fingerprint evidence." Brooke studied his face. "What happened?"

"A lot."

Callie stopped beside them. "We're in the conference room, Sean."

He didn't even acknowledge the comment as Callie walked off. He was too busy staring down at Brooke.

"Come here." Sean took her hand and pulled her into a break room. It was empty, luckily. Brooke tugged her hand free.

"We've had some new developments." Sean rested his hands on his hips.

"Is this about the body at the lake?"

"You heard about it?"

"Just what was on the news."

He gazed down at her, and she realized he wasn't going to tell her more because she wasn't officially involved in that case.

She huffed out a breath. "You need to talk to Rachel. You need to convince her to leave Cameron alone. She wants to sit him down with a sketch artist."

"I know."

"*Sean*. Think what could happen. He could end up dragged into a trial."

"He might not have to testify. We may just need the sketch to help get an ID."

Brooke's stomach clenched. "Are you hearing yourself?"

"What?"

"You were there last night! You saw him in the hospital, for God's sake."

"And?"

"And I can't believe I'm the only one concerned about this boy's safety."

"That's not true, and you know it."

The muscle in his jaw bunched, and she could tell

she'd struck a nerve. Good. She wanted him as pissed off about this as she was. Maybe he'd stand up to the damn prosecutor.

"A sketch is a tool for investigators," he said. "It doesn't mean he's going to trial or that he's going to be dragged into anything."

"You sound like Rachel."

"Rachel's right. I'm right." He raked his hand through his hair. "Look, I hear what you're saying, but you're not used to seeing cases from this angle. This is a homicide investigation, and we need to use every lead available to close in on a suspect and get that person into custody."

Brooke crossed her arms. "So . . . that's it? She's right. You're right. I don't know what the hell I'm talking about, even though I was *there* when this child and his mom got gunned down in their front yard, but who cares? My opinion means nothing?"

"I didn't say that."

"You didn't have to. I've seen this before. My way or the highway, right?"

Anger sparked in his eyes. "*Don't* do that. Don't compare me to him."

"Sean?" Callie poked her head into the break room. "Sorry to interrupt, but we're meeting now."

"You're not interrupting," Brooke snapped. "I'm on my way out."

• • •

Sean watched her leave, pissed at himself for letting the conversation go off the rails. She didn't need this right now. *He* didn't need this right now. He had a fresh homicide on his hands, and a prosecutor to deal with who wasn't going to like anything he was about to tell her.

Callie waited outside the conference room, practically tapping her foot, and Sean followed her into the meeting.

"Hey," Ric said, looking them over as they grabbed chairs. Sean knew from Ric's expression that he could tell something was up. "We're updating Rachel on the leads we're pursuing."

"And the ones you're *not* pursuing," Rachel added.

"New development," Sean said, glancing at his lieutenant. "We've established a link between Samantha Bonner and Jasmine Jones."

"Who's Jasmine Jones?" Rachel asked.

"The DOA from Lake Wiley," Callie said. "Her body was recovered this morning."

Rachel looked at Reynolds. "Why am I just now hearing about this?"

"They just completed the autopsy," Sean said.

"What's the cause of death?" Ric asked.

"Manual strangulation," Callie told him. "She'd been beaten beforehand and then dumped off the dam, it looks like. The time of death estimate is twenty-four to thirty-six hours from when the body was recovered, so sometime Saturday night or early Sunday morning."

Rachel arched her eyebrows. "And there's a connection between her and Samantha Bonner?"

"Jasmine was at Samantha's funeral Saturday," Sean said. "Turns out, both victims were friends from AA, and they had the same social worker, who also happened to be at the funeral that day."

"A social worker?" Rachel leaned forward on her elbows. "Man or woman?"

"Woman," Callie said. "Her name is Farrah Saunders. She's been in the job twelve years, and we checked her out. Spotless record."

"So what's the extent of this connection?"

"It goes way back," Sean said. "Both victims were removed from their biological parents as children and placed in foster care. Farrah Saunders was their social worker when they were teens, and the judge overseeing their cases was Eric Mahoney."

Silence settled over the room.

"Mahoney," Ric stated. "As in . . . a relative of James Mahoney, whose DNA is a partial match with what was found under the vic's nails?"

"Whoa. Wait." Rachel held a hand up like a stop sign and turned to Sean. "You're telling me you think Eric Mahoney, the *judge*, had something to do with these murders?"

Sean didn't respond. He simply watched her, waiting for her to process everything. The logic of it all was undeniable.

She turned to Reynolds. "Are you hearing this?"

The lieutenant darted a look at Sean, clearly startled by everything he'd said. "What kind of evidence do you have to back that up?"

"I'm working on it."

"Like hell you are." Rachel slapped her file shut. "Don't think for one minute that you're going to go after a *sitting judge* with some half-baked theory based on questionable DNA evidence."

"Nothing wrong with the evidence," Ric said, obviously not liking the jab at his wife's laboratory. "The DNA on Samantha Bonner is a partial match with a profile that's sitting right there in the database."

"A *partial* match! As in, the man in the database is not our suspect." Rachel turned to Reynolds. "You think you can just go around arresting people named Mahoney on a hunch? I need facts, not hunches."

"It's not just a hunch," Sean said. "The DNA under Samantha's nails *and* the DNA on the knife used to kill her share key genetic markers with a convicted felon named Mahoney. And Judge Eric *Mahoney* knew both the victims because he presided over their cases when they were teenagers."

Rachel's eyes widened as she leaned toward him. "What are you suggesting, Sean? That the judge had some kind of . . . of relationship with these girls, and now they've somehow ended up dead?"

"Your words, not mine."

"Is that seriously your case theory?" Rachel glanced around the table, visibly shaken for the first time since Sean had known her. "To even *suggest* such a thing would be career suicide." She looked at Reynolds. "For both of us."

Sean shook his head. "But the DNA—"

"*Don't* talk to me about that DNA! It's a partial hit, and I can't use it as probable cause for a warrant. And you can be damn sure I'm not going to demand a DNA sample from a sitting judge."

"We could get a sample without him knowing," Ric said. "A drinking straw or a cigarette butt, something like that."

Rachel shook her head. "We went through all this earlier. Even *if* you got a hit, you would have targeted this man as a suspect merely because he shares a last name with someone who's in the system. The whole thing is fruit of the poisoned tree. It would get tossed out of court in a minute, especially given Mahoney's connections on the bench."

An uneasy silence settled over the room.

Sean leaned back in his chair. "It's not a hunch, Rachel. Think of all the coincidences we're talking about here. The same social worker, the same judge, the murders within a few days of each other. So, this DNA lead isn't one hundred percent? Don't use it at trial, then. But it *is* a lead, and we can't ignore it."

Rachel took a deep breath and blew it out. She looked around the table, and her gaze settled on Sean.

"You think Judge Mahoney had something to do with these murders? Fine. Show me. Show me something in the victims' phone records or emails. Show me a neighbor who saw his car out in front of Samantha's house. Show me a suspect sketch from the kid who was there that night. You believe in this theory? Then get me something usable, God damn it, or don't bother asking me to put my head on a chopping block!"

• • •

Callie watched the prosecutor stalk out the door. Then she turned to Sean. "Well, at least she didn't freak out."

He shot Callie a look, obviously not appreciating her sarcasm.

"God damn it, Byrne." Everyone's attention turned to Reynolds. "Don't come in and drop this shit in my lap with the DA here."

Sean lifted an eyebrow. "You planned to keep her out of the loop? Aren't we going to need her when it's time for a warrant?"

Reynolds leaned forward, getting red in the face. "Don't give me your smart-ass crap, Byrne. She's right. There's no way we're using a partial DNA hit for any kind of warrant against a judge. Not on my watch. So you better be ready to roll up your sleeves and do some real detective work."

"I thought I was."

Reynolds turned and jabbed a finger at Callie. "Get

on the Bonner girl's computer. We need it turned inside out."

"Yes, sir."

The lieutenant turned to Ric. "Get working on those cell phones. I want a dump on both victims' numbers going back twelve months. Calls, texts, everything."

"I'm on it."

"And get that boy in here for an interview." Reynolds stood up and glared at Sean. "I want a suspect sketch on my desk by tomorrow."

CHAPTER 18

Brooke returned to the lab, but she felt too agitated to be there. She worked her way through two evidence envelopes, all the while replaying the exchange with the prosecutor. Of course, in hindsight it was easy to think of all the perfect retorts that had eluded her in the heat of the moment.

Roland plopped a drinking glass on the worktable beside her. “You missed a print.”

She glanced up at him. “I did not.”

He switched off the spotlight above her head. Then he took out a flashlight and aimed it through the glass at an oblique angle, illuminating a partial fingerprint that had somehow escaped her black powder.

“Oh.”

His eyebrows shot up. “That’s it? ‘Oh’?”

“What do you want me to say? I made a mistake.”

“Yeah, no kidding. What the fuck’s with you today?”

“Nothing.”

“Bullshit.” He went back to his table.

Brooke stared at the glass. Roland was right. Her concentration was crap this afternoon and so was her work product. And she had no right to be sitting here handling evidence.

She stopped what she was doing and put it away for

tomorrow. Then she packaged up the drinking glass to reexamine later. She grabbed her purse and left the lab without a word. It was almost five, which was ahead of her typical departure time, but she was better off leaving early than staying here and screwing things up.

On the way to her car she scrolled through her phone until she found Kaitlyn Spence's number. By the third ring, Brooke's heart was racing. When Kaitlyn finally picked up, Brooke felt a wave of relief.

"Hi, it's Brooke Porter."

"Hi." Kaitlyn sounded surprised but not hostile. For some crazy reason, she didn't seem to blame Brooke for what had happened last night.

"I just wanted to check on you and Cameron." From the background noise, it sounded like Kaitlyn was in her car. "How's everything going today?"

"You really want to know? Terrible."

Brooke slid behind the wheel, but didn't start the engine. She heard shuffling noises and then Cameron's voice in the background asking for McDonald's.

"I told you, Cam, no more fast food. . . . Brooke? Sorry, you're on speakerphone. We're in the car." Kaitlyn sighed. "It's been a bad day."

"What happened?"

"They want us to spend the night at the shelter again. And I'm missing another dinner shift, but my boss won't reschedule me. But who cares, right? It's only money." Brooke heard the stress in Kaitlyn's voice. "And to top it off, I just left the police station, where they totally *grilled* me like they think I'm some drug dealer or something. Or maybe they think Sam was. Those guys need to get a clue. Sam didn't touch drugs or even alcohol. She ate freaking veggie shakes for breakfast."

"I'm sorry you're dealing with all this. Is there anything you two need? I can swing by the shelter."

"Oh. Thanks." Kaitlyn sounded taken off guard by the offer. "I think we're good."

"How's your arm?"

"Fine," she said, but Brooke caught something in her voice and wondered what the answer would have been if Cameron weren't listening. It had to be painful for her to do her job with fresh stitches in her arm.

"Well . . . let me know if I can do anything. Do you guys need me to check on Fenway?"

"Yes!" Cameron yelled. "Can you bring him over?"

"No, she *cannot* bring him over, Cam. I told you, they don't allow dogs."

"Please, Mom?"

"No. . . . Sorry, Brooke? Don't worry about Fenway. Our neighbor is taking care of him."

"Okay, well . . . if you need anything, please don't hesitate to call me."

"Thanks. That's nice of you to offer."

"You guys take care."

Brooke ended the call and analyzed the conversation as she drove home. She hated that they'd had such a miserable day. But Kaitlyn had mentioned nothing about a forensic artist, so maybe that wasn't happening, which eased Brooke's worry, as did their plans to spend another night at the shelter. The place had an armed guard and plenty of security. They couldn't stay there forever, but at least Brooke knew they'd be safe tonight.

The tightness in Brooke's shoulders started to loosen. She didn't feel relaxed—not by a long shot—but she felt better as she swung by the grocery store and picked up some ingredients for dinner. By the time she made it home, she was looking forward to a restful evening.

Until she stepped through her door and confronted the mountain range of laundry in her living room. It had been weeks since she'd done any chores. Her entire house was in disarray, just like her personal life, and she couldn't stand it another minute.

Brooke deposited her groceries on the counter and changed into yoga pants. She hauled four overflowing laundry baskets into the utility room and dumped them onto the floor, then sorted everything by category—towels, clothes, and delicates. She heaved a load into the machine and got it going.

Next, she poured herself a generous glass of wine and started chopping. Brooke didn't cook often, but when she did, it relaxed her. Tonight was all about comfort food, and she was making one of her grandmother's soup recipes. She cut up vegetables, letting her mind wander as she sliced and diced. She sipped her merlot and tried to unwind, but her thoughts kept going back to Sean.

Don't compare me to him.

She'd hated the look on his face when he'd said that. And she'd hated the words, too, because he was right.

She tried to block out everything and focus on the task at hand as she sautéed onions and celery. She rinsed a batch of Roma tomatoes and started carving out the stems. The recipe made way too much for one person—maybe she'd take some over to Owen and Lin.

The doorbell rang, and Brooke's hands froze.

Sean.

She grabbed a dish towel and wiped her fingers. Then she smoothed her hair before hurrying to the door. Her pulse pounded as she checked the peephole.

Not Sean, but Maddie.

"Hey, stranger," Maddie said as Brooke let her inside. “I had to come check on you. You missed our coffee klatch.”

Brooke gasped and put her hand to her mouth. “Oh, my God, it’s Monday.”

“Yes, it is.”

Brooke had a weekly coffee date with her friends at Delphi.

“I totally forgot.” Brooke sighed and closed the door. “You want a glass of wine? Or a beer?” She led Maddie into the kitchen. “I’ve got Corona, but no lime.”

“Corona sounds good. And something smells incredible. What are you making?”

“Tomato bisque and grilled cheese. Can you stay for dinner?”

“Yum. Wish I could, but Brian’s bringing home steaks.”

Maddie took a stool at the counter while Brooke retrieved a beer from the fridge and popped off the top.

Out of all of Brooke’s girlfriends, Maddie was the easiest to talk to, especially lately. She was a newlywed, but she wasn’t all starry-eyed and gleefully playing house with her husband. This was a second go round for her. Years ago, Maddie had lost a child and gone through a messy divorce. She tended to have a realistic, grounded outlook on life.

“Sorry about our coffee klatch.” Brooke set the Corona in front of Maddie. “I completely blanked. It’s been a crazy day. Two days, actually.”

She brought Maddie up to speed on everything, including the shooting, but omitting the part about seeing Sean afterward.

“Wow. Forget coffee. I’m surprised you didn’t call in sick today. You okay?”

“Pretty much. Mind if I chop while we talk?”

"Go ahead."

"So, how are *you* doing?"

"Um, nice try, but we're not done with you yet." Maddie smiled. "How's Sean?"

Brooke continued chopping, stalling for time. "How do you know about Sean?"

"I *knew* it! Alex owes me five dollars."

Brooke stopped chopping. "You guys made a bet?"

"She said you were still off men, but I told her I thought you and Sean had a thing."

"Where'd you get that?"

"Oh, please. I've seen the way you look at each other."

"What way?" Brooke took a sip of wine to hide her reaction.

"Oh, I don't know. Like you want to eat each other alive?"

Damn it, who else had noticed? Brooke set her glass down and took a deep breath. "I spent last night at his house."

Maddie slapped the counter. "You did not!"

"I did."

Brooke's stomach flitted with nerves. It felt strange to tell someone. Talking about it somehow made it more real, and it would be harder to chalk it up as a one-night stand.

"And?"

"And what?" Brooke rinsed some basil leaves.

"And how was it?" Maddie grinned. "I've always wondered about that man."

"Hey. Stick to your FBI agent."

"Ha! Jealousy, too. This sounds serious."

"It isn't." The instant the words were out, Brooke felt guilty.

"So . . . was it okay? Better than okay?"

Brooke felt her cheeks warm as she tore basil and sprinkled it into the soup. "I don't really have words to describe it."

"Try."

Brooke sighed. "He's very . . . thorough." She smiled and picked up her wine.

"Oh, my God." Maddie fanned her face. "That is so hot. And I'm so damn happy for you."

Brooke set down the glass, and the nerves were back in her stomach.

"What's wrong? You look all worried."

"Well, I am."

"I won't tell anyone. My lips are sealed."

"No, not that. Although, please don't tell anyone. I just . . ." Brooke leaned back against the counter and combed her hands through her hair. "I feel like this is happening way too soon."

"Too soon after Matt, you mean?"

"Yeah."

"It's been four months." Maddie sipped her beer.

"Yes, but I'm still just getting out of it with him. He was here the other night."

"Here as in *here*?" Maddie set her bottle down.

"He's still lurking."

"Damn it. I should have Brian talk to him."

"No. It's fine."

"It's not *fine*, Brooke."

"I can handle everything with him. It's Sean I'm confused about. My head's all over the place and I feel like I'm making a mess of everything."

Brooke stirred the soup with a wooden spoon.

"It sounds like me when Brian and I first got together." Maddie shook her head. "I was a wreck. After

Emma died, I was basically in emotional lockdown. I stopped caring about my job, my marriage. When Brian met me, I was completely missing in action emotionally."

"I can't imagine what you went through. I'm sure my problems seem silly by comparison."

"They're not silly at all. In fact, it sounds familiar. I liked Brian a lot, but that alone confused the hell out of me, and I kept pushing him away."

"So, what happened?"

"He saw straight through my bullshit and called me out on it."

Brooke thought again about her argument with Sean. *Don't compare me to him.* "I keep thinking I need to follow my plan, which was to take some time off for myself to get my footing back. Whenever Sean's around, though, all that goes right out the window and all I want to do is be with him."

"So, be with him."

"But the logical side of me knows I'd be making another mistake by rushing into something like I did when Matt and I started. I'd be falling into the same pattern I had with Matt."

"Well . . . is Sean like Matt?"

"No. They're completely different, and I think that's what scares me."

Maddie watched her, looking pensive. "For years I convinced myself every guy I met was going to be just like the guy I divorced. Kind of put a damper on things. I had to stop listening to my brain so much. When Brian came along, nothing was logical, so I had to suck it up and go with my heart."

Brooke stirred the soup, and her throat tightened as she thought of Sean. Why was she so conflicted?

Maybe that in itself was a sign she shouldn't be getting involved with anyone new right now.

"I hate how indecisive I am. I never used to be this way. I used to set my sights on something I wanted and just go for it. It pisses me off that he took that away from me. That I *let* him take that away from me."

Maddie gave her a worried smile. "You'll get it back. You're going through a transition right now."

"I *hate* that. I feel like I'm in limbo."

Maddie's phone dinged and she dug it from her purse. "Well, dinner calls. I need to get home." She walked over to Brooke and gave her a hug.

"Thanks for coming by." Brooke led her to the door. "And sorry about our coffee klatch. Any good gossip?"

"Oh, yes. We got to hear all about Kelsey's sexcapades. She and Gage are trying to have a baby."

"Sorry I missed that."

Maddie smiled. "You get a pass this time. But don't miss the next one or we'll be forced to talk about you."

• • •

Brooke was home. The front windows were dark, but Sean saw the warm yellow glow from the kitchen spilling out onto the driveway. He parked at the curb and checked his watch as he walked up her sidewalk and rang the bell.

"Hey," she said when she pulled the door back.

"Hi."

Sean could tell he'd surprised her, but he couldn't tell if that was good or bad. Her hair was down and she'd changed into yoga clothes—some tight black top that clung to her breasts.

She caught him staring and raised an eyebrow. "Would you like to come in?"

He stepped into the darkened living room, and for a moment they just stood there, looking at each other.

"Something smells good."

She yelped and rushed into the kitchen. He trailed behind and found her at the stove, flipping over a perfectly golden-brown grilled-cheese sandwich.

Sean's mouth began to water as he looked around. Something simmered in a pot on the stove, and a glass of red wine sat beside a cutting board.

Sean spotted the half-empty beer on the counter.

Brooke noticed his look. "Maddie was here."

"Oh, yeah? How's Maddie?"

"Good."

She avoided eye contact in a way that told him they'd talked about him, and Sean wished to hell he knew what Brooke had said.

She slid the finished sandwich onto the cutting board. "The soup's almost ready. Have you had dinner?"

"No, but I can't stay. I'm working."

She looked at him. "Still?"

"We're running surveillance on a suspect. I got stuck with the late shift."

"Who's the suspect?"

"No one you know."

"Try me."

"Guy named Eric Mahoney."

Her eyebrows shot up. "The *judge*?"

"You know him?"

"I was in his courtroom once to give expert testimony. Oh, my God, you have *his* DNA under Samantha Bonner's fingernails?"

Sean frowned. "How do you know about that?"

"Ric mentioned something in the meeting today."

"First of all, no, we don't have it. Not for sure, anyway. And you can't repeat that name to anyone, you got me?"

"The DA must be flipping out."

"Brooke, do you understand?" He stepped closer. "That information is confidential."

"I understand." She gazed up at him, and he could see her wheels turning.

"Don't even go there."

"Go where?"

"Wherever you're going in that brain of yours. This phase of the investigation doesn't involve you."

"I know."

Sean stared down at her as he battled his urges. Brooke smelled amazing, her kitchen smelled amazing, and he wanted nothing more than to stay here all night filling up on her.

"Stay for a bite."

"I can't." He checked his watch. "I'm late already."

"Then why did you come here?"

He gazed down at her. "I needed to see if you were still pissed."

"I'm not."

"And I needed to check something." He pulled her against him and dipped his head down to kiss her, all the while gauging her reaction.

It wasn't just one reaction, but a whole string of them, starting with surprise, then hesitation, and finally a slow, delicious opening as she relaxed into the kiss. She tasted so damn good, like wine and spices and that woman flavor he remembered from last night, and he wanted to lift her onto the counter and do her right there. He gripped her hips and pulled her against him, and she moaned into his mouth.

Why did he have to go? He wanted to stay. He

wanted to keep her up all night again. And he wanted to watch her eyes go hazy as she clutched him inside her body and screamed his name.

Finally, he eased back, and her heated look erased the moment on the porch this morning when she'd flinched. For the first time in hours Sean felt like he could breathe.

She smiled slowly. "That's what you had to check?"

"Yeah."

He wrapped his arms around her, and she rested her head on his chest.

"Sean, about what I said earlier—that 'my way or the highway' thing. That wasn't fair. And you're right about why I said it."

He pulled back to look at her.

"I think . . ." She cleared her throat. "I'm a little freaked out about last night."

"Me too."

"Really?"

"Yes. I've been thinking about you all day."

Heat flared in her eyes, and he had to kiss her again. He couldn't resist, not when she was right there in front of him and he'd been replaying their night together all day long. She slid her arms around his neck, tempting him to stay, and it was physically painful for him to step back and let her go.

"I need to get back."

She nodded and led him through the dark living room to her front door.

"Oh, wait!" She rushed back into the kitchen before he could object.

Sean checked his watch. He was so freaking late, Ric was going to kill him. And he still hadn't told Brooke his news.

She reappeared with a can of Coke and a plastic baggie containing a grilled-cheese sandwich sliced diagonally in half. Sean's heart squeezed.

"For your stakeout."

"Thanks." No one had ever given him homemade food for a stakeout before. And now he felt guilty for the rest of what he had to tell her.

"Listen, I talked to Kaitlyn Spence tonight. She agreed to bring Cameron in for a session with a forensic artist."

Brooke stiffened. "When?"

"Tomorrow. After he finishes school and Kaitlyn gets off work at the coffee shop."

The look in her eyes chilled.

"Reynolds pushed hard for this. I stalled him as long as I could, which is why this is happening late tomorrow. If we get lucky, we'll catch a break before then and we won't need him."

Brooke pulled the door open. No touch, no kiss. Sean stepped out into the cold, wondering if he'd just undone all the progress he'd made with her.

"Be careful tonight," she said crisply. "I hope you catch that break."

CHAPTER 19

Callie parked in the shadow of a huge oak tree and looked up and down the street. She sent Sean a text to alert him before getting out of her SUV and trekking up the dark driveway where the minivan was parked.

The door slid open silently, but the interior light didn't come on. Callie climbed inside. No heat. No radio. Only a soft snick as the automatic door eased shut.

"Damn, it's an icebox in here." Callie slid into the front passenger seat as Sean lifted a pair of binoculars to his eyes. "Brought you some coffee." She set a cardboard cup in the console.

He muttered a thanks.

Callie glanced around, expecting to see the typical heap of discarded food wrappers. But the van was fairly tidy. She looked at Sean, who seemed to be in a foul mood. Not that she could blame him. He had seven hours left on his shift, whereas she was on her way home to a warm apartment.

"So, what's the lay of the land?" She noted the FOR SALE sign in the front yard beside the driveway where Sean was parked. "Is this house vacant, or are the people out of town?"

"Vacant." Sean lowered the binoculars. "Mahoney's house is across the street and to the right."

"That's a pretty big lot."

"A full acre. There's a long driveway leading up to it, gated at the top. That's the only way in or out by car. The gate's been closed since he got home around seven thirty."

"You've been here since seven thirty?"

"I got here after nine. Ric was here before that. Wife pulled in at five, probably coming from tennis, based on what she was wearing. No one's been in or out since seven thirty."

Callie stared at the two-story brick house with black shutters. It looked expensive but not ostentatious. An autumn wreath decorated the front door, and spotlights illuminated two giant oak trees in the yard.

"I did some checking," Sean said. "No dark red Ford or black Chevy pickup registered to the judge or his wife."

"Of course. That would be too easy."

"Yep."

"You really think he's our guy?" She looked at him.

"Don't know, but I plan to find out." Sean lifted the binoculars again. "How'd it go at Delphi?"

"I dropped off Samantha's computer."

"You give Alex Lovell a heads-up?"

"Yes, and she wasn't happy that we don't have either of the victims' phones."

"She'll work around it."

"Also, I confirmed the forensic artist for four thirty tomorrow. That's what you told Kaitlyn Spence, right?"

Sean didn't respond.

"Right?"

"Yeah."

"What's the problem?"

He rested the binocs on his lap and stared at the house. "Brooke thinks we should skip the artist."

"Why?"

"She thinks the kid's traumatized by the murder he probably witnessed and then yesterday's shooting. She's worried about him."

"Aren't you?"

"Honestly? No." Sean looked at Callie, but she couldn't read his expression in the dimness. "I met him at the hospital. He seems like a tough kid. I think he can handle it. It might even be good for him, like talking to a shrink. Could be cathartic."

"Wow. That's very evolved."

"What?"

"Every cop I know hates shrinks and avoids them like a root canal."

"Yeah, well, sometimes you can't."

She looked him over, remembering the department-mandated psych visits he'd had to go through following the shooting several months ago. Sean seemed to remember, too, and shifted in his seat to stretch out his leg. He squeezed his eyes shut.

"Your leg bothering you?"

"No."

"You don't have to give me that crap, Sean. I won't tell anyone."

He sighed heavily. "It hurts like a bitch. All this sitting makes it stiffen up."

"You could tell Reynolds you're not up for surveillance right now."

"No." Sean picked up the coffee and took a sip. "This wasn't his idea in the first place. Ric and I had to talk him into it."

She turned in her seat to face him. "Are you *serious*?"

"Yeah."

"Well, hey, thanks for consulting me on this. I've got an eight-hour shift tomorrow. So does Jasper. So does Christine."

Sean shook his head. "Sucks to be you."

"You know, just because you don't mind wasting your time in some minivan doesn't mean everyone else wants to."

"It's not a matter of want. We've got a viable suspect in the killing of two women. I'll be damned if we're letting him out of our sight."

Callie turned to stare at the house. She knew Sean was right, but she really, *really* wasn't looking forward to her shift tomorrow.

"A little surveillance work won't kill you."

"Easy for you to say. You're a guy. The whole world is your urinal. Try sitting in a car for eight hours without a bathroom break."

He smiled but didn't look at her.

"And how long are we planning to do this? This thing could drag on for days. Or weeks."

"It could. But I'm counting on Alex to come through. If there's a digital connection anywhere between the judge and these victims, she'll sniff it out. She's diligent."

"Speaking of diligent." Callie dug into her bag. "I brought you a little reading to keep you awake out here." She handed him a manila file folder. "Samantha's case file. Jasmine's is in there, too—separate binder clip."

He set the binoculars aside and opened the folder. "Farrah give you any trouble?"

"Surprisingly, no. I think she felt guilty. Like maybe

if she'd cooperated sooner, we could have cracked this thing before something happened to Jasmine."

Sean wasn't listening. He'd taken out a red tactical flashlight and was already examining the papers.

"These are copies?" He looked at Callie.

"Farrah wouldn't part with the originals. I made copies of my own to take home tonight." She huffed out a breath. "The joys of single life. It's not like I've got anything better to do than go home to my cat and my Netflix."

"You know, you don't have to do it this way."

She looked at him. "What way?"

"You don't have to be married to the job. You should keep some balance in your life."

"Sounds a little hypocritical coming from a man who traded his girlfriend's warm bed for stakeout duty."

Sean adjusted his leg again, then leaned back to look at the house. "She's not my girlfriend. Yet."

Callie smiled. "Listen to that can-do attitude of yours. I like that. It's a good predictor of future success."

"Don't try to change the subject. If you don't like the single life, how come you never go out with anyone?"

She bristled, even though she knew he was just trying to needle her. "Maybe no one's asked me. You ever thought of that?"

"That's an excuse."

"How would you know?"

"You're an assertive woman. If there's someone you want to go out with, why don't you ask him?"

"Maybe I will."

She thought of Travis Cullen with his beautiful forearms. They were tan and muscular, and she liked the way they'd looked folded over his big chest as he'd stood in his lab talking to her. And his voice . . . That low, masculine voice had been on her mind all day.

"You've got someone on your radar. Who is he?"

"No one."

"So, you can dish it out, but you can't take it, huh?"

"Whatever." She didn't want to get sucked into this conversation, mainly because Sean had a point.

"Listen to your own advice. If there's something you want, go for it. If you've got your eye on some guy, ask him out. Don't be such a wuss."

"You're right." She sighed and turned to look at him. "Sean . . ." She rested her hand on his leg. "Will you go out with me?"

His jaw dropped. He glanced down at her hand. "I . . . um—"

"Kidding!" She burst out laughing. "Oh, my God, your face! That was priceless."

He scowled at her, and she laughed so hard she felt tears coming.

"That was awesome." She dabbed her eyes. "I needed that."

"Hey, glad I could entertain you."

She patted his knee. "On that note, I'm out. Enjoy your sleepless night." She opened the door and a gust of cold air rushed in. "I hope you've got thoughts of Brooke to keep you warm."

• • •

Brooke arrived at the lab before dawn, already alert and caffeinated. With no one around to distract her, she got straight to work on the cart full of evidence envelopes, powering through seven separate cases without even breaking for coffee.

The highlight of her morning was envelope three, a difficult lift on the curved lip of a beer bottle. Experimenting with casting silicone again—clear this time—she was able to lift two good fingerprints from the ridged surface. Because the material was transparent instead of white, Brooke didn't need to reverse the print with digital photography. She was able to make a comparison right away with a suspect's fingerprint card. She got a match, too—which was going to make the detective on the case very happy.

Brooke was back in the zone.

When lunchtime rolled around, she was immersed in her music, humming softly as she typed some notes on her laptop. She turned and peered into her microscope, adjusting the lens to bring dozens of spherical-shaped particles into focus.

"I knew it," she murmured, typing her observations.

A shadow fell over her and she got an overwhelming whiff of campfire. She turned to see Roland standing behind her in filthy gray coveralls.

"You reek." She plucked out her earbuds.

"Three-alarm fire up in Williamson County." He took a swig of Gatorade.

"Any fatalities?"

"Negative." He eyed her suspiciously and nodded at the evidence envelopes lined up on her worktable. "Don't tell me you've done all those."

"Okay, I won't."

"No shit. Really?"

Brooke smiled as she entered a final observation before closing out of her document. Eight cases down. She'd hit her goal.

"What's this you're working on? You look smug."

"I am. I just found a detective his smoking gun."

"Which case?"

"The home invasion from Kerrville. Residue from the shoe print on the door matches the suspect's boot. Here, take a look." She stepped back to let him see, and he was so tall that he had to hunch to get eye level with her viewfinder.

"What is this?"

"Particles of polyurethane mixed with sawdust. I'd bet money this guy's in construction. He's got this stuff all over his boots, and it's a perfect match with the material recovered from the victim's door."

"Damn. Nice work." Roland eased back and looked at her. "You're killing it today. What time'd you get here?"

"Five thirty."

His gaze narrowed.

"What?"

"What are you up to, Brooke?"

"Nothing." She switched off her microscope and removed the slide from the stage. She dropped it into an evidence envelope and resealed it, then scrawled her initials on the label with the date and time.

"Brooke?"

She turned to Roland.

"Seriously, what's up? And don't say 'nothing,' because you've done two days' worth of work in one morning."

She slid off her stool and gathered up all the envelopes she'd processed. "I'm taking the afternoon off." She replaced the packages on the cart to be returned to the evidence room.

"Why?"

"There's something I need to look into. And trust me when I tell you, you don't want to hear about it."

"A secret mission? Now you definitely have to tell me." He leaned back against the counter and waited.

"Actually, I don't."

"Brookie . . ."

"Whatie?"

"This wouldn't have anything to do with the floater from yesterday, would it?"

She wondered what exactly he knew about it. "What have you heard?"

"Nothing much. Just that the same team that's investigating the Samantha Bonner murder is also investigating the woman they found near the dam yesterday morning." Roland swigged the rest of his drink and lobbed the bottle into a trash can. "Let's see, that would be Callie McLean, Ric Santos, and your new boyfriend. What's his name again?"

Brooke didn't comment as she shut down her computer.

"I'm right, aren't I? You're involved with him."

She rolled her eyes.

"So, what's he got you doing for him, rushing evidence? Running samples for free?"

"None of the above. This has nothing to do with him."

"Except that it's related to his case, right?"

She sighed. "Don't you have work to do?"

Roland grinned. "This is better. Tell me about your mission this afternoon."

"It wouldn't interest you."

"Why not?"

She crossed her arms. "Because it's completely outside my job description, and I know how much you hate that. It's also ethically questionable."

"Sounds right up my alley."

"And as an added bonus, it has the potential to screw up my personal life as well as my job."

Roland smiled. "This could be interesting."

"It could also be a disaster, and I don't need an accomplice, so you're off the hook." She grabbed her purse from the back of her chair. "I'll catch you tomorrow, okay?"

"No way. Whatever you're up to, I'm in."

• • •

Sean sidestepped puddles as he walked through the alley that smelled of piss and garbage.

"Yo, Sean."

He turned around to see Jasper approaching him. He wore street clothes instead of his typical uniform, but Sean noted the pistol bulge under his plaid shirt.

"Thought you worked the night shift," Jasper said as he caught up to him.

"I did. I'm just checking in with Ric. Are you taking over for him?"

"Yeah, at two o'clock."

They walked together down the alley toward the minivan where Ric was set up.

"What's with the tie?" Jasper asked.

"I've got a deposition."

"Bummer."

Bummer was right. Sean was in a severely shitty mood right now, and only part of it was due to lack of sleep.

Today's deposition was for the case in which Sean had taken a bullet and fucked up his leg, one of the worst days of his life. Rehashing it all with a bunch of attorneys was the dead last thing Sean wanted to do right now.

What he *wanted* was to fall into bed. Preferably with Brooke. He wanted to have mind-blowing sex with her and then sleep for about a week.

Would it be a violation of their "casual" relationship if he showed up at her house for the third night in a row? He sure as hell hoped not, because he needed to see her. Soon. He was feeling desperate, and the hours he'd spent in that freezing minivan thinking about her had only made it worse.

When they reached the minivan, Jasper rapped on the panel. The door slid open, and they climbed inside.

"How's it going?" Jasper asked as he squeezed his bulk into the front passenger seat.

"It's going," Ric mumbled, staring through the binoculars. He lowered them to his lap and turned to look at Jasper, then Sean.

"What's with the tie?"

"I've got a deposition. Where's Mahoney?"

"Still having lunch at Cajun Jay's. He's been there almost two hours with a couple buddies. Callie's got eyes on him inside the restaurant."

"Man, a two-hour lunch? Must be nice," Jasper said.

"Yeah, he wrapped a big trial this morning, so I think he's in celebration mode."

Sean gritted his teeth. He couldn't wait to take this guy down.

"Who's he having lunch with?" Sean asked Ric.

"Tom Moore and Dave Garver."

"You're kidding."

"Who's that?" Jasper asked.

"Moore is another judge," Sean told him. "Garver is a sheriff's deputy."

"*Retired* sheriff's deputy," Ric corrected.

"Total dirtbag," Sean said. "We caught him up in an

undercover operation—what was it, four years back?"

"Five," Ric said. "We did this sting op at a motel off the interstate, busted a prostitution ring. Lot of the girls were minors, one as young as fourteen."

"Garver's car was in the parking lot," Sean said.

"He claimed he was there meeting a girlfriend, not a hooker, and we could never make anything stick," Ric said. "But I always suspected he was there for one of the kids."

"A few months later he took early retirement," Sean said. "I'm pretty sure his brass knew what he was up to."

"What, like, he had a track record?" Jasper asked.

"Probably something like that. Whole thing smelled bad from the beginning." Ric looked at Sean. "Kind of like this."

Sean stared across the town square at the restaurant where Eric Mahoney was probably eating crawfish and sucking down beers. And meanwhile Jasmine Jones was laid out cold in some funeral home by now. Sean didn't have a clear picture of the judge's connection to the most recent victim—or to Samantha Bonner—but he had some ideas.

"Check it out," Jasper said. "He's on the move."

Sean leaned forward in his seat so he could see through the windshield. Mahoney stood in front of the restaurant now, slapping his buddy Garver on the back. Moore stood beside Mahoney, handed him a cigar, then offered him a light.

After shooting the shit for a few minutes, the trio split up, with Garver heading north toward some parking meters and the two judges heading south toward the courthouse.

Ric's phone beeped and he dug it from his pocket. "Callie's on her way. She slipped out the back."

Sean watched with disgust as Mahoney and Moore continued down the sidewalk, puffing their cigars. Moore was short and stocky, but Mahoney was tall and in pretty decent shape for a fifty-year-old. Once upon a time he'd played football for UT El Paso, and he still carried himself like a jock.

"Be nice to have that cigar," Jasper said. "Think I should follow him?"

"No," Ric said.

"Why not? Maybe he'll toss it before he goes inside."

"Doesn't matter. We can't use DNA for a warrant this time." Ric looked at Sean. "Any word from the cybercrimes unit at Delphi?"

"Alex is still working it."

A sharp tap, and then Callie opened the door. "Hey, look. Everyone's here." She squeezed past Sean and slipped into a seat. "What are you doing here? I thought you had a deposition this afternoon."

"I'm getting an update." Sean checked his watch.

"Man, that was a long lunch." Callie rubbed her stomach. "I ate that whole damn po'boy *and* dessert. I think I might throw up."

"Hey, take it outside," Jasper said. "I'm in this van for the next eight hours."

"What's the word on Mahoney's lunch bunch?" Callie asked Ric.

"Nothing new on either of them. I ran their records."

She leaned forward. "You know about Garver, right? About the rumor he got caught in a prostitution sting a couple years back?"

"He was never charged," Ric said.

"Yeah, but still."

"We'll look into it. Do you think any of them saw you in there?"

"I had a corner booth in the back. None of them noticed me." She looked at Sean. "Neither did Brooke."

Sean got a sick feeling in the pit of his stomach. "What do you mean?"

"She was in there, too. Showed up right after the judge."

"There she is now," Ric said.

Sean grabbed the binoculars to see for himself. And there was Brooke exiting the restaurant wearing a baseball cap, shades, and an oversize brown jacket. She glanced around before heading north down the sidewalk. Then she stopped at a meter and hopped into a black Toyota 4Runner. Some guy was behind the wheel, but Sean didn't have a good view of him.

"What the hell is she doing?" Sean looked at Callie.

"I don't know. I was hoping you could tell us."

CHAPTER 20

Brooke was stepping out of a steamy shower when the doorbell rang. She hurried into her bedroom and threw on some clothes before grabbing her wallet on the way to the door. The delivery guy was early.

But it wasn't the delivery guy on her doorstep.

"Hi," she said, letting Sean inside. He wore dark slacks and a tie, and she started to ask where he'd come from, but the expression on his face stopped her cold. "What's wrong?"

"Sit down. I need to talk to you."

She narrowed her gaze at him.

"Please," he added, but his voice was terse.

She closed the door and took a seat on her sofa. He sat on the chair beside her and rested his elbows on his knees for a long moment as he stared at the floor. Then his gaze met hers, and the stormy look in his eyes had her heart racing.

"Where is it?" he asked.

"Where is what?"

"The drinking glass. And *don't* lie to me."

She pulled back. "What the hell? Don't accuse me of *lying* to you."

"Where is it?"

"At the lab."

He closed his eyes, and the muscle at the side of his jaw twitched. "God damn it, Brooke."

"What?"

He started to say something, then shook his head. Suddenly he stood up. "I need to go."

"Wait, that's it?" She looked up at him and laughed. "Discussion over?"

"If I open my mouth right now, I'm going to yell at you."

She got to her feet and plunked her hands on her hips. "Yell all you want. I won't break."

He shook his head and looked away.

"Obviously, you're ticked off. I can understand, but—"

"Ticked off? That doesn't even *begin* to describe what I am right now, Brooke. I'm fucking furious—" He stepped back and held his hands up. "You know what? I'm not doing this. I need to go. I almost didn't come over here in the first place because I'm so goddamn mad at you right now."

Anger swelled in her chest at the idea that he'd avoid her because he thought she couldn't handle a conflict.

"*Be mad*, Sean. Go ahead. Yell all you want."

He shook his head and wouldn't look at her.

"*Yell*, Sean. Say what's on your mind!"

His gaze snapped to hers. "Fine! I can't *fucking* believe you did this!"

"What, exactly?"

He sneered. "You should stick to lab work, Brooke, because you are *not* a detective and you suck at undercover."

"Who said anything about undercover?" she demanded. "I'm not hiding anything."

"Oh, yeah? So, you weren't trying to be all stealth

about it? So, you don't care if a brutal murderer knows you're tailing him around and collecting his DNA?"

She rolled her eyes. "He doesn't know that."

"No?" Sean stepped closer. "I talked to that waiter, Brooke, and it took me all of *thirty seconds* to figure out what you did. If I can do it, so can Mahoney."

"He didn't even see me there."

Sean tipped his head back. "Jesus Christ. How can you say that?" He gaped at her. "I saw you there. My whole team saw you there. The entire staff of that restaurant saw you there. How could you be so damn reckless? You could have gotten hurt. You could *still* get hurt!"

The bell rang. She tore her gaze away from Sean to look at the door.

"That's my dinner." She grabbed her wallet from where she'd dropped it on the couch and hurried to the door. After taking the warm paper bag of Thai food, she tipped the delivery guy and sent him on his way with a phony smile.

Brooke closed and locked the door, barely glancing at Sean as she strode into the kitchen. He followed her. She set the bag on the counter and started unpacking the cartons, not bothering to hide her emotions as she slapped everything out on the counter.

"You know, I thought you might be annoyed, but I also thought you *might* be a tad bit grateful."

"Grateful." He folded his arms over his chest.

Again she wondered about the tie. "Yes, grateful. Appreciative. *Thankful* that I put a rush on some tests for you so you'll know whether you're focused on the right suspect."

"I *already* know I'm focused on the right suspect! You want to know how? Because I'm a detective and

I've got years' worth of experience doing what you tried to do this afternoon with absolutely no training whatsoever, which is close in on a suspect, build a case, and ultimately obtain an arrest warrant."

She rested her hand on her hip. "So, you're not grateful at all to have a DNA sample to help you do that?"

"We're using other means."

"Why?"

"A lot of reasons, none of which concerns you. Or didn't until you decided to barge into the investigation."

"You see it as barging, I see it as helping. Whatever." She got two plates down from the cabinet. "Anyway, DNA evidence is much more conclusive than anything else you're doing, and that's a scientific fact. I took a calculated risk and it was worth it."

He shook his head.

"What?" She opened a carton of noodles.

"We'll have to agree to disagree on that."

His words hit her smack in the center of her chest. Yet another example of how totally different Sean was from Matt.

Brooke looked up at his eyes, simmering with frustration, and she felt guilty. He was truly worried about her, so much so that he'd worked himself into a fury over it. But he didn't deal with his emotions the way Matt did. Not at all.

She stepped closer to him, and he watched her warily as she rested her hand on his chest. The starched cotton felt warm under her fingertips.

"I'm sorry you don't agree with my tactics. I'm not sorry for what I did, though."

"Brooke—"

"The results should be in sometime tomorrow, and you guys can move forward one way or another. And if Rachel has a problem with what I did, then she can ignore the findings. But at least you and your team will know whether you're wasting valuable time."

He took a deep breath and blew it out. Then he combed a hand through his hair.

"Stay for dinner."

He looked at her for a long moment, and she saw the emotions warring in his face. "I should go."

She turned to the cabinet and took down a wineglass. She poured a glass of merlot and handed it to him.

"Stay with me, Sean. Please?"

• • •

Sean didn't need wine. Or food. He just needed her to look at him with those seductive blue-green eyes that promised him the world.

She was so damn beautiful, and he needed to turn off the anger coursing through his system because he couldn't stand for her to see him lose his temper.

He took the wineglass and set it on the counter beside him. He was still pissed off, and he had no business being here when he felt this way. He never wanted her to think he was one of those tightly wound guys who would lose their shit in the heat of the moment.

"Relax." She stroked her palm over his chest again.

"I can't. I'm worried about you."

Worried was an understatement. In the past week, Sean had watched two young women get zipped into body bags, and the idea of Brooke crossing paths with the man responsible made Sean queasy with fear.

He removed Brooke's hand from his chest, needing

her to focus on what he was saying. "What you did was dangerous, Brooke. I don't want you on that guy's radar."

"Don't worry, I'm not."

She slipped her arms around him, filling him with the tantalizing scent of her wet hair. She rested her head against him, and he couldn't resist squeezing her tight. All day long, he'd felt this aching hole in his chest. And she seemed to know right where it was because she rested her palm over the spot.

"You're dressed up." She smoothed her hand down his tie. "Where were you today?"

"A deposition," he said, allowing himself to be lured into a change of subject.

"Oh?" She eased back and looked at him curiously. "Want to talk about it?"

"No." She lifted an eyebrow at his sharp tone. He was shitty company tonight, and he needed to make up a reason to leave.

"How'd it go with the interview?"

"Interview?"

"Cameron and the sketch artist."

"It didn't happen. Cameron threw up in the car on the way to the police station. His mom says he has a nervous stomach."

Brooke's brow furrowed with worry.

"They rescheduled for tomorrow afternoon, and they're going to try again."

She rested her head against his chest. He didn't tell her she'd been right about the kid being traumatized, because she obviously knew. But they needed him anyway, so traumatized or not, they planned to get him in front of the sketch artist.

This case was so fucked-up. Sean hated that an

innocent little boy was right in the middle of it. He hated that Brooke was right in the middle of it. But she wouldn't let it go, and Sean's inability to stay away from her wasn't helping matters. He needed to leave.

She tipped her head back to look at him, pressing her breasts against his chest.

"Brooke—"

She kissed him, cutting off the lame excuse he'd been about to give her.

He wasn't going anywhere. Not when she had him wound up like this—a tight ball of nerves and frustration. He'd been like this all day, but worse since he'd seen her outside that restaurant, only footsteps away from the prime suspect in two vicious homicides. What the hell was she thinking?

He gripped her shirt, insanely relieved to know she was safe and in his arms, where nothing bad could happen to her, at least for this moment.

She seemed oblivious to his struggle as she dug her fingers into his hair. Her mouth was hot and seeking, and he pushed her back against the counter, pinning her there as he gave in to the need that had been hounding him for days. Her hand was up at the knot of his tie now, loosening it, and he didn't bother to help her because he was too busy devouring her mouth.

She tasted so good, even better than last night, and he remembered the fantasies that had haunted him during his endless stakeout.

She tugged the tie loose and jerked it free from his collar. She tossed it on the counter and went to work on his buttons as Sean pulled her T-shirt over her head, revealing a sexy black sports bra. She pushed his shirt off his shoulders, but the sleeves got caught at his wrists. He stepped back to unbutton the cuffs and toss the shirt aside, and the instant he was free, she was in his arms again. He stroked his hands over all that smooth, warm skin he'd been craving, but damned if he could find the clasp of her bra. While he was busy searching for it, she stripped his white T-shirt over his head and fastened her mouth on his chest with a little moan.

God, she was hot. Sean lifted her onto the counter, pushing her thighs apart so he could position himself where he'd wanted to be for days, and she smiled down at him.

"In a hurry?"

"Yes."

He gave up on the bra and simply jerked the strap down her shoulder, uncovering a pale, perfect breast that fit right in his palm. He bent his head down and sucked her nipple into his mouth, and she made another of those sexy moans.

"Sean. Ohhh . . ." She wrapped her legs around his waist and pulled him closer, digging her fingers into his hair while he kissed and licked her. He pulled the other bra strap down, and she arched her back and offered herself up to him. He loved kissing her—and especially loved the sounds she was making. Then she surprised him by wrestling the bra right over her head and flinging it away.

"No clasp," she said breathlessly.

He took her mouth again, kissing the smile right off her face. Cupping her breasts in his hands, he rasped his thumbs over her nipples as she arched against him.

She was hot and eager, and he couldn't stop kissing her. Emotions churned through him—anger, lust, frustration—as he recalled the choking fear he'd felt when he looked through those binoculars and realized what she'd done. And part of him still knew he shouldn't be here, that he should leave her alone tonight. But the other part of him knew he wasn't going anywhere when he so desperately wanted to be right here, right now. He dragged her hips to the edge of the counter and reached back to unhook her ankles so he could slide the stretchy black pants off her body and drop them on the floor. One look at her, completely naked and panting and flushed on her kitchen counter, sent a surge of need through him.

He kissed her again—harder than he should have—but she wrapped her legs around him and brought him in close. He felt her hand fumbling with his belt buckle.

"Sean." She pulled back and glanced over her shoulder at the window behind her. "We can't do this. Not here."

He went still, his hand at the top of her thigh as he took in the scene and realized what she meant. Anyone could see them through the blinds.

She slid down from the counter and grabbed his hand. "Come to the bedroom."

CHAPTER 21

Brooke's heart was racing as she pulled him down the dim hallway leading to her room. She was naked—*naked*—towing him through her house and into her most private space, and she realized she might be making a mistake. But she glanced over her shoulder, and one look at the desire etched on his face banished her doubts. Mistake or not, they were doing this now. She quickened her pace, towing him faster as they neared her room.

"God, I love your ass." He reached out and caught her around her waist with one hand, while the other squeezed her butt.

"You do not."

He swatted it, and she yelped at the sting.

"Wanna bet?"

She laughed and fell forward onto the bed, and he came down on top of her, caging her in with his arms. She flipped onto her back and wrestled him, and in no time he had her pinned underneath him with her wrists clamped against the mattress.

She smiled up at him, but he didn't smile back, and when he kissed her, she tasted all that pent-up anger he'd been trying to keep in check. Something was different tonight. There was something raw and possessive, and she'd never liked that with anyone before, but coming from him, it thrilled her. The realization that it did sent a jolt of excitement through her body. She bit his lip, and when he jerked back in surprise, she yanked her hand free and burrowed it between them so she could unfasten his pants.

He pulled back and looked at her, his gaze narrowing as she smiled up at him and eased down his zipper.

"Sneaky," he grumbled, then kissed her again, giving her lip a nibble of his own, and when her fingers curled around him, he groaned into her mouth.

She loved the way she felt with him—powerful and in charge and exhilarated, like she could do anything she wanted. And in this moment, she wanted *him* and nothing else. She wanted his powerful body and the thrumming sexual energy she felt coming off him in waves.

He murmured something and pushed up and off the bed, watching her with that heated gaze as he kicked off his shoes and stripped off the rest of his clothes. She propped on her elbows to watch him as he dug into his wallet for a condom and tossed it on the nightstand, and soon he was back at her side, stroking his hand down the front of her body. It came to rest just below her navel, and her heart did a little dance of anticipation.

He eased on top of her, using his knees to push her legs apart as her rested his weight on his arms and kissed her—starting with her mouth, then sliding down her neck and lingering at her breasts. He'd obviously noticed how sensitive they were, and he stayed there teasing and licking and suckling her until she was writhing under him, dizzy with need. She arched up, pressing her hips against him.

"Sean," she said, hoping he heard the impatience in her voice.

He pulled away and sat back on his knees, watching her intently as he pulled on the condom. Then he stretched out over her and entered her body with a powerful stroke that had her gasping.

He adjusted her legs and did it again, and she tipped her head back and slid her hands up his back. He felt good, so amazingly perfect inside her, and she wrapped her legs around him and pulled him as close as she possibly could as he drove into her again and again, making the bed shake. She tipped her head back and tried to keep up with him as he hammered into her.

"Brooke . . ." His voice was strained and the muscles of his shoulders bunched under her hands. She clenched herself around him as hard as she could and felt herself start to come.

"Yes. Yes, Sean, *yes*."

He thrust into her again, and she saw stars behind her eyes and the orgasm blazed through her.

He groaned and collapsed, catching his weight on his elbows as he buried his face against her hair.

She didn't move. She couldn't. She could barely breathe with his body pinning her beneath him. Then he pushed up on his palms and stared down at her, breathing hard.

"Did I hurt you?"

"What? No."

He gazed down at her for a moment, then rolled onto his back, closing his eyes and dropping his arm over his face.

She propped on an elbow and looked at him, taking a moment to catch her breath, too. She had no idea what he was thinking right now, and when he let his arm flop onto the bed, he looked dazed and winded and, yes, still stressed-out.

"Hey."

He turned to look at her.

She trailed her finger along the stubble covering his jaw. "I'm sorry you were upset earlier."

His face tightened. He sat up on his elbows, and she could tell he wasn't ready for the past tense. He was still upset with her.

He got up and disappeared into the bathroom for a moment, then returned and tossed a pair of throw pillows to the floor. He stretched out next to her and pulled her against him, nestling her head against his chest.

"You're not sorry for going behind my back and meddling in my case, though, right?"

Now she wished she hadn't brought this up so soon. She could have at least waited until they were dressed again, or under the covers, or *something*, rather than lying here naked together.

"I told you. I took a calculated risk that I believe was warranted by the situation."

He looked at her. "Again, we're going to have to agree to disagree."

What, exactly, was happening here? His responses were all over the map.

"Let's drop it."

"You mean that?"

He sighed. "I'm resigned to the fact that you don't want me or anyone else telling you what to do."

She tipped her head back and ran her fingertip over his jaw again, watching the tension in his face.

"But you're still angry."

"Yes." He stared up at the ceiling, then looked

down at her. "The thought of something happening to you—" He shook his head, as though he couldn't find the words.

Emotion swelled inside her. "I know."

He looked at her.

"This summer when I heard you'd been shot . . . I couldn't breathe. I felt like my heart was being squeezed in a big fist." She settled her cheek against his side, and for a long, quiet moment they just lay there.

Sean ran his fingers through her hair, and she closed her eyes to enjoy it. She loved the way he touched her. She loved the way he made her feel cared for, but not weak.

"Brooke?"

"Hmm?"

"How come you never said anything about coming by my hospital room?"

She opened her eyes and looked at him. "You knew?"

"I saw you."

"I thought you were asleep."

"I was in and out."

"Oh." She cleared her throat. "I don't know."

She'd gone to the hospital without even deciding to. As soon as she'd heard what happened to him, she hadn't been able to stay away.

She couldn't explain it now any better than she could then.

"I don't know why I never said anything." Her words sounded inadequate, even to her. "When I was there, I thought you were out cold. And later . . . I thought you might think it was weird. It wasn't like we knew each other that well then."

He pulled her closer. "I'm glad you came."

"Why?"

"Gave me something good to think about when I was ready to throw in the towel on my physical therapy."

Her chest tightened. "Was it bad?"

"Excruciating."

She stroked her hand over his pecs, hating that he'd had to go through that. She knew that he'd worried he might never make a full recovery, and she'd been elated for him when she heard he was back on the job.

A hard lump lodged in her throat. He'd thought about her during his PT. Why did knowing that send a flutter of anxiety through her?

She was so confused. All her emotions swirled together in a big tornado inside her—fear, dread, hope. What the hell was she doing? They'd established the ground rules for what this was, and she shouldn't be having all these thoughts.

"Hey." He squeezed her shoulders. "You're all uptight. What's wrong?"

She closed her eyes. "I knew I'd be bad at this."

"What?"

"This casual-relationship thing. Just having fun."

He looked down at her and lifted an eyebrow. "You're not having fun?"

"No. I *am*." She sat up and pulled away. "But I can feel myself getting attached to you."

"And that's bad?"

"Yes. I told you, I don't want a relationship right now. The timing's all wrong."

"Maybe the timing's perfect," he said quietly. "Maybe this is just what you need right now to move from an unhappy place in your life to a place where you feel good." He eased her back against his chest and stroked his hand down her arm. "You deserve to feel good, Brooke."

His words put a knot in her stomach. "You sound . . ."

"What?"

She pulled back to look at him. "Are you really serious about this? About us?"

"Yes."

The solemn look in his eyes when he said it made her chest ache. "But you said you wanted casual. I never thought . . ."

"What?"

"I didn't think you wanted a big commitment or anything. You've always seemed like . . ."

He smiled. "Like what?"

"I don't know. Kind of a player."

"I've changed."

She looked at him for a long moment. Then she leaned her head against his shoulder because it was easier than looking him in the eye when he was telling her all this stuff. She didn't want to hurt him. Or disappoint him.

"I spent years steering clear of anything serious. I'd pretty much perfected the art of keeping things casual, playing the field."

She felt a tug of relief. It hadn't been just her. He'd definitely projected that image when she first met him.

"I basically dodged commitment of any kind—with the exception of my job. *That* had my full attention. But when it came to relationships? You're right, I was like that. *Was*."

She tipped her head back to look at him. "What happened?"

Seconds ticked by as he stared at the ceiling. Then he looked at her. "The shooting changed me, Brooke. It changed everything."

His whole body felt rigid now, and she waited for what he would say. He'd never talked about this with her, not in any detail. She stroked her finger over the scar the bullet had left on his shoulder.

"I was there, pinned in that truck, clutching my Glock in my hand and waiting for that sniper to come finish me off."

She shuddered at the image and pulled her hand away from his scar.

"The gunshot wound, that wasn't the worst part. My leg was so fucked-up, I can't even describe the pain. And the whole time I'm trapped there, all these crazy thoughts are racing through my head. I'm thinking about my parents. My sisters. I'm thinking about my brother and my nieces and nephews, everybody. I was so sure I was going to die. I was *certain* of it. And I was smacked in the face with the realization that there was so much more I wanted to do with my life . . . so many things I've never done or never said to people. Things I never even thought about, because I was so cocky and arrogant and I always thought I'd have plenty of time."

She envisioned him pinned in that truck, bleeding and sweating and believing his life was about to end. Her pulse was racing just thinking about it.

"And then by some miracle I *didn't* die, but I ended up in that hospital and then in rehab, where I seriously *wanted* to die. . . ." He shook his head. "Rehab was bad, but I had a lot of time on my hands and I did a lot of thinking. I'm not proud of some of the things I've done. I took my family for granted a lot. And I hurt people, including some nice women who didn't deserve how I treated them."

"How did you treat them?"

"I basically took what I wanted and didn't stick around for anything else. I avoided whatever wasn't easy."

He shifted to look at her. "I'm not like that anymore. I don't take anything for granted now. Not a single day." He laced his fingers through hers. "Not one night."

Brooke stared at him, completely at a loss for words. She wasn't sure what he was trying to tell her, and she had no idea how to respond.

"This doesn't happen every day, Brooke. We're lucky." He squeezed her hand. "Don't throw it away because you're afraid."

She sat up and scooted back against the pillows. "I . . . I honestly don't know what to say. I'm confused, Sean."

"Why?"

"Because I hear what you're saying and I even agree with a lot of it. I know this—whatever this is—doesn't come along all the time. At least, it hasn't for me." She sighed. "But every time I've invested in a relationship, every single time, I thought it was special and I thought it would work and I did everything I could and it still went sideways. And I just got out of a situation like that. I'm still getting out of it, and I can't bring myself to trust anyone right now."

"That's okay."

She gaped at him. "*How* is that okay?"

"I told you, I'm a patient man." He lifted her hand and kissed her knuckles.

Brooke stared at him, speechless. In all her life, no one had ever shown her such caring, such tenderness. Not Matt, not Joshua—*no one.*

Until this instant, she'd considered tenderness a weakness. It was something that made her roll her eyes when she saw it in movies. But right now, in this moment with Sean, she realized it was an expression of strength. He was so confident in himself—and, even more amazingly, in her. He was so determined to wait for her to get over her fears and let this thing between them take its natural course. But she knew all too well that the course could result in hurt and disappointment for both of them.

Where did he get this faith in her? In them?

"What are you thinking?"

"I'm thinking . . . that I wish I could be more like you. More trusting."

He stroked his fingers down her hip and gently cupped his hand under her thigh to pull her lower on the bed. He hovered over her, watching her in the dimness.

He smiled slightly. "Stop worrying so much."

"I can't."

"Try."

"I knew you were faking it earlier."

"Faking what?"

"I knew you wanted more than 'keep it casual' and 'no pressure.' "

"Okay, honestly? You're right. What I wanted was for you to give me a chance."

"I feel like I'm a mess right now, Sean. Something's wrong with me and I'm numb."

He traced his fingertips over her breast and down to her hip, and a warm shiver went through her. "Not everything's numb."

"I'm not talking about sex."

"I am." He glided his hand up her body, brushing his thumb over her nipple. "I found your weakness and I plan to take full advantage." He lowered his head to her breast, and she felt the hot pull of his mouth as his hand slid between her legs.

"Not fair. You play dirty."

He groaned against her skin. "Dirty? You have no idea." He moved her thighs apart and settled between her legs, pressing his erection against her. "The first time I saw you at a crime scene, you were in dirty coveralls and work boots and you had soot all over your face, and I was hard for hours."

"Yeah, right."

"I was."

"That was that house-fire scene. That was months ago."

"I know."

"You've really been thinking about—"

"*Yes*, Brooke. I've been thinking about us for months, wishing we could do what we're doing right now. And not just this—although I could do this all night. But there are so many things I want to do with you, if you'd give us a chance."

She felt a pinch in her chest. This wasn't just sex to him. He wanted a real relationship. And he was steadily chipping away at the protective shell she'd grown around her naturally hopeful heart.

Why was she letting him do this to her? She felt a renewed sense of panic. She wasn't prepared to go on this roller-coaster ride again.

"Stop." He reached up and smoothed the crease between her brows. "I can tell you're thinking again."

"I am."

"I told you, I'm patient. We don't have to figure all this out now."

"I can't help it! I analyze things, Sean. That's what I do."

"I have an idea."

"What?"

He kissed her forehead, then her mouth, then her neck. "How about less thinking and more kissing? Think we could try that?"

"We could try."

CHAPTER 22

Sean was already late for work, but he had a stop to make, and it couldn't wait.

It had only taken one phone call for Sean to learn that Matt Jorgensen belonged to a local gym popular with cops and firefighters. Pulling into the parking lot now, Sean immediately spotted the black F-250. He slid into a nearby space, checked his watch, and got out to wait.

Sean no longer believed Jorgensen might be responsible for the drive-by shooting. Not only did his vehicle not match, but Sean's contact in the Burr County sheriff's department had told him Jorgensen had been on duty that night. It wasn't an airtight alibi, but combined with what Brooke had said and what Sean had dug up on his own, it made him believe Jorgensen wasn't a fit for the crime. Sean had done some subtle poking around, and the picture he was getting of Brooke's ex was more consistent with that of a hotheaded asshole than a cold-blooded killer.

Jorgensen emerged from the gym. Right on time. It was exactly one hour since the desk clerk inside had called to give Sean the heads-up. Jorgensen was distracted with his phone, and Sean took the time to look him over. The man was bigger than he had expected and pumped up from his workout, and Sean began to second-guess his decision to do this alone. He'd thought about bringing Ric or Jasper, but this move was strategic. It wasn't about muscle.

Even so, Sean knew there was a chance he was about to get his nose broken.

Jorgensen glanced up and noticed Sean watching him. His gaze went to Sean's badge and gun, but there was no recognition or even suspicion—which was good news because that meant he hadn't been following Brooke's every move.

Sean pushed off his truck and walked over. "Matt Jorgensen?"

Suspicion kicked in. "Yeah?"

Sean stopped in front of him, blocking the path to his truck. The man had three inches and at least fifty pounds on him, but Sean's detective shield counted for a lot in cop circles.

"Sean Byrne, SMPD. You and I need to talk."

Jorgensen looked mildly annoyed. "What about?"

"Brooke Porter."

The light came on as Jorgensen realized this wasn't something work related. He crossed his arms, and Sean noted the scars Brooke had told him about.

"What about her?"

"Brooke's a friend of mine. Which means I'm watching out for her."

Jorgensen's gaze narrowed.

"And when I'm not around, my friends are watching out for her. And when they're not around, *their* friends are watching out for her. You need to leave her alone."

Jorgensen stared down at him. Sean didn't blink. Several seconds ticked by, and finally Jorgensen looked away.

"Look, you can tell Brooke I don't give a shit what she does anymore."

Sean studied him, trying to get a read. To his surprise, the man seemed genuine. Maybe he had come to terms with the situation and decided to cut his losses. Or maybe not. Only time would tell.

Jorgensen nodded at the door. "Do you mind?"

Sean stepped back. Jorgensen slid into his truck, started it up, and drove away.

• • •

"You're late," Callie hissed as Sean dropped into the seat beside her.

He glanced at the clock on the wall, then at the faces around the conference table. The whole team was here, with the notable exception of Christine, who'd pulled the overnight shift at the judge's house, and Jasper, who was on surveillance right now.

"It's always better if you have the devices," Alex Lovell was saying. The cybercrimes expert sat at the head of the table with a laptop open in front of her. "But since those haven't been recovered, I used data from the phone company to get an overview."

Sean glanced at Callie, who was watching him closely. He'd gone by his house to shower and change, but something told him he hadn't managed to erase the evidence that he'd been up most of the night.

"Anything interesting in the phone records?" Ric asked Alex.

"A lot. The records show that these victims were in contact with each other several weeks before they were murdered. I found phone calls on November first, third, and tenth."

"Any record of them texting?" Sean asked.

"No."

"What about any calls to Eric Mahoney, our prime suspect?" Callie asked.

"No, but I found some other communications you might be interested in."

Around the table everyone perked up.

Alex tapped some keys on her computer. "Okay, so it doesn't appear that Jasmine Jones owned a computer."

"We didn't find one," Ric said. "She was renting a room in a girlfriend's apartment, and her possessions were minimal. She'd sold her car after losing her job a few months ago, and it looks like she was pretty close to broke."

Alex nodded. "But I *was* provided with a laptop belonging to Samantha Bonner. She had an email account through the university, where I understand she was a part-time student."

"That's right," Ric said. "But I thought we checked those emails. You're saying we missed something?"

"That edu email wasn't her only account. A detailed search of her browsing history turned up a Gmail account that she used infrequently."

"How infrequently?" Sean asked.

"The in-box is mostly ads and spam. So I'm guessing it's a secondary email address she gave out to stores and companies that she didn't want cluttering up her primary account. The in-box is full of junk and the out-box is empty, *however*"—Alex tapped her computer and an email message flashed onto the large display screen on the wall—"the drafts folder contained this unfinished message, dated October thirtieth."

Sean's pulse quickened as he read the words:

Time's ticking. You know what you have to do. We have the—

"It cuts off in midsentence," Callie noted.

"Like I said, it appears to be a draft she never sent."

"Who's johnjohn9987?" Sean asked, reading the recipient address in the header.

"I don't know."

"It says 'we,'" Ric pointed out. "You think she's talking about herself and Jasmine?"

"Could be, although I found no email communication between the two of them, only phone calls."

Ric turned to Sean. "Sounds like some kind of extortion plan."

That had been Sean's first impression, too. "We need more on this johnjohn person. Clearly, it's a guy."

"You can't necessarily assume that. But after running down this account, I'd say it's a good bet."

"What do you mean 'running down this account'?" Callie asked. "You hacked into it?"

Alex smiled. "Let's just say I accessed the account through creative means." She tapped her computer, and another screenshot came up behind her. This one showed an in-box filled with unopened messages. "As you can see from the subject lines, whoever has this johnjohn9987 account is getting bombarded with ads for erectile pills, sex toys, online dating sites."

"I get some of that stuff, too," Callie said. "That doesn't make the account holder a guy."

"True. But as far as the username, the one attached to this account is a John Green."

"Sounds phony," Sean said.

Alex nodded. "I agree. So, we're basically left scouring the account itself for clues. Thing is, there's no record of an email from Samantha Bonner's Gmail address in here. So, if she ever sent a message like the one in her drafts folder, it looks like johnjohn9987 deleted it. *However—*"

Sean was beginning to like how Alex said that word, and he watched with interest as she clicked into another screen.

"I found *this* interesting message in johnjohn's junk folder. Looks like it got caught in the spam filter, so johnjohn might never have seen it."

Sean leaned forward as he read the message:

Clock's ticking. You know what you have to do. We have the proof so don't make us go public.

"Now that definitely sounds like extortion," Ric said.

Sean read the sender name, JMJFlowergirl. "Those are Jasmine's initials. Jasmine Michelle Jones."

"And her name is a type of flower." Callie looked at Sean. "The second victim sent this. And it's almost identical to a message in the first victim's drafts folder."

"And look at the timing, November second," Sean said. "That's right after the draft message. Samantha and Jasmine were working together to extort this guy. Wonder what this 'proof' is they're threatening to make public. Maybe pictures or video or something?"

"But where's the money demand?" Callie asked.

"Maybe a separate email that got deleted. If this message ended up in the Junk folder, maybe they emailed him again sometime later." Sean looked at Alex. "Is that possible?"

"Yes."

"Okay, but who are they trying to shake down?" Ric asked. "We have no link to our prime suspect, Eric Mahoney. Or am I missing something?"

All eyes turned to Alex, and Sean liked the satisfied look on her face.

"I traced the IP to find out where these johnjohn emails are being pulled. Only two locations came up. One is a location in Marshall County, about a hundred miles south of here. The second location is in Burrville. The specific network is maintained by the county justice complex."

"That's the courthouse," Sean said. "That's our warrant right there."

"Hell yeah, it's our warrant." Ric pushed back his chair. "I'm going to go call Rachel, give her the update, see how fast she can move on this. Alex, will you talk through all this with the DA?"

"Of course. But are you sure you're ready to bring her in? I mean, yes, the courthouse is on this network, and that would include Eric Mahoney's office. But I can't trace this to him specifically. At least not yet. I know you guys are in a hurry, but I've got some more work to do here."

"Keep working." Ric got to his feet. "But in the meantime I'm going to see what we can do with what we have."

He left the room, and Alex watched him go with a look of concern.

"Don't worry," Sean told her. "Rachel makes a habit of dotting all the *i*'s and crossing all the *t*'s." He turned to Callie, who was staring at the screen on the wall. "What's wrong?"

"I'm still not convinced."

"How can you not be convinced? Alex just linked both victims to our prime suspect with an extortion scheme."

"Walk me through it," Callie said. "I want to play devil's advocate."

Sean summoned all his patience, when what he

wanted to do was race over to the courthouse and drag the judge off in handcuffs. "Okay, so we know these victims knew Judge Mahoney when they were teenagers. And Mahoney associates with crooked cops who have been known to hook up with underage prostitutes."

Alex looked startled. "He does?"

"*Allegedly,*" Callie said. "But fine, keep going."

"So, say he somehow manipulated these girls while he had control over their cases. It's a classic abuse of power. These girls are isolated and vulnerable, they're in trouble with the law and have zero credibility. So he demands sex from them."

"Where?"

"Could have been a lot of places. I've seen some sick stuff over the years when it comes to abuse. The point is, these were troubled teens, and that's why he picked them. A lot of kids like that end up on the streets or on drugs, in jail, you name it. They slip through the cracks, which is why they appeal to predators like Mahoney."

Callie shuddered. "That's twisted."

"I see it all the time with internet predators," Alex said. "They have a knack for finding victims who are trapped in bad circumstances, and they manipulate them into keeping quiet. You wouldn't believe how often it happens."

"But then these two girls crossed paths at some point," Sean said. "Maybe they compared notes along the way, maybe through AA, and realized they'd been abused by the same man, who's still sitting in his position of power, probably still doing it. So, they decided to confront him and shake him down for money. We know Jasmine was nearly broke. Maybe she convinced Samantha to help her, and together they confronted

Mahoney. When threatened with exposure, the man snapped and killed them. First Samantha. And then Jasmine."

"What about the drugs in Samantha's car?"

"Like we said at the beginning, that could be a plant to throw off investigators."

"I think you have a long way to go to prove all that," Alex said.

"We'll get there," Sean said. "Wait until we get a warrant for the judge's phone and computer, and we can start connecting all these dots. I'll bet he has a pair of shoes with a herringbone tread pattern and an empty sheath from that hunting knife we recovered. We need to search his home, his car, his office."

Alex didn't look convinced as she packed up her laptop. "I've got to get back to Delphi. I'll let you know when I dig up more, but I figured you guys would want to know about this."

Sean got to his feet. "Thanks for coming in."

"I'll be in touch." She walked out.

Sean turned to Callie. "I knew this was going to happen today. I fucking knew it when I got up this morning."

"*Sean.*"

"What?"

"Nothing's happened yet. And this isn't enough for a warrant."

"Are you kidding? I bet we have something by lunchtime."

Callie stood and put her hands on her hips. "Sean, *think*. We still don't have conclusive evidence that Eric Mahoney is our guy."

"Did you listen to a word Alex said?"

"Yes, I did, as a matter of fact. She said those emails

were pulled from two locations, and one of them happens to be the courthouse."

"Exactly."

"Yeah, and who else has a reason to be in and out of the courthouse? *Bradley* Mahoney. The lawyer. Who practices law in Burr County, among other places, and also happens to be the judge's nephew. Who's to say that guy didn't sit down at some clerk's computer to check his email? Or duck into his uncle's office to use his computer? Or, for that matter, it could be anybody. Right now we have no way of knowing exactly who was actually sitting at that computer terminal logging on to the Gmail account that's receiving extortion messages from JMJFlowergirl."

"I can't believe you're dragging your feet on this. Don't you want to arrest this scumbag? He's probably still operating this whole scheme."

"Yes, but I want to do it by the book."

"We are."

Callie crossed her arms. "Is it or is it not possible that some other person besides the judge could have logged on to an email account from a computer at the courthouse?"

"Sure, it's possible."

"So, until we know for sure that Eric Mahoney is our killer, I don't think this is enough. And I think we need to tell that to Rachel. She's not even aware that one of the suspects we've looked at is an attorney who is in and out of that same courthouse."

Sean stared at Callie. He couldn't believe she was putting up this much resistance.

"At the very least," she said, "we need to get corroboration from another source, such as the DNA on that drinking glass that Brooke is testing."

"*Brooke* is not testing anything. Her lab is. And I don't want her involved in this."

"She's already involved. And we'd be a lot better off if we have those results back so we know for certain we're right before we rush out and execute a warrant in the office of a sitting judge. This is a sensitive case, Sean. It could be a career wrecker if we botch this up. Why do you think Brooke went to all that trouble to get us that drinking glass?"

Sean ran his hand through his hair. "God damn it."

"I don't care if you think I'm being a pain in the ass. You're going to thank me if it turns out that DNA doesn't match and we're targeting the wrong guy."

Ric poked his head into the conference room. "Rachel's all over it. She said she'll have something for use within two hours."

He left, and Sean looked at Callie and said, "Go to Delphi and track down those DNA results."

"And where are you going?"

"To the courthouse to sit on this judge."

Sean swung by his desk to grab his jacket and was rushing out the door when Marjorie flagged him down.

"Sean, don't go anywhere."

He glanced at his watch.

"There's someone here to see you," the receptionist said. "Farrah Saunders? She says it's urgent."

Sean switched directions and headed for the lobby. "Where is she?"

"I put them in conference room A."

"Them?"

"She's got someone with her."

Sean crossed the bull pen to the conference room, where Farrah stood outside the door. She wore a black pantsuit and had her hair in a messy bun, and Sean could tell by the look on her face that she was in crisis.

"What's going on?"

"I have a question for you." She gazed at him and swallowed nervously. "Is Eric Mahoney the target of your investigation?"

Sean glanced at the closed door. "I can't discuss an ongoing—"

"Sean, please. I need you to be straight with me here. Is the judge a suspect?"

Sean paused for a moment. "Yes."

She closed her eyes.

"Farrah, whatever you've got for me, I need it now. I'm on my way to execute a search warrant."

She nodded. "I've got someone you need to talk to."

"Who is it?"

"Let me introduce you, and you can hear what she has to say."

CHAPTER 23

Sean could tell at a glance that Hannah Lipsky didn't want to be here. The nineteen-year-old wore ripped jeans and a black hoodie, and her sleeves were pushed up to her elbows, revealing an intricate vine tattoo on her skinny arms.

Sean introduced himself, and she watched with a sullen look as he took a seat.

"Thanks for coming in."

She didn't respond.

"I'll wait outside," Farrah said.

Hannah looked panicked. "Wait, you're not staying?"

"Would you be more comfortable?"

"Yes."

Farrah glanced at Sean before pulling over a chair from the corner of the room. She positioned it so that she was between Sean and the witness, as though she were a mediator or maybe a court-appointed attorney.

Hannah had brown hair dyed black at the ends, and hostile blue eyes, which she settled on Sean. "So . . . what do you want to know?"

"Why don't I start with some background." Farrah looked from Hannah to Sean. "Four years ago, Hannah was arrested as part of a drug raid over in Burr County."

"You were fifteen?" Sean looked at her. She could have passed for fifteen now with those bony arms, and Sean noticed the parallel scars inside her wrists.

"Almost sixteen. I was at my boyfriend's place, and these cops kicked in the door and cuffed everyone up." She shrugged.

"Hannah appeared in Judge Mahoney's courtroom following her arrest. She had no prior record at that time—"

"Shoplifting," Hannah cut in.

"Oh. Excuse me. Shoplifting." Farrah nodded. "Anyway, the judge gave her probation with thirty hours of community service." Farrah paused and looked at Hannah. "Why don't you tell Detective Byrne what happened after that?"

Hannah shifted in her chair and refolded her arms. Sean watched her, hoping he was wrong about what she planned to say.

"So, then"—she cleared her throat—"about three weeks later, or maybe it was a month—I don't know—but I was still on probation, and I snuck out of my house to go to the park with some friends and this cop rolls up, and he's, like, 'Hey, who's got the weed?' "

"Which park?" Sean asked.

"Mayfield. Over by the train tracks."

"It's in Burrville," Farrah said.

Sean nodded.

"So . . . he starts patting us down, you know. I had a bag on me. He told my friends they could go, and then it's just me and him, and he asks me my name and I tell him, and he runs me and finds out I'm on probation, and then he's, like, 'What are we gonna do about this, Hannah?' "

Sean gritted his teeth as she shifted in her chair again.

"And then he's, like, 'Think we need to take you to see the judge.'"

Sean looked at Farrah, and she was watching Hannah intently.

"And where did he take you?" Sean asked.

"It was late. Maybe eleven or something, so I thought maybe he was taking me to the police station, but he took me to the courthouse. He parked around back and said the judge was in his office." She looked down at her arms. "We went up, and there he was sitting behind this desk with a green lamp on it. And he"—she hesitated a beat—"he waved me over and he wanted me to blow him, so I did."

"He asked you for oral sex?"

"He didn't *ask*. But it was obvious, all right? He had his pants unzipped and he was just hanging out there, like, waiting for me to do it."

"Where was the officer at this point?"

"In the hallway. On the other side of the door." She looked away.

"Hannah."

She met his gaze.

"Did the officer ever identify himself to you?"

She shook her head. "He was big. I remember that. He looked like a skinhead. I don't know his name, but he had a gun and a badge and his car smelled like vomit."

Farrah cleared her throat, and Sean looked at her. "We walked through the incident this morning, in great detail. Hannah let me record our session on my phone."

Sean nodded. "What happened after that, Hannah?"

She shrugged and looked away. "That was it. He zipped up. And he said, 'You're free to go.' And I walked out, and the cop was waiting for me."

"Where did he take you?"

"Back to the park. He dropped me there and told me to stay out of trouble or I'd have to go before the judge again. I remember that, 'go before the judge,' like it was a trial or something."

Sean clenched his teeth as he watched her. His gaze went to the scars on her wrists. He thought of Jasmine's file that he'd spent half the night reading in front of Mahoney's house. Jasmine had been admitted to the ER for a drug overdose when she was fifteen, the same summer she first appeared in Mahoney's courtroom.

Sean took a deep breath. "So, he dropped you off in the park . . . and then what did you do?"

"You're asking if I went to the police?" She sneered. "Who would believe me?"

"That's not what I'm asking. But where did you go?"

She brushed a tear from her cheek and looked down. "I wanted to go to my boyfriend's but . . . I couldn't. I didn't want to tell him, so I went home. My mom was passed out. She never even knew I was gone."

• • •

Brooke knelt beside the ditch and collected a shard of glass with a pair of tweezers. At the sound of footsteps, she turned to see Roland standing behind her finishing off a sandwich.

"Hey, thanks for joining us."

"I was at lunch." He dusted off his hands and crouched beside her. "What's the scoop?"

"SUV versus pedestrian. Hit and run."

Roland grimaced. "Damn."

"The paramedics just left with the victim. She was in bad shape." Brooke nodded at the pool of blood on the asphalt a few feet from where Maddie was setting up her tripod. A uniform had put down cones to reroute traffic.

"This the headlamp?" Roland asked.

"That's right. I've got this area covered, but you could go help Maddie. We haven't had time to measure the tire marks yet."

Roland stood and walked off as Brooke's phone chimed in her pocket. She sealed her evidence envelope and dropped it into her kit, then pulled out her phone.

"Porter."

"Brooke, it's Kaitlyn. Kaitlyn Spence."

The distress in her voice made Brooke stand up. "What's wrong, Kaitlyn?"

"Has Cameron called you? Have you seen him?"

"No, why?"

"Oh, God."

"Isn't he in school?"

"*No.* I just came from there. I was supposed to pick him up after lunch for his interview with the police artist and I went by to get him and he wasn't in the office and his science teacher says he never showed up for fourth period—"

"Kaitlyn, where are you right now? Have you called the police?"

"I'm almost there. Maybe he went over there without me. But why would he do that? The police station is, like, two *miles* from the middle school!"

Brooke's heart was racing now. "Yes, but . . . maybe he's there. Cameron walks everywhere, right? Two miles isn't a long distance for him."

"But he's not answering his phone."

Brooke looked at the congested road where a uniformed officer directed traffic around the accident scene. "Kaitlyn, listen to me. When you get to the police station, if Cameron's *not* there, ask for Sean Byrne or Ric Santos right away. Tell them what happened."

"I don't know what happened! He's just *gone*! Why isn't he at school? Are you sure you haven't missed a call from him?"

"I'm sure, but why would he call me?"

"He's been begging me to call you to see if you could bring Fenway to the shelter to visit us."

Brooke felt a swell of hope. "Maybe he went to see Fenway. Did you call your neighbor who's taking care of him?"

"She was my first call. I thought maybe Cam cut class to go visit the dog, but Mrs. Nance hasn't seen Cam since we were there together on Monday. Where could he have gone?"

"I don't know." Brooke packed her evidence kit and clicked the lid shut. Roland was going to have to take over with this crime scene so she could follow up on this.

"I have to go now, Brooke. I just pulled into the police station."

"Maybe Cam will be there," Brooke said, trying to project a calm she didn't feel.

"Brooke, he wouldn't just disappear like this! There's something wrong."

CHAPTER 24

Ric called as Sean and Jasper were rolling up to the courthouse.

"The warrant came through. Where are you guys?"

"We just pulled up," Sean told Ric. "Anyone heard from Callie?"

"No, but we're ready to move."

"Okay, we'll meet you in the lobby."

Sean got out of the car as a call from Callie came in. Last time he'd talked to her, she'd been headed to the Delphi Center.

"Hey, Callie, what's the word?"

"I talked to Mia's assistant in the DNA lab. The profile from the drinking glass matches the profile from the victim's fingernails."

Sean stopped on the sidewalk in front of the courthouse. The Honorable Eric J. Mahoney had killed Samantha Bonner. And they had proof because Brooke had tailed the man yesterday and collected his DNA.

All of Sean's suspicions were confirmed, but the relief he'd expected didn't come. Instead he felt a heavy ball of dread in the pit of his stomach.

"Sean?"

"I'm here."

"We've got the son of a bitch! Why aren't you excited?"

"I'll be excited when he's in custody." Sean nodded at Jasper and they crossed the street. "We're at the courthouse now with the warrant. We've got another team at his house, waiting for the green light. Why don't you head over there and help with the search of the residence?"

"Okay, see you back at the station."

They entered the lobby, flashed their badges at the guard, and walked around the metal detector. Ric and Christine came in through the back entrance and met them at the elevator.

"Everything in order with the warrant?" Sean asked.

"I skimmed through," Ric said. "Looks like she's after everything but the kitchen sink. Computers, cellular devices, clothing, shoes."

"The knife sheath in there?" Jasper asked.

"Yep."

The elevator emptied and everyone stepped on. Sean jabbed the button for level two—luckily no civilians were riding up with them.

"Same as we talked about?" Ric asked.

"That's right. I'll handle the search and the inventory," Sean said. "You take the judge aside and try to convince him to come in for an interview."

"No judge is going to give an interview without a lawyer present," Christine said.

"You'd be surprised," Ric told her. "Some people think they're smarter than everyone. This judge might just waive his right to counsel."

"I'm not counting on it," Sean said, "but I *am* counting on you to keep him under control while we paw through his office."

"This should be fun," Jasper said as the doors dinged open.

They stepped off and turned onto a long corridor, and Sean imagined fifteen-year-old Hannah Lipsky walking this same route late at night in the presence of a cop. Courtrooms lined the left side of the hallway. They passed Judge Mahoney's courtroom, which was empty at the moment, and reached a glass door for a private office.

"Ready?" Sean asked.

Everyone nodded.

Sean strode into the waiting room and cut straight to the reception desk.

"Detective Sean Byrne, SMPD, for Judge Mahoney."

The receptionist looked alarmed by the sudden crowd of people, two of whom were uniformed officers.

"Uh . . . I'm sorry. You're who?"

"Where is the judge, ma'am?"

"The judge . . ." She glanced around, flustered. "He's out right now. Would you care to—"

"We have a search warrant for his office." Sean slapped the paperwork on the counter as Ric walked past the reception desk.

"Sir? *Sir*?" The woman jumped to her feet. "You can't just go back there! He can't go back there!" She turned to Sean with a frantic look. "What is the meaning of this?"

"Where is the judge?"

"He left. After his hearing ended."

Sean's gut clenched. "*When* did he leave?"

"Uh, I think . . . it was about eleven?"

Ric returned to the waiting room. His gaze locked on Sean's and he shook his head. No judge.

What the fuck? Sean turned to Christine. "I thought you had eyes on him this morning?"

"We did. We do." Now Christine looked flustered. "His Escalade is parked right down there in the parking lot."

Sean jerked his head at Jasper. "Get started on the office."

"Down the hall and to the right," Ric told him.

"Where's the judge's assistant?" Sean demanded.

"That's me."

"What is your name, ma'am?"

"Connie Hudson." She was still standing, and she reached for the phone beside her computer.

Sean leaned over the counter and stopped her. "Not so fast. Where, exactly, did the judge go?"

Her cheeks flushed crimson. "I don't *know*. He didn't tell me. He went into his office and hung up his robe and left."

"Where's his bailiff?" Ric asked.

"He left, too. He said he felt sick and needed to go home."

Ric looked at Sean.

"When was this?" Sean asked.

"About, I don't know, an hour ago? Not long after the judge."

Ric pulled out his cell phone. "Tell us his name."

• • •

Brooke swung onto Cameron's street, searching for any sign of the boy or his dog. She was driving too fast and nearly hit a silver Audi backing out of a driveway as she pulled up to Cameron's house and parked.

Should she try Cameron's or the neighbor's house

first? Her question was answered when the neighbor's front door opened and Fenway darted out, straining against the leash held by an elderly woman. The dog was yapping wildly and trying to drag the woman down the steps.

"Mrs. Nance?" Brooke crossed the lawn, and Fenway turned his attention to Brooke, barking and lunging.

"Fenway, no! Stop that!"

Brooke stayed out of biting range. "Mrs. Nance, I'm a friend of Kaitlyn's and I'm trying to locate Cameron. Has he been by here?"

"Kaitlyn called me," she said, looking confused. "*What* is this all about?"

A long horn blast pulled Brooke's attention down the street where a minivan narrowly missed the speeding Audi as it blew through a stop sign.

Brooke stared after the silver car. Suddenly her blood turned cold.

"I haven't seen Cameron. Isn't he in school?"

Brooke looked at Mrs. Nance. "I . . . um, excuse me."

Brooke ran back to her car and jumped behind the wheel. She grabbed her phone to call Sean. Putting it on speaker, she tossed it into the passenger seat, then threw her car into gear and sped away.

"Come on, come on. Pick *up*," she muttered, barely slowing at the stop sign.

"I can't talk right now," Sean said. "I'll call you back."

"*Wait.* Where is Mahoney?"

Silence on the other end.

"Sean? Do you have eyes on him?"

"No. Why? Where are you?"

"I thought he was under surveillance!"

"He gave us the slip. Brooke, where are you? What's wrong?"

She gunned the gas and tried to catch up to the silver Audi that was quickly fading from view.

"*Brooke*?"

"I'm at the Spences' house. Or I was. Cameron is missing, and a silver Audi just went tearing out of here—"

"What do you mean, *missing*?"

"Sean, what kind of car does Mahoney drive?" She floored the pedal as the Audi hung a left at a stoplight.

"A black Escalade. You said a silver Audi? Hold on."

She heard muffled conversation on the other end as Sean talked to someone.

"Joe Hurd drives a car like that. That's the judge's bailiff. You think Cameron is with him?"

"I don't know." She slammed on the brakes, and her car rabbited to a halt at the intersection, nearly hitting a pickup truck in front of her. Brooke smacked her steering wheel.

"Where are you, Brooke?"

"I'm at"—she glanced around—"Cherrywood Road and Market Street. Sean, you have to get someone over here. They just turned south on Market. They're getting away!" She glanced in her rearview, then threw her car into reverse and shot backward. Shifting into drive, she maneuvered around the pickup truck, prompting a chorus of honks as she drove onto the median and hung a left in pursuit of the Audi.

"We're sending patrol units now. Did you actually *see* Cameron in the car?"

"No. I haven't seen him at all." She swerved around

cars, trying to catch sight of the Audi, but she couldn't spot it. "I don't even see the car anymore. Sean, what if they have Cameron?"

In a flash of silver the Audi came into view. Brooke punched the gas, barely making the next traffic light as it turned red.

"Brooke, are you listening? We have units en route. You need to pull over."

"Are you crazy? They'll get away!"

"Brooke, *pull over*. You're going to get hurt—"

"I'm not letting them out of my sight, Sean. They might have Cameron!"

More muffled voices as he talked to someone.

The Audi hung a left onto a state highway.

"They're turning onto Highway 46 southbound. Can you tell your people?"

"Brooke—"

"I'm not pulling over, so save your breath." She swerved around a delivery truck.

"Okay, just . . . listen. Whatever you do, you cannot let them see you. Do you understand? We think the judge and his bailiff could be in that car. We think they're armed and dangerous. Hang way back, and do not confront them, whatever you do. Got it?"

"Yes."

"I have to jump off, but I'll call you back."

Brooke tossed her phone aside and focused on driving. Her heart raced. Her hands felt slick on the steering wheel as she waited for a break in traffic and made the turn onto the highway. The Audi was far ahead now, but with a fair amount of traffic on the four-lane road, she hoped she could keep from being spotted.

Maybe she'd been spotted already. She wasn't trained

in covert vehicle pursuit. She wasn't trained in any of this, and Sean was probably right that she should pull over and let the police handle it.

Only the unshakable certainty that they had Cameron in that car with them kept her going.

She eased into the right lane, where she'd be less conspicuous as she kept a steady pace behind the Audi. Minutes passed as they neared the outskirts of town. Where were the cops? Were they on their way? Or maybe they were already in pursuit in unmarked units. Brooke glanced around at the other vehicles on the road, but none looked like a cop, undercover or not.

She nudged her speed up as she trained her gaze on the silver sedan in the distance. It was just driving. Not erratically, not too fast. It was moving only a few miles per hour above the speed limit, as though the driver had no idea she was back here following him.

He hadn't spotted her.

She took a deep breath and tried to calm her nerves. It didn't work. Brooke knew, in her heart of hearts, that Cameron had been grabbed and that he was *in* that vehicle. It belonged to Mahoney's bailiff, and it had been speeding away from Cameron's house. Now that the driver was out of Cameron's neighborhood, he seemed to want to blend in with traffic.

Had Cam cut class and gone home to see his dog, as his mother suspected? Had he been avoiding the police interview?

Whatever had happened, Brooke had no doubt he'd crossed paths with some dangerous people.

A horrible thought jumped into Brooke's mind and she gripped the wheel tighter.

What if Cam *wasn't* with them? What if he hadn't

been kidnapped at all? Maybe whoever was in that car had already hurt him and was speeding away from the crime scene when Brooke showed up?

Brooke passed a sign for an upcoming juncture. They were nearing the interstate. The Audi slowed suddenly. Was it turning? Brooke tapped her brakes, struggling with what to do as the Audi pulled into a gas station.

She clutched the wheel. Should she follow or drive on? Were they checking for a tail?

Brooke drove past the gas station, which was busy with cars and pickups and a few long-haul rigs. She spotted the Audi as it glided up to a pump.

They were fueling up. At least, that's what it looked like. Brooke kept the gas station in her rearview mirror as she moved through the intersection. After less than a mile, she made a U-turn and doubled back.

The Audi was still at the pump, the driver's-side door open and a fuel hose attached to the tank. She took a deep breath and turned into the gas station. She stayed on the perimeter, edging around a large Suburban and curving around to park on the far side of the convenience store.

Brooke got out and scanned the area and quickly realized she had no idea what Joe Hurd looked like. She'd been in Mahoney's courtroom, but she couldn't remember his bailiff. She darted a glance inside the store, but she didn't see Mahoney among the customers in line at the register.

Brooke stopped and peered around the corner of the building at the gas pumps. Still no driver inside the Audi. A man sat in the front passenger seat talking on the phone. Was it Mahoney? He wore a baseball cap, and Brooke couldn't be sure.

"'Scuse me." A tall, heavyset man stepped past her, carrying a bag of ice on his shoulder.

On impulse, Brooke stayed at the man's side, casually walking with him across the lot toward a pickup truck with oversize tires. He gave her an odd look, and she smiled and then ducked behind a van parked at the pump beside the Audi.

Brooke crept around the van, then glanced around the side.

Baseball Cap Guy was still on the phone. Suddenly the door opened, and he got out. He wasn't Mahoney. The man was tall and barrel-chested, and his hair was black instead of silver. The baseball cap concealed part of his face, so she couldn't get a good look at the rest of his features.

He glanced around the parking lot, then checked his watch and ended the call. His gaze zeroed in on the Audi's trunk.

And Brooke *knew*. Cameron was in there. Alive or dead, he was in that trunk.

Another furtive glance around, and the man hurried into the convenience store.

Brooke's heart pounded crazily as she studied the car, looking for any movement in the trunk. After glancing around, she made a decision. She wiped her sweaty palms on her jeans, then ducked low and scuttled toward the back of the Audi. Softly, she tapped on the trunk.

No response. She glanced at the store again, but no one was coming out.

She crept alongside the car and peered into the back window. Nothing in the backseat. She crept to the trunk and tapped again.

Thud.

Brooke's heart skipped a beat. She ducked lower and tapped again, a rapid *tap-tap-tap*.

Another *thud*.

Adrenaline flooded her. He was in there! He was alive! She had to get help before—

A burst of pain blinded her.

CHAPTER 25

"God damn it. Why aren't they there yet?" Sean asked the dispatcher.

"They haven't spotted the car. Right now both units are heading southbound on Highway 46."

Sean ended the call and brought up a map on his phone, desperate for something to do as they sped across town and tried to catch up to Brooke.

"Where would they be going?" Sean looked at Jasper behind the wheel. "What's their destination?"

"No idea."

Sean zoomed out on the map. "Hays County, Seguin, *Marshall* County. That's it! That's where they're going. Has to be."

Sean dialed Callie, who answered right away. "Where are you?" he asked.

"I just left Delphi. Why?"

"Go back. Find Alex Lovell."

"What? I'm on my way to the judge's house to help with the search warrant."

"Mahoney's missing and so is his bailiff. We think they may have kidnapped Cameron Spence and are now heading southbound on Highway 46, in the direction of Marshall County."

"Wait, *what*? Why would they—"

"We don't know! We don't even know if it's them yet, but you need to find Alex and get her to pinpoint the location of that Marshall County computer network Mahoney was using to check his email. Maybe he's got a second home there, or a buddy does or something. The bailiff's name is Joe Hurd."

"But—"

"Just do it and get back to me." Sean lowered his voice. "We haven't caught up to them yet. Brooke is tailing their car, and I'm going crazy here."

Silence as Callie digested this news. "Okay, I'm on it." She clicked off.

Jasper switched on his siren briefly as they shot through an intersection. "Think that's where they're going? Marshall County?"

"I don't know."

"Why would they go there?"

"I don't know that either."

Sean looked out the window as acid churned in his stomach. Why hadn't their patrol units spotted the Audi yet? He picked up his phone to contact Brooke as a call crackled over the radio.

"Shit, what was that?" Sean turned up the volume.

The message came again—multiple reports of a carjacking at Benny's Truck Stop on Highway 46. The vehicle was a silver Audi.

Sean's heart lurched.

"A *car*jacking?" Jasper glanced at him. "What the hell?"

Sean reached over and switched on the siren. "Floor it."

• • •

Pain roared through Brooke's skull, so loud it dominated all her senses. It had a sound, an odor, a taste. It had a definite *feel*, like someone thumping relentlessly against her brain with a hammer.

Where am I?

Her thoughts were murky, as if she were waking up from a dream or a nightmare to the world's worst hangover.

But it *wasn't* a nightmare. No. With an icy blast of clarity, she realized this was real. She wasn't asleep and she wasn't hungover. She was awake and in agony and . . . moving. The surface under her vibrated, adding a steady hum to the bursts of pain already pulsing through her head.

She tried to open her eyes. But she couldn't. They wouldn't move. Panic zinged through her until she realized they *were* open, and she was staring into darkness because she had something over her head. That realization brought another zing of fear.

Breathe, she told herself. *Don't panic. And definitely don't move.*

She wasn't sure why or how, but she somehow knew that moving wouldn't be good. Moving would draw attention, and she was better off staying still.

Brooke's body jolted, sending darts of pain everywhere. She realized she was in a car.

Cameron.

The silver car.

The man with the ice.

Flashes of memory emerged from the void, but she couldn't get a clear picture.

Where the hell am I?

She squeezed her eyes shut, trying to force her brain to remember. She pictured the bumper of the silver car as she approached it. She pictured tapping on the trunk, and she remembered the burst of hope at the answering *thud.*

Cameron was in this car with her.

He was in the trunk, and she . . . was in the backseat. Curled on the floor with something dark wrapped around her head. A blindfold? A T-shirt? She didn't know. Slowly, carefully, she tried to move her hands, but they wouldn't budge. Her wrists were bound together in front of her, bound so tightly she couldn't feel her fingers as she tried to flex them.

And there were voices. Low, male, close by. They'd notice if she moved or made the slightest sound.

Cold sweat seeped from her pores as she tried to think of what to do. She was bound and blindfolded, being taken to an unknown place for an unknown purpose. The pain pulsing through her brain made it impossible to think, much less come up with a plan.

Another jolt. Another stifled yelp.

The voices stopped. She heard a squeak of leather as someone turned to look at her.

"She awake?"

A fresh spurt of panic went through her. Brooke bit down on her tongue and tried not to scream.

• • •

Sean felt like he was going to jump out of his skin.

"Where's the chopper?" he yelled above the noise around him.

"We're working on it," Reynolds said over the phone. His department didn't have a police helicopter, so they had to coordinate with the county, and multiple agencies meant multiple delays. The first 911 call had come in thirty-two minutes ago, and still no one had spotted the Audi. "Should be soon. And the Amber Alert should be up any minute."

Sean got off with his lieutenant and crossed the

parking lot to the white pickup truck where a sheriff's deputy was interviewing a man who had witnessed the "carjacking" that had actually been a kidnapping.

Sean had already talked to the guy. The man had watched as a young woman was struck in the head and then shoved into the back of a car. While the witness was calling 911, the car sped away and turned west onto the frontage road that picked up the interstate.

"And you're *sure* it was west?" the deputy was asking him.

"I'm sure."

Sean couldn't listen to him anymore. The guy was easily six-two, 210 pounds. If he'd rushed to intervene, he might have saved Brooke, but instead he'd stood there with his thumb up his ass.

Sean stalked back to the patrol car, where Jasper was on the radio.

"Still no sign of them," Jasper told Sean.

State troopers and sheriff's units had been combing the interstate in both directions for twenty minutes, but no one had seen the Audi, and Sean was beginning to think they were looking in the wrong place.

"Gimme your keys," he told Jasper.

"Why?"

"I have to get out of here. I have to look."

"I'll come with you."

"Fine, but I'm driving."

Jasper tossed him the keys, and they jumped into the car. Sean peeled out of the lot, hooking a right onto Highway 46.

"I thought the witnesses said they got on the interstate?"

"I think they got off."

"Why?"

"We've got half a dozen units looking, and no sign of them. I'm headed south."

Sean hit the gas as he checked his phone. Still no Amber Alert. He looked up at the sky. And still no sign of the police chopper.

He glanced at Jasper. "What?"

"Isn't that a gamble? Going south when all the witnesses said they went west?"

Sean didn't answer. Instead he stomped the gas.

• • •

The sharp pain had morphed into a sickening lump in Brooke's stomach, and she fought the urge to throw up. She didn't want to draw attention to herself on the floor of the car as they bumped along the road.

The noisy highway had given way to uneven asphalt many minutes ago. Then that, too, had disappeared, and now they were bumping along on a severely rutted road that was making Brooke dizzier by the minute.

She thought of Cameron in the trunk with his nervous stomach. She prayed he was alive and hadn't succumbed to suffocation or anything else. Had he been injured when they put him in there? Had they come up behind him with a blow to the head? Or maybe they'd threatened him with a gun.

Then again, he was little for his eleven years, and maybe they'd simply grabbed him and tossed him in the trunk.

You're not alone, Cam. I'm here.

CHAPTER 26

Callie was about to leave the Delphi Center when she got a call from Sean.

"Where are you?" he demanded.

"Hey, nice greeting."

"Brooke and Cameron have been kidnapped!"

"Are you serious?" she asked. But she could tell he was by the panic in his voice.

"She got grabbed at a truck stop. Where are you now?"

"At Delphi. I talked to Alex Lovell, and she ran down some info for us."

No answer.

Callie glanced around the lobby, which was busy with geeky-looking people hurrying to and fro. Some wore lab coats, others were in jeans and pocket protectors. Many carried cups from the coffee shop, which was where Callie had met with Alex just a few minutes ago.

"Sean? Did I lose you?"

"I'm here. What'd she say?"

"Alex traced the location of that Gmail user to an internet-café-slash-barbecue-joint in Latham, Texas. That's in Marshall County."

"Internet and barbecue?"

"Weird combo, I know. It's a small town."

"What's there? Any address listing for a Mahoney?"

"I tried that. I tried the name Hurd, too, but no luck." Callie stepped away from the traffic flow to stand beside the lobby windows. She put her phone on speaker so she could manipulate the maps app on her phone.

"So, what the hell's in Latham? Why would Mahoney go there? I need a destination, and I need it ASAP."

"I'm working on it." She zoomed in on the map, scanning the various streets and highways. The town was so small, almost no businesses were labeled. There was a post office, a grocery store, a meat processor. On the outskirts of town was a taxidermy shop.

"There's not much here," she told Sean.

"I need a lead. Have you talked to Mahoney's wife? She's bound to know why he goes down there."

"I haven't talked to her. Last I heard, she wasn't home, but Christine was trying to get her whereabouts from the maid who answered the door."

"*Shit.*"

"I know you're worried, Sean."

He didn't respond, but she could feel his anxiety coming straight through the airwaves.

"We'll locate them, okay? Sit tight." Callie glanced up at all the people bustling through the lobby.

Travis Cullen stood out. Broad shouldered, athletic. He stepped onto an elevator and turned around. His gaze settled on Callie as the doors slid shut.

"Sean? I need to check on something. I'll call you right back."

Callie stuffed her phone into her pocket and darted for the elevators, grabbing one just as the doors were closing. But it was headed up, of course, and she waited impatiently for everyone to get off on their various floors before she jabbed the button for the basement level where Travis worked.

She got off and jogged down the dimly lit corridor, accompanied by the *pop-pop* of gunfire coming from the firearms lab.

The door to the tool-marks lab was closed and locked, but Callie pounded on it anyway. He had to be here. She'd just seen him.

"Looking for someone?"

She turned around. Travis stood in the doorway of the firearms lab down the hall. He wore eye protectors and held a black pistol at his side.

"I need help."

His brows arched.

"It's urgent," she added because she was obviously interrupting something.

He disappeared from the doorway, then reappeared a moment later without the gun or the eye protectors. In a few strides he was beside her, using his badge to swipe into the office.

"What's the problem?"

"We've got a missing person. Two." Callie didn't have time to go into the whole story, so she jumped ahead. "That hunting knife you tested for us. You found human and animal blood on it, correct?"

He switched on a light and led her into the office. "The four-inch serrated blade, full tang."

"That's right. Any chance you know what kind of animal blood that was?"

He walked to a laptop sitting open on a counter and tapped a few keys. She hurried over to watch as he pulled up the report.

"*Odocoileus virginianus*," he recited. "Whitetail deer."

"*Yes!*"

"That's good news for you?" He gave her a puzzled smile.

"Maybe." Callie whipped out her phone and called Christine. "Hey, it's Callie. You get hold of the wife yet?"

"She just showed up," Christine said in a low voice. "I'm standing in her living room while she talks to the maid in the kitchen."

"Does she know what's going on?"

"Only that police are looking for her husband. The lieutenant didn't want to freak her out, so I'm here by myself, but she seems pretty alarmed to see me. She's got card tables set up here, and I get the impression she's having friends over this afternoon."

"Whatever. Listen, I need you to get her alone right now. Don't give her time to call her attorney or anyone, you got that? Get her alone and ask her the location of her husband's ranch property in Marshall County. It might be a deer lease."

Pause. "Mahoney has a deer lease?"

"We have reason to believe so, but we don't know where it is. Only that it's most likely in Marshall County. Ask her. Now."

"Hold on a sec."

Callie glanced at Travis, who was sitting there watching her with those nice forearms folded over his chest. She couldn't read the look in his eyes. "Sorry to interrupt you. You work in the ballistics lab, too?"

"Only when they're backlogged. Which is pretty much always."

"You like guns?"

He nodded. "You shoot?"

"Not if I can help it."

He gave her a funny look, and Christine was back on the phone.

"Okay, she's hedging, I can tell. Not exactly what you would call a cooperative witness."

"What'd she *say*?" Callie gripped her phone, hoping for something usable.

"She claims she knows nothing about a ranch in Marshall County. Her husband *used* to have a deer lease there that he shared with his brother, but she said his brother died, and her husband hasn't gone there in years."

"Bullshit he hasn't." Callie huffed out a sigh. "I need an address."

"I asked her that, but she swears that's all she knows."

"She's lying. Talk to her again. Tell her if she doesn't give you a location, you're going to haul her ass to jail and charge her with obstruction of justice, child trafficking, and conspiracy to commit murder."

"You seriously want me to say that to a judge's *wife*? I mean, she's got ladies in pearls showing up here for bridge right now."

"You say it or I will! Put her on the phone. We need this information, and we don't have time to dick around being polite!"

"Okay, just . . . hold on."

Callie closed her eyes and waited, trying not to grind her teeth to nubs. Her phone beeped. It was an incoming call from Sean, but she ignored it.

"Callie?" Christine sounded breathless as she got back on. "Okay, she spilled."

"Tell me you got an address."

"I'm texting it now."

"*Yes!* You're my hero."

She hung up with Christine and glanced at Travis, who was watching her with an amused look on his face.

"Thanks for your help," she said as she rushed for the door. "I owe you."

He smiled. "Definitely my pleasure."

• • •

With every bump and lurch, pain rocketed through Brooke's body. It seemed like hours now that she'd been knocking around on the floor of this car. With every minute that passed, she knew the chances of Sean or anyone else finding her were growing more and more remote.

Tears burned her eyes, but she squeezed them back, even though no one could see her crying beneath the hood or the T-shirt or whatever they'd wrapped around her head.

Breathe. Be calm. Think!

She had to come up with a plan. For Cameron. Whatever faint chance they had to get out of this depended on her, and she refused to lose hope. *Refused.* Even though logic told her it would be next to impossible for someone to find them in time. If someone had witnessed them leaving the gas station, that would be one thing. But there had been no sirens or even evasive maneuvers to indicate the driver was trying to outrun somebody.

No, they were off the grid. Defenseless. Just Brooke and an eleven-year-old boy and at least two armed men who were taking them somewhere extremely remote to do God only knew what.

Bile rose up in the back of Brooke's throat.

She couldn't let this happen. She had to do something. She pictured her body being dumped into a shallow grave. Then she pictured that grave being excavated. She pictured Sean standing nearby as people in white Tyvek suits dug her remains from the earth. He'd never get over it. He'd feel responsible, as though somehow this were *his* fault, even though he'd warned her over and over to stay away from his case.

She thought of sweet young Cameron, and her eyes filled again. She had to get it together and *do* something. He wouldn't even be here if it weren't for her. She'd felt connected to him ever since she'd crouched inside that pantry, staring at those cookie crumbs and imagining how events had unfolded.

Why had she been so clever? So tenacious? So intent on proving to Sean and everyone else that she could glean every last speck of evidence from every crime scene? Deep down, she knew. She'd wanted to show off, to earn their respect. And by doing so she'd endangered the life of an innocent boy.

Think.

She sucked a breath through her nose, trying to get oxygen to her brain without making a move.

An idea flickered in her mind. She drew in more air, fueling the idea as it started to grow.

Brooke sank her teeth into her tongue until the coppery taste of blood filled her mouth. She swished it with saliva and then quietly spit into the cloth wrapped around her head. She dug her fingers into her palms until the nails bit into her skin and she felt the welcome wetness of blood. Whatever happened here or anywhere else, she would leave her DNA behind for investigators.

A sharp dip, and her head smacked against the floor. She sucked in a gasp as the car rattled over something. A bridge? Too small. It had to be a cattle guard.

Brooke's pulse raced. Her palms were damp now, from a combination of blood and sweat and the pure fear seeping out of her with every passing second.

The ride grew bumpier and more painful and seemed to go on and on until she wanted to scream.

They jerked to a stop. Brooke held her breath. She listened. Doors opened, weight shifted, doors slammed shut.

She stayed perfectly still and listened. She heard nothing but the frantic pounding of her heart. Minutes ticked by. Had they been abandoned?

The door opened. Big, sharp hands dug under her armpits and dragged her out, then released her to smack her head against the ground.

The air was cold. Damp. It whipped through her shirt and chilled her sweat-soaked skin.

A low grunt near her ear as someone dragged her backward and leaned her against the car.

"Don't move." The voice was harsh and commanding, but it didn't belong to the judge. His bailiff, maybe?

A metallic *pop*.

Brooke went rigid with fear as she listened to something being pulled from the trunk.

Then a squirming, sniveling body was lowered to the ground beside her, and Brooke's heart squeezed because, thank God, he was *alive*.

Their shoulders didn't touch, but Cameron's warmth penetrated her skin, along with his terror. His breath came in short, choppy gasps, and she hoped he wasn't having an asthma attack.

Calm down, Cam. It's okay. I've got you, she tried to tell him with her mind, although it was utterly absurd, and she didn't have anything, not a damn *thing*, that would get them out of this situation. But he had to calm down. She shifted her leg and pressed her knee against him.

You're not alone. I'm right here. I'm—

The cloth over her head was whipped off.

Brooke blinked into the brightness.

A dark silhouette loomed over her, blocking out the sun. She squinted up at him.

And found herself staring at the barrel of a gun.

CHAPTER 27

Brooke's mouth went dry. She stared at the round black hole, immobilized with terror.

A screen door slapped shut, and she turned toward the sound as a bulky, black-haired man stepped from a ramshackle cabin nearby.

Where the hell were they?

And who was *he*?

He had brownish skin and jet-black hair, and his brown eyes zeroed in on her as he approached.

Brooke glanced at Cameron beside her. He had a black T-shirt wrapped around his head, and his shoulders were hunched forward as he buried his face against his knees. Blood had seeped through a rip in his jeans, and Brooke noticed what looked like vomit on the sleeve of his red sweatshirt.

The black-haired guy was talking to Baseball Cap, who still had the pistol pointed at Brooke. A Glock nine-mil. Having processed countless bloody crime scenes, Brooke hated guns. But at this moment she longed to snatch that thing out of his hand.

She shifted her gaze to the black-haired guy, who was watching her closely with those odd brown eyes. There was something odd about his skin, too. Almost as if . . .

Mahoney.

It was him.

He'd dyed his hair and spray-tanned his skin and put in colored contacts . . . But the cocky way he carried himself couldn't be disguised. He looked at her with contempt, as though her presence here was an unexpected pain in the ass. His gaze moved to Cameron, and he barked an order at Baseball Cap, who had to be his bailiff.

Hurd reached over and yanked off the T-shirt covering Cameron's head.

Cam gave a startled gasp. He blinked rapidly, and the tear tracks on his freckled cheeks made Brooke's heart ache. She couldn't resist leaning into him to offer some kind of comfort, but he wasn't focused on her at all. Even more surprising, he wasn't focused on the pistol pointed at him by Hurd.

No, his entire focus was on Mahoney.

The stark terror on Cameron's face eliminated the last shred of doubt in Brooke's mind. Cameron had witnessed a savage murder. He knew a secret, and now Brooke knew it, too.

And Eric Mahoney planned to make sure they took that secret to the grave.

• • •

The car ride had seemed endless, but now everything seemed to be happening too fast. Mahoney was in the shed, a corrugated-metal building that might once have housed a tractor or a couple of ATVs. A black pickup truck was parked there now, and Brooke watched it silently, recalling the heart-stopping moment when it had slowed in front of Cameron's house.

Cameron recalled it, too. Brooke could tell because

his whole body stiffened when he noticed the truck.

"Cam," she whispered.

"Hey!" Hurd pointed the pistol at her. "Shut the fuck up."

Cam darted a fearful look at Brooke. She wanted to talk him through some things, but Hurd wouldn't let her speak.

Mahoney crouched beside the back bumper, unscrewing the license plate. Brooke's heart drummed in her chest as she watched his brisk movements. The window was closing on her chance to get them out of this.

She looked up at the pistol still pointed at her. At the beast of a man holding it. He outweighed her by at least a hundred pounds. And he held that weapon like he knew how to use it.

Even armed, Brooke probably wouldn't stand a chance against him.

Brooke rested her hands on her knees. Her wrists were bound together with a zip tie, and she could no longer feel her fingers. She took a deep breath and shifted her jaw, which was sore from being clenched shut.

Brooke looked at Mahoney. "You know, I testified in your courtroom."

"Shut the fuck up."

She ignored the bailiff and focused on the judge. He was the alpha here even though he wasn't holding the gun.

Mahoney tossed a look over his shoulder. "I don't remember you."

"You should listen to your expert witnesses." She refused to look at Hurd because the judge had given her tacit permission to speak. "Really, we know what we're talking about. Every contact leaves a trace."

The judge darted an annoyed look at her. He tossed

the license plate into the shed like a Frisbee and picked up a Mexican license plate, and Brooke's heart skittered as another element of his plan fell into place.

"You're not going to get away with this. We've left DNA all over the place. In that backseat, in that trunk. On the ground here."

Mahoney got to his feet and disappeared into the shed. He returned with a red plastic gas can, which he set on the ground right next to her.

She was getting under his skin. She could tell. And she needed to get deeper.

"So . . . you plan to torch the car, is that it?" She shrugged. "Won't work. Not completely. We're leaving traces all over the place, just by sitting here breathing. You, too. You left skin cells on that gas pump. And fingerprints. And your face is on the surveillance tape."

Mahoney shot her a knowing look.

"You think a disguise will help you? Sorry to break it to you, but you're wrong about that, too."

Hurd eased closer. Brooke ignored his gun and plunged on, even though her mouth felt so tense she was surprised she could talk.

"Might fool a few border agents, maybe. But long-term? That won't work either."

Mahoney darted her a glare now as he tromped into the wooden cabin. The screen door slapped shut, and Brooke looked at her knees because she didn't want a confrontation with Hurd.

"You think you can talk your way out of this?" He turned and spit in the dirt. "Not going to happen."

A slight whimper beside her. Cameron hunched deeper into himself. His shoulders were practically at his ears now, and his face was buried against the torn knees of his jeans.

Mahoney was back with a shotgun slung over his shoulder. The easy way he carried it made Brooke's blood turn cold, and she immediately pictured him swinging the weapon up to shoot birds out of the sky. She pictured bursts of feathers and little carcasses raining down.

Hurd kicked her feet with his boots, and Brooke's confidence wavered. She'd been on a roll, but now she felt insanely reckless for opening her mouth.

Mahoney popped open the trunk and pulled out a black duffel bag. From the way he hitched it onto his shoulder, Brooke could tell the bag was heavy. Was it filled with weapons? Ammo? Money?

He unzipped the bag and pulled out three thick stacks of bills, which he handed to Hurd.

"You think they won't come after you? They will."

Mahoney dug some keys from his pocket and handed them to Hurd, too, and Brooke felt her window closing even further.

"Even plastic surgery won't help you! Certain things *can't* be disguised. The space between your nostrils, your pupils. The shape of your ears." The words spilled out of her as she looked at that shotgun. "Facial-recognition software will pick you up in a minute, and it's all over the world. There's nowhere you can hide. You think you're smarter than everyone, but you're wrong and your game is up!"

Mahoney swung the shotgun back and *whack*.

Brooke fell sideways, knocked breathless. Stars swam in front of her eyes. She pressed her bound hands against the ground and forced herself up. When her eyes were able to focus again, she looked at him.

It was working. She was getting in his head and

pissing him off. She was buying time, but it might not be enough.

Sean, Ric, Callie, somebody find us! She wanted to scream at the top of her lungs, but she forced herself to just stare defiantly.

Brooke knew this man better than he realized. She'd figured him out. His need for control was his Achilles' heel, and she had to use that to her advantage. It was the only advantage she had.

He stepped over to her, swinging the shotgun back and forth, missing her battered face by mere inches as he smiled down at her, enjoying her fear.

He stopped the motion with a loud *smack* of his hand against the barrel. The smile disappeared and his eyes turned cold as death.

"On your feet, bitch."

• • •

Sean skidded to a stop on the dirt road and checked the mailbox.

"It skips a number," Jasper said.

"This has to be it." Sean shoved the car into reverse and then hung a right onto the dirt road. They bumped along, passing several locked gates until they came to one that was propped open with a rock.

"Here?" Jasper looked at him.

Sean checked his phone again. Callie had sent him a satellite map of the area, and Sean checked it against the nearby landmarks.

"The third gate past the low-water crossing. This has to be it." Sean pushed open his door and looked at Jasper. "No noise."

They got out and looked around. Sean checked the sky, but still no sign of the police chopper that was supposedly combing the area. Several Marshall County sheriff's deputies were supposedly on the way, too.

Sean went around to the back and opened the trunk.

"Shouldn't we wait for backup?" Jasper asked.

"You can, but I'm going in."

"I am, too, then."

"Your call."

Sean reached into the trunk and grabbed the two long guns, a Remington 870 and a Ruger Mini-14 rifle.

"Which do you want?" Sean asked.

"I'm better with the Ruger."

Sean handed Jasper the rifle and took the shotgun for himself, along with a box of shells. Jasper combed through the trunk. He found a box of bullets and stuffed some in his pocket. Sean grabbed the Kevlar vest and handed it to him.

"You have it," Jasper said.

"No."

"Really, man." Jasper tried to hand it back, but Sean wouldn't take it.

"I outrank you. Put the damn thing on."

Jasper shook his head and pulled the vest on, tightening the Velcro straps as he glanced around.

"Remember the layout we talked about," Sean said. "There's only one road in. I'll keep to the western property line and circle around to the house. I expect they'll either be there or by this shed near the pond." Sean tapped the satellite map on his phone. "You come from the north, but keep off the road and try to stay out of sight."

"Roger that."

The distant hum of an engine had them both turning toward the open gate. Someone was on the move.

"Listen to me." Sean clasped Jasper's shoulder. "To Mahoney, prison with a bunch of convicts is a fate worse than death. You understand? He's going to feel cornered and desperate when he realizes we're here."

"I got it."

"Be careful." Sean gripped Jasper's shoulder. "And don't hesitate."

• • •

Brooke lay on her stomach in the truck bed beside Cameron as they bounced along the road, picking up speed. Where was Mahoney taking them?

"Cameron," she yelled over the noise.

He turned to face her, and he was crying. Brooke squirmed closer to him and used her bound hands to check his bindings. His zip cuffs looked even tighter than hers. But at least their feet were free.

She glanced at the back window of the truck cab to make sure Mahoney wasn't watching, but his attention was on driving.

"Cameron, I'm going to create a distraction, okay? When I signal you, you need to run for cover. Did you see all those scrubby-looking trees and bushes? Run there. Get as far away as you can and then *stay hidden.*"

The truck jerked to a halt. Mahoney jumped out. Then the tailgate opened with a squeak and he grabbed Brooke by the ankles. She scrambled out of the truck, landing hard on her tailbone. Mahoney seized her arm and hauled her to her feet, then grabbed Cameron by the ankles.

Brooke glanced around frantically. Nearby was a large pond surrounded by grass on three sides. The nearest tree cover was at least thirty yards away.

"Move!" Mahoney shoved her, and she tripped forward. He shoved her again, and she felt a sickening sense of déjà vu.

Her pulse raced as she struggled to formulate a plan. A weathered wooden pier stretched out over the water, and a small metal skiff was tied on the shore beside it.

She glanced at Cameron, then Mahoney. "You won't get away with this."

Another shove. "*Shut up.*" Mahoney pointed the shotgun barrel at the ground beside a wooden shed. "Sit down."

Cameron sat. Brooke lowered herself into a crouch, but Mahoney poked her shoulder with the gun, pushing her off-balance and onto her butt.

He tromped across the grass to the shed, which evidently had a door facing the water. She heard what sounded like a padlock rattling as she glanced around. She noticed a rock on the ground in front of her and snatched it up.

Mahoney reappeared with yet another black duffel bag, which he dropped beside the pickup.

"You think you're so smart?" Brooke yelled. "They *will* come after you! Everyone will. You're a disgrace to the justice system. You're an embarrassment. Every law enforcement officer in the state will track you to the ends of the earth."

He returned to the shed, and Brooke glanced at Cameron. She lifted her bound hands, showing him the rock. He nodded.

Brooke waited, trying to time the moment perfectly. She glanced at Cameron, who was perched on the balls of his feet now, ready to spring.

Mahoney returned to the truck, this time carrying a metal toolbox, which he heaved into the truck bed. The moment his back was turned, Brooke lifted her arms over her head and hummed the rock at the metal boat.

Ping!

Mahoney turned and jerked his gun up. He frowned in the direction of the noise and walked slowly toward it, pumping the shotgun with a loud *sch-schick*. Brooke's heart hammered in her chest as he moved past her and approached the boat. One step, two, three.

Cameron took off. He darted behind the truck, and Brooke held her breath, waiting for Mahoney to turn around.

A few seconds later, he did. His face flushed red when he realized Cameron was gone.

"God damn it." He stomped over to Brooke and kicked her ribs so hard she fell sideways. "Where'd he go?" When she didn't answer, he reached down and hauled her to her feet, sending a bolt of pain up her arm.

"On the pier. *Move!*"

Brooke forced herself not to look in the direction Cameron had fled. Instead, she looked at the pier. She took a tentative step forward. Then another. Thoughts raced through her brain faster than she could process them.

But as her foot touched the wood, everything slowed to a crawl.

All at once, she understood. She understood the remote location, the water, the pier.

"It won't work." She looked at him over her shoulder. "The cadaver dogs, they can sniff out anything. Even twenty feet deep. I've seen them do it."

He snugged the gun against his shoulder and took aim. "Shut up and walk."

Brooke's legs quivered. Her heart pounded. The blue-green water glimmered in front of her, and she thought of Sean. Her throat burned and she wished she'd told him. Why hadn't she told him everything she felt?

He would get here. She knew it. Maybe not in time for her, but in time for Cameron.

Please, Sean. Please, please, please.

Brooke swallowed a lump of fear in her throat. She pictured Cameron making a dash for the trees, and with every drop of hope left in her, she prayed he would make it.

She forced her feet to move, even as her lungs seemed to stop working. The shimmering water was closer and closer and closer, and she desperately wished she could stop time, but she could do nothing but hold her breath and brace for the blast. How fast would it happen? Would she even hear a sound?

The end of the pier loomed in front of her, and calm settled over her. She would never take those last steps for him. She wouldn't do it. No matter how futile it was, she was going to—

Crack.

Brooke lunged for the water.

• • •

The sound stole the air from Sean's lungs. He ran toward the gunshot and heard it again as he burst from the trees just in time to see Mahoney hobbling toward a black truck, clutching his arm to his chest.

Sean raised his shotgun and fired, but Mahoney ducked behind the cover of the vehicle. He heaved himself behind the wheel, and Sean fired again, shattering the back window.

The truck peeled away in a cloud of dust.

Movement caught Sean's eye, and he sprinted for the water.

"Brooke!"

She struggled toward the pier, using her legs to propel her.

Sean ran to pull her out. "Are you hurt?" He hauled her up and out of the water, and they collapsed into a wet heap on the wood.

"Cameron," she gasped.

"Are you okay?" His gut clenched as he got a look at her face. It looked like someone had hit her with a baseball bat. "Jesus Christ, what happened?" He whipped out his pocketknife and cut through her bindings.

"I'm fine," she choked. "We have to find Cam."

Sean wiped the wet hair from her face and took a good look at her. She was clearly injured, but she was talking and breathing, and already scrambling to her feet.

"I'll find him," Sean said, pulling her up. He helped her off the pier and glanced around for any sign of Jasper.

"There's two of them," Brooke gasped. "Mahoney and Hurd. Mahoney's in a black pickup. Hurd took off after he got paid."

"I saw Mahoney right after Jasper shot him. He's wounded and he's trying to make a break for it." Sean led her to the shed. "Brooke, listen to me. I have to go help Jasper. There's only one road out of here, and there's bound to be a confrontation."

"Cameron—"

"I'll look for him." Sean put the shotgun in her hands and wrapped her fingers around it. "Stay here. Stay low behind this shed. Have you ever fired a shotgun?"

"No."

Sean wished he'd taken the damn Kevlar so he could leave it with her.

"Sean, we have to find Cameron. He's hiding. He's—"

"First, I need to neutralize the suspects. Do you understand? If anything threatens you, point and shoot."

She looked down at the gun in her hands. She looked up and nodded, and Sean's heart swelled. She was bruised and beaten, but she was *alive*, and he was determined to get her out of here that way. Cameron, too.

He pulled his Glock from his holster and checked it. Then he kissed her forehead.

"Go," she said.

"I'll be right back."

• • •

He sprinted for the trees, and Brooke watched him disappear into the foliage. She stared after him, trying to catch her breath. The wind whipped through her wet clothes, and she felt cold all over.

She couldn't believe Sean was here. How had he found her? And why were he and Jasper alone?

She glanced down at the gun in her hands and pushed away from the shed. Her legs felt wobbly, but they weren't injured. Her face was another story.

She squeezed her eyes shut and remembered the crack of gunfire. She'd thought it was a shotgun blast. But it was Jasper shooting at Mahoney. Another second or two, and she would have been dead.

A shudder moved through her.

She took a deep breath and glanced around. On the ground near the spot where the pickup had been sat a black duffel bag.

He'd left it. Or dropped it in his haste. Brooke walked over and picked it up. It was heavy, and she wasn't surprised when she unzipped it and found two pistols inside, along with several spare magazines. She also found four, five, *six* thick bundles of cash, like the ones Mahoney had given Joe Hurd. Brooke couldn't leave the weapons there for anyone to grab, so she hitched the bag onto her shoulder and glanced around.

A flash of red near the trees caught her eye.

Cameron?

Brooke moved toward it. She gripped the shotgun in her hands and ducked low as she jogged toward the brush.

In the distance, the distinctive crunch of metal. Brooke froze and listened. A car crash? Was Sean involved? Maybe someone had intercepted Mahoney or Hurd as they'd tried to flee.

Brooke darted into the trees and glanced around for the red. It was Cameron's sweatshirt. Had to be. She pushed through some mesquite bushes and ducked between oak trees and cedars. Thorns snagged her clothes, and she swatted the branches away as she searched for Cameron.

In the distance she heard yelling. Then the faint wail of a siren. *Finally.*

A glimpse of red caught her attention, and she looked up to see Cameron sitting in a tree, wedged into the V where the limbs split.

"Gimme the bag," a gruff voice said.

Brooke whirled and lifted the gun just as Mahoney wrenched it from her hands.

His eyes were wild. Blood saturated his right arm, which hung limply at his side. His left arm held her shotgun with the stock resting against his hip.

"Take the bag off your shoulder and loop it over my head." His words were labored but forceful. She started to resist, but then she thought of Cameron in the tree. Had Mahoney seen him?

"Now."

Never taking her eyes off the judge, she slowly lifted the bag from her shoulder and held it out to him. He stepped closer.

"Loop it over my head."

He couldn't do it with his injured arm, not while keeping the gun pointed at her.

Brooke looped the bag over his head. Then she backed away, hands up.

A blur of red as Cameron leaped from the tree and landed on Mahoney, knocking him to the ground.

"No!" Brooke screamed, and lurched toward them.

Boom.

Fire tore through her leg. She rolled under some bushes and crashed into a tree trunk. Through the branches, she saw Mahoney charging toward her.

Pop.

Mahoney staggered back, clutching his shoulder. He collapsed with a yowl. The next instant was a blur of movement as Sean burst through the bushes. He landed on Mahoney, flipped him onto his stomach, and pinned his arms behind his back.

"Brooke!"

"Over here," she shouted.

"Brooke, *stay there*!"

More grunts and howls as Sean cuffed Mahoney and frisked him for weapons. The judge was bleeding and bellowing about his shoulder.

Brooke swiped the branches away and tried to sit up. She scooted out from under the bushes as pain blazed up her leg.

Then Sean was there. He dropped to his knees and

yanked his jacket off. “Jasper, get an ambulance! Now!” He leaned over her. “Brooke, you’re hit.”

“I know. I think . . . I think—” Her leg was on fire, and she couldn’t think at all. “Cameron . . .”

“Jasper’s got him. He’s fine.”

“Are you sure?”

“I’m sure.”

Brooke closed her eyes, and the relief was so intense it almost eclipsed the pain.

“Jasper!” Sean stripped off his shirt and started wrapping her leg in a tourniquet.

Jasper stepped through the bushes. “Paramedics on the way. ETA five minutes.”

“Get the boy out of here,” Sean ordered. “Take him to the sheriff’s units over by the gate, and then lead the paramedics back here. Got it?”

“Got it.”

Brooke groped for Sean’s hand and found it. “Stay with me. Please.”

“I’m right here. I’m not going anywhere.”

CHAPTER 28

Sean trained his gaze on the gray doors, willing them to open, but they wouldn't move.

"Sean." He turned around to see Callie stepping off the elevator. "What's the news?"

"Still nothing."

She had a cardboard coffee cup in her hand, and she held it out to him, but he shook his head.

"You sure?"

"Yeah."

She took a sip and turned to look at the doors. "I thought they said an hour?"

"They did." Sean glanced at his watch again. It had been nearly two hours since Brooke had gone into surgery, and still no updates. With every minute that ticked by, acid was eating away at Sean's stomach.

He glanced across the waiting room at Brooke's brother and his girlfriend, who were sitting in chairs beside a television no one was watching.

"Mahoney's out."

Sean looked at Callie and tried to process the words. "Out . . . ?"

"Of surgery. Sounds like his shoulder and arm are torn up, but otherwise he's okay. Doc says he'll be cleared to go later. Jasper and Ric are going to take him in. And Hurd is being booked as we speak."

A bitter lump clogged Sean's throat. Mahoney was going to be okay. Meanwhile, Brooke was still stuck back there—

The doors pushed open. A woman in blue surgical scrubs emerged and scanned the waiting room.

Sean rushed over, joined by Owen and Lin.

"How is she?" Owen asked.

"She's in recovery." The vise around Sean's heart loosened. "The surgery went well."

Lin slumped against Owen. "Oh, thank God."

"She's very lucky she missed a direct hit. It looks like several shotgun pellets deflected off the ground and caught her in the lower leg, one fracturing her fibula. We removed the fragments, set the bone, and did our best to repair the tissue damage. She'll have some scarring."

"How's her head?" Sean asked.

The doctor looked him over, taking in his badge and sidearm. "She's not ready to be interviewed, if that's what you're thinking."

"No, I mean . . . she took a blow. She said something about a shotgun stock when the paramedics were with her. Did you do X-rays?"

"We ran a number of tests, and it looks like she's got a mild concussion."

"Mild?" Owen asked.

"We'll keep her under observation tonight, but if everything goes well, she should be ready to leave tomorrow."

"Can we see her?"

"She'll be awake soon, but very groggy. You can see her, but it's best if you keep it short." The doctor turned to Sean. "Are you Detective Byrne, by chance?"

"Yes."

The doctor handed him an envelope. "Before we put her under, she made me promise I'd give you this."

"What—"

"The fragments. She said you'd need them as evidence."

Sean stared down at the envelope. The doctor answered more questions from Owen, but Sean wasn't listening. He just wanted to see Brooke. He tucked the envelope in his pocket and looked at her brother.

"You first," Owen said.

"You mind?"

"Go ahead. I need to call my parents."

Sean pushed through the doors and didn't stop at the nurses' station. He'd been in this wing of the hospital not long ago, and he didn't need directions. He strode down the hallway to the recovery rooms.

At the first door, he stopped cold. Brooke lay on a gurney under a light blue blanket. She had a bandage wrapped around her head, and dark purple bruises stood out against her pale skin. She looked asleep.

Sean's chest tightened as he stepped into the room. He knelt beside her and slid his hand under hers. Her fingers felt warm, but she didn't move.

"Brooke," he whispered.

Nothing.

He glanced behind him and dragged a chair over. He sat down and reached over to touch the side of her face that wasn't injured. "Brooke, honey, I'm here."

She was still. Silent. But with every gentle rise and fall of her chest, Sean felt like he could breathe again.

He kissed her hand and held it. Then he settled in to wait.

• • •

Callie caught Sean in the bull pen. He'd been scarce since yesterday, and she was surprised to bump into him at work. She'd expected him to take at least a few days off.

"Got a minute?" she asked.

"Not really."

"This won't take long. But I need to show you something."

Not waiting for an answer, she stepped into the nearest interview room and waited for him to close the door. She took a chair and he reluctantly followed suit.

"How is she?"

He sighed. "Doing better. She had a rough night."

"I won't keep you." Callie pulled out her phone and opened up a photograph. "Take a look at this."

Sean took the phone and stared down at the picture of lined paper filled with loopy handwriting. "What is this?" He glanced up.

"Samantha's journal from when she was fourteen."

"How—"

"Amy Doppler brought it in. She spent yesterday over at Samantha's house, packing up her things. She came across this journal tucked between some textbooks."

Sean skimmed the words and his expression darkened when he got to the part about going to see the judge. Fourteen-year-old Samantha Bonner had used the very same words as Hannah Lipsky to describe the encounter. Her description of the cop who escorted her to the office fit, too.

As part of his deal with prosecutors, Joe Hurd had identified Mahoney's other accomplice as Burr County sheriff's deputy Craig Petok. Like Hurd, the man had been on the judge's payroll for years.

Sean glanced up. "Did you see this about the cop who picked her up, the guy with the shaved head?"

"I know. It has to be Craig Petok."

"Holy shit. She even mentions the green banker's lamp." Sean shook his head. "Has Rachel seen this?"

"Not yet. But this is the 'proof' they were talking about, Sam and Jasmine. Some of the passages are marked with sticky notes. I'm thinking maybe she took pictures of the pages and sent them to the judge as part of their extortion plan."

Sean handed back the phone, then leaned back in the chair and scrubbed his hands over his face. The man looked beat, and Callie doubted he'd slept at all last night.

"How the hell did we miss this? We turned that house inside out."

"Yeah, but we were looking for drugs," Callie said. "The dogs aren't exactly trained to sniff out an old diary. And anyway, it was tucked between some textbooks. Amy wouldn't even have noticed it if it hadn't fallen out while she was packing up Samantha's things."

"So, where is it now?"

"Jasper's got it. He's taking it to the lab for fingerprinting. Samantha's prints are all over it, I'm sure, but there's a chance we could even find Jasmine's. Not that we need any more evidence against Mahoney now that Hurd is talking, but every bit helps."

"Hurd is cooperating?"

"Rachel's using him as leverage against the judge. Turns out Hurd has a dark red pickup truck registered to his name, supposedly keeping it for his son who's away at college. Hurd claims Mahoney borrowed the vehicle from him the week of the murders, claiming his car was in the shop. I think Rachel's positioning Hurd to testify against the judge. From what I hear, she's determined to nail Mahoney on everything, no deals."

"Good for her." Sean glanced at his watch. "Listen, I have to go. I'm picking up Brooke."

"She's being discharged?"

"At noon, supposedly. I'm taking her home."

Callie arched her eyebrows. "Home as in . . . ?"

"My place. If she agrees." He blew out a breath. "I've got some convincing to do."

"Hmm." Callie tilted her head to the side. "Interesting tactic."

"What is?"

"Taking her to your place. She doesn't strike me as someone who wants to be babysat."

"She isn't. But she needs help, even if she doesn't know it yet." He shook his head. "She's medicated and she's on crutches. I've been there. There's a lot that's hard to do, and the first few days are the worst. The exhaustion comes out of nowhere and knocks you flat, and I want to help her through that."

"You look exhausted yourself."

"*Me*? I'm fine." He raked his hand through his hair. Then he checked his watch, and she realized he was nervous more than anything. "I'd better go."

He was in love. Callie could see it. She hoped Brooke could, too, and that she was ready for it because Sean Byrne didn't do anything halfway.

Callie smiled at him. "Tell Brooke I said hi. And good luck with your convincing."

He smiled slightly. "You think I'm going to need it?"

"Absolutely."

• • •

"You're rushing it," Roland told her.

"No, I'm not," Brooke insisted.

"I disagree."

"Well, it's not up to you, is it? So, are you going to help me?"

He sighed on the other end of the phone. "Fine. But for the record, I think you're rushing it. Text me if you change your mind."

"I won't."

Brooke tossed her cell phone onto the coffee table and stared at her laptop. She had 286 messages in her in-box, and it had been less than three days.

The doorbell rang, and she startled at the unfamiliar sound. She looked at Sean's front door. He usually used the back door, and he had a key. She debated for a moment before grabbing her crutches and heaving herself up. She loped over and peered through the peephole and was shocked to see Maddie, Kelsey, and Alex.

Brooke unlocked the door and clumsily pulled it open.

"Surprise!" Maddie stepped past her, carrying a tray of cardboard coffee cups. "We decided to bring our coffee klatch to you."

Brooke smiled. "But it's Friday."

Kelsey kissed her cheek. "We needed an emergency session."

"Plus, we wanted an excuse to check out your new digs," Alex added.

"They're not really *my* digs," Brooke said, leading them into Sean's living room.

But she could tell her friends didn't buy it. Brooke's laptop was on the coffee table, her jacket was draped over a chair, and her favorite magazines were stacked on the end table beside her phone charger. She'd made herself quite at home in Sean's space. Temporarily.

"Wow, this is nice." Maddie looked around. "Great view of the greenbelt."

"Yeah, not quite the bachelor pad I imagined." Taking a seat on the armchair, Kelsey quirked an eyebrow at Brooke. "Who knew Sean Byrne had a domestic side?"

"Nice alarm system," Alex said from the foyer. "This thing's top-of-the-line."

"Leave it to you to notice his electronics," Brooke said.

Maddie sat on the sofa and passed out coffee cups and muffins. "We got you a chai latte."

"Thanks."

"In exchange, we want the full story, uncensored," Kelsey said. "How are things with you and the sexy detective?"

"Good." Brooke leaned her crutches against the end table and lowered herself onto the couch. "How are you? I understand you and Gage have a new project under way."

"You see what she did there?" Kelsey looked at Maddie and sipped her coffee. "The baby-making mission is going fine, thank you very much."

"Any news?" Alex asked.

"Not yet. But Gage is taking the whole operation *very* seriously. The man is determined."

"Give a SEAL a mission . . ." Maddie smiled and bit into a muffin.

"But enough about my tireless husband." Kelsey put down her cup. "We're here to talk about *you*. How's the fibula?"

"The fibula is fine, Dr. Quinn. Thanks for asking."

"And how's everything else?" Maddie asked with a worried look.

"Fine. Or better, I should say."

Brooke knew what Maddie was asking, but she wasn't ready to talk about Sean. He'd seemed so pensive lately. So quiet around Brooke. She worried something was wrong, but whatever it was felt private between them.

"They had an article in the paper this morning," Kelsey said. "Evidently, they think Mahoney may have had dozens of victims over the years."

"I saw that." And even if Brooke hadn't seen the article, Sean had been keeping her updated on the case.

"It makes me sick," Maddie said. "It's always the most vulnerable people. I hope they throw the book at him."

"That's the plan." Brooke picked up her tea. It was her favorite kind, but she didn't feel like drinking it. She still didn't feel back to normal yet. Maybe she never would.

"How's Cameron Spence doing?" Kelsey asked. "He's, what, ten years old?"

"Eleven. I talked to his mother yesterday, and she said he's doing okay. Some nightmares about what happened, which I guess is to be expected."

"And you?" Maddie asked.

Brooke shrugged. "Some."

"Your doctor should be able to prescribe something for that," Kelsey said.

"I don't know. Sean's been good about it. I'd rather have him than a pill."

All three of her friends smiled at her.

"Aww . . . that's so *sweet*." Kelsey dabbed her eyes.

"Oh, God. Are you actually *crying*?" Maddie asked. "Maybe you are pregnant."

"What? It is sweet."

"It's not sweet, it's hot," Alex said. "I'll take sex therapy versus a pill any day."

"Damn, me too." Maddie winked at her. "Especially with those sexy law-enforcement types."

A noise at the back door had everyone turning to look at the kitchen as Sean walked in. He wore jeans and a leather jacket and had his badge clipped to his belt. The layer of stubble on his jaw reminded Brooke he'd been called out of bed early this morning.

"Speaking of . . . ," Alex mumbled.

Sean seemed unfazed by all the women in his living room. "Ladies." He nodded at them.

"Hey, Sean," Maddie called. "Hope you don't mind we invited ourselves over."

"Don't mind at all." He deposited a brown sack on the kitchen table and walked into the living room and leaned over the back of the sofa to kiss Brooke's cheek. "Brought you some lunch."

"Thanks."

He returned to the kitchen as her friends watched her, every one of them grinning.

"Well, look at the time." Kelsey jumped up. "Better get back to work."

Alex and Maddie stood, too, and Brooke grabbed her crutches.

"No, don't get up," Maddie said. "We can see ourselves out. Bye, Sean. Take good care of Brooke for us."

"Will do."

Brooke rolled her eyes and followed them to the door, where they said good-bye with hugs and teasing and even a few tears from Kelsey. Then Brooke crutched her way over to the kitchen, where Sean was unpacking deli sandwiches.

"You guys were talking about me."

"How would you know?"

He gave her a sly smile. "I'm a detective."

He grabbed a Coke from the fridge and popped it open. "What did you tell them?"

"That's confidential." She propped the crutches against the counter and leaned into him. He wrapped his arms around her and pulled her close, and she felt a familiar rush of warmth. She loved the feel of his arms around her.

"Missed you this morning. I didn't even have time to make coffee."

She pulled back. "You didn't have time to shave, either."

He rubbed his jaw.

"I like it." She leaned her hip against the counter. "So, hey, I wanted to let you know I decided I'm going back to work on Monday."

"Already?"

"I'm getting way behind."

He took out a few plates and put the sandwiches on them. "I thought your doc said no driving for another week."

"Roland can drive me. He lives across the park from here, so it's on his way in."

Sean lifted his shoulder. "Makes sense."

Brooke watched him, trying to read his reaction. "That's it? You're not going to try to talk me out of it?"

"Sounds like you've made up your mind."

"I have."

"Then, I hope you'll take it easy until you're back to feeling one hundred percent."

She tried to read the expression in those hazel eyes of his. "So . . . you don't have an issue with Roland?"

"Why?"

"I don't know. Matt always had a thing about him. I'm glad you're not the jealous type."

"I'm totally jealous."

She pulled back. "You are?"

"Hell yeah. Roland gets to see you all day." Sean slid his arm around her and cupped her butt. "I only get to see you at night and on weekends."

She smiled. "But they're very good nights."

"They are." He kissed her. "And I have a confession to make. I didn't just come here to bring you a sandwich."

"No?"

He lifted her up and carried her into the living room. Taking care with her cast, he set her down on the sofa where they'd shared those first intimate moments. Then he lowered himself beside her.

He kissed her, and her entire body responded. She slid her hands around his neck and pressed against him, drinking in everything she'd craved this morning when she woke up in an empty bed.

He tipped her head and took her mouth with a kiss that was greedy and possessive and tender, all at once.

"You taste so good," he said against her lips. "I can never get enough of you." He kissed her chin, her neck, her collarbone, and his hands eased underneath her sweater.

"Sean . . ."

"Yeah?"

"I love you."

He stopped and stared down at her. She could tell she'd surprised him, and her throat went dry because she'd surprised herself, too. The silence stretched out, and nerves rippled through her. She didn't want to pressure him by saying it too soon.

He kissed her, and the raw need in the kiss made the nerves disappear. She felt light. Free. Exhilarated—like she always felt when she told him something in her heart. Even if he didn't say it back, she was glad she'd told him.

He broke the kiss and looked down at her. "I love you, too."

"You don't have to say it just because I did."

"Are you kidding? I've been *waiting* to say it. I've been choking back the words for weeks."

"Weeks?"

"Yes." He framed her face in his hands. "Brooke. You are the bravest, smartest, sexiest woman I have ever known. I think I've been in love since the day I met you."

She sighed quietly and closed her eyes. When she opened them again, he was watching her.

"What's that look?"

"I'm just . . . relieved." She smiled. "You've seemed so, I don't know, preoccupied lately. I thought something was wrong."

He brushed her hair out of her face and his gaze lingered on the ugly bruise along her cheek. "Something is wrong. I keep replaying everything that happened and how close I came to losing you. Every time I think about it—"

"I know." She kissed him to stop the words. "I get that way, too." She rested her hand against his chest. "I keep remembering how I felt walking toward the end of that pier knowing my life was about to end, and all I could think of was how truly sorry I was that I never had the guts to tell you how I felt about you and us and everything."

He gazed down at her, and the love in his eyes made her heart feel swollen.

"And how do you feel about me and us and everything?"

"I feel . . . grateful. So grateful, I can't even put it into words."

He kissed her. "You don't have to. I know."

Turn the page for a sneak peek at Laura Griffin's latest scorching-hot thriller from her brand-new action-packed series, Wolfe Security!

Available in June 2018 from Gallery Books!

CHAPTER 1

Jen Ballard planned to get lucky tonight.

The thought made her heart do a little hopscotch as she pulled her Volvo sedan into the driveway and checked her surroundings. No news vans. No beat-up hatchbacks belonging to reporters. She skimmed the street in both directions but saw only familiar cars in familiar driveways. She glanced in the rearview mirror to the driveway across the street, but it was empty—which might or might not be a good sign.

Jen pulled into her spacious garage and gathered her groceries off the passenger seat as her phone pinged with an incoming text. David.

Running late. ETA 20 min.

She breathed a sigh of relief. Perfect. Now she'd have time to shower and change into something more alluring than the charcoal pantsuit she'd worn to work.

She slid from the car and hurried into the house. Even laden with groceries, she felt empty-handed this evening. She had no briefs to read, no pre-trial motions to consider. She'd left everything at the office, including her laptop, which felt good for a change.

Jen stashed the steaks and salad ingredients in the fridge, then washed the potatoes and put them in the oven. She checked the clock. Fifteen minutes. She uncorked the merlot. It needed to breathe anyway. Really.

She poured half a glass, then made her way to her bedroom as she sipped a little liquid courage.

David liked merlot. And he was allergic to bees. Funny the things you learned about your neighbors over the years. She also knew he was divorced, had no kids, and he was one of the top cardiologists in Dallas.

Jen set her glass on the en suite vanity and turned on the shower, twisting her thick hair into a bun because she didn't have time to dry it. She stripped off her clothes and stepped under the hot spray.

A date. *Tonight*. Her stomach fluttered with nerves, and she wished she hadn't sampled the wine.

She'd bumped into David at Home Depot last week, and he'd asked her out right there in the light bulb aisle.

We should have dinner sometime, he'd said with his easygoing smile.

She'd been so shocked that she stood there staring at him for a full five seconds until *I'd love to!* popped out of her mouth.

It was impulsive. And ill-timed. But once the words were out, there was no going back.

She'd told him they should probably wait until her trial was over, but his blank expression made her realize he might not even know about it. How could he not, though? Didn't he read the papers? Or was he too busy saving lives to take notice of the media circus that had been going on in her courtroom for the past four weeks?

His utter obliviousness to her professional life appealed to her. A lot. She liked the prospect of seeing someone who didn't think of her as Judge Ballard or Your Honor. Most men were intimidated by the robe, and she hadn't had a single date in the two years since she'd been elected to the bench.

Jen stepped out of the shower and wrapped herself in

a towel. Nerves fluttered again as she opened her closet and skimmed the endless rack of suits.

"Crap," she mumbled, combing through the hangers. Everything was drab, even her weekend clothes.

Very few women could exude sex appeal in the courtroom and still be taken seriously. Brynn Holloran came to mind. The auburn-haired defense attorney wore low-cut blouses and spiked heels, and everyone knew she was a force to be reckoned with. Jen had always dressed down, in muted colors and sensible shoes, even during her prosecutor days. She wanted people to focus on her brain, not her boobs, but lately she'd felt sick to death of the whole conservative-jurist shtick.

Her gaze landed on the coral sheath dress she'd worn to her niece's graduation. It was pretty. Feminine. She remembered feeling confident in it. She grabbed the hanger and before she could change her mind, slipped into a lace thong and pulled the dress over her head. She tugged up the zipper and rearranged her breasts because the tight fit didn't leave room for a bra.

Jen checked herself out in the mirror. Not bad. She freshened up her makeup and fluffed her hair into a breezy style to match the dress. She slid her feet into sandals and downed a last sip of wine.

Her phone chimed from the bedroom, and she rushed to check it. Maybe another update from David. But instead it was Nate Levinson, a former colleague. What would he want? She'd missed two calls from him while she'd been in the shower, as well as a call from a Beaumont area code. She let Nate's call go to voice mail. It was business, no doubt, and she was taking the night off.

She looked at the mirror one more time before heading to the kitchen. The house felt warm, and she stopped at the thermostat to turn up the AC. The clock read 7:25.

David would be here any minute, and she still needed to season the steaks and throw the salad together. She walked into the kitchen and felt a crunch under her feet.

She looked down. What the . . . ?

Glass. All over the floor. She glanced at the patio, and a warm waft of air turned her blood to ice.

"Hello, Jennifer."

She whirled around to see a black pistol inches from her face. Her heart leapt as she looked at the man holding the gun. *Dear God, no.*

The calls from Nate, from Beaumont, all made sense now.

The man stepped forward. "On your knees."

"Don't hurt me."

"*Now!*"

Her legs folded, and she was on the floor, chunks of glass biting into her skin. *This can't be happening. How can this be happening?* Her heart hammered wildly in her chest.

"Don't hurt me." She gazed up at him, and the utter calm on his face made her stomach quiver.

He brought the muzzle of the gun to her forehead. It felt cool and hard, and bile rose in the back of her throat.

"Please," she croaked. "I'll do whatever you want, just—"

"That's right." His eyes were flat and soulless. "You will."

• • •

Friday morning.

The sun was bright, the sky was blue, and the temperature hovered at a bearable eighty-five degrees. But despite the weather, Brynn Holloran couldn't seem to get into her typical TGIF mood as she drove to work.

A Wonder Woman ringtone emanated from the cup

holder. She turned down the relentlessly cheerful morning DJs and answered a call from her sister.

"Hey, Liz, what's up?"

"Oh, nothing," she said, which Brynn didn't buy for a minute. "Just wondering what you're up to this weekend."

"I'm loaded with work."

"Again?"

"Yep."

"Isn't this the third straight weekend? Reggie's a tyrant."

"It's not him, it's me," Brynn said. "Our trial starts Monday in Dallas."

"Oh." Her sister sounded disappointed. "Are you ready for it?"

"Not even close."

"Then I guess there's no chance you'll join us for dinner tomorrow?"

Us was Liz and her husband. Brynn loved them dearly, but she didn't love being a third wheel.

"Mike's got a college friend in from out of town," Liz continued, "and we thought it would be fun to take him out for Tex-Mex."

Brynn turned into the parking lot beside her office and whipped into her customary space. "I wish I could, but I'm slammed."

"You're just saying that because you think it's a setup."

"Well, isn't it?"

"It's Tex-Mex and margaritas. Totally casual. And this guy's cute, trust me. You two will hit it off."

Not likely. Liz and Brynn had a special language when it came to men. "Hot" meant drool-worthy alpha. "Cute" meant a teddy bear, and the last "cute" guy her sister had set her up with had been three inches shorter than Brynn.

Not that it should matter. Who cared what he looked like if he was decent and smart and managed to get through the evening without burping or bad-mouthing his ex? Brynn was the problem here. She wasn't ready to get out there.

"I really have to work. And I'm not just saying that. But you guys have fun, okay?" Brynn slid out of her car just as her phone pinged from a text.

"Okay, well . . . I'll call you tomorrow, just in case you change your mind and need a break."

"Sounds good."

Brynn hung up and checked the text. Ross. As usual, her partner's message was short and to the point: *Perez a no-show.*

Brynn cursed and stomped her foot. The trial started in seventy-two hours, and their star witness was missing.

Reggie was going to go ballistic. He was going to blame her, and with good reason. He'd warned her Perez was a flight risk, but Brynn had been so preoccupied that she didn't listen.

She strode across the lot, careful not to catch her Jimmy Choo sandals in any of the potholes. She dropped her phone in her purse as she mounted the steps to the converted Victorian that housed the offices of Blythe & Gunn.

Reggie had bought the property three years ago when he moved his law practice from Dallas to Pine Rock, a sleepy bedroom community north of Houston. From the street, the place looked charming. But years of dealing with leaky windows and temperamental plumbing had dampened Brynn's enthusiasm for the architecture. The building was originally a boarding house, but Reggie had renovated it to accommodate six lawyers, two paralegals, an administrative assistant, and a receptionist—not to mention the steady flow of clients who drifted in and out seven days a week. Big trials were the firm's gravy, but Saturday night arrests were its bread and butter.

The waiting room was empty of tearful mothers and hand-wringing spouses this morning. The receptionist's chair was empty, too, and Brynn followed the smell of fresh coffee back to Reggie's office.

Faith sat behind her mahogany desk, dabbing her eyes with a tissue. Brynn stopped short. Reggie's assistant never cried. She was an island of calm.

"Faith?"

She glanced up, startled, and her usually perfect mascara was streaked down her cheeks.

Brynn's stomach knotted. It was Faith's boys. Had to be. Her two teenage sons were constantly getting into trouble, and Faith had started to worry that her oldest was on drugs.

Brynn walked over and knelt beside her, taking her hand. "Faith, what happened?"

She squeezed her eyes shut and shook her head.

"Brynn!" Reggie's voice boomed from his office. His door jerked open, and her silver-haired boss stepped out. "Brynn, get in here."

She shot him a glare and returned her attention to Faith. "Are you all right?"

She dabbed her nose. "Yes, just . . . go on."

Brynn rose and followed Reginald H. Gunn, Managing Partner, past the nameplate bearing his title. Shelves crammed with law books lined the walls, and towers of file boxes crowded every corner. Reggie walked behind his cluttered desk, and Brynn noted the pin-striped suit jacket hanging on the back of his chair. The pink silk handkerchief in the front pocket told her he planned to be in court later.

"Close the door, would you?"

She followed his gruff command, taking one last peek at Faith as she eased shut the door.

"Sit down."

She crossed her arms, staying in place. "I'll stand. What's up?"

Reggie's leather chair creaked as he sank into it. Then he ran a hand through his thick hair.

"Nate called me." He glanced up. "Jen Ballard was killed last night."

Brynn sagged back against the door. "What—"

"I don't have all the details yet, but she was murdered sometime yesterday evening in her home."

Murdered.

Brynn's blood turned cold. Beautiful, witty Jen Ballard *murdered*. The words didn't belong in the same sentence.

She stepped closer to Reggie's desk. "How—"

"I don't know, okay? I haven't even had time to call the police up there. And there's something else—"

A sharp knock at the door. Ross leaned his head in and immediately zeroed in on Brynn. "You tell him yet?"

"Tell me what?" Reggie asked.

Ross stepped into the office, oblivious to the tension hovering in the room. "Perez is MIA. We were supposed to meet at eight to run through his testimony, but he didn't show."

"Try his girlfriend."

"She hasn't seen him in a week." Ross looked at Brynn and frowned. "What's wrong?"

She cleared her throat. "Jen Ballard."

"What now?"

Anger flared in Reggie's eyes. "She'd dead, Ross."

Ross's face went slack. "*What*?"

"She was killed in her home last night. Up in Sheridan Heights, right outside of Dallas," Reggie said. "I just got off the phone with Nate Levinson twenty minutes ago."

Ross shot Brynn a look, as if she might somehow make sense of what he was hearing, but she couldn't. The forty-two-year-old woman who'd once been their boss, their mentor, their *friend* was dead.

"What's the other thing?" Brynn asked Reggie. "You said there was something else?"

Reggie stared at Brynn. A veteran trial attorney, he had a talent for creating drama, but the somber look on his face was all too real.

"What?" Ross demanded.

"James Corby is out."

Brynn's eyebrows shot up. "*Out*?"

Beside her, Ross made a strangled sound.

"He escaped."

"Are you fucking kidding me?" Ross clutched his head with his hands. "*How* do you escape a fucking maximum-security prison?"

Reggie's gaze locked with Brynn's. "I don't know."

But he *did* know. And so did Brynn. As an assistant prosecutor, Brynn had tried James Corby's case alongside then-lead prosecutor Jen Ballard. Brynn had learned that James Corby was not only violent and sadistic but also smart. Frighteningly smart. And the prospect of him slipping out of prison had lurked in the darkest corners of Brynn's mind for years.

Her chest felt tight. She placed her hand on her sternum and tried to breathe. But it was Ross who bent at the waist and looked like he was going to puke.

"Shit!"

"Hey," Reggie snapped. "Don't throw up in here."

Ross straightened and shook his head. "This is insane. Where the hell are the marshals?"

"They're on it," Reggie replied. "That, I *do* know. Nate tells me they've been working this thing from the beginning."

"And when was that?" Brynn asked.

"Wednesday."

"He escaped *Wednesday*, and we're just now hearing about it?"

Ross let out a blistering string of curses. He was starting to grate on Brynn's nerves.

"What does this mean for us?" Ross demanded. "Our trial begins in Dallas in *three* days, right down the goddamn road from Jen's murder—"

"It means we have to take action," Reggie said. "I've already started."

"What do you mean?" Brynn couldn't keep the skepticism out of her voice. She'd dealt with plenty of criminals and considered herself fairly streetwise. But what kind of "action" did Reggie think they were going to take here? Was he planning to jump in his Mercedes and hunt down an escaped convict?

"I'm hiring protection," Reggie said. "The best money can buy."

"*Bodyguards*?" She blinked at him. "You can't be serious."

"I am." He checked his watch and picked up the phone.

"Wait, *stop*." Brynn held up her hand. "Before you rush off and hire anyone, we need to talk to the sheriffs up there about protection. This falls on them, doesn't it? Our courthouse is in their jurisdiction."

Reggie gave her a dark look. "This law firm doesn't exactly have a lot of friends up there. As you well know."

"Yes, but . . . it's their *job*."

"Yeah, and it's our job to win this trial. I won't have my two top attorneys worried and distracted."

Brynn was still in shock. But not so much that she couldn't imagine the major pain in the butt that having a bodyguard trailing her around was going to be. This was the biggest case of her career. Reggie had put her in charge of everything, from jury selection to the closing statement. She'd spent countless hours preparing and still had work to do.

"Yes, but . . . *bodyguards*? As in plural?" She played the money card. "That sounds expensive."

"It is."

"Listen, Reggie, I appreciate the thought—" She glanced at Ross. "We both do, but—"

"No buts. And it's not a thought. I already made the call." He looked at Ross. "Now, about this Perez thing, did you get Bulldog on it?"

Ross shook his head, and Reggie jabbed at his desk phone.

Bulldog, aka Bull, aka John Kopek, was the private investigator Reggie kept on speed dial. Brynn shook her head. She felt like she'd been sucker punched, and her boss was already back to business.

"Bull, it's Reggie. I need a locate." He muffled the receiver against his shirt and gave Brynn a sharp look. "You've got a trial to prep for. Better get to it."

• • •

Erik Morgan was almost out when everything went sideways.

An earsplitting *boom*.

A billow of smoke.

He halted in the narrow corridor and adjusted the body that was slung over his shoulder. The air around him swirled with grit. Sweat seeped into his eyes. But he pushed the distractions out of his mind as he and his teammate moved into position.

Weapon raised, Erik darted around the corner, instantly spotting two silhouettes. To his right, a man holding a pistol. To his left, a teenage girl holding a cell phone. Erik fired two rounds at the guy, hitting him square in the chest.

"Clear!"

He ran for the door, stopping at the threshold to scan for hostiles.

"Clear!" he repeated, then took off down the stairs.

One flight. Two. A door slapped open above him.

Boom!

Dust rained down as Erik adjusted his load and kept moving. They were running out of time. He could feel it. More smoke, more shouting. He heard his partner's footsteps behind him.

"Go, go, go!" someone yelled.

Boots thundered as four men carrying more than eight hundred pounds of dead weight bounded down the stairwell. At ground level, Erik stopped at the plywood door. His teammate kicked it open and peered out to scan the area.

"All clear!" Hayes yelled.

Erik followed him through the door, exiting the kill house with a cloud of smoke and dust. He sprinted the last fifty yards to a concrete barricade, then dropped to a knee in the dirt and lowered his load to the ground.

"Two minutes, forty-six seconds."

Erik glanced up to see Jeremy Owen looming over him with a stopwatch. The former Marine sharpshooter did not look happy.

The man playing the role of Erik's protectee groaned and sat up. "What the fuck happened back there?"

Hayes shook his head. "I couldn't see." He glanced back at the kill house, a building made up of rooms, hallways, and stairwells, where they practiced closed-quarters battle-and-rescue scenarios. Flash bangs and smoke grenades were tossed into the mix to ramp up the chaos.

Erik had watched Hayes work, and visibility wasn't

his only problem. Hayes's protectee had a paint splatter on his shirt the size of a soccer ball. If they'd been facing live rounds, the man would be dead.

"Okay, everybody up," Jeremy ordered. "Hit the hoses, and we'll reconvene on the south range at 1500."

Erik got up and helped his teammate to his feet. He wiped the sweat from his face with the back of his arm and glanced at the sun. It was ninety-eight degrees today—hotter inside the kill house—and his clothes were saturated.

Everyone grabbed their gear and moved out. Jeremy caught Erik's eye and signaled for him to walk back with him on the trail.

"How'd it go with Becker?" Jeremy asked when they were deep in the woods.

Hayes Becker, twenty-six, of Roanoke, Virginia. As a team leader, it was Erik's job to help evaluate candidates who wanted to join the elite ranks of Wolfe Security, and Hayes had made it to the final round.

"He's not ready yet," Erik said. "But he's getting there."

"What's your take on his skills?"

"His tactical driving's good. PT scores are off the charts. It's his shooting that needs work."

Jeremy grunted. "That's the problem with these FBI hires."

"So, we're keeping him?"

He nodded.

They made their way along the running trail and O-course. Set among the towering East Texas pines, the course had been modeled after the SEAL obstacle course at Coronado. The pinnacle in terms of height and effort was a seventy-foot cargo net, which a couple of new recruits were clawing their way up right now. They wore olive-green BDUs to differentiate themselves from real Wolfe agents, who wore all black.

Erik reviewed this afternoon's session, making a mental list of the areas where Hayes needed work. Any team they deployed on a job was only as good as its weakest member, and new hires either had to get up to speed or get out, simple as that.

"I'll spend some time with him," Erik said. "We can burn through some mags on the range, see if I can pinpoint his problem."

"Good. I'll give Liam the heads-up."

Erik walked into the clearing as a silver BMW 5 Series sped by, leaving a cloud of red dust in its wake. It curved along the dirt road and pulled up to the sprawling log cabin that served as their business headquarters. A man climbed out from behind the wheel. Average height, medium build. From his Ray-Bans and suit, Erik pegged him for a corporate executive. Then the passenger door opened, and a woman stepped out of the car.

Erik halted. Her long, red hair caught the sunlight as she turned around. She wore tight black jeans and a silky white shirt, and she had a big leather purse slung over her shoulder. She was several inches taller than the guy with her, partly because of her mile-high heels.

"Who is that?" Erik glanced at Jeremy.

"No idea."

They got all kinds of VIPs at the compound. Pop stars, politicians, athletes. Some of their clients were just ordinary rich people who'd picked up an enemy along the way and decided they needed protection. Judging from their looks, this couple fell into the last category. They mounted the steps to the building, peeling off their shades as they went inside.

"Yo, Erik."

He turned to see Tony Lopez jogging up the trail. In a black T-shirt and tactical pants, he was dressed just like Erik, only he wasn't sporting a layer of dirt and soot.

“The chief wants you in his office,” Tony said.

“Now?”

“Yeah, ASAP.”

Erik’s gaze narrowed. “This have to do with the Five Series that just pulled up?”

“You got it.”

“Know who they are?”

He smiled. “I hear they’re a couple hotshots from Dallas.”

“Shit.”

“Think they’re attorneys,” he added.

“*Shit.*”

Tony grinned and slapped him on the shoulder. “Better you than me, bro.”